Large is the Smallest We've Got

A Jigsaw Puzzle

Jed Hamilton

Large is the Smallest We've Got - A Jigsaw Puzzle
Jed Hamilton

Paperback Edition First Publishing in Great Britain
in 2015 by aSys Publishing

eBook Edition First Publishing in Great Britain
in 2015 by aSys Publishing

Disclaimer

This is a work of fiction. Names, characters, businesses, places, events and
incidents are either the products of the author's imagination or are historical
events which are a matter of public record and/or used in a fictitious
manner. Any resemblance otherwise to actual persons, living or
dead is purely coincidental.

ISBN: 978-1-910757-14-7
aSys Publishing
http://www.asys-publishing.co.uk

To my dear sister Margaret, who for two years listened patiently while I talked of nothing but 'my book'.

And to Robin and Selina, who with great kindness and tact steered me away from the inadequacies of my first draft.

The Jigsaw Pieces

Part Nine

One

1

Rome

"Then why did you stay there so long?"

After a short pause, in which the old man himself began to wonder why, he said: "I think I fell in love."

"You?" said his godson, laughing. "I find that hard to believe!"

"*Impertinente!*"—The old man was Italian.

A long time ago, a very long time ago, he had been Oscar-nominated for a 'best foreign language film' which he had both starred-in and directed, set in Copenhagen; so it was only natural that on his arrival in Los Angeles they called him 'the Dutch guy'. When he decided to stay, and make his home and career in Hollywood, the name stayed with him.

"No-one '*thinks*' they fall in love," said his godson. 'You do or you don't. Trust me."

He, on the other hand, was from America. And at an age (not yet twenty) when a new-found confidence, risking impudence, finds itself indulged—encouraged almost—by those nearer the end than the beginning of their lives.

"So! The arrow has pierced your tender young heart already? *Povero bambino!*" said the Dutch guy, resorting to his native tongue.

"Just a glance. Don't make a big thing of it." The young man was also at that age.

"Mine was more than just a glance, you should understand," said his godfather. "But it was what you in America call 'a love-hate thing'."

"Oh. One of those. Been there. T-shirt. *Una cosa di amore-odio.* Isn't that how you say it?"

His Italian was excellent, but his godfather never acknowledged it, and insisted they talk in English 'because he found it difficult to understand him otherwise'. Upon hearing his godson's quite remarkable translation from idiom into idiom, all he said was -

"Since you were a child you have been coming to Rome, and yet you have the accent of a tour-guide."

They were sitting in the old man's apartment, a short walk from Piazza di Spagna. They had spent over an hour skirting around a subject they knew they would have to come to, sooner or later. An October sun shone through the open windows, and the bustle of morning rumbled in the streets below.

"Will you stay for lunch? We can 'send out' if you like?"

"I have to go pack." His godson shrugged what passed for a refusal.

'All day?' he wondered, silently. But he resigned himself to a finality in the young man's voice that offered no hope of a longer visit.

"Check-in tomorrow is at the crack of dawn," added his godson.

"What merciless words. 'The crack of dawn.' As though she had a whip! *Peccato* . . . But thank you for coming. It meant—"

"Please don't go all Italian on me! Not twice in one morning! I *wanted* to come. No-one back home will talk about it. And I wanted to see you again. True."

His godfather's look could not have been more fond, nor more pained, no matter how hard he tried to disguise both. To see him again—before . . . ?

An awkward silence, then—"So who did you fall in love with?" asked his godson.

"It's not that simple. And it was a long time ago."

"I should hope it was!"

The significance of that careless reply did not even cross the old man's mind. He stared out of the window, allowing himself to be blinded by the morning sunlight; and with his eyes half-closed he began at last to speak about the things his godson had flown across the Atlantic to hear.

"It was because of Madison that I met your mother," he said, almost to himself. "And then, it was because of me that your mother met Scott. Strange! A late train, a longer shower, a red traffic light, you take the stairs instead of the elevator—who can say?—*Una pochissima differenza*, a delay of a just a few seconds, and we may never have met. Unless it was always to be. Do you believe in destiny? '*La Forza del Destino*'? Maybe the earthquake was always going to throw us together, no matter how long we spent in the shower, eh?"

"What earthquake?"

"Madison came to your mother's wedding," he said suddenly. "*Risplendente* she was." Drifting deeper into memory, and with the trace of a smile on his face, he repeated—"*Risplendente*."

"What earthquake?"

2
Madison

Madison was from Wisconsin, and had unimaginative parents. Had she been born in Florida they might have called her Tallahassee. She arrived in Hollywood, full of the usual hopeless hope, back in the early nineties.

The peak of Madison's academic achievements had been her selection as a High School Cheer-leader; and the photographs of her in that flamboyant role (snapshots she still takes out to show visitors) tell us that, as college drop-outs go, she must have been a very pretty college drop-out when she boarded the aeroplane to Hollywood. A little less pretty, perhaps, when she stepped off at LAX after a heavenly duty-free flight. But she being the first of them to make a home in West Hollywood, they never got to see that prettiness 'face to face' before the sun-dried, drink-dried skin drew tight around her bones. The early 1990's, one must remind oneself, were Pre-Botox. There was a rumour going the rounds recently that they are re-calibrating Los Angeles years, ditching BC and AD, and replacing them with BB and AC—*before botox* and *anno collagen*.

The origins of any suggestion that Madison might become an actress have proved impossible to trace. Her claim that 'she'd always wanted to act ever since she could remember', is unhelpful in that regard since she was usually incapable of remembering anything before the previous night, and often not a great deal about that either.

Her conviction—that, having seen Jessica Lange in "Tootsie", twice, and looking quite like her, there couldn't be much else to it—wasn't in the least dented when Caryn (who had *not* been a cheer-leader) suggested that going to a classical concert, twice even, fell a little short of the training required to play the piano. Madison said that was *totally* different—but in her heart of hearts she could see the strength of the argument if the analogy had been with a violin.

From an objective distance, I hope it is not too unkind to suggest that Madison may have gone into acting because it didn't seem likely she was capable of going into anything else

If there's one benefit every child in America gains from a High School education, it is the ability to write a lying resumé. With the help of a few friends, Madison cobbled together a couple of impressive looking pages and sent them, along with some touched-up photos, to every agent listed in 'Variety'. No one replied. Madison had yet to learn that in LA silence means 'no'. (She never came to learn that in LA 'yes' sometimes means 'no' too, and that it is futile for anybody to try to come up with a formula explaining when.) She thought that not getting a reply from any of them was _most_ encouraging, and went about Wisconsin boasting that '_she'd not had a single rejection_'.

Then one damp day the mail brought her a scented envelope, with a scented letter inside it, from an address in Sunset Boulevard—saying (as Madison summarised it to her friends) that Sunset Creative Arts—**Sunset Boulevard Caryn!**—were very interested and would be delighted to be able help her, and if ever she found herself in Los Angeles she should be sure to come and see them, but she had to understand that neither they nor any other agency was going to be able to take her on as a 'remote' client, if she knew what they meant, and had she ever thought of moving to Hollywood?

We can put Madison on an aeroplane to California immediately, because she boarded an aeroplane to California immediately. But even in the short space of time between the scented letter and the departure lounge, Sunset Creative Arts had forgotten all about her—perhaps because the one-man outfit known as Sunset Creative Arts was a little further up Sunset Boulevard than you might think, past Formosa where the transvestite hookers hang out, past the drug-dealers near the pharmacy at the free hospital, past that strip where no sane person would stop his car no matter what colour the traffic signal, and round the corner on Eastern Avenue, in a small office (on a temporary lease) at the back of the seedy Motel opposite the gay bath-house; and the 'one man' was Wendle Stein, a middle-aged gentile who gave himself a Jewish name for the credibility of the Agency, and who never discouraged young aspiring actresses (ideally with absolutely no experience) from coming to see him, on the off-chance he might get laid.

It was Madison's great misfortune to have packed too many suitcases, and to lose one of them in transit. Inquiries at LAX established that the mistake had been made and discovered back in Wisconsin, and the bag was already in the air and would be arriving in a couple of hours. They were very sorry, but they hoped she would understand these things happened. Some vouchers for the restaurant were thrust on her in the hope of staving off any demand for real compensation—to which, if only they'd known Madison, they'd have known she had no idea she would be entitled.

Rather than sitting in a low chair at a nice little table eating one of today's specials, Madison spent her vouchers sitting on a tall stool at the even nicer bar drinking a number of today's cocktails. Sitting, that is, until she couldn't find the footrest on the stool and slipped right off, and the barman said "*Don't you think maybe you've had enough*?" She gave him a withering look, left no tip, and zig-zagged over to Baggage Reclaim to pick up her delayed case.

That's when she made the unwise decision to go straight away to see 'her agent' (as she called him in Wisconsin) before checking-in to her temporary accommodation.

The cab pulled up outside the Sunset entrance to a Eastern Avenue motel which displayed the same address as that on Wendle Stein's letter, in big numbers above a doorway with an arrow pointing to 'Reception on Eastern', and a blue neon sign that flashed "VAC NCY". There was no trace at all of Sunset Creative Arts, nor any other possible claimant to the address on the letter; so a confused, tired and tipsy Madison lugged her bags through the door into an area about the same size as, and not dissimilar to the smell of, the men's restroom at a gas-station.

In an even smaller anti-room, in a torn leatherette armchair that leaked dirty yellow stuffing onto the dirty rug on the dirty floor, sat a woman who was watching daytime TV, and slowly shoving so-called 'fast food' into her mouth from a cardboard container. She saw Madison soon enough, but took her sweet time wiping the grease from her face onto her fat fingers, then from her fat fingers onto her stained thighs, and easing herself out of the chair and plodding through to the desk, looking at Madison's luggage and complaining -

"The entrance is on Eastern. Are you blind or something? How many nights?"

"Oh . . . I'm not checking in . . . " Madison smiled nervously, "I'm here to see Mr. Stein." Then more confidently: "*He's my agent!*"

Madison waved the scented letter at the woman, who took it, smelled it, glanced at the top and the bottom of it, but never the middle of it. (She didn't need to: she'd seen it a hundred times before.) She grunted, shoved the letter back to Madison, and disappeared—which is a wholly misleading word, for which I apologise, if it is taken as having been intended to imply the slightest impression of speed. After some minutes, during which Madison could hear distant voices shouting at each other, the woman returned.

"Follow me."

She who divided her time between watching TV as the Motel's receptionist, and watching TV as Wendle Stein's secretary, led Madison out into a small courtyard with a filthy swimming pool and a Jacuzzi bubbling brown froth, through to the equally splendid offices of Sunset Creative Arts.

Madison was not looking her best. Any potential for kindling Wendle's attraction could neither be described as immediate nor likely to be future, even if he was desperate. And although the actual meaning of his speech was 'Get the bitch outa here', the words Wendle Stein chose to convey that meaning were -

"Madeline, my dear girl, thank you SO much for coming to see me. This has got to be one of the most exciting days for me this . . . how do I know? . . . and I cannot TELL you how excited I am to be meeting possibly one of the most exciting new talents to arrive in Hollywood this . . . you tell me!"
Madison wasn't entirely sure what she was meant to tell him. But before she could speak –

"The thing of it is, you've come at a very bad moment. I got one of my young actresses doing a screen-test at Universal in . . . " He looked at his watch. "Like NOW! Geez! And I just HAVE to be there. Like I will be for you, sweetheart. Take this card. It's my private number . . . ." (It was a card with a direct dial to an answer service no-one ever checked.) "Ring me ANY time. I cannot TELL you how excited I am! But I gotta run." A final press of her hand, and he finished with "Any time. I MEAN that."

Wendle nodded to his 'secretary', who abruptly took the disoriented Madison by the arm and manoeuvered her to her baggage in reception and from reception out into the bright sunshine of Eastern Avenue, with -

"This way. Sweetheart. Don't get too excited."

***

When she was dumped so unceremoniously, even dear, innocent Madison had a rough idea she might be best-off heading straight back to Wisconsin. But the shame of it! She had enough savings to seek fame and fortune in Hollywood for . . . three weeks? So she decided to stay and try her luck.

Someone back in Wisconsin had told her not to bother pre-booking accommodation, because there are so many bargain motels to be found in LA—she had just had first-hand experience of one!—and she took a cab instinctively Westwards (and so right she was), asking the driver if he could recommend somewhere cheap but clean. He drove her to a nice little owner-managed motel off San Vicente in West Hollywood, which is where she checked-in.

She promised herself, and meant it, that if things had not worked for her by the time her money ran out, she would make the shameful journey home and brave Caryn's snide comments with as much dignity as she could muster.

Her little room was immediately adjacent to a large sky-blue swimming pool, chlorine-fresh, auto-skimmed and sparkling in the LA sun. Determined to take a plunge as soon as she could, to refresh her from her long journey and (if she were honest with herself) to rid her of the lingering odour of Sunset Creative Arts, she showered—then realised she had not packed any swimming wear. She collapsed jet-lagged and despondent (and not entirely sober) onto her bed, with only a towel to cover her, where she fell asleep in seconds and awoke after several hours, just before dawn, a little hung-over but refreshed and ready for the challenges ahead.

After a good breakfast on Santa Monica Boulevard, and with her unfailing optimism restored, she called the number on Wendle Stein's business card as soon as it was reasonable to assume he would be sitting at his desk. She listened to the answer machine (telling her that Sunset Creative Arts valued her call), left a short message, and waited by the telephone all morning for a call-back. But Sunset Creative Arts did *not* call back. Did you think they would? Not that morning, not in the afternoon, not in the evening; nor the next morning, afternoon and evening; nor the day following, or the one after that.

Wendle had no idea she'd even dialled the number on the useless card he'd given her.

3

Rome

"The first time I saw Madison it was immediately before she was mugged."

"Excuse me . . . ?"

"It was entirely her fault. We were in Silverlake, where Hollywood Boulevard meets Sunset. I was in my car and she was at a *Bancomat*, an ATM machine, stuffing dollars into a small purse. A couple of young robbers with knives had no difficulty in persuading her to give them her purse, and they disappeared down a road behind the shops. Poor Madison stood there like a rabbit, as you say. She didn't shout or scream, she just stood there."

"Like a rabbit?"

"*Esatto*. And when I drew up alongside her, I truly believe she thought I was going to rob her as well."

"Did you call the cops? Or a Vet, at least."

"A Vet?"

"My dearest, esteemed godfather, it was a joke. What did you do?"

"I got out of my car, spoke to her calmly, and very softly, told her I had seen everything, and asked her if she was alright and if there was anything I could do. She flung her arms round me and burst into tears—great salt-water drops all over the front of my shirt."

"Your shirt! Dude! Were you OK?"

"This is more of your joking, eh? It is very amusing."

The young man apologised by grinning at him; and then feigned the demeanour of as rapt a listener as any raconteur could wish for.

"Please go on."

"I couldn't understand what she was saying at first," said his godfather. "I had only been in America a few months you see, and she spoke very quickly."

"But you called the cops, right?"

"When she at last slowed down her speaking it was clear to me she didn't want the *polizia*—she said there was no point, and I had to agree with her. The robbers would never be found, it was obvious. Then she burst into tears again and said the money was the deposit for a car and she was afraid someone else would buy it. She kept saying she didn't know what to do. Again and again. '*I don't know what to do!*' She was so small and so fragile and vulnerable. Who except a monster could not be *simpatico*? Eh? Don't look at me with that . . . that . . . *faccia da scemo*."

"You lost me there."

"I am Italian. Are you unhappy with that? *Va bene*. I said she mustn't worry. I would take her to the car showroom and she could explain everything. They would understand, I told her.—And what did I say to deserve that look you gave me?"

"Calm down, my dearest godfather! *Piano piano*. I get it. She was the one you fell in love with. It's cool."

"Nothing is so simple," said the old man, becoming agitated. "I know you are not much older than a foetus, but surely even you have learned? Everything in life is complicated. The more simple it looks, the more complicated it is. There was no car showroom. Naturally there was no car showroom. Why did you think there would be a car showroom? *Stupido*. It would have made things easy. She took me to a . . . what do you say?... 'dilapidate'?... Is that a word? '*Dilapidate*'?

"More or less."

"A dilapidate motor-vehicle business, with a solo-pump gas-station attached in the front, oil-drums and shredded tyres lying everywhere, curled iron sheets leaning against the walls like huge slabs of steel *lasagna* (I have not an idea what they were for), and a small *piazza* at the back, which was devoted—it was like a mortuary—devoted to the selling of vehicles recovered from . . . help me . . . you understand what I am saying? . . . .damn your language!... *incidente stradale*."

"Traffic accidents."

"*E cosi*. And so badly damaged—and it seemed to me it was the whole point of the thing—it was not cost-workable to make them good again. It was as though they scraped them up from the road! Madison told her story to the ruffian at the back of the garage and I confirmed it was true. *Santo cielo*! He only had to see the stains on my shirt!"

"They'd have done it."

"But he said he still needed a deposit, because there were other people who were *very* interested in this *magnificent* car—which was lies!—wait until I tell you what car she wanted!—he pleaded if someone made for a sale he had no choice—all that nonsense—you can imagine the lies he told—and Madison believed every one of them. She offered her watch, her rings, anything she had that might be worth a few dollars, but the man said he wanted cash. Which I can't say I blame him, because the jewellery was trash. Then the poor little thing, she turned to me."

"Please don't tell me you gave her the deposit?"

"What else could I do? Besides, I lent it to her. I didn't give it to her. She told to me that she was an actress (and she *looked* like an actress), she was out of work at the moment (and she *looked* out of work), and she needed a car to go to audition the next week. Her parents were rich and were sending her the money by Western Union but it hadn't come through, *e cosi, e cosi*. The deposit was only $300, but that was the maximum she could take from the ATM and it had been robbed from her, which I had seen for myself, and she would pay me back the next day."

"And you believed her?"

"*Naturalmente*. What was there not to believe? And she *did* pay me back, just like she said. So."

"I'm amazed."

"Save your amazement until I tell you about the car! *Mio Dio*! It was only $600 to <u>buy</u>! The deposit was half! It was a disaster! I begged her not to buy it! What are those military cars we always see in the news?"

"A Jeep?"

"No. *Più grande*. The fat cars that men with tattoos drive round West Hollywood, playing loud music."

"A Hummer?"

"Eh?"

"A Humvee."

"*Esatto*! A Humvee. With an engine that sounded like a dying grandmother, no spring –"

"Suspension."

"Are you a mechanic now? But worst of all, unbelievable of all in fact, it was painted over—someone on drugs, it had to be—all over, from top to bottom, with the American Stars and Stripes!"

"Not the Italian Stars and Stripes?"

"Now you are a comedian. *Bravo*. I am corrected. *The* Stars and Stripes. It looked . . . what would you call it . . . ?"

"*Stupidissimo*."

"Or a word that exists. *Imbecille*."

"Why was she so keen on that old whip?"

"Ah! I know you too well, my crafty young godson. You tempt me to challenge the existence of that *espressione*. Eh? '*Old whip*'? I know you, little *Scottino*. I am right. Your face says it to me. So I do not accept the challenge, and your clever trap doesn't work. She wanted '*that old whip*' as you call it, because it was the least espensive '*whip*' they had. $600. Two journeys to the ATM—even you can see the point? The deposit one day. The car the next day. No Western Union. No rich parents. To me it was . . . transparent."

"But you gave her the $300 all the same."

"And I was right. I drove her back to her motel, and she promised to pay me as soon as her parents sent the money. I didn't believe the nonsense about the rich parents, obviously, but I trusted she would pay me from the ATM, and I gave her my *numero di cellulare*. Three days later, she calls and invites me to lunch to say thank you, and she gives me every last dollar."

"Lunch, not dinner?"

"You will not give up, will you? You are determined to throw us together, eh? You have closed your soap-opera mind, I can see. But listen to me. No Italian could ever be in love with anyone who cooked like Madison."

"Looked?"

"Cooked. The lunch. It was *spaghetti alla Bolognese*, in my honour she said. In my honour! *Spaghetti alla Bolognese!* Meat the size of tennis balls, and pasta so soft, so 'al dentures', it melted into the *parmigiano*. Explain, please, what do you mean, '*lunch, not dinner*'?"

The young man grinned wider still. "Have we hit a raw nerve?"

"*Ragazzo ridicolo*! No we have not! And I can tell you whose raw nerve will be hit if you carry on with this nonsense! Of course I used to see her, every '*now and then*' as you like to say, driving around West Hollywood; and she sounded her horn and waved at me—as she did at everybody. But we never met again, not to talk to, until by chance— "

"By chance?"

"I discovered she had moved into my apartment block. It must have been several months since we had spoken."

"My poor godfather! Several months?"

"*Ragazzo ridicolo!*"

4

ThePatriotic Hummer

There was something appropriate, even poignant, about Madison driving herself around the sprawling town of Los Angeles in a falling-apart vehicle painted up as 'Old Glory'. But she loved that old wreck of a car, and it was soon the joke of the parking lot at San Vicente.

One lunchtime, she was returning from Jon's (the cheapest convenience store in town) with a car-load of brown-paper bags containing 'can't be beat' priced groceries, when she pulled up at the junction of Fountain and Hollywood, where they happened to be shooting an on-the-spot news item for a local TV station. Madison stuck her head out of the window and waved at the camera. She sounded her horn, and as the reporter turned round she gave him a smile and drove off.

The anchor-man back at the studio said to the on-the-spot reporter—"Who's the blond in the patriotic Hummer?"

And that's all it took.

The following day the anchor-man, short of anything else to say at the end of a segment, but needing to say something, *anything*, blurted out to the reporter—"Who *was* that blond by the way?" They both laughed, as television presenters often do, at nothing, in case they lose the momentum of their repartee. 'The blond in the patriotic Hummer' became a catch-phrase on the programme, to be spoken at random—"*Would that be the blond in the patriotic Hummer, Bob?*"—"*I guess that wasn't the blond in the patriotic Hummer, Jolie?*"—"*Well that looks like its all we got time for, Larry, but I need to ask you . . . who was that blond in the patriotic Hummer?*"

In no time at all, the totally meaningless set-piece banter was ping-ponging its way around every news-station in LA. The rule of thumb was, when you can't think of anything else, ask: "*Who's the blond in the patriotic Hummer?*"

Los Angeleans would say it to each other and guarantee a chuckle: "*By the way . . . I've been meaning to raise it with you . . . who's the blond in the patriotic Hummer?*" Shameless LA newspapers desperate to fill space would have a picture of Madison in her car, a 'still' from the first TV moment, with a caption

15

asking the same stupid question. The joke, if joke it was, even made it into the scripts of the big chat-shows on the Networks: first the West coast, then the East. The simple, unexplained words—"Who IS that blond?"—would get a laugh in the warm-up sessions.

Madison was unaware of any of this, because her diminishing funds could not afford cable TV and she never read a newspaper. She did begin to wonder, though, at what seemed to be a totally uncalled-for increase in the honking of car horns, even by LA standards. And the 'Hi's from people in the parking lot were much more familiar, for some unaccountable reason, than she could ever have expected from less than a month's living there.

Slowly, but surely, her small savings dwindled, and the day drew near when she would be forced to return home. She gave notice to the motel, told her mother she was coming back soon, and used all but her last few dollars on a budget flight to Wisconsin. Then, from left field, on the Tuesday morning of her final scheduled week in LA, she picked up a message on her answer-service telling her to call a number that meant nothing to her at all. The message said to call urgently. So she called at once.

> "Madeline, my dear! It's Wendle. Where have you been? I've been trying to track you down everywhere, like . . . how do I know? I finally got a hold of your number from your folks. I only hope the heat hasn't gone out of it."

Wendle? Her AGENT? Calling HER? She gushed some kind of reply, which was of no interest to him.

> "I've arranged the shoot for this afternoon. Take down the address and be there at 1.30 prompt."

Wendle Stein, spurred-on by the ridiculous 'who's the blond?' mania, had dreamed up the even crazier idea of a poster campaign, to 'take it to the next level'. She would appear on bill-boards all over Los Angeles, sitting in her now famous car, head out of the window, smiling and waving. That's all. Nothing else. Other than the caption: '*Who's the blond in the patriotic Hummer?*' Wendle said they would run it for a couple of weeks, to 'test the temperature'. His only concern was, as he kept saying—"I only hope the heat hasn't gone out of it."

But it hadn't. And the meaningless poster campaign stoked up the fire very nicely indeed. Soon Madison had a small income, in the strange way that celebrities in Los Angeles often do—by being celebrities. Of course she was a very small fish of a celebrity in a big pond full of great-white-shark celebrities, but she made enough money from opening convenience stores, attending 'B-list' film premiers and allowing local newspapers to make up nonsense stories about her, to move herself out of the motel in San Vicente and into her very own apartment. And she was sublimely happy there, having no ambition for anything better.

Then came the earthquake.

5
Monologue

"*You remember the earthquake in Los Angeles, back in 1994? The Northridge quake? Twenty or so killed outright?*

"*We were living in Larrabee, off Sunset, most of us. A block up from where River Phoenix died outside the Viper Rooms the year before, and all those flowers got piled up against the wall. Remember that? Poor guy. I read somewhere he had about six different narcotics in his bloodstream. Didier can take ten. But there won't be any flowers for Didier, you can count on that.*

"*04.31 Pacific Standard Time on January 17, 1994; I'll never forget it; everyone in our block got shook out of our beds, and the whole building juddered for a full 45 seconds that seemed like 45 minutes and we all stumbled out onto the sidewalk in boxer shorts and stuff, through broken glass—remember all that broken glass?—with the power off and a couple of guys with torches shouting at everyone to put their cigarette lighters out because of the gas. I hated those guys.*

"*And oh boy! Was it cold out there on the 'pavement'!—That's what Tom always called it. He was kinda smart-ass, don't you think, about not becoming an American?*

"*It was one of those January nights in LA when you can find ice up in the Hills. And all of us dressed for a pool party, freezing to death on the sidewalk. Then Tom snuck back into the block when the cops and the firemen weren't looking. Typical English. But it only took that one fella to lift up the colored 'keep out' tape they'd wound round the building, and sneak in, and the rest of us followed, like sheep. All of us—'the earthquake people'; a little hysterical, if I'm honest about it. Scared shitless, more like, but giggling in the dark like schoolgirls. Least, Madison was. You said 'I don't care if I die. I need my bed. I need to sleep.' (It WAS you. You always say it was the Dutch guy, but it was you.) Truth is, none of us cared. We were young back then. 'LA young' anyways. No matter how big the spread of ages, we all thought we're 'young', huh? Weird. Who gets old in Los Angeles?*

"*One by one we fumbled through the pitch black in different directions, and the group got smaller and smaller—I remember it so clearly, even now, like it was yesterday—like we were in some Agatha Christie, or 'Alien'—until there was just the two of us, you and me. We said our goodnights, and good lucks, and felt our different ways into the dark of our different rooms, and the comfort of our different beds.*

"That's when the aftershock came.

"It was just as bad as the quake. You gotta remember that! It had to be every bit as long. Shook me clean out of bed all over. I put on my bike helmet this time, and crouched under the doorway like they always tell us to. But the frame started cracking up, so it had to be back outside. Back into the freezing cold. I pulled on some jeans and a sweatshirt. I didn't think the pool-party look was right. Not for the sidewalk at five in the morning. Not on the borders of Beverly Hills.

"How you lied to the cops about not having left the building the first time! They knew you were lying, and we knew they knew you were lying, and Scott didn't even TRY to sound like he was telling the truth—and Madison still giggling didn't help—and we didn't give a damn, except there was no way they was going to let us get back in again, back to our warm beds.

"So Scott rounded us up, and said we should try to find somewhere for an early breakfast. Remember? He said: 'We'll turn this round and make it a good thing.' (He used to say that all the time. 'A good thing, not a bad thing.' That was him all over. I liked Scott.) 'Cept nothing around Sunset and Larrabee was open, so he took us off to Beverly Hills in his truck, on the basis that, according to Tom anyway, it being Beverly Hills an' all, they'd probably had the San Andreas Fault removed by lazar surgery. Funny guy. Not too sure I liked Tom, though. But he was funny, that's for sure.

"But you know what? He was damn right about Beverly Hills. There was a diner open all hours in Wilshire Blvd. That dirty old dump on the corner. Remember that diner? We poured in, tired and hungry and dusty, not knowing if we had homes any more, looking like the street-people that maybe we'd become for real. With the waitress who hated Tom SO much—for no reason 'cept he was Tom. You gotta remember her! The more English and polite Tom got, the more she hated him. So he just got more and more English and polite, didn't he? And when he did his full-on Hugh Grant thing, she snarled at him

'What d'ya want?'

'Do you, by chance, have any fresh orange juice?'

'Of COURSE we got orange juice. Large?'

Tom smiled—'No, small will be fine, thank you.'

She folded her arms and fired back at him: 'Large is the smallest we've got.'

"And that's how we met. That's how I see it, anyway. I mean MET. Properly. Weird, looking back. Not like the way we'd said 'Hi' over and over by the elevator. Meeting is different.

"I know, I know, Scott was never out of Chloe's apartment. And no-one ever bumped into the Dutch guy unless he was with Madison. But the way I see it, all of us met that morning for the first time. It's when we became . . . damned if I know if they even got a word for it . . . greater than the sum of the parts and all that crap. No-one thought about it then, you wouldn't, but the quake that tore Los Angeles apart was what pulled us together. Weird.

"And we were something else those days, huh? Madison called us the earthquake people; you preferred 'The Seismic Seven'; but Tom's was best: 'The Quakers'."

The nurse comes in, really quiet, and whispers to him 'would he would like a cup of coffee?' He shakes his head. She says the chair by the window is more comfortable and he helps her drag it to the bedside, and it catches the corner of the venetian blind, making little bands of shadow and sun rock backwards and forwards on the wall.

He asks her –

"Do you think . . . ?"

She anticipates what she has heard many times, from many a bedside.

"No one really knows. But maybe. For sure, maybe."

He nods a substitute for 'thanks'.

"Use names," the nurse tells him. *"Try not to say 'you' or 'me'. Most times you get something back it's because they heard names."*

"Is that right?"

She gives him a smile that is meant to be reassuring, and leaves the room, closing the door behind her so carefully it doesn't even 'click'.

He sits in the comfortable chair and pulls it even closer to the bedside. Only the slightest movement of the sheet indicates the slightest of breathing underneath it; and the pulsing machine confirms life, of a sort, despite the closed eyes and a face that could be a waxwork. He dims the lamp and continues—saying 'you' and 'me' before he can stop himself.

"*Did you know there could be so many aftershocks to an earthquake? The first, the big one, was no different than the quake. They would have called the movie 'Quake 2: Aftershock'. Someone told me it did even more damage, 'cause the buildings that the quake just put cracks in, the aftershock came in and demolished. I guess it was one of those movies where the sequel is better than the original.*

"*But I'd never have thought the franchise would extend to 'Aftershock 50' or perhaps it was 100? Maybe 300? OK, some of them were way smaller, but then you'd get a big one again, outa nowhere. Remember that time in a restaurant on 3rd, the whole gang of us was sat by the window when the 5.2 hit, and the window rippled with vibrations that started small enough, but turned into these big waves, waves as big as the surfers come in on, well almost, and everyone was screaming and running out into the street - 'cept us? Madison was so drunk she didn't give a damn; and Tom said "I don't care if I die, I need to eat!" - in your voice—because it was you said that back in the apartment block, not the Dutch guy. Remember now? You gotta remember now! The window didn't crack, though. Nothing broke, 'cept a glass or two that jumped off the sides of tables.*

"*The aftershock stopped juddering just as quick as it started; the waves rolling down the window turned back to ripples, then to solid glass; and the people outside came drifting in from the street, a bit sheepish, what with all of us still sitting like nothing had happened, while they had ran for their lives. Then, just as they are all inside, there was one of those silences—like you get in movie theatres, even sports grounds, when suddenly everyone stops talking for no reason—and while the people are picking their way through the restaurant to their seats, and there is this weird silence all of a sudden, Tom holds his wineglass by the side of his face, with his elbow on the table, and looks at us all serious, like he's replying to something one of has only just said, as if we'd been in deep conversation throughout the whole damn thing and not noticed it, he holds his wineglass to his head and says, so quietly the whole restaurant listens in, 'But of course, that has to be right!' Like we'd never noticed anything and had just kept on talking through it all, while they were panicking and screaming. Well that breaks the silence and everyone laughs and a few guys start clapping their hands and some of us stand up and take bows—for being so brave, I guess. I wasn't too sure, but I took my bow anyway.*

"*That was a great night. I loved that night.*

"*I loved it when there was a really small aftershock, 2.3 say, and the news channels were short of stories and tried to pump up the 'shock' to something newsworthy. Like the time we all went down to Newport Beach, and Chloe was going through one of those moods where she wouldn't share with Scott, so Scott came and shared with me, and Madison burst in around 6 a.m. before it was even light? All over-the-top dramatic like she always was, and announced, in the same way you'd announce an asteroid was hurtling towards Earth, Madison burst in with 'There's been another earthquake !!'*

"*So we turned on the TV to catch the coverage. And we found out it was only a poxy 2.3 aftershock. The epicenter was in downtown Pasadena, and the 'shock had hit at around 5.00 a.m. The local news station had a reporter just one hour later 'at ground zero'—which was only downtown Pasadena, but 'ground zero' sounded better—interviewing the owner of a corner grocery store. All for a little wobble of a 2.3! Can you believe it? A newsflash for a 2.3! The guy said -*

'I locked up like I usually do, last night. And everythin' was like it usually is, nothin' special to write home about. Then when I came in this mornin' and opened up the store, there was this can of baked beans layin' clean off the shelves in the aisle . . . shaken clean off it was.'

(Cut to can of baked beans on the floor of the aisle.)

'You can see the dent in the side of the can.'

(Close-up of dent.)

After a long pause, in which he stares out of the window with something like a smile on his lips for the first time that day (and many days before), he turns towards the bed and asks -

"*Who's idea was it go spend the night on the Queen Mary?*"

***

"*Everyone in LA dreaded those friggin' aftershocks, specially the first ones, even though we made jokes about it. How many would there be? How big? How many more buildings would be rubble by tomorrow morning? And how many of us crushed by the rubble? The same could be asked at any time during the day, 'course it could—but the answers were much more scary if they crept up on you in the dark.*

"*No-one wanted to go to bed. Remember? Not even Scott and Chloe. And they wanted to go to bed 24/7. Most nights, anyway. 'Cept when they was fighting.*

"*Someone (was it Madison?—sounds more like Tom.) came up with: 'Why don't we spend the night on the Queen Mary?' I doubt it was even floating then. What d'you think? In dry-dock? I remember it was next to the Spruce Goose, and that sure as hell wasn't floating. Anyway, we just assumed the Queen Mary was on the water, being a ship an' all.*

"Tom said we wouldn't feel any tremors, even the big ones, and we'd just heave side to side a little, like we were on a cruise to Acapulco, sleeping like nothing had happened. Bobbing up and down like a fisherman's float, so Tom said. Tsunamis weren't fashionable back then—I'd never even heard of them—and anyway the epicentre was 30 miles inland.

"So we all trooped down in the back of Scott's truck to the docks in San Pedro . . . 'cept . . . Remember? They wouldn't take his dog. Do you think that's when Chloe started to go cool on Scott - like, for real this time? When he left her on the boat and drove off to find a motel for him and his dog?

"Anyway, there we all are in the bar, Madison queening it, smiling at fans, doing the autograph thing and loving it, and a guy no one knows comes up, offers her a drink, gives her his card and asks if she would like to be a guest on some daytime chat-show no-one watches. That was Didier all over. You would have thought he produced the show. Never liked him from the get-go. Creepy kind of guy. But he was one smooth operator, that's for sure. She takes the bait quicker than a backwater catfish, and before the end of the week we're sitting in Larrabeee, round at the Dutch guy's place watching Madison on TV—'cos the dude had cable. Remember? Like the earthquake never happened.

"The world gets weirder and weirder. That's what I think, anyway."

6
Rome

"Who are you trying to kid? It's obvious! You fell in love with Madison. My most amorous godfather! *Bravo*! Cool! She still on TV? Star fucker!"

"Don't be an *imbecille*. I adored Madison. We all did. But I didn't fall in love with her. And your language is despicable."

"But you Italians fall in love with everyone."

"We also fall in hate."

"Now we're getting to it! Who did you hate? Not Madison, I hope? Please don't tell me you came to hate Madison. Not fragile and vulnerable little Madison?"

"*Che Schifo . . .* ! There is no word strong enough for . . . the *sirena* I came to hate. You would not know, because you have no passion. You do not *know* hate. Of course not Madison. Anyway, all of that comes later. Much later. How do you say *odio viscreal*?"

"A bad smell. But that's a guess."

"Now you are mocking with me." The old man looked at his watch impatiently "You had better go. You have a plane to catch."

"You can't leave it there. Christ! It was only a joke."

"Always you joke. And always in bad taste."

"At least finish about Madison? Jesus!"

It need hardly be said that now his godfather was into the story there was no power on earth that could stop him telling his godson *all* about Madison, and much more besides. But the little ritual of persuading him had to be gone through first.

"There's nothing to finish," said the old man. "*E non profanare*! How many times do I have to ask you?"

"Then tell me about the woman you hate instead! I have to know about *her*. Isn't that why I'm here?"

"Is that so?" said his godfather, rising to his feet. "You need to pack, you said?"

"Whoa! Packing can wait. You can't stop there. *Please* go on. Please. I'm sorry. Most venerable godfather, I'll behave."

The old man took a deep breath, stared at his godson, and sighed.

"I'll tell you about Madison," he said, "but that's all."

"I ask for nothing more." (A blatant lie.)

"It is, in fact, charming. Perfect for your lukewarm blood." He returned to his chair. "Prepare yourself for a fairy story. *Una fabia.* Then you go."

7
Ghosts

Madison would be wholly unable, now, to tell you which of the prime-time chat shows signed her up first. After all, it is a long while ago, and a whole lot has happened since.

Whichever of the 'big three' it was that first answered the question on the lips of Los Angeles—who *is* "the blond in the patriotic Hummer"?—she was soon scooped-up for guest appearances on all of them; initially, it has to be admitted, with the idea of a mockery driving the chat, rather than anything that might further her career in Hollywood. But to everyone's surprise, and the vindication of the few who had championed her, she was gloriously entertaining in interview. Her trick was never to let the words galloping out of her brain take any detours into truth or reality before racing down the home-straight towards her mouth. She was made in heaven to sit on the studio sofas and chairs, and say the first thing that came into her head; and that 'thing' was either funny, or interesting, or both.

Of all the spontaneous nonsense pouring out of Madison, most popular with the audiences were: a twin sister (Madison was an only child), who was born dead, but with whom she felt she had some kind of affinity she couldn't understand, and certainly couldn't explain; a great-uncle who taught her to sharp-shoot (she had never in her life handled a gun)—who didn't exist but had overcome that difficulty and gone on tour with Buffalo Bill; her mother (who out of a bourgeois respect for biology did exist) for whom she gave up two years of her life, nursing her back to health after she was bitten by a black-widow spider and nearly died; and the great-great-grandmother who had a letter signed by Abraham Lincoln—"No! She hadn't considered its value. And it was far too precious to put on eBay! You're kidding me, right? You're *bad!*"—and to the adoring studio audience, in an inexplicable southern drawl: "He's *bai-yud!*"

The variety of ways in which people respond to life's little absurdities is well illustrated by the buxom, rosy-cheeked, never-been-ill-in-her-life, possibly immortal mother of Madison, watching the program from back in

Wisconsin, vividly recalling those non-existent two years of near-death as if they had been yesterday, as well as the great uncle on the road with Colonel William Cody—although she couldn't quite remember where she'd put Abraham Lincoln's letter.

Madison's tour of the chat-show circuit and her guest appearances on panel-games made her a familiar face on TV, day and night. Wendle called and said he had decided to double the number of billboards—"To fan the flames my dear". Whether the caption, now she was a celebrity, should *state* 'The Blond in the Patriotic Hummer', rather than ask the original question 'Who's the Blond in the Patriotic Hummer?', exercised Wendle's brain more than usual, distracting it from almost everything else; and he fretted over the dilemma vocally one afternoon in bed with his secretary. She, secretly hoping for its failure, suggested they stick to the old wording.

"Worked like it was, didn't it?" she said. "An' if you change it, what d'you do 'bout the ones already up there?"

Wendle was persuaded, and opted for the tried and trusted words on the original posters. In less than a week Madison was smiling and waving from her patriotic Hummer (restored and re-painted) high above every street in LA.

***

"Ghost Trail" was a TV programme of a kind known the world over, and it had a loyal following in spite of never managing it all its years to capture on film anything more exciting than the performers' *reaction* to supernatural occurrences, rather than the occurrences themselves.

The wobble of hand-held cameras gave a *cinéma vérité* feel to dimly-lit scenes in abandoned houses, old prisons, underground caves—all filmed by the light of torches, and equipment that bathed the fuzzy picture in a green glow, even though full studio-lighting was available if they had cared to use it. Black and white was the preferred medium, other than for the night-vision green and the orange/red images from heat-sensing cameras.

The ghost-detecting equipment was an integral part of the show. Dauntingly scientific in name, it could in fact be purchased online for a few dollars from outlets advertising their products in a very matter-of-fact way, with insouciant headings such as:

Ghost hunting equipment: below is a list of *the most commonly recommended* items for use in ghost hunting:

- **Particle detectors**

- **Ion detectors**
- **Infrared motion detectors**
- **Infrared thermometers**
- **Dowsing rods**
- **Mel meters**

Those were "The most commonly recommended". Less commonly recommended was equipment which one can only assume it would be irresponsible to sell to amateurs.

The cast of Ghost Trail liked to refer to the tools of their trade by initials whenever possible. DVR, EVP, EMF.

"My DVR is showing activity."—"I'll take a reading on my EVP."—"There is an unusually strong EMF."—"We'll catch it on the IMD."

The Mel Meters, of course, were Full Spectrum. They would have been utterly useless otherwise.

Pieces of kit not much larger than a cell phone (they might have *been* cell phones) that glowed in the dark, and verified—without any doubt at all—that there was *energy* present. Energy that was trapped! In a wall, a paving stone, or the air itself. The presence of energy meant the presence of 'spirits'. As Bradley frequently explained –

"Technically, Spirits are energy that hasn't been used."

It was a shame he never gave a non-technical explanation so we might all understand.

The long-running success of 'Ghost Trail' was in no small measure due to the skill—cunning, almost—with which the team was assembled:

A psychic, Kaitlyn, who could be relied on to know if spirits were present, even without the aid of a DVR. In fact, Kaitlyn had no faith in DVRs. (Or EVPs, if you pressed her.) She just *knew* if there were any spirits around. And who could contradict her?

A skeptic, Dr. James, whose role was to create an impression of balance by raising doubts (only little ones) about there being anything supernatural happening at all, and counteract the rock-solid certainty of Kaitlyn with the mildest of plausible alternative explanations for the various shocking incidents the team was exposed to.

Bradley. A hard-nosed, hard-hatted, bruiser of a man, with a tough-guy name, and no end of things clanking from his thick belt. A no-nonsense firm believer in the spirit-world, who was always the first to put himself in danger (such as opening a creaking door and fearlessly entering a room in which they had had a pre-production meeting that afternoon). Wholly inarticulate in post-investigation discussion, but verbally liberal when in action, to the point of Tourettes, with his repeated battle-cry "*Ok Man. Let's Do it.*" cranking up the excitement, immeasurably, when things seemed to flag.

A medium, Courtney. Her function was to hold séances, and even to become possessed if an accommodating spirit happened to be passing that way; which tended to be when any other member of the team looked like upstaging her. The skill was to keep the fits appropriate to the level of possession, and to the character of the possessor—by which I mean (to adopt European Union terminology) no more than was necessary and proportionate in pursuit of the legitimate aim, viz., preventing anyone from stealing her big scene.

The repertoire of shocking incidents was no different from those in the dozen other TV shows of a like kind, and included -

- **Cold-spots** (that no-one could disprove)—"Do you feel that?"—"Yes. I feel it."—"I'm *so* frigging cold, man!"—"So am I"—"Oh my God!"

- **Sound recordings** which were made in an empty room, but when they were played back there was *noise* on the tape—such as the squeaking of a loose spool in the crude recording device—"Oh my God!"

- **Invisible beings** brushing against the performers—"Something just touched my hand!"—"Mine too!"—"Oh my God!"

- **Footsteps**—"Listen to that!"—"What is it?"—"Footsteps."—"Yes! I hear them."—"Oh my God!"

- Most important of all—***the sound of heavy breathing***. This was provided off-screen by Vince, the cameraman, and rather too often it descended into the sound of Vince's badly suppressed laughter. (Oh my God.)

When they visited a room and had exhausted all touchings, footsteps, trapped energy, EMF, cold spots, heavy breathing—someone would say, with unprovoked passion, "*I need to get out of here. Something doesn't want us to be here.*" Or—"*I can't breathe!*" This heralded an off-stage BANG or an unexplained scream, and the team would quickly move on to the next fantastic phenomenon, with no explanation at all for what had just happened—or not happened, depending on your perspective.

Sometimes they reached the door to a room, and improvisation (rather than courage) failed them altogether, and they would say things like "*There's something evil in there. I can feel it!*" This might or might not be corroborated by an EVP reading. In any event, they would leave the door unopened—and whatever was on the other side unexplored and unexplained.

In a period of crisis 'Ghost Trail' itself had a near death experience, and came close to slipping into the afterlife of TV shows—doomed for eternity to be repeated on cable channels with bigger and bigger numbers, until so far down the TV listings no-one could seriously be thought to watch them, and advertising space was more or less free. Kaitlyn, the psychic, was arrested by the IRS for a tax fraud—(she never saw that coming)—and hit the bottle the same day the story hit the tabloids. Unless they filmed it from a police-cell in Van Nuys, the show was in real difficulties. Either she was replaced, and quickly, or the Network would have no choice but to pull the plug.

Enter Madison.

Her existing, albeit fragile, celebrity, and her natural ability to lie on tap, convincingly, which the chat-shows had scarcely begun to exploit; coupled with—most important of all—her relationship with her dead twin sister; spurred the producers of 'Ghost Trail' into the high-risk strategy of throwing Madison to the spirits, in a desperate make-or-break bid to keep the show on air.

She quickly saw the danger of being resented by the existing cast, even though she might more charitably have been thought of as their saviour. She came onto the show a higher-ranking celebrity than any of them: they were known faces, but only to a relatively small audience: and none of them had been on Letterman. When Madison walked into a diner she could expect heads to turn: the cast of 'Ghost Trail' walked in begging for recognition, and often acted as though they *had* been recognised by diners who hadn't the faintest idea who they were, and didn't care much either. So Madison had to battle against an initial unhelpfulness from the whole team and, in particular, a determination in the jealous Courtney to make her fail.

To the irritation of them all, Madison took to her supernatural role like a duck to water, or maybe a bat to moonlight is more appropriate. She was, of course, an only child, and there had never been any twin, dead or alive. Which made it all the more remarkable when she was warned, and with such urgency, on the very first show, by the spirit of her dead twin sister, not to enter a certain room with a shimmering green door that the night-vision camera was pointing at. The mystery was deeper than anyone in the TV audience could possibly have fathomed. Not only was there a ghost trying to stop Madison entering the room—but the ghost was lying about being her sister.

"Are there any spirits here? Speak to us!"

Why any spirit should even contemplate doing so, having nothing whatsoever in common with any of them, was a bigger mystery than 'Ghost Trail' ever cared to explore.

"Spirits. What are you trying to tell us?"

Vince, the cameraman, had his ideas, but kept them to himself.

"Quiet everyone! Do you hear that?"

Madison assumed a dramatic intensity more like Lillian Gish than Jessica Lange.

"Hush! Footsteps! Do you hear them?"

You should understand that it was the accepted role of anyone who was off-camera at such a moment to walk either towards or away from the microphone, so that those who were on-camera could legitimately get themselves in a lather about a ghost pacing up and down somewhere out of picture. It happened to be Courtney who was off-camera then, and whose clear duty it was to start walking; but she was so put-out that Madison was surviving her initiation with panache that she stood with her arms folded across her chest, and refused to provide the slightest aural confirmation of footsteps, either towards the microphone or away from it, or on the ceiling for all she cared.

"Footsteps?" said Bradley, with an angry stare at Courtney, which carried every commanding ounce of his hallmark expression "OK, Let's do it!"

Courtney stood her ground, and didn't do it.

"I'm not sure . . . " faltered Dr. James, and Vince stifled a snort. But Madison, wholly un-phased, came riding to the rescue -

"Is that you, Alice?"

Alice! A seminal moment in TV history. Madison, from nowhere in particular, had dreamed-up a name, never before mentioned, for her non-existent dead twin sister. (The researchers put in a good few hours checking interviews to make *sure* Madison had not previously given her sister a different name. Happily, no other christening was found, so the never-born, but dead, Alice was baptized accordingly.)

"Alice. Speak to me. Why don't you want me to go into that room?"

Alice, had she existed, would not have cared less if Madison went into the room or went shopping on Rodeo Drive. The room was empty, except for a broken wicker table buckled over its three remaining legs, some orange boxes stuffed with decayed papers of no importance to anyone, and—of course—energy. Loads of it. Trapped energy. Energy that 'hadn't been used up'.

Courtney was not to be outdone. She staggered into view, like *Lucia di Lammermoor* in her mad scene, <u>possessed</u> by Alice!—who, it would seem, was suffering from an extremely heavy chest-cold.

"Don't . . . go . . . there. Don't . . . go . . . there," she rasped using only the longest and deepest-sounding of her vocal chords.

Now each of these two rival girls was in the power of the other. Madison could easily have exposed Courtney as a fraud by asking 'Alice' questions about her family, which she knew Courtney could not answer. And Courtney could have 'let slip' some embarrassing revelations, of her own invention, about Madison's past. But both of them were troopers, and the show went on, as it had to, with the benefit of their mutual assistance.

Madison made a wise decision to ignore Courtney's hostility towards her, and even came to her rescue by interrupting a torrent of spiritual explanation as to why no-one should go into the room—which was about to become preposterous even by that show's standards—with a sudden, and indisputable proclamation –

"She's gone! She's gone!"

– which Courtney had the sense to understand meant 'shut the fuck up'.

A long sigh, and a wistful look at Dr. James:

"She's gone," repeated Madison sadly, with a shake of her weary head and a courageous smile. "Boy that was tough!"

Dr. James put a comforting arm round the emotionally shattered surviving twin.

"Are there *any other* spirits here?" asked Bradley, rather feebly, giving Courtney the opening for another fit, had she been inclined to have one.

But Courtney was smarter than that—Alice had left her drained too, and she leaned against the wall in a semi-trance, drawing deep, other-worldly breaths.

Not everyone subscribed to the view that there was at that very moment a small sub-sonic vibration on the wooden floor of the old shack where they were recording. Possibly the smallest-measurable of aftershocks. But those who *were* sure of it screamed their heads off in response.

Unfortunately, Vince burst out laughing at the same time, and the producer had to shout "Cut".

"I'm telling you Vince. One more time . . . "

"I'm sorry. I'm sorry." Vince controlled himself for a second or two, then buckled up in helpless laughter again, and the producer said 'he meant it', in a really stern voice.

Madison managed to light a cigarette in the short break, so when the cameras started rolling again, although she quickly stubbed it out, there was a residual haze of nicotine in the air.

"Do you see that?"

Courtney had made a complete recovery; and, grateful for having been rescued by Madison, chimed in with a fearsome—"I see it!"

"Oh my God!"

"Oh my God!"

The camera swung round to catch the dissipating cigarette smoke. Bradley, who in younger years had taken minor roles in porn films, liked to be macho with the spirits -

"Come on! Show yourself! We're not afraid!"

The last of the cigarette smoke evaporated.

"Big guy, huh?" sneered Bradley. "Too scared? We're not going anywhere!"

I am sure we are agreed, it is not in the least remarkable for a speck of dust to float in the disturbed air of a long-deserted house, especially if it has had a film crew stomping around it all day long. One such spec drifted into the beam of light shining from Bradley's torch. A *tiny* speck of dust. I cannot begin to describe how tiny it was. Almost microscopic. It innocently meandered across the camera lens, and for the two seconds it caught the light from Bradley's torch it caused mayhem.

"Oh my God! Oh my God!" screamed Madison and Courtney, in unison.

Vince waved his camera around, as though he were using it to swat a fly. Which was visually effective, and commendable in so many ways, but unfortunately it caught some of the crew sitting on a nearby bench nonchalantly drinking from bottles of Rolling Rock.

"You like to play games with us, huh? You like that?" shouted Bradley, to the emptiness.

It was his turn, now, to drift, along with the speck of dust, dangerously close to the dialogue more familiar to him in his pornographic film days. Vince couldn't resist saying, and saying too loudly -

"Yeah, you like that, don't you!"

The whole crew guffawed, and the producer 'gave up the ghost' and called it a wrap up for the day.

Courtney was far too savvy not to realise that Madison was going to be a hit, and she made no further attempt to sabotage her success on the show. She even apologized, saying she wasn't feeling too well and didn't know what had possessed her to behave the way she had. When Madison replied that it must be the first time *anything* had possessed her, they fell about laughing and became the firmest of friends.

Madison's role on 'Ghost Trail' was assured. She was a natural. The risk had paid off, and the producers were satisfied that she could be relied on to react, violently, to nothing, for an indeterminate number of episodes in the future. When it would all come to an end, neither Madison nor Courtney, nor any of them—not even with the help of the DVRs, EVPs, EMFs and the Full Spectrum Mel Meters—could tell.

But the irony was not lost on the newcomer that, whilst not a single one of them had the slightest belief in the psychic nonsense they served up to their sad viewers, each of them predicted with unerring certainty that Kaitlyn would be found guilty of revenue fraud and sent to jail.

8

Madison's Oscar Party

Madison's new-found celebrity, with a small-by-Hollywood-standards, but nonetheless substantial income attached, moved her into a modest penthouse apartment at the quieter end of Larrabee, with a balcony big enough to have breakfast on, and a view over the pool to a tiny corner of the old Spago's restaurant where Swifty Lazar gave his famous post-Oscar parties.

Madison, too, gave an Oscar party on her first Oscar Night in her new home. She provided a grandstand view of the awards on her huge TV screen (the largest money could buy—about the size of '*The Night Watch*'). And even better, she gave her guests a vicarious sense of being at the heart of things, which TV audiences were denied: she made available, for three or four at a time on her balcony, a real-life, up-close sight of that tiny corner of Spago's the other side of the pool; and her guests could hear the actual sounds, as they happened, not broadcast on TV or radio, of the scaffolding being set up for the cameras to catch the stars as they made the rounds after the Governor's Ball. It was only necessary to touch the hem of Oscar's robe, so to speak, to have a part of Him.

Madison invited Wendle Stein to her party (who, mercifully, came alone), for whom she had a soft spot. She wanted to acknowledge publicly, and thank him in a little speech she had prepared, for being the engineer of her success. Alcohol overtook her memory, however, and she never gave the speech.

She also asked a handful of those neighbours who she saw most frequently, as well as some of her new friends from behind-the-scenes of television—who, to be frank, only came when they heard the size of her TV screen. Other than Courtney, the front-of-camera folk were beyond the reach of friendship and weren't asked.

The party was not a failure, but the groups did not mix particularly well—which can happen when you bring people together from different corners of your life: they have little in common, except you, and each corner is covetous of your friendship, and resentful of whatever relationship you have with the other corners.

Wendle alone was as affable with Madison's show-biz friends as he was with her Larrabee neighbours—which may have been due to the fact that his affability was so perfectly insincere it could be spread everywhere equally. It was never too long after he started talking to someone, before Wendle asked –

"Do you have representation?"

"I'm sorry?"

"My books are—if not overflowing, I don't know what they are. But if . . . "

"I teach history of art at UCLA."

"My dear, I thought you were one of our bright young aspiring actors at . . . wherever they're at these days, you tell—"

"He said he's a teacher," said a scruffy behind-the-scenes-of-TV youth, who clearly regarded teaching as a contemptible occupation and vastly inferior to shifting scenery.

"But he has the looks of a leading man, my dear." (Scruffy youth as pissed-off as pissed-off can be.)

Wendle shuffled away, working the room all night in the hope of 'filling his overflowing books' from another source—any source.

"There he is! There he is!"—The cry went up from the girls grouped round Madison's TV, as one of the up-and-coming heart-throbs was mobbed by reporters.

"Who represents him?" asked Wendle.

We can be fairly certain that the animals filed into Noah's Ark in less time than the stars walked the Red Carpet into the Kodak Theatre: but eventually they were all herded inside (the film stars), and the long wait began before the Award ceremony itself.

In the interval Wendle made an interesting proposition, to an unlikely person.

"I hesitate to ask," he said to a dark-haired woman who was putting a hot dog and salad onto a plate for her small son, "but is your delightful boy already in the business?"

"He's only eight years old!" replied the woman, laughing.

"Think Shirley Temple my dear," said Wendle.

"I wouldn't want him to be *that*," the mother protested.

"I don't mean . . . you know what I mean . . . what do I mean? . . . not a girl my dear . . . of course . . . think . . . think more like . . . "

"George Burns?" suggested an extraordinarily tall woman in black salopette-style pants. (She had been introduced as a production assistant but had said '*it was a little more complicated, but a long story*', with a closed eyes and a mysterious smile that left no one in any doubt, that whatever it was she did, it was pretty damned important.)

"Younger, of course," said Wendle. "But you're not serious. Are you?"

The tall more-important-than-production-assistant, who had misheard the conversation, and had been utterly serious, gave a careless shrug indicating that she had been teasing Wendle, and that he should count himself fortunate to have been noticed by her at all.

"I guess you're thinking more on the lines of Hayley Joel Osment?" said the good-looking teacher, pointedly smiling at the dark-haired woman.

"What did you have in mind?" she asked Wendle, having no interest whatsoever in the answer, but amused to string him along nonetheless.

"There's a show they call WEBNBC," said Wendle.

"I haven't seen it."

He explained - "'What Every Boy Needs' my dear, W . . . E . . . B . . . N, on NBC. It's an acrylic."

"An acrylic?" asked the art teacher, raising an eyebrow at the boy's mother. There was something cute going on between the two of them from which a discerning observer might have concluded that this was not their first encounter.

"WEBNBC . . . it spells out What Every Boy Needs NBC . . . or it should . . . you get the point, I'm sure," said Wendle. "They've collided the two ends."

"I'm on the production crew," said one of Madison's TV friends. And she said it bitterly. "I shouldn't repeat this, but I'm drunk, so I will." Then she emptied her glass and tottered away without saying what she shouldn't repeat, but would.

"I *have* seen it," said the teacher. "They get the kids wound up about stuff. And then the kids pester their parents to buy it for them."

"How wicked," said the boy's mother, archly.

The teacher retaliated –

"What every boy needs, of course, is a dog."

"And a mother who allows him to have a dog," she replied.

"Oh please, please mom, please," cried her son.

"What a truly delightful thing it is," said Wendle. "Children and animals. Delightful. There's an episode on WEBNBC . . . "

"Children and *any* animals?" asked the boy's mother.

"Dogs. Ideally dogs. Chimpanzees work. And . . . "

"Snakes?" suggested the good-looking teacher, never taking his eyes off the dark-haired woman.

A fanfare of music drowned Wendle's reply. The Awards had begun in earnest, and further speculation on the subject of 'what every boy needs' was
brought to an end. But Wendle had just enough time to pass the dark-haired
woman a card.

"They're scouting for new talent. I was thinking Johnny . . . "

"Billy."

"Whatever you say my dear."

And the big opening number started. And all conversation stopped. And
the long haul through the presentations and speeches began.

Everything went as it usually did on Oscar nights, with the inevitable arguments about who hadn't deserved to win, and who had been overlooked; the
TV crowd asserting a superior right to any opinion on the subject—"it's rather
obvious, surely?"—with an tired indulgence to those not in show-business, as
much as to say '*I will give you a few seconds of my time, but there really isn't any
point discussing this with you.*'

The 'best picture' was a foregone conclusion (because it centred on
disability and ethnicity) and it aroused no interest at all, except for an inflam-
matory comment from the more-important-than-production-assistant, who
said she hadn't seen it and wild horses would not drag her to see it—which
prompted a limp debate. The award having been received, the whole world
thanked, the closing music played, the end-titles rolled, and with the com-
mercials shouting at them from the TV, Madison's Oscar party was over, and
her guests drifted away.

There is a nice convention, by which people who meet for the first time at
an acquaintance's house and have taken against each other on sight, when it
comes time to leave, affect to part as though they were the best of friends and
can hardly wait until they meet again. That nice convention, however, was
not observed at Madison's Oscar party. The different groups left with scarcely
a look at each other—and certainly no pretence of friendship—and with sufficient a degree of ill-feeling that if there happened to be an unfortunate
mixture of them at the elevator, those from one group would take the stairs
rather than share the elevator with the other group.

The chief advantage of the alcoholic haze through which Madison saw
everything that night was that she was blissfully unaware of the depth of
ill-feeling between the two branches of her LA society. She could just about
see that not *everyone* liked each other—but that's how the world is, and it
didn't bother her at all. The party, she thought, had been a *great* success.
She closed the door on the last of them and lay on her bed listening to the

loudspeaker announcements of the film stars arriving at Spago's, until she fell asleep dreaming she was there amongst them.

When she heard a voice booming over the speakers—"*Ladies and Gentlemen, Mr. and Mrs. James Stewart!*"—greeted by cheers and applause, and no doubt a genuinely modest wave from the man himself—Madison thought that life could get no better.

It got much worse, of course.

Two

1
Rome

"I am responsible for your mother meeting Scott."

"You told me that much," said his godson.

"It was during the 'Rodney King' riots," said the old man, as if it were mitigation.

"Before my time."

"But you know about it?"

"Sure. There was some looting and stuff."

"*Non ci credo!*" exclaimed his godfather. "The whole of Los Angeles saw the filming of it!" He put on an exaggerated display of astonishment, which might perhaps have been appropriate if a young American had not heard of George Washington. "Four *polizietti* beating, kicking, and . . . what is it called? When they lash out with their guns?"

"Pistol-whipping."

"Pistol whipping! What kind of people could have *una espressione special* for such a thing? Eh? And 'pistol whipping' someone without weapon, completely harmless! *Indifeso!*" (The more emphatic he became, the more Italian he used.)

"I wasn't defending—"

"Your Los Angeles had also taken note of a number of other *polizietti*"—he screwed his mouth around the word, as though he were eating a bad piece of meat—"close by, seeing all, *non fanno niente.*" (Now he worked himself up into a froth of melodramatic anger, which his godson found both amusing and annoying.) "Bored animals with full stomachs at another animal's kill."

"It's not *my* Los Angeles."

"And your Los Angeles had, *dare il colpo di grazia*"—he landed on the first syllable of each word, as though jumping from verbal stepping stone to verbal stepping stone—"seen the trial of the *polizietti* on TV, and the freedom of them—how do you say it?"

"Acquittal," helped his godson, if a little reluctantly.

"And at the acquittal of these *monsters*,"—he all-but shouted the word—"Los Angeles drew a sharp breath that made the whole city shudder."

"You sure picked the right night to introduce my mom to Scott."

"It is no joke, little *Scottino*," said the old man, calming down. "I found it was difficult, impossible—and it was the same for many others—model citizens, who go to church and ask God to bless America—it was difficult even for them, not to be . . . *comprensivo* with the sense of . . . of hopelessness. Hopelessness that turned to anger, anger that exploded into *furia*"—(with a magnificent flourish of his hand)—"*furia* that took to the streets in riot. If what was done to Rodney King was not a crime, what was? Eh? What could ever be a crime, committed by white *polizia* against a black man? It is not much altered now, is it not?"

His godson made no attempt to deny it. The spectre of Ferguson Missouri haunted the room, with a New York Grand Jury incandescent alongside it.

"But you are closer to the truth, by accident, than you might think. Los Angeles came out onto its rooftops and stood watching the fires and the explosions, glad to be at so safe a distance I am sure. Some had children on their shoulders to get a better view. A few came out with drinks in their hands, glasses of wine, bottles of beer, as though the rioting was a party, *una festa*.

"I went up onto the roof of our block in Larrabee and took Madison and your mother. We stood watching alongside Scott, who had a small boy hoisted up over his head, with a woman close by, holding the boy's hand to steady him. Now and then there was a distant flash of fire, and a roar—almost a cheer!—came from a handful of people close by.

"Scott muttered—loudly—'*It's not a Fourth of July firework display,*' in a disgusting voice."

"Disgusted."

"As you like. Then Chloe edged towards him. None of us knew him, not then. '*It's terrible, isn't it?*' she said. '*From every perspective,*' said Scott. The boy gave Chloe a quick glance. Scott half-turned when he spoke, but kept his eye on the flames. The woman ignored Chloe completely.

"Chloe nodded to Scott but received no acknowledgment in return, so we moved away and had no further exchange with him, or any of them, that day."

* * *

"The second night of the riots, as it became dark, Madison knocked on the door of my *appartamento*. Chloe was with her. They asked if I would go up with them and see how things looked. We climbed the little stairway leading onto the rooftop. There were a great many more people this second night: not so much drinking, and no cheering at the 'fireworks'. The flames had moved closer, you see—half as close as they were the day before. But no-one talked about that. It was not possible that a riot starting in Watts could creep up to the very borders of Beverley Hills. Eh?—Was it?

"In the streets below, the *polizia* stood around and did nothing, *come Nerone*, while LA burned.

"Scott was on his own, leaning over the rail, and Chloe casually led us towards him. They made eye-contact, and Chloe asked him 'Where's your boy?'—'Oh, he's not mine,' Scott smiles at her. 'They've high-tailed it out of LA . . .'—'*high-tailed it*'! I shall never forget! An explosion on La Brea masked the rest of his words.

"Chloe said—'I couldn't leave. Not now. It would be like deserting a sinking ship'. So she said to him, or something similar. That her fine sentiments might show her in a good light—and make a pleasant contrast with the woman who held the *bambino's* hand the previous evening, and had run from the city, eh?—'high-tailed it'—I am sure nothing like that ever crossed your mother's mind."

"She hit on him that quick?"

"*Hit on him* is not fair. But no doubt there was what you call '*chemistry*'. I could see that. Madison could see it too. Scott was very good-looking, you understand. So was your mother, of course, with big eyes like Claudette Colbert—who I suppose was also before your time?"

"Never heard of her."

"*Naturalmente*. Everything is before your time, eh?"

The old man sighed a long sigh. He was a master of the long sigh.

"But your mother would not allow the conversation to stop there, so she made another advance at him: 'Did you see Rodney King on the TV asking '*can we all get along*?' she said. 'Can you see anyone doing a goddam thing to stop what's happening?' says Scott, and he shuffled back towards the building. He turned at the doorway and called 'have a nice evening' over his shoulder.

"I don't think he was being sarcastic with us, but he was angry, for sure. We stayed for a half-hour or so, until it became unbearable to watch. Down on Sunset, and on Santa Monica and Melrose Boulevards, on Pico and on La Brea, sprawled across Highland and Third, we saw the fire-engines, the patrol cars, the National Guard, all spectators from their safe distances—always as before, doing nothing, and with no more intention of doing *anything*, so it would seem, than the rest of Los Angeles' watchers, looking at events on TV or from their roof-tops, shrinking from the rioting the way they run from their summer bush-fires."

* * *

"In the morning of the third day the cars parked on Larrabee were covered in a grey-brown ash, still floating down from the sky where it had floated up from the burning city the night before.

"I saw Chloe getting into her vehicle, at the same moment as Scott came out of the building. 'It looks like snow,' she shouted at him gaily; and before I had time to say to her 'No!' she pulls the lever that squirts soapy-wash over the windscreen—and just one swipe of the blades turned the 'snow' into a thick brown soup. A half-gallon of screen-wash, I am certain not a drop less, finally cleared her view—but by then her quarry had gone.

"I took her to the rooftop again that night. But Scott was not there."

* * *

"On the fourth and fifth nights there was a dusk-to-dawn curfew. South Central suffered massive power cuts. By now you could *hear* the screams and shouts of the rioters if you stood-still on the Larrabee rooftop; and the nearest explosions could be measured in hundreds of metres rather than numbers of miles. The National Guard was at last called into action—*grazie a Dio!*—and Marines from Camp Pendleton patrolled San Vicente and Holloway.

"A few in our block gave 'curfew parties' to pass the hours and comfort each other throughout our imprisonment, and sometimes even these parties were plunged into darkness by a power-out.

"Chloe gave a little party on the fifth and last night of this terrible time. I suggested to her that I should invite Scott, even though we still didn't know him. I did it for your mother, you understand? And he came.

"I was talking with her when there was another power-cut; and in the sudden dark I heard a soft male voice, *molto affettuoso*, say—'*Are you OK?*' Chloe was standing next to me, but I somehow don't think the man was concerned for me, eh? Then he said to her—'*Hey, come here!*' and pulled her into a nice little hug and patted her back. The lights flickered on and . . . *Santo Cielo!* He was *not* who she thought it was! She shook herself free and without thinking spouted out these words to Scott—who was the other side of the table, and it made him smile when he heard them—she said to him '*I thought it was you!*'—which was perhaps a little embarrassing for her, don't you think?"

2
Scott & Chloe

There are some people in life who almost everyone seems to be in love with. The reason for this may have something to do with the fact that they, the loved ones, seem to be in love with almost everyone else. Scott was just such a loved and loving person. People of both sexes came alive when he joined them, and like Cole Porter '*died a little*' when they said goodbye. It's more than Platonic, but less than carnal. Whatever it is, we see it often enough, and never more so than when such a person is, as Scott most certainly was, extremely good-looking.

He had his bundle of faults, like the rest of us. He was somewhat vain; determinedly self-reliant; and almost rude to anyone who tried to help him or give advice—'interfered', was how he saw it. And he could be stubborn, very stubborn—"*as stubborn as a pasta stain on a white t-shirt*", Tom used to say.

A trait which some found admirable, others plain silly, was that when things went wrong for Scott he determined to find *something* positive in whatever had happened, and affected to turn events to his advantage. "*We'll make it a good thing, not a bad thing.*" It was his 'trademark phrase'—or so Tom called it.

He was no Pollyanna. He feared the worst in people, and his fears were too-often justified. He could be ultra-critical. More frequently disappointed than gratified. But he always forgave—or seemed to forgive—and Tom often remarked that there was no one he ever met who didn't want Scott's approval.

Chloe most certainly wanted his approval—and a whole lot more besides. She wasn't as beautiful, in the classical sense, as he was handsome; but the sheer joy of her, the liveliness, the fun, the mischief (never unkind, unless it was *really* funny), the huge dark eyes, and the sudden contralto notes that bubbled into her mezzo voice, gave her more than her fair share of a different kind of beauty, and made her the natural enemy of a great many women.

Scott had no-one special in his life when Chloe moved into Larrabee, if you discount his dog, who slept on Scott's bed down at his feet, and growled when Scott turned over. Chloe, similarly, had no-one special in her life—no dog nor any other animal—although she had left a string of bruised hearts behind her when she, and her contralto notes, and those eyes, moved up to LA from Orange County.

Alone in her room on the last night of the riots, still mortified by her gaffe, Chloe lay in her bed thinking how maybe it could be through his dog that she finally broke the ice with Scott; and she began working-up a first line of 'nice-dog' dialogue that didn't sound too corny. If she said the dog had beautiful eyes, what were the chances Scott would say . . . ?

And with that unfinished thought, she fell asleep.

* * *

Chloe was saved the risk of further embarrassment if her over-rehearsed remarks about the cuteness of the dog's eyes did not come off as well as she hoped. A few days after the riots had ended, and LA had settled itself back into the familiar rhythms of unreal life, Scott and Chloe ran into each other in the mail-room, and Scott's dog effected all Chloe could have wished for, in a few easy seconds. He did so by growling at her: fiercely, on sight, and wholly without cause.

"Hey! Behave!"

"That's OK. I'm great with dogs."

She moved to pet him; but a ferocious snarl, turning into a vicious SNAP of the teeth, sent Chloe reeling backwards.

"HEY!" yelled Scott, and pulled the dog to heel.

Chloe, who had jumped against the wall and dropped her mail, said a less than convincing "Good Girl".

"Boy."

If dogs grin (and I think they do) the dog grinned. Ear to ear. He tugged at his master's leash, pawing at the door to get away from *that ridiculous woman*; and Scott allowed himself to be pulled out of the mail-room, with a 'catch you later' that caught Chloe's heart with no 'later' about it.

So the shape of better things to come which Chloe had striven for took form all by itself. That same afternoon Scott sent her a small bunch of flowers, with a note that read—

The mutt says sorry. (Growl)

The chance meetings in the mailroom became longer, and their small-talk became more intimate.

She told him how she worked as an assistant director for the movies.

(*'Although she wasn't working now, and hadn't for a while, but that's the movies for you!'* -- *'The movies? That's great! He was sure something would come up soon.'*)

He taught History of Art at UCLA.

(*'He wanted to paint more, but he had to make a living, and you don't do that by slapping colours on a canvass, unless you're a Picasso, which he was the first to say he wasn't.'* -- *'She was sure he was doing himself down and couldn't wait to see his work.'*)

The first date took a while to materialise, but went well; the second date even better, breaking the 'less than carnal' rule. And Chloe and Scott became what is carelessly called 'an item'.

They didn't move-in together, and kept their separate apartments; but Scott's dog certainly had a bed to himself more often than he liked, and he missed being shoved around by Scott's smelly feet. He sometimes growled all on his own up there in the dark, under no provocation at all, just for form's sake.

All in all, however, an acceptable *ménage a trois* was established amongst them.

3
Valeria

You need to know more about Valeria—the mother of the boy sitting on Scott's shoulders the first night of the Rodney King riots—the dark-haired woman at Madisons' Oscar party

Valeria and Scott had been college sweethearts for a brief time at the University of Southern California. If college sweethearts were for sale at the corner sweetheart shop, in her three years at USC Valeria probably ate her way through a half-pound bag of them.

Her study of Law may be thought to have impacted on her development as a human being: she saw everything in terms of legal entitlement, enforceability and non-enforceability; and in the small print—especially when it came to her dealings with boyfriends. Her relationship with Scott, drawn up as a contract, would have stated—

PREAMBLE

WHEREAS Valeria (insert full name) of (insert address) and Scott (insert full name) of (insert address) have agreed to be friends . . .

'Friends' would be loosely defined in the Interpretations Section.

IT IS AGREED THAT . . .

The body of the document would then have contained innumerable clauses beginning 'PROVIDED that Valeria is not . . . (small print); and 'PROVIDED that no commitment of any kind . . . ' (very small print); and NO PROMISE, express or implied . . . ' (print so small it couldn't be read in strong light under a magnifying glass).

Scott's understanding of the relationship was imperfect because, figuratively speaking, he signed Valeria's contract without reading it.

Valeria broke up with Scott at the end of her studies: suddenly, brutally, before graduation, and entirely without ceremony or any of the usual talk about 'staying friends' or 'keeping in touch'. It was important she handled things somewhat clinically, you will understand, because her imminent wedding to an Ivy League young man, from an old family with old money, who had a glittering career ahead of him in the military, where all the males in the family enjoyed glittering careers, was scheduled for the following month. So it made sense that none of her undergraduate dalliances turned up at the church. She had, after all, 'kept herself' for her fiancé—in much the same way as her fiancé had kept himself for her whilst at West Point.

Her husband's parents did not like Valeria, and she was acutely aware of it. She was penniless—but worse than that, she had no 'family' and was self-educated. They had been against the relationship ever since its unambitious teenage beginnings—and she had sensed that too. They put no hurdle in the path of their son's happiness, however, when it appeared he had set his heart on marrying her, and they tried to welcome Valeria into the bosom of the family as warmly as they would have welcomed the bride of their choice—but Valeria gave them no credit for that: she had astutely tuned-in to their unspoken, undemonstrated disapproval, and she never forgave them for it.

It was destined to be a short marriage.

It was blessed by an early child; but it was tragically curtailed by the death of her military hero husband in Iraq during the first, George Bush Senior, conflict. A few weeks after her husband's body was flown back home and buried with full military honours, a baby boy was born. Valeria called the boy Billy, out of defiance to her in-laws. Her dead husband had been Edward, and his father was an Edward, and his grandfather was an Edward too: indeed, the Mayflower was tethered to her husband by an unbroken line of Edwards. So Valeria chose the name 'Billy' for her son—not even William—to spite the whole pack of them.

After a couple of months' mourning, followed by a long period of indecisiveness with regard to the various options offered her by her in-laws, all of which were rejected (she needed, but didn't want, their help, and she took a bitter-sweet pleasure in rejecting it); and after several failed attempts to stimulate any serious male interest in her; Valeria moved herself, her war-widow's pension, her law degree and her boy (and something of a reputation) away from her Massachusetts disasters and back to LA, with a fully-formed but only half-admitted intention of rekindling a relationship with whomever of her former boyfriends might take her. That she should have persuaded herself she was returning there to look for work is endearing, but difficult for the rest of us to believe: there are more lawyers in Los Angeles than there are grains of sand on Malibu beach.

On that first night of the riots, when Chloe found the three of them, Valeria, Scott and Billy on the rooftop, Valeria had been in LA for a year, but had only recently moved-on from a failed mission in Marina Del Rey. Set back, but not dispirited, she took an apartment in Larrabee because she heard Scott was living there. They met, for the first time since their break-up, at Madison's Oscar party.

"Scott! I don't believe it! The same apartment block! Have you ever *heard* of such a thing?"

* * *

"I'm so sorry," Scott said to her one night, when she told him the story of the years since they last saw each other (or rather, her version of it). "And the family won't help, not at all?"

"Nothing," said Valeria. "They don't like me, and they're glad to be rid of the shame of me."

"That itself is shameful. Not even for sake of their own grandson?"

"Nothing," she lied, with a downturned mouth and a careless shrug.

The meal was romantic. The story heartrending. Any lingering resentment at how he had been spurned had no chance of survival against Scott's sympathies, which were engaged to the fullest. But whatever had been between them at USC was not rekindled, not in either of them—not the slightest spark of it. Valeria had thrown too-cold a bucket of water over the flames when she abandoned Scott for a better match, and the awkwardness of that hung over the table throughout their candle-lit dinner.

She was not despondent, however, even after the unequivocal 'keep in touch' of their parting; and she still regarded Scott as one of the plentiful fish in the Los Angeles ocean who might yet be hooked.

The bait, if ever she should reel Scott in, was her son. She watched and waited to see if Scott's affectionate nature should turn paternal. On the first night of the riots, when he lifted Billy onto his shoulders on the Larrabee rooftop, things certainly looked promising. And had Chloe not appeared on the scene with her own agenda, the course of Valeria's untrue love might have run smooth indeed. But her ill-timed departure from Los Angeles gave Chloe the field, and it was arrogant of her to think her off-hand little snub had sufficiently seen her potential rival off.

Valeria hadn't, as Scott thought she had (because that's what she told him), returned home at her widowed mother's urging, to keep her, and especially Billy, away from danger. She had accepted an invitation from a quite different quarter, another 'ex' from her college days who she bumped into at Billy's school; recently divorced, with a girl about the same age as Billy. An 'ex' who she had already dated a couple of times, even while she was casting flies at Scott. An 'ex' who had suggested that Valeria and Billy join him at his ranch north of Los Angeles until the rioting was over. An 'ex' with a bank-vault more money than Scott ever had, or ever looked likely to have. It nearly came off, because Billy and the girl were already friends at school; but her hoped-for husband did not like Billy, and Billy did not like him. The man put up a good disguise of this uncomfortable truth; but the boy, wonderfully lacking in guile, made no secret of his antipathy; and the romance dwindled to an inevitable breakdown.

The moment she returned to LA and saw that Scott was caught on some other fisherwoman's hook and was beyond any immediate chance of release, Valeria's interest in him waned as though it had never been. Her adventure in the ranch north of LA had come to nothing and she resumed her search for a husband and provider, caring little for what had been stolen from her while she was away. '*Anyway,*' she reminded herself, '*Scott was an insurance policy, not her preference.*' So she played the field again—but was astute enough to wait, like a trap-door spider, ready to pounce if the opportunity came her way to snatch him back, and (more importantly) if the need arose to do so.

Those who underestimate dogs say they will wag their tails at anyone who feeds them. But Scott's dog was much more complex than that—and much more interesting. Let the under-estimators take note: Chloe could have turned a whole pig into sausages and fed them to him, and his tail might not have wagged a hair's breadth—but if Valeria had offered him the sausages, Scott's dog would have turned his back on her without even sniffing them.

4

Rome

"It must have been well over a year before I saw her again. It was on the morning of the earthquake. I was not aware she had returned to Los Angeles, less still to the same apartment block—I had not seen her collecting mail or waiting for the elevator, or in the parking lot, *or anywhere*: I don't know how long she had been back; but she came out onto the pavement on that morning with her small boy, and they made two of the little group who Scott drove to Beverly Hills for our *colazione*, and who slept on the Queen Mary in San Pedro to escape the aftershocks, and who became such friends with each other."

"Friends? C'mon! She's *gotta* be the one you hated."

"If you don't object, I will tell the events in my order. She may be, she may not be. Wait."

"It's frigging obvious."

"She called herself Valeria, but her given name was probably something less . . . *affascinante*."

"Friends. Sure."

"If Chloe had ruined her schemes and stolen Scott from her while she was away, she gave no sign of it. She didn't make any play for him, any more than she made any play for me, or Didier or Tyler."

"And who the hell are Didier and Tyler?" interrupted his godson. "You keep on about them, like they were some comedy duo—who the hell are *they*?"

"Wait! They were no comedy duo! But wait. Please. Now you have made me lose my thread."

"Valeria made no play for Scott," prompted his godson.

"Or for Tom."

"For Christ's sake! *Tom?* Now you're just being mean."

"It is my turn, eh?"

"So she made no play for any of them?"

"*Esattamente.* No obvious play. But I noticed something much more subtle. More importantly, so did Chloe notice it. So did everyone, I think, eventually. Valeria was always pushing Billy to Scott. Do you understand what I mean?"

"No."

"At a table when we met in a restaurant, she might sit far away from Scott, almost ignoring him, sometimes going to great effort to talk with anyone except him—but she would make sure *Billy* sat next to him. *Si?* Remember how she had Billy up on Scott's shoulders in the Riots? It was like that. There was nothing I could do, of course—nothing anyone could do, who saw it—what *should* we do? *What had we seen?* There was never anything to seize hold of, to make a complaint about, to . . . *Non capisco.* It was so subtle, as I said. So, so, very subtle. But it was there. Tom said that Billy was Valeria's *Trojan Horse.* But exactly when Valeria intended to jump out and capture Scott, we didn't like to think."

"Didn't he wise-up?"

"The only one *not* to see it was Scott. It is always so. Chloe pretended it wasn't happening—although I could sense it unsettled her. Every 'now and then', as you like to say, Chloe would put up some resistance, with a '*no, you come and sit by me, Billy*' or such like; but when she did fight back, it was somehow a victory for Valeria. I don't know why it should have been, but it was. I once saw Valeria smile to herself when Chloe made her little fuss. Not a nice smile, *Scottino.*

"Then came the famous day at Venice Beach. The big storms, they were still gathering, but on that day there was the sound of distant thunder, for sure."

5

Venice Beach

Venice Beach. Early spring. Dazzling mid-morning sun. Strings of mirrored 'shades' swinging from the sunglass-huts, flashing secret sunbeam signals to each other.

Ice creams and spun sugar. Children with pink-candy-coloured mouths, chocolate sauce and sticky syrup on their fingers.

Street performers of all sorts, small mid-week crowds watching, listening. Musical acts. Mime. Jugglers. Dancers. Magicians. Fortune-tellers.

'Muscle-Beach'—enormous men on steroids lifting and dropping enormous weights, with grunts and groans and motivating shouts of "*One more!*"—"*Yeah!*"—"*Great workout!*"

Surfers far out at sea, shimmering in the sun like the mirages on the over-heated tarmac of the Pacific Coast Highway; appearing, disappearing, bobbing up and down, waiting to catch that wave.

A pavement café by the cycle track. The smells of breakfast. Orange juice, coffee, waffles, pancakes, cinnamon, crispy-bacon.

* * *

It is Madison's birthday. Tom has arranged a birthday brunch for her at the beach, and he invites the Dutch guy, Chloe and Scott to join the party. Scott calls Chloe and tells her to get a ride from Madison, because he is picking up Valeria and Billy.

"*It'll be great for the kid,*" he says.

"*Fine,*" says Chloe. "*See you there.*"

But when Madison goes to collect Chloe, she says she can't come after all. She is snowed-under with work (she says). She gives Madison a card and a neatly-wrapped birthday present tied with a small, *very tight*, pink bow; and she asks Madison to make her apologies to the others.

"*I'm sure they'll understand,*" she says, waving her hand towards to a pile of utility bills on the table. She doesn't mention Scott by name—just 'the others'.

* * *

They sit down at a table by the white picket-fence separating the café from the track. Scott's dog is on the other side, tied to the cycle-stand: every few seconds there is a SWISH as some rollerblader roars by, and the dog barks his lungs out. Billy throws bits of bacon to him, even though Valeria has told him not to. Scott gives Billy secret supplies from his plate when Valeria isn't looking.

* * *

The boys go to hire rollerblades. The girls stay at the table. Madison would have liked to join the boys, but Valeria says 'no way' is she going rollerblading.

"*No way*," she says, and pulls her sunglasses up over her forehead, and leans back in her chair, eyes shut, to catch the sun—and for the next hour or so she completely ignores the birthday-girl who has stayed to keep her company.

* * *

Scott rollerblades up to the café, with Billy sitting on his shoulders.

"*Mom! Mom! Look*!"

Valeria shakes herself out of her slumber, annoyed that she has been woken, and calls out to Scott -

"*Put him down! Scott! For heaven's sake*!"

* * *

Mid-day. The sun is at its highest, and everything is red and sunburnt and glowing and tired and lazy—even the white sun-baked paint peeling off the picket fence yawns and stretches and gets itself a tan.

* * *

Billy runs towards Scott's dog, laughing, exhilarated, bubbling-over with giggles. Scott rollerblades up behind him. The dog yelps and barks.

"*Oh Scott! Now you've got Billy over-excited. He'll be sick*!"

Billy giggles and bubbles even more, and races over to Valeria with his arms held out. Scott, still on his blades, follows close with smiling appeasement on his face—but as he slows down to a stop he loses his balance and falls over, for no apparent reason. He picks himself up, a little dazed and dizzy.

"*See what might have happened*?" says Valeria.

* * *

Now the sun is sinking and the air is cooling. They walk to their cars past the shacks and shops and near-derelict houses painted blue and pink, with broken gates and litter in the front yard and crude graffiti on the walls. A folksy-looking woman accosts Scott and asks him if he wants to know his future—he says '*if she was any good she'd know the answer*'. They all laugh, and she curses them; so Scott puts a couple of dollars in her hand anyway, and so does Madison, because they feel guilty for laughing.

The dog tugs at his leash, pulling them on to the next trash can, the next MacDonald's carton; and they meander along the strip until they disappear out of our view; looking at the street-acts, listening to the music, not giving another thought to the curse, or what might have made Scott lose his balance and fall over, for no apparent reason.

6
Everything He Wanted

Scott drove back to Larrabee. Having dropped-off his dog, and fed him, he went straight to Chloe's apartment. He knew Chloe had been lying when she said she couldn't come to the beach, and that '*she had too much work to do*'. The truth was, and it was all-too obvious to him, that Chloe had kept herself away because he had invited Valeria and Billy to join them, and Chloe had to take a ride with Madison, and not drive down with him.

"Why couldn't she understand," he asked himself, "that he'd only done it for the kid? He has a bad enough time, what with no dad. Why couldn't she see that?"

And anyway, he reasoned, although Chloe may not like Valeria, *he* was fond of her, and was sorry for her, and admired her for how she coped on her own, bringing up her boy. And she was doing a great job—Billy was turning out alright—more than alright. Scott was glad to have given both of them a day out. Yes he was *glad*. It was 'a good thing', and Chloe should be less prickly and more understanding.

But for Chloe, shut in her apartment on her own, thinking about them having a fun day at Venice without her, it was 'a bad thing'. And Scott saw that he needed to coax her round to the Chloe he loved; give her the reassurance that he was all hers and she was all his, and there wasn't and never could be anyone else—*yada yada*—if that really was the kind of foolish nonsense that had kept them apart all day.

"My! You've caught the sun!" she said, looking up from a table of utility bills which she contrived to be paying just as soon as she heard his key in the door-latch.

"We missed you." He gave her a peck on the cheek.

"Did you have a good time?" she asked, a little too enthusiastically. The sort of repressed hysteria Ingrid Bergman was so good at.

"Great. You should have seen Billy! He's a natural on blades."

(*Not a good subject Scott. Move on to something else. Quickly.*)

"You took him blading? That was brave. I bet Valeria didn't like that!"

"What?"

"Taking Billy rollerblading. I bet Valeria kicked up a fuss about that!" (Her little laugh belies her deepening displeasure, or betrays it if you know her well enough.)

"Did you get everything done?" Scott looked over Chloe's shoulder and she stacked together all the paper that had not needed, and had not been given, any attention the whole long day.

"Just the moment you arrived," she said. "All done."

"Perfect timing! So where shall we go?"

"Go?"

"I want to give you a treat for being stuck on your own all day."

Another peck on the cheek.

"Don't be silly." (In her head she is choosing the main course.)

"I won't take no for an answer. Come on. Where would you like to go? Anywhere. You name it."

Scott always imagined the nicest thing he could possibly do was to give the choices—restaurant, cinema, weekend break—to Chloe. He saw it—which, in fairness, it was—as a complete subjugation of his own preferences to the desires of his lover. Chloe, on the other hand, ached for Scott to present her with a pre-planned package, to be whisked off to somewhere Scott had chosen for her, with every last detail arranged in advance.

"You choose," she said.

"No. It's your night. Where would you like to go? *Really* like."

"*La Traviata.*"

Now *La Traviata* was, at that time, one of LA's fashionable hot-spots. Incredibly expensive. But Scott took the mischievous request in his stride and telephoned the restaurant there and then for a reservation, without any outward sign that his heart had sunk to his stomach.

The scorn with which his request for a table for two was rejected, and the gratuitous information that the restaurant was booked for the next month, unless they wanted to dine at 5.30—but the table would have to be vacated by 7.15—might in other circumstances have rattled Scott; and the sharp voice at the other end of his call might have known of his irritation, in blunt language; but relief was dominant, and he pretended polite disappointment—devastation, even—and said he would try on another night. The voice couldn't resist a final stab at him, "*You'll have to book well in advance,*" it said—which Scott ignored.

"I heard," said Chloe, when Scott hung up. "Another night then."

An endearing feature of their relationship was that they spent so much of their time trying to make each other feel good—(if you discount the time they spent trying to make each other feel bad). Softened by his ready show of willing, and thinking it was her turn, now, to take the role of soothing *his* disappointment, Chloe said—

"Here. My treat."

—and straightaway she led him by the hand, out of her apartment, into the elevator, through the doors onto Larrabee, down the hill and round the corner, to a little Italian Trattoria (so it called itself, as well as "*La Dolce Vita*"); where, when they entered, they were greeted with all the welcoming fuss that would have been given a pair of film stars.

They were seated at a pretty table for two by the window, lit with a candle in a blue jam-jar made of mottled glass. From the simple menu they selected equally simple antipasto, pasta, *pesce*, and *dolce*; and from the wine list (printed at the bottom of the menu) they chose the red one, rather than the white one.

With their single espressos, and rock-hard mint chocolates in the saucers, there came complimentary shot glasses of hideous *Limoncello*, which they had no opportunity of tipping into the flowering jasmine because the generous, grinning waiter was hard-by, and so pleased with his little touch that he offered them a second glass, which they felt they could not politely refuse.

After dinner they crossed the road to a short strip of businesses on Western Sunset Boulevard, North of Holloway, which included a 24-hour printing service (it was before home-publishing became so easy), a small but classy Hamburger joint (with Valet parking, no less), and a dry-cleaners that had Jerry Seinfeld's poster in the window. Behind the strip was a quiet service road, full of trashcans, half-locked rubbish skips, and rats. Leading off the service road was a dirt track opening onto a yard full of pot holes—unlit, in spite of a steep drop at its rear—where couples parked their cars perilously near the edge, ostensibly to gaze at the host of twinkling street lights stretching all the way to the airport, but to judge from the steamed-up widows and the lascivious bouncing of the cars' rear-suspensions, I doubt that much time was spent in admiration of the light-show.

It was to a low wooden bench at the edge of the precipice that Chloe and Scott often strolled down the hill from Larrabee on a warm evening; and there they *would* sit and gaze at the twinkling lights, each with an arm round the other, their heads tilting and touching; and there they would talk the night away making plans for the future. And it was to that very wooden bench, on that very night of dinner at *La Dolce Vita*, that they took themselves, hand in hand and happy as could be—happier than any diner at *La Traviata*, you can bet your last dollar.

Their silence was as eloquent and affectionate as any lovers' talk, in any language; and it lasted just as long as the reader might want it to; until -

"As soon as we can afford the deposit, we should buy a small house, out of the smog, with a back yard" she said, leaning back on the wooden bench and resting her head on Scott's shoulder.

"We gotta have a back yard. And *definitely* out of the smog," he beamed at her.

"Or maybe rent."

"That'd do it!"

"We could probably rent faster than we could save for a house."

"Much faster, I'd think. So let's go for rental first, while we save for a deposit."

Although he could hardly be said to be unsupportive, and was even enthusiastic, Chloe wished Scott would sometimes offer an idea or two of his own, rather than always listening to, and accepting fully, hers. After another long, pensive pause, in which she didn't seem even to breathe, she prompted him with -

"What would you like? If you could have anything you wanted, what would it be?"

Scott answered, perhaps too quickly for such a question -

"I'm one of the lucky people," he said, his eyes reaching for something far beyond the lights, and beyond the aeroplanes landing and taking off over the horizon, and even beyond the stars peeping out behind them. "I've always had everything I wanted."

He wrapped her in his arms and hugged her like a bear. They kissed, as young lovers do on a park bench in the night, then he turned his eyes back to the edge of the universe, losing himself in a total absence of thought, perfectly content and at ease, oblivious to any possibility that Chloe might not be so lucky as he, and might want something more.

7

Rome

"It was a while before our little gang of earthquake people met again. I picked up a message from Chloe suggesting a long overdue—how do you say it?—'get-together'—at the weekend. I returned her call, of course, and she said to me *everyone* was going over to Wilshire Boulevard on Saturday to play the role of 'extras' in a low-budget film they were making at the old Ambassador Hotel.

"To my mind she was just a little too enthusiastic about "*everyone*"; and I always thought (afterwards, perhaps) that she made sure Valeria and Billy were included to demonstrate to Scott that she was secure in their relationship—which was, of course, nonsense!—rather than out of generosity of spirit.

"But she was working again as first assistant director, which was nice, and she said she could easily fit us in among the crowd of paid extras, unnoticed. 'It'll be a laugh,' she said. I will leave you to judge how much comedy there was in it.

"The *mise en scene* was a restaurant. The stars were Yin and Yang—you know of them? I had not seen them before or since."

His godson said - "I used to watch their show on TV when I was a kid. They were a couple of Chinese-American comedy detectives. But soon as I realised the murderer was always the guy who *no way* could possibly have done it, I kind of lost interest."

"At the age of . . . ?"

"Ten or twelve."

"So there you have the measure of the film they were making. Yin and Yang were to meet an informant there, in the usual clichéd way. A dozen or more tables were filled with extras, like us, who had nothing to do except sit and pretend we were eating and talking.

"I saw a different Chloe that day, doing her job. She was good, I thought. I would certainly have used her. Perhaps. Maybe she was *un po' brutale*. Very confident, very sharp with the crew, and not much nicer to us extras. She explained there was no budget for putting the dialogue into the scene afterwards, so they would be making a live recording of the conversation between Yin and Yang: that meant the extras should *not talk*, she told us (like a drill-sergeant) but only *pretend* to talk; and we should not make *any noise* with our knives and forks, but only *pretend* to eat. The requirement was mime. '**Savvy?**' she said, in a voice that did not ask for an answer, and she marched away to bark instruction to someone else. She was impressive—*formidable*—do you think, maybe, she was trying to impress Scott?

"She placed us all together at a table at the back of the old ballroom where they were filming the scene, some distance from Yin and Yang, because the paid extras were very anxious to have their faces seen by the cameras (so Chloe told us) and they would make a problem for her if they found out her friends were given the best positions. And anyway, she said, Madison was too well-known to be an extra and risk recognition. We made a pleasant little group, I think, to fill the blurred background of the picture.

"Chloe's plan went wrong within seconds. The director pointed to our table and shouted—'I want that good looking guy and the kid closer. Who's the mother?' Valeria put her hand up, as though she is still at school. No-one else laid claim to being 'that good looking guy': it was obviously Scott. 'The kid' identified himself by his size.

"Chloe was at once in a panic, for no reason anyone else could know, not even the detectives Yin and Yang; but of course *I* knew. She spouted the words—'Do you think that's such a good idea?'—'Yes. I do,' says the director. Firmly. And Chloe backs off. She went a little red in the face, I remember.

"A female stagehand with thin headphones and microphone strapped round her head (which had practically no hair, I mention *en passant*) ushered Scott, Valeria and Billy to a little family table for three, right behind the stars; and she readjusted our nice table so that I filled Scott's empty seat—still in the distance, but with my back to the camera. The director said 'now the table looked empty', so the stagehand plucked three extras from around the room to make the group again, and fill the table with strangers—and ruin the enjoyment for the rest of us.

"Now I come to the part I do not like to talk about. You know how I am sensitive to the slight loss of hair at the back of my head . . . "

"Slight!"

"There you go. You torture me with it ever since you are too big for me to slap you."

"I don't know why it bugs you so much."

"Well it does, and it did. *Va bene.* It took an eternity for the lighting to be settled; and it got hotter and hotter in that un-air-conditioned old ballroom. I was not the only person sweating—but I confess I did sweat. Beads of it breaking out all over the top of my head, if I am honest with you, and rolling down my face and down the back of my neck. So the director bellows 'I'm going blind here!'—because of the lights, you see—'Get some powder on that bald guy's head.'"

"That is just *too* funny!"

"I am glad you enjoy it. The humiliation was as bad as anything you have ever inflicted on me—not least because there was no doubt the director meant me; and the extras, and Yin and Yang too, had a laugh at my expense while my head was patted with powder."

"My mom said it would be a laugh!"

"'*Yeah right*' is, I believe, your expression, *impertinente bambino.* Eh?

"*Allora.* The director's hope had been for a quick morning, so Chloe told us. We had booked a table for lunch afterwards. It was a very short scene, she said. But take one was "CUT!" almost as soon as he had said "ACTION!" The requirement not to speak aloud had caused almost every extra to mouth their pretend conversation in huge exaggerated facial expression, the way you might speak to a deaf person trying to lip-read. In addition, because they were not actually saying anything, the extras believed it was necessary to accompany their mute contortions with massive hand and arm gestures: so if one of them thought it would enhance the overall dramatic effect of the scene if he asked another to pass the salt, he lifted his arm high, *come questo*, index-finger outstretched, and then he slowly brought it down towards the salt—as though he was reaching for it the other side of a tennis net—from the serving line!—while he moulded his lips round all the silent shapes of 'pass the salt' you can possibly imagine. Whether the request for salt was better or worse than the way it was passed is a matter I leave to your imagination.

"'CUT!' shouts the director.

"Chloe explained to the extras that everything had to be toned down; that it was unrealistic for everyone to be pretend-talking at once; that often—though not always in Los Angeles, she admitted—one talked and the other listened; and it didn't matter if most of us sat there and did nothing.

"As though he had heard not a word of this instruction, an extra at our table turned to me (and I was one of the few who *had* been sitting and doing nothing!) and he said—

'*I can't act with you.*'

'*Scusi?*' I say.

'*I can't act with you. I'm getting nothing back.*'

"I couldn't help but smile.

'*I suspect the audience is going to be more interested in Yin and Yang,*' I said.

"The man turned from me and for the next few takes 'acted' with one of the professional extras; and between the two of them they acted enough for all of us who were sitting there, and a table-full more besides."

"But now I want you to look at Chloe. What is that change that seems to have come over her? Eh? Has her sharp manner become too brittle? Is the self-assurance that had dressed her with such command, is it turning to . . . how do you say . . . not panico . . . what is the word?"

"Bluster."

"Say again?"

"Bluster."

"As you like. But could these things have *anything* to do with the perfect domestic scene at the table for three immediately behind Yin and Yang?

The table that looked so natural. That had the director going especially over to them and saying they were 'doing great'.

"They were *bonding*! Chloe saw it with her own eyes. And I saw it with mine. Valeria was thrusting Billy into Scott's attentions without shame, and he was just lapping-up his role as 'dad'. Billy was the happiest little eight-year old you could ever see. And Chloe could do nothing about it. Even as it grew stronger and stronger by the minute, she was powerless. She would have given the world to separate them, I am sure—but the director was in love with his precious idea to have the nice family sitting behind the stars of the show.

"Chloe hovered at the camera. To me she was waiting for an excuse to regroup the table—but none came. How she must have longed for a take the director was satisfied with, so they could wrap the wretched business up! But he wasn't satisfied with any of them: he went for take after take after take, *moto perpetuo*, with the smallest adjustments to the script, and 'You're doing great' after 'That's great' after 'Aren't they perfect?' for Scott, Valeria and Billy. Every time. Yin (maybe it was Yang) said they were 'as American as apple pie'.

"Chloe shouted an order to the boom operator in such an unpleasant tone of voice that, as I remember it, had even the dolly grip saying he thought it was a little unnecessary."

"You can be *so* camp, you know that?" said his godson.

"I do it for your amusement," said the old actor, now throwing himself heart and soul into one of his grand performances. "Then came an incident that might have turned things round, if Chloe had not handled it so badly. During yet another take, Scott's wrist caught the edge of his wine-glass and spilled the contents onto the table—and it splashed onto Valeria's blouse. He didn't know how he had done it. No one did. These things happen. *Si*?

"Valeria let out a little shriek. Scott let out a little 'Fuck!'. The Director let out little 'CUT!' And Chloe saw her opportunity. 'Right. We need to move you,'—meaning Valeria. 'Can you come over?—meaning a young woman at a near table. 'It's no problem,' protested Valeria, holding her ground. 'It's only a splash, ' she says, smiling at *il direttore*. 'No no. You have to swap places . . . ' says Chloe. 'Whoa!' bellows the director. 'They look great together. Are you OK to go on, honey?'—Valeria smiles back at him 'Absolutely'.

"Then it comes. *Il momento fatale*. Chloe butts in with—'It's impossible!' The director whips round and stares her down. 'Who's directing this movie?' should have been a sufficient warning, eh? Chloe ploughed on, recklessly. 'But it looks ridiculous!' The room froze.

"The director walked slowly over to behind the camera, and stared through the view-finder. 'I can't see the problem. Here,' he says to the cameraman. 'Does anything look ridiculous to you?' The cameraman squints his eyes through the lens. 'Not to me.'—'What about you?' The director summons another, it doesn't matter who. 'No,' she says, looking through the camera.

"The director then asked another to look, and another, and everyone within reach, one after the other, if it looked 'ridiculous'—and each said no, because it didn't. It was, as Valeria had said, only a splash, and it was invisible behind the comedians Yin and Yang.

"Chloe stood still, *come una statua*, through each humiliating hammer-blow, redder and redder in the face. The ballroom at the old Ambassador Hotel was as silent as it can ever have been. Everyone was staring at Chloe. When the director said to her maybe they had different ideas of what 'ridiculous' meant, and maybe she should look somewhere closer to home if she *really* wanted to see 'ridiculous', Chloe hesitated . . . then marched off the set—and out of the film, it was inevitable of course.

"Scott's face was a little drama all of its own. It seemed to me he was torn between supporting Chloe (who had been treated harshly, but *was* in the wrong) and letting down his table, and letting down the director who had been so nice to them, letting down Billy (who was in heaven) and also Valeria, and even Yin and Yang; and while for a moment I thought he was going to go after Chloe, the balance must have fallen in favour of staying where he was. I am not sure he did the right thing, even though I could understand his reasons, if I have guessed them correctly.

"Valeria had a hand on his arm, saying it would be alright, even before the director was shouting 'Action!'"

"Matters can not have been made better, no one should be in any doubt, by the long delay before Scott could arrive at Chloe's apartment—even though I saw he was on edge to get away so he could join her. The delay was caused in this way: the caretaker of the empty hotel used to take visitors, if they desired, to the actual place, a back of house pantry, where Robert Kennedy had been shot. It was a gruesome, *voyeurismo* fascination he satisfied, and not one of us except Valeria wanted to go on the excursion he offered. I took Valeria to one side and whispered if she thought it was a suitable thing for Billy. 'It's history,' she said. 'Anyway he has to grow up some time.'

"I pressed my point, nonetheless. But she was insistent. I think she *wanted* the delay, you see. 'It's only a kitchen we're going to,' she said to me. 'Not a morgue.'

"She had her way, *come faceva sempre*, and we were led through the same back-passageways Robert Kennedy had been led through—for his own safety so they said!—to the very place were he was gunned down by Sirhan Sirhan. When the caretaker stopped and invited us to look at a stain on the floor no-one did; except Billy—who must be forgiven; and Valeria—whose forgiveness I find more difficult. It was in fact most uncomfortable, shifting from foot to foot, looking at anything except the floor.

"Tom broke the silence with—'*What a fall was there!*'

"It was Scott who gave the missing line—'*Then I, and you, and all of us fell down.*'

"No-one spoke another word.

"The caretaker led our solemn procession back to the main entrance of the Hotel, and into the early-evening shadows of Wilshire Boulevard, and the sulphurous smell of the tar pits in Hancock Park."

8

Monologue

"Scott sure as hell had a thing about them, even if you didn't. Remember that time up in Malibu? Alice's Restaurant? Like the song."

He sings a couple of bars from 'Alice's Restaurant Massacree'.

"I think him and Chloe had one of their rows the night before, because they were such great company, so _funny_, the life and soul and all that crapola; but they never once looked at each other or spoke more than two words, just kept on laughing and messing with the rest of us, like they was in a competition to see who didn't care most.

"Then these dolphins swim by, and Scott gets all excited and makes us go to the windows to look at them. Remember that? There must have been about six. Maybe seven. And everyone came and did their 'oohs' and 'oh my Gods', like they do in Hawaii with the humpbacks, 'cept these were only dolphins, like I said.

"But Chloe didn't come and look. I mean **didn't come**, like in a big way. She just sat there and ate faster, smiling to herself, which really pissed Scott off, because it had to be deliberate, not coming to see the dolphins in order to get back at him. She could be real mean, Chloe.

"So Scott retaliates—'Hey! Billy! I'll lift you up so you can see.' And Chloe eats faster still and says—'I don't know what all the fuss is about. They're only fish.' Then Scott says—'They're mammals, Billy, just like us'. And Chloe says—'Just like us! How true. One minute you see them, the next minute you don't.' And Scott says—'Mammals are warm-blooded, Billy: we're not cold fish. Most of us.'

"Boy. That was some journey home from Alice's Restaurant. Total silence. All the way.

9

Tremors

Chloe lay back on her pillows the next morning, wide-awake, staring at the ceiling. As soon as Scott came in from the bathroom, she closed her eyes.

Scott, fully dressed, crept around the way you do when you don't want to wake somebody; but he overplayed it in the hope she could see him. He sat at the dressing table, where there were two separate arrangements of bottles and jars, and various plastic tubes of cream. He went to the smaller arrangement, selected a jar, gingerly so as not to make the slightest noise, and like a good LA boy born and bred, applied moisturiser to his face. Then he took a squat, cylindrical tube and squirted onto his fingers a tiny droplet of a precious transparent amber liquid, which he carefully smoothed around the areas of skin under his eyes—the places where, if he didn't apply the miracle compound daily, he thought there would be bags (and had so believed since the age of seventeen).

From the bed came—"You use more of that stuff then I do."

"So you *are* awake."

A pause.

"I thought so," he added, to consolidate his little triumph.

Another pause, before Chloe complained -

"Why do you have to go so early?"

"I need to walk the mutt before I go to work. You *know* that."

"Sometimes I think—"

"Don't say it. *Please* don't say it!"

A short, sardonic laugh from Scott—to himself, with a tiny shake of the head.

"Say what?" challenged Chloe.

"Sometimes you think I love 'that dog' more than I love you, yada, yada, yada."

"That is so NOT what I was going to say!" she lied.

A long pause this time, while she waited for Scott to ask her 'what it was then?' But Scott didn't ask; and he continued, with annoying attention to detail, to apply anti-ageing cream to the sides of his eyes (where no crow had ever stamped its feet, and was not likely to for a decade or so).

Chloe caved in -

"You know what I think?"

Now she was prepared to wait forever; and Scott, doing his best to make it look like it was in his own time, was eventually forced to answer—

"No I don't."

But he continued to work moisturiser around his eyes, just as carefully (in fact, much more carefully) without looking at her. So she remained silent. Until he turned and said -

"*What* do you think?"—with a benign smile that was as provocative as Hell to Chloe, and was meant to be. So she told him -

"I think it would lend a great deal to your credibility, Scott, if you left a longer gap between saying you love me, and asking if you can borrow my car."

"Here we go!"

"Where's that?"

"And *they're off!*"

"I haven't the faintest idea . . . "

"Jesus! Of course I love you. How's this?" He went to the bedside and kissed the top of her turned-away head.

"I love you."

(Kiss.)

"I love you."

(Kiss.)

"I love you."

(Kiss.)

"I love you."

(Kiss.)

"I love you. One—two—three—four—five—six—seven—eight— nine—ten. Gap long enough? Can I borrow your car or not?"

"Now you're being childish."

"I'll pick up a rental. One of us has to work."

(That hurt.)

"Of course you can borrow the car."

"I'll rent."

"Scott!"

He left without looking at her, and slammed the door behind him.

Chloe flung her head back on the bed and punched her temples—one might say savagely, except that she was careful to soften the blows with pillows—but her muttered self-torment met no such barriers, and became more bitter and ridiculous with each blow --

"Fool—Stupid—Fool—Overweight—Fool—Fat—Ugly—FOOL."

* * *

Scott was miserable all day, and Chloe was miserable all day.

He hated himself for letting—what? It was nothing. Nothing that could begin to justify the row between them, nothing that really mattered when you looked at it dispassionately—he hated himself for letting that 'nothing' escalate to such a pitch of bad feeling; and he hated himself for losing his temper, and for making that cruel remark about Chloe walking out of her job, and for not accepting her offer of the car, and for slamming the door when he left.

She hated herself for letting—what? Letting him get away with it. That's what! "Scott-free". Oh yes! They didn't invent that expression out of nowhere! His utter selfishness. His sarcasm. His arrogance. His total lack of feeling. His stubborn refusal to accept *any* blame . . . His . . . His ... Maybe she hated herself for not hating *him*?

Scott did what many a guilty male lover will do to make everything better—usually making everything worse—and he tried to patch things up as though nothing had happened. On his way home, he bought Chloe a bunch of flowers. To his credit, it wasn't a quick and careless purchase, as these olive-branches so often are: he didn't buy them at a gas station, in the traditional way: he took his time in a Melrose florist, selecting flowers he knew she liked, and even tried to find a bloom having associations with her name—to the bafflement of the florist, who knew of no such flower.

Earlier in the day, when he couldn't get a reservation at the *Café La Traviata* on Santa Monica Boulevard, he had asked Madison if she could pull some strings, and she had secured for him not only a reservation, but what is called an 'A' table.

Flowers and dinner. What could possibly go wrong?

Chloe did what many a wronged female lover will do, and regretted, with increasing intensity as the day wore on, that she had failed to speak her mind, and instead retreated into a stupid, futile dumb-sulk; that she had failed to let Scott know in plain English, who was in the wrong and who was in the right on this one; and had failed to make it clear to him *leaving no room for doubt* just why she was so angry. And who wouldn't be?

But none of her bitter regret, none of her perceived failures, none of her self-awareness, played the slightest role in shaping her future conduct of the battle, which she waged precisely as before. She contrived to be out and unobtainable from early evening until late at night.

Instead of throwing the flowers into the trash when he saw his attempted truce thwarted, Scott decided to display them as prominently in his own apartment as was consistent with his self-image (and with the black truck he drove), hoping for their accidental discovery if Chloe should call-by before the display faded (and he prayed to God she did call by!), and realise that their originally-intended home was hers. But his bachelor pad was light on vases. So he popped down the corridor to ask Valeria if she had a spare he could borrow. Not only did she have a *choice* of spare vases to offer him, she insisted on coming over and arranging the flowers herself.

('Don't be ridiculous! He couldn't arrange a single rose in a bud-vase! No: she *insisted*!')

While she was fidgeting with minute adjustments which, to Scott, made no difference whatsoever to the general effect, he was inspired, recklessly, to ask her if she was doing anything that night, because he had a reservation for two at *La Traviata* which he was about to cancel, because --

He got no further. When a *diem* came along, Valeria was quick on the *carpe*.

"I'd love to," she said. "What a lovely surprise!" And every cell in her brain went into immediate and furious overdrive, accurately putting together an entire jigsaw of which she had been given only two pieces.

"How lovely!" she said.

She took the bold step of leaning forward and kissing Scott on the cheek, and said 'she couldn't go to *La Traviata* looking like this!' and she would be back in ten minutes.

As soon as Valeria left the room Scott had qualms that perhaps this wasn't such a good idea; but he couldn't cancel Valeria two minutes after he had invited her; and he surrendered to the un-chivalrous thought that it would serve Chloe right. He determined to enjoy himself thoroughly: a frame of mind that, in a man particularly, and in an angry man especially, has been known to lead to excessive drinking.

Which was indeed where it led Scott, and way beyond, that silly, fateful night.

10

Didier

Necessity requires that a few words are now given to a description of Didier, to whom some brief reference has already been made. Happily, there is not much that needs be said about him at this precise moment, because he plays only a cameo role in what is immediately to follow. You must think of this as a short prelude to the more substantial fugue (or two-part invention) played by Tyler and him later in these pages.

Three things attracted Didier more than anything else: celebrity, other peoples' money, and a select circle of young male whores. It is tempting to call him shallow, but the word implies at least some depth.

Separated from a life-long relationship with an older man—a prominent (and rich) entertainment-lawyer—every month he received a large palimony check, which by careful economy he managed to eke out until towards the end of the first week. Those who disliked Didier put it about that for the remaining three weeks of the month he was kept in funds by an implied blackmail of his rich ex-lover, which threatened his leaking to the newspapers what they had done when younger men, and with whom. But this was mere supposition by the enemies: the ex-lover kept Didier in funds because he had a kind heart, remembered the best of times, and could afford it. Reasons quite incomprehensible to most of Didier's friends, and to all of the select circle of male whores.

His detractors said Didier was lazy, but that is simply not true. He attended every Hollywood gathering worth being seen at; and it would be preposterous to suggest that at those gatherings he was idle. He worked them harder than did the children who made the cheap sweatshirts he wore.

And one must not forget his 'Aids Benefits', in which he was extremely active; and his industry, as well as his thoughtfulness, could not be better illustrated than by his utilising the proceeds, in part, so as to ease the financial burdens he placed on his ex-lover.

Other than that he was Austrian, of medium height, unctuous to those he thought useful, dismissive of almost everyone else, and somewhat stout in build (despite sporadic bursts of activity in the gym—and despite an over-indulgence in cocaine and crystal methamphetamine, which might have made him thinner), there is not much else to say about him.

11

Aftershocks

The morning following her manufactured unavailability, and Scott's selecting Valeria as her substitute for dinner at *La Traviata*, Chloe's agent called her. An offer of a job, so soon after walking out of her last one, was not to be rejected; even if she was a second-choice, the first-chosen having fallen sick a couple of days before shooting. That they were filming on location—in Quebec!—and she would be away for a month or more, and that she had to fly as soon as she could pack, meant that Chloe *needed* to make up with Scott; and the truth (which is as you would hope it to be) is that she sorely wanted to, as soon as she possibly could.

She had one of those 'Love Is . . . ' cards in a drawer somewhere—she knew it was corny but didn't care; and inside it she wrote the single word: *"Ceasefire?"*. But before she left her apartment to slide the card under Scott's door, so he would find it the moment he came back from work, her telephone rang for the second time: it was Didier.

"I hope you managed to get Scott back safe and sound? I hear he was quite a handful. Is he OK? I just called him at the Campus, but he's off sick and he's not picking up at home. Poor lamb!"

"Slow down! What are you saying?'

"Last night, at *La Traviata*. My spies tell me you both had quite a time of it! Is it true you had to stop him driving? My dear! How DID you manage that big truck?"

"Your spies don't follow my movements carefully enough, Didier. I was at the movies last night—and I have no idea what you're on about." (Which was a lie: she had a pretty accurate idea.)

"Are you high?" she spat at him.

"Ooops! Wrong number! And no, I'm not."

"Good bye, Didier."

"OK, I am. High as 'a *elephant's eye on the fourth of July*'. What's new?"

"Didier, I am in a mad hurry. I have to go. If you want to find out what happened to Scott, at *La Traviata* or anywhere else, ask Scott."

With which, she hung up.

After five minutes' pacing in her apartment, Chloe decided to knock on Scott's door and wake him from his hangover-bed. Poor Chloe, she guessed (rightly) that *La Traviata* might have been hers, and guessed (wrongly) that Scott allowed himself to become drunk whilst pretending to have a good time with her substitute, but in reality having a miserable time without her; and in her heart of hearts all she really wanted to do, desperately before she left, was to make-up with him. The new job was *'a good thing'*, as he would say, and they should be celebrating, not feuding.

Even though she had her back to Chloe, there could be no doubt it was Valeria who slipped out of Scott's apartment and closed the door so gently behind her. An identification forcibly confirmed when she tripped gaily down the corridor to her own front door, and opened it with a quiet call to *"Billy?"*

It is just as well Valeria did not turn round, because the curl of her lips might have suggested, to eyes disinclined towards charity, a smirk rather than a smile—with a hint of triumph, to the close observer.

Chloe retreated to the elevator; which she had left only seconds earlier so full of hopes for reconciliation, and so nearly-happy.

The remainder of the last, precious day before she flew to Quebec was spent shut in her apartment packing, and hoping for a call that never came; and she passed her last night even more alone—if that makes sense—mostly awake, and about as miserable as it is possible for a young woman to be.

The "Love Is . . . " card was torn to shreds.

* * *

Scott learned from a pencilled note on a piece of scrap paper, ripped from its cheap pad and only half-slid under his apartment door, that Chloe had been called away urgently to replace a sick first assistant director on a Hallmark Hall of Fame TV movie, and that she would be gone for at least a month.

The last of the few words scrawled on the note were "Both of us have to work."

12
Wonderful News

Chloe had been away for six weeks, and no one had heard a whisper from her in all that time. Then, out of the blue, Madison received a picture-postcard of a breaching whale, with a short message written in a carefree style that a cynic might have suggested was a trifle forced. This is what it said -

> *"Hi Madison! Working socks etc. but time off (when I get it) is great!! Saw whale like this on boat trip with some of crew!!! Staying at the Tadoussac on the St. Laurence. Come visit!!!! Fab!!!!!"* C

"She wants you to go visit her," said Madison to Scott.

"Then why not ask me?"

"You know why," said Madison. "It's not always easy to say 'sorry'."

"And which one of us do you suggest should say 'sorry'?"

"Both of you."

"Chloe has a problem with saying 'sorry' because she's never in the wrong. She's never had to say 'sorry' in her life," said Scott, increasingly tense.

"Write to her, Scott. Why do you think she's given us her address? She's reaching out. Can't you see that?"

"Then let her reach out to me," said Scott; and the topic was closed.

Madison wrote to Chloe and delicately suggested she get in touch with Scott. She received no reply.

* * *

The next postcard was addressed to Tyler.

> *"Can you do me a favour? We have to re-shoot some stuff in a couple weeks, so no point coming back home and out again. Can you go check my mail and forward anything looks important? Big Kiss. C"* (ps Tadoussac Hotel)

"Dude, she wants you get your ass over there," said Tyler.

Scott finished his beer in silence.

* * *

The third, and final postcard Chloe sent from Canada was again addressed to Madison, and was much shorter than the first—

"Off skiing between shoots. Breathtaking. Spending Christmas in Montreal. Back to work in two. Ugh! Happy Holidays. C"

It was one of those cards where the customer supplies a photograph for the picture. The photograph was of Chloe and three others at the entrance to a *téléphérique*, holding their skis and poles.

Chloe and three others. On a skiing holiday. Two boys and two girls.

Madison realised the postcard was almost certainly intended to be passed-on to Scott in order to make him jealous, and goad him into coming over; but she thought it would probably strengthen his determination to stay put, so she decided not to tell him about it, or anyone else. But she did have another go, in her own homely style, at persuading Scott to hold out the olive branch.

"I know you mean well Madison," interrupted Scott, before she had spoken five words, "so don't take this the wrong way. It wasn't me who got up and left town. She knows my address, my phone, my message service, my goddam work-number. And she writes to you and Tyler? You and Tyler? I really, really don't want to talk about this any more."

Madison changed her mind about Chloe's postcard, in one last-ditch attempt at spurring Scott into making the first move. She showed it to him.

"Don't you think you ought at least to do *something* Scott?"

He got up and left the room.

* * *

Chloe had not been in touch with any of them since her 'Happy Holidays' postcard. She had been away from Los Angeles for nearly nine weeks, and in all that time there had been no contact whatsoever between Scott and her, other than the cards intended for his eyes, but sent to others'.

Then one night when Madison returned from an unusually hard day's recording of 'Ghost Trail' (in which Courtney had been possessed by Eleanor Roosevelt), there was an unexpected message on her answer service. On hearing it, Madison collapsed into a chair and remained seated for some minutes, staring at nothing, doing nothing. The message was from Chloe -

"Madison—I've got wonderful news!—I'm engaged!—I'll tell you all about him when I get back—I'm so happy!—I had to call and tell you!"

And that was that. The line cut dead.

13

Rome

"We sat around Madison's kitchen table most of the night, trying to piece it all together and listening to Chloe's answerphone message, it must be for a hundred times.

'*Do you think she <u>sounds</u> happy?*" asks Tom.

'*It's so short,*" says Madison. '*I can't tell. I just can't tell.*'

"Again and again she said the same thing: 'I just can't tell.'

"Then there was something strange. I've never told anyone before, because—well *Scottino*, perhaps you will understand why—but it was, to me, very strange. Not frightening. Not good, either. Strange. *Singulare. Ma molto strano*.

"It happened when Madison emptied a bottle of *vino rosso* into her glass—which was not exactly unusual for Madison, eh?—and then began to open another, which she took from a wooden wine-rack fixed to the wall. I couldn't have told you then, and I can't now, why I particularly noticed what was to all appearances an insignificant moment—Madison pulling a bottle of red wine from the wooden wine-rack fixed to the wall of her kitchen. We are talking about Madison, *si*? There was nothing remarkable about the way she did it, nothing remarkable was said when she did it, and I had seen her do the same thing, *essatamente cosi*, a thousand times: but that three-second action of hers caught my particular attention; everything else, it seemed frozen; the moment somehow stepped out of the scene, as though it was saying to me 'remember this!' And I did remember it. And I often wondered why it had buried itself in my memory, and why it sometimes crept into my dreams.

"Then Tom spoke, and the moment was gone.

'*You couldn't tell what was going on in Chloe's head if she was right here in front of you,*' he said. '*Right here, saying she was 'engaged' and saying she was 'so happy'. Right here in your kitchen.*'

'*You never know for sure with Chloe,*' said Madison. '*What she's thinking, why she's doing what she does, or anything else.*'

"We listened to the message again: '*Madison—I've got wonderful news!—I'm engaged!—I'll tell you all about him when I get back—I'm so happy!—I had to call and tell you!*'

'*Chloe should learn the difference between playing hard to get, and playing impossible to get,*' was Didier's helpful contribution.

'*Maybe it's for real,*' said Madison—she was so desolate. Poor Madison.

'*Maybe she thinks it's for real,*' said Tyler, '*but I doubt it. She's fucking with him.*'

'*I hope she isn't,*' said Madison.

'*You <u>want</u> it to be for real?*' said Didier, testily; his unattractive Austrian 'r' rasping more than usual when he landed on '*real*'.

"Madison was on the brink of tears.

'*Of course not. Of course I hope she isn't engaged. But I hope she isn't . . . fucking with Scott . . . And I hope she isn't engaged, either. I don't know what to hope.*'

'*She's fucking with him*' said Tyler again.

"If she was, we were of a single mind in wondering what in God's name she thought she was going to achieve by such a childish stunt: no one believed for a moment that Chloe had suddenly found 'Mr. Right'—

'*Not two and a half thousand miles away,*' they said.

'*Not in just nine weeks,*' they said.

"Pah! As though either of those two random measurements could possibly work against her finding Mr. Right—or Mr. Wrong for that matter—and getting engaged to him in Quebec.

"But it was done, and all the speculation in the world as to why it was done could not undo it.

'*Who's going to tell the boyfriend?*' asked Tyler.

"The task was left to me, as I suspected it would be."

* * *

"I arranged to meet Scott, with Tyler for support, for a drink after his work the next day—in Westwood, which I chose deliberately because it was near to where Scott taught at UCLA. I hadn't thought-through why that might be a better place to tell him than anywhere else: it was instinct. I suppose it had something to do with Westwood being Scott's own—how do you say it?—his 'back-yards'. *Suo territorio*. It belonged to him more than it belonged to us, and I thought maybe that was where I should break him the news. Over a beer in a bar where Scott was usually—as you like to say—'top dog'.

"I told him about the message soon after we sat down, but only when we had each emptied a bottle of Budweiser, and Tyler had brought us back a second. I didn't build to it, or dress it up, or make any comment of any kind about it. I simply told Scott, in plain words (it may be I was *un po' come una tragedia Greca*, but it doesn't matter now), I told him he ought to know that Madison had a message from Chloe, which I then summarised.

"Scott's face was expressionless—

'*Is that right?*' he said.

'*She's fucking with you, man,*' said Tyler.

'*Want another beer?*' asked Scott.

* * *

"When Chloe returned to Los Angeles it was without a fiancé, but with a diamond on her left ring finger."

The old man raised his eyebrows, cocked his head slightly, and added -

'

'Es ist eine alte Geschichte,

Doch bleibt sie immer neu;

Und wem sie just passieret,

Dem bricht das Herz entzwei.'

"I . . . don't know too much German," said his godson. The old man translated for him:

'It is an old, old story

It's not exactly new;

And all it does to our young man

—Is break his heart in two.'

"Or something similar," he said.

Three

1

Tom

It was a good few months before the earthquake that Tom first mentioned to anyone that he thought he might be going mad. But he wasn't being serious. Not seriously serious. Not back then. It was simply that in Los Angeles he found himself saying things with no expectation that anyone would understand him—but he went ahead and said them anyway. That, he once confided to Scott, must be a sub-set of madness.

Ever since he arrived in America he had found that the cultural gap between the UK and the States was considerably wider than he'd appreciated—which may have been true, but didn't in all fairness take matters very far because his appreciation of the States didn't stretch beyond California, and his appreciation of California no further than Los Angeles, and his appreciation of Los Angeleans was mostly limited to people working in the film industry, or waiting tables, or both. There were many in LA more cultured than he; and in all truth he was a tad precious about such culture as had rubbed-off on him in England.

Tom's everyday conversation was packed with irony. He was bemused, and uncertain how to respond, when he said the opposite of what he meant, for comic effect, and his circle of American friends took his words literally. You mustn't think Tom was showing off, or trying to be clever: he wasn't, though many thought he was; and a great number in his new American society '*didn't get him*', and even disliked him for no other reason than the '*smart ass*' way he talked.

He came to the attention of Hollywood with an animated children's fantasy that used 'animatronics' rather than drawing or computer imagery. It was an overnight success and brought him a nomination for a Special Achievement Award from the Screen Animators' Guild of America. His innovation was the use of free-standing voice-activated puppets—'*The Nurslings*'; and he created an imaginative and highly original universe for them to inhabit, where they played-out modern morality tales in which good doesn't simply triumph over evil, it changes evil into good.

It may have been children's fodder but adults flocked to it along with their kids, and it cleaned-up at the box office. (Hollywood isn't renowned for giving awards to film-makers who *don't* clean-up at the box-office.)

The most advanced of the *Nurslings*, and the lead role in the film which had caused such a stir, was a character called 'Nimrod'. Half elf, half boy.

You may say: 'Oh come on, we've all seen that before'. But in creating him Tom had achieved something extraordinary, and even he didn't fully understand exactly what he had done, or how he had done it. Nimrod was strange, mystical, and unearthly—J. M. Barrie might have said '*he was carved from a tree that had a nymph enslaved in it*'—and at the same time he was mischievous, funny and quintessentially human. We *hadn't* seen it before; and Nimrod was never to be replicated.

And he was free-standing!

And he talked!

I refuse to use the word 'robot' to define him because Nimrod was as alive as any mortal you are likely to meet, and more alive than some of them. It was his interaction, his seeming *interest* in what was said to him and his *response* to it that set him apart from his nearest puppet rivals—by leagues.

"What's so clever about Nimrod", Tom explained to a Discovery Channel interviewer, "If it isn't too awful of me to boast" . . . he genuinely meant that, and genuinely blushed . . . "is that there's a chip inside him that allows him to increase his own vocabulary."

"Vocabulary?"

"If he hears a new word, in a tone of voice he knows, he'll guess its meaning *and respond accordingly*. If his reaction is not corrected, the new word goes in his memory, and he'll respond the same way whenever he hears that word. He's learning all the time. Like a 12 month old baby."

"For real?"

"It's totally unreal, but that's what he does. And he's the perfect actor. He knows his lines and he takes direction."

"And you take his earnings."

"Just a percentage."

* * *

The Screen Animators Guild Awards were held in May 1991: (the same merry month when Paula Jones stepped into a Little Rock hotel room with Bill Clinton, and whiled away some time with him which it took her three years to complain was not quality time.)

The Studio Executives insisted that Tom and Nimrod should *not* walk the Red Carpet together because the appearance of Nimrod beforehand would ruin a choreographed surprise. And that was true. But it was not the whole truth. They also thought Tom was likely to let the Hollywood side down: they did not want him on camera with his cut (rather than styled) hair, his un-straightened English teeth, his scruffy Tux, and his refusal to wear a lapel-ribbon commemorating the *cause du jour.*

It never crossed Tom's mind to be driven there. He turned up in the car he had hired at the airport—a bronze Toyota Cherry—with Nimrod in a large black case on the back seat (for the purposes of concealment and surprise). The uniformed guard at the gate shouted at him '*where did he think he was going?*'—the implied words being '*in that car?*' The guard made no attempt to disguise his irritation when Tom produced a valid pass, but still he wouldn't raise the barrier, because (to his immeasurable delight) a chauffeur-driven Humvee—*chauffeur driven!*—the Stars and Stripes painted over the entire body of it, and a glamorous woman with blond hair sitting in the back passenger seat of it, pulled up alongside Tom's Toyota and was ceremoniously waved through ahead of him. The uniformed man gave the woman a long, pointed, unnecessarily deferential salute as she passed.

She smiled a sweet smile at Tom though, and her eyes sparkled in counterpoint with her jewels. The Humvee drew up to the Red Carpet, and the Toyota Cherry drove down into an underground car park. And while Tom wheeled Nimrod's coffin-like case through a back-alley to the stage door, the blonde ran the gauntlet of the press-corps—with no visible sign of her having pre-loaded a couple of miniatures of neat vodka a only seconds earlier.

Madison had come a long way since her first faltering steps in Hollywood.

* * *

The awards. Tom back stage. Madison in a front-row 'A-list' seat. The celebrity hostess talks intimately to the cameras, but she completely ignores the live audience. They *feel* ignored and don't give celebrity hostess an easy ride. She is in full flow -

"*The focus tonight is on the boys and girls behind the scenes—and the young man behind Camera number 2, I'd focus on him any night! Uh-Humm!*"

As she flirts with the cameraman, the mildest of audience laughter has to be supplemented by a large dollop of the canned. She continues—

"*The faces you don't see up on the big screen. Those names that roll by to beautiful music while you're all scrambling to leave the theater, and get a free refill on your diet coke.*"

This places a heavy burden on the canned laughter.

"*Every so often Hollywood is privileged to discover someone working back stage who by sheer force of talent can lead us into new and exciting journeys. Someone who can take the ordinary, raw material we all know, and like . . . excuse me . . .* "

The audience does not disguise its *shadenfreude* as she struggles with the auto-cue.

"*Rumpled?*"

A man in black-tie walks on stage (to applause) and whispers in her ear. Celebrity Hostess speaks to the audience for the first time—

"*I got this wrong in rehearsal!*" she tells them, intimate and coy.

More laughter, coupled with a sprinkling of slow hand-clapping. Black-tie man whispers in her ear again—before and between each syllable of . . .

"*Rumple—Stilt—Skin*"

Black-tie man leaves the stage to his own round of jeers and wolf-whistles. She picks up the auto-cue where she left off -

"*Someone who can take the ordinary, raw material we all know, and like RUMPLESTILKSKIN*"—(she is magnificent in her triumphant peroration, and there is thunderous applause)—"*spin it into gold.*"

"*Tonight the Guild is proud to honor such a person, under whose direction animatronics has transcended craft to become the highest art. The raw material? A block of wood. Some wire . . . and OK . . . A computer chip or two!*"

What in God's heaven made her pause for a laugh? For *that* line? A voice in the audience shouts "And a million dollars!" (Now they laugh.) She soldiers-on, and the auto-cue is again the entire focus of her attention as she navigates through the lines—

"*But from these create he can
Forms more real than living man,
Nursling of immortality.*"

"*Members of the Guild, Ladies and gentlemen, the Screen Animators' Guild of America is proud to present this year's Special Achievement Award to . . . Tom Hart.*"

The clapping is short-lived, because the stage and auditorium suddenly go dark, a spotlight shines on an entrance at the back of the stalls, and into it steps . . . Nimrod!

He saunters down the aisle and climbs the steps to the stage—effortlessly. The audience is wowed: A puppet! No strings! STEPS!!

All but a pair of eyes are transfixed on Nimrod. Madison's are the exception. She peers around and into every corner and finally catches sight of Tom in a small control room, working the dials on a complex panel and from time-to-time speaking into a microphone. The extraordinary thing is his face and demeanour. He is ecstatic, almost to the point of embarrassment if anyone took the trouble to look at him. He *is* Nimrod.

Now begins the much-rehearsed dialogue scene between a celebrity hostess and a puppet. Only the puppet is word perfect.

With an exaggerated expression of surprise, which goes some way to explaining why celebrity hostess has never won anything for herself, she exclaims -

"Nimrod! What are you doing here? Where's Tom?"

"I came to collect the award. After all, I do all the work."

"Don't get smart now!"

"Well, the truth is, I came to make a proposal."

"A proposal! What kind of proposal?"

"When I grow up, will you marry me?"

(Much laughter. Whatever else she isn't, Celebrity Hostess is a head-turner.) She makes a nervous reference to the auto-cue . . .

"Do you know, that's what a four year old Mozart said to Marie Antoinette?"

"Yeah! And look what happens to them. She gets her head chopped off, and he gets talked to death by F. Murray Abraham."

"Nimrod! Don't you think it's time you said a few 'thank-yous'?"

"Oh yeah! I'd like to thank an oak tree in Virginia, a tin-mine in Arizona, and everyone in Silicon Valley."

"I think it's past your bedtime."

Celebrity hostess takes a bow. Nimrod takes two. And they walk off-stage, she holding Nimrod by one hand and the award by the other, to a delighted, rapturous standing ovation.

* * *

All in all, the evening was reported as a great success, the one complaint being that Tom himself never appeared.

But Madison had seen him; and just as she did on the way in, so she did on the way out, and drew up alongside him in her chauffeured Humvee by the gated entrance. Things were much the same as earlier, with three major differences. Firstly, the surprise was over and Nimrod didn't need to be hidden anymore, so he was slumped in the front passenger seat, fish-eyed and lifeless, secured upright by his seatbelt, and staring out of the windshield. Secondly, although the uniformed gate-keeper did everything in his power—and those powers acknowledged no limits—to waive Madison through ahead of Tom, she insisted Tom went first. And the third and most important difference of all was that Madison had a few words with Tom through her open window.

"That was simply amazing. Congratulations. You must be *very* proud."

"Well, it's all down to him, rather than me." Tom patted Nimrod on the head, and the head flopped down sideways onto its chest and stared at nothing on the ground outside the passenger window—almost as though he wasn't listening.

Madison said -

"I had to admire the hostess. I mean, '*Nurslings of immortality*'!! How did she manage to *say* that? Who wrote the script?"

"Shelley."

"Honey, trust me, get rid of her."

"She'll never work in this Town again."

Madison held a pen and a programme out of the window, towards Tom, and apologised . . .

"Would you mind? It's for my niece . . . "

"Sure." Tom smiled diffidently, and scrawled on the front of the programme, and handed it back. Madison screwed her eyes (which should have been wearing glasses) and read the signature -

"You signed "Nimrod".

"Who's 'Tom Hart'?"

Although their vehicles separated at the first junction, and Tom thought little of Madison until months later, when he found they were sharing an apartment block in Larrabee, Madison thought a great deal about Tom, that night and for many nights to come.

She was smitten.

* * *

The first signs of Tom's being pathologically unsuited to the taking of forbidden narcotics (to which he was introduced behind the scenes at the Kodak Theatre, to boost his confidence) occurred while he was driving home from the awards. But the adverse effects were in proportion to the short lines he had snorted, and his hallucinations were comparatively mild.

He swung his Toyota Cherry off the 10 Freeway onto Pico, feeling relaxed and contented: Nimrod strapped safely in the front passenger seat, and the 'Screen Animators Guild' Award bouncing around in the back.

"Strange woman!"—meaning Madison. To Nimrod - "What did *you* make of her?"

The pre-sets on Tom's radio had all been re-tuned by the thoughtful mechanics at a 'Kwik-Fit' tyre-change to exactly the same Country and Western station. But Tom was content to sing along with Roy Rogers—

> "*My Palomino Pal, my Palomino pal,*
> *A horse is a cowboy's best friend.*"

There was more of a Western 'twang' in Tom's pronunciation than in Roy's -
"You'll always be my *fray-ind*, won't you Nimrod?"

He veered off Pico onto La Brea. A blur of coloured disks appeared, skipping on the horizon.

> "*He's trusty and loyal,*
> *From his nose to his tail,*
> *My country-bred quadruped*
> *Palomino pal.*"

Tom smiled at Nimrod—and Nimrod turned and smiled back at him. (According to Tom.)

He ruffled Nimrod's hair -

> "*My digital fray-ind,*
> *My digital fray-ind...*"

The coloured disks got nearer—stop lights at the next junction—cycling Red, Amber, Green. Red, Amber, Green.

Nimrod swayed along in time to the music.
(According to Tom.)

> "*My solenoid, silicon, digital fray-ind...*"

The shop-windows either side of La Brea *pulsated*, flooding white light into the road, as if a thousand giant refrigerator doors were being opened and closed by a thousand giants.

> "*I don't give a damn if I go round the bend...*"

The Toyota wove side to side, swaying along with Tom and Nimrod.

"With my wonderful two-footed digital -"

A sudden crash.

The pulsating shop-lights cut out on impact. A rhythmic buzzing crescendo'd in Tom's head, louder and louder until it was unbearable, then it faded to nothing.

Normality.

Tom had ignored the red stop-sign at a junction and driven into the side of a truck. Not much damage, considering the noise it made. One of the Toyota's headlights smashed. A couple of dents to the truck. Tom's head grazed, nothing worse.

The angry truck-driver yelled at Tom 'what the hell did he think he was doing?' and muttered about calling the cops, while Roy Rogers belted out *'My Palomino Pal'* from the truck-driver's radio—(Tom had crashed into a Kwik-Fit recovery vehicle.)

"And we'll ride side by side
To the end of the trail . . . "

Nimrod was unhurt: saved by his seatbelt. He sat there just as he did when leaving the awards, fish-eyed and lifeless, staring at nothing out of the passenger window.

2

Orange Blossom

When, an age later, Tom met Madison by chance in the parking lot at Larrabee, and they discovered they had lived in the same block for months, and hadn't noticed each other, *'which was unbelievable'*, and Tom found he was *'really pleased to see her again'*, and they talked about this, and about that, and about the awards night, and Tom became bashful, and Madison became coy, and *'wasn't it amazing, we've been chatting for nearly an hour?'*, and Madison asked if one day she could maybe come and visit his studio . . . Tom said:

"Right now, if you like."

Madison suggested six o'clock; so Tom gave her the address and headed straight there, excited as a teenager on his first date, to prepare it for her visit and make it magical.

Back then, before he moved up to Mulholland, Tom rented a space in the old Motown Hitsville studios in West Hollywood. It was there he once saw Keannu Reeves playing basketball in the yard, and Jane Fonda recording the sound track for one of her workout videos; and it was at the urinal in the gents' toilet that he famously stood next to Bruce Springsteen. So when Madison arrived in her 'Patriotic Hummer', whilst it attracted a few curious glances, it was not the sensation—in that starry place—that it so often was when she pulled into other parking lots.

Dusk was becoming night, and on the urban flats of Los Angeles the scent of orange blossom made the air itself giddy.

Tom was waiting in the studio lobby when Madison arrived precisely as scheduled, not a minute early nor a second late. He was sitting next to Nimrod and to all appearances talking with him, to the delight of the receptionists and the various passers-by. The moment Madison came through the revolving doors Tom stood for her (as in England they did then) and Nimrod stood too, and gave Madison a little bow.

"How do you do that?" she asked.

"What?" said Tom.

Holding Nimrod by the hand, he escorted Madison along a corridor and down an elevator into a small basement studio littered with Nursling puppets, perched on shelves, sitting on chairs—even suspended from the ceiling, making fairy-tale shadows on the walls.

It wasn't (as she expected it to be) a cold or clinical place. It was comfortably furnished with warm colours, and fully carpeted. Several polished wooden tables were arranged asymmetrically in the room, each standing on its own Persian rug. A confusion of machinery, half-made puppets, computers, the innards of computers, tools, saws, wire, Da Vinci-style drawings and diagrams. On every table a monitor—the screen not a cold blue, but a soft, glowing ochre. From the back of every screen a single lead, attached to a 'mother board', held securely in place by an old-fashioned tripod. Thermostats and humidifiers were jotted here and there. And even they hummed *melodiously*.

Madison, for all her recently acquired world-weariness, was unable to repress a sense of awe, which Tom echoed by speaking to her in a hushed voice:

"These are embryo Nurslings."

"Embryo?"

"They're not finished. Not born."

Madison eyed the banks of sound-recording equipment, tape machines, microphones, and a long mixing console.

"Is this where you make them so they talk? Program them? What?"

"No. Not at all. This is the maternity ward. Right now I don't program them, so much as give them the capacity to learn. Later. For themselves."

Madison said she didn't understand. Tom explained -

"It's the same with us. You don't know anything when you're born. But you were pre-programmed, so you could *learn*. Anything and everything."

Madison protested that 'she's not a computer'.

"Sure you are. A computer that can re-produce itself."

Madison blushed. Tom, oblivious, continued—"With a shelf life of about 70 years."

"That's horrible."

"No it's not. It's beautiful. A tiny rose seed is just a computer—brilliantly programmed."

"Programmed?"

"To produce an infinite number of roses. We've got a more complex design—with a less attractive program. It's still beautiful though... Or it could be. Don't you think these have a sort of beauty about them?"

Madison said 'yes she did'.

"When they're fully fledged—"

Madison interrupted him: "Born?"

Tom smiled at her. She smiled back. She's falling under the spell. And he, in his own odd way, is falling under hers.

"When they're born! . . . The others will teach them everything they know."

Madison laughed and said 'he's gone too far'. Tom didn't seem to hear her. He was lost in his imaginary world, gazing with a mixture of pride *and wonder* at the creatures he had placed in it.

"They'll teach each other? You're serious?" She hesitated, as ready to believe him, for a brief moment, as a child is to believe in Santa Clause.

"Absolutely."

A moment's silence. Which breaks when Tom speaks—

"That's how it *grows*. I hook them up every night. And whatever any one of them has learned, he passes it on to the others. They talk to each other."

"Oh, come on! Talk?"

"What else would you call it? Sometimes even I don't know what they're saying."

He's kidding her, of course. And the dreamy, wondrous gaze has been replaced by an arch expression he puts on to signal his 'English sense of humour'.

"I do know that some of the older ones scare the youngsters with horror stories, about one day human beings taking over."

"You're funny!" A pause. "How do you dream them up? Where does it all come from?"

"There are two types of people. One looks at a fire hydrant, and sees a fire hydrant."

"Not the kind of mistake you'd . . . "

"Type two", says Tom, "looks at a fire hydrant and sees a small yellow man, with a big nose, sticking his chubby little arm out." He demonstrates.

"Is that what *you* see?"

"Good God no! I see a fire hydrant. D'you think I'm crazy?"

In the quietest corner of his brain there is the faintest rhythmic buzzing.

"You make these things yourself? Just you?"

"Just me."

"You write the stories too?"

"No. I think of things for them to do. There's a whole team turns it all into a storyline."

"I gotta tell you, if my little niece knew I was up here—"

"Don't tell her! It'll ruin the magic."

"I won't say a word."

The buzzing in Tom's head slowly fades to nothing.

3
Tyler

Say what you like about Tom, but let no-one think that Tyler was even a little crazy. He wasn't. He was the sanest of them all and the cleverest man you'll ever be likely to meet. You have to understand he only did it for a bet, and it got a little out of hand. That's all.

There used to be a truly *dreadful* daytime reality show on Los Angeles TV, which filled its 30 minute slot by dragging onstage a series of freaks—of all kinds, physical and mental—who were then ridiculed by the host, Artorio. The more cruel the mockery, the happier the studio audience. Best of all was when the poor victims got an inkling that the joke was on them, and the laughter was at them. That's what they tuned-in for, said Artorio, in their millions. (The number was possibly an over-estimate.)

They called the show 'The Artorio Collection'.

The programme had, *de rigueur*, people who had been abducted by aliens; as well as people with an extra toe, or tongue; televangelists prophesying the Apocalypse (now); and a troop of people who had had sex with their parents, children and siblings. The show featuring people who had had sex with their pets was thought of as distasteful, and never aired other than in leaked clips on U-Tube.

One day, the televised half-time promotion put out a call for people who claimed to be the Devil, and gave a number to call, in the usual way. That's when Tyler accepted the regrettable bet.

The researchers corralled a nice collection of lunatics and show-offs in costume (horns and tails); and they even found a man who had had an operation to remove benign brain tumours, which left him with two bumps either side of his crown that could be mistaken for incipient horns—but the operation must have taken out a generous slice or two of brain in the process, to judge from his TV debut.

Tyler was very canny about how he answered the call-back, and put on a crazy off-the-wall performance at the audition that guaranteed him a place in the show. His performance before the *cameras*, however, was completely different, and was '*so not what they wanted*' it would have been cut from the broadcast, if it hadn't been for the incident.

Dressed in a jacket and tie, answering Artorio's questions with a sane urbanity that reminded Tom of Gore Vidal, Tyler didn't surrender a single laugh to Artorio. Worse still (or better still, depending your stance on these things) Artorio gave the audience a glimpse or two of his own nasty, irritable little self.

"What really interests me, Arterial," said Tyler. "You don't mind if I call you by your first name?—or is it your last name?"

"Never mind about that, *what* interests you? I sure hope it interests this good audience here, who've been waiting for some time to be interested."

The enthusiastic applause was not, by any means, in support of what Artorio thought he had said.

"What really interests me, Arterial, are the changes in mankind's behaviour that I've observed throughout the ages."

"Well, sadly, we haven't got ages, we've only got—"

"Many, many years ago—I'm guessing it was some time before you were born—thousands of years—a man did what he wanted to do, without reference to ethics or laws or anything else."

"Ethics? I think you're on the wrong show, bud!" Artorio was becoming reckless.

"Then came the age when man decided what to do by reference to right and wrong. The Christian Age."

"I think some of the good folks watching this show would be offended if . . ."

"Then," Tyler was on a roll, "then came the age we have only recently passed through, *and we have passed through it*, when man made his choices merely by reference to what was lawful or unlawful—regardless of the rights and wrongs. How many immoral politicians have we heard say 'it isn't against the law'?"

The applause is all Tyler's

"So what age do you say we are at now?" asked Artorio, with a wink at the audience.

"Ahh! The age we have entered is an age where a man decides what to do by reference *only* to whether he can get away with it."

The first big laugh of the show—and not the kind Artorio was looking for.

"But it's the age that is *about to be* fascinates me the most, Arterial, because it is almost upon us, and it is my all-time favourite."

"And what might that be?" Artorio has no intention any of this will get aired.

"A man will soon do what he wants to do without reference to ethics, or laws, or getting away with it, or anything else. He'll just do it. Like an animal. We've come full circle, don't you see?"

Applause. Artorio is on the ropes.

"So why should this audience believe you're the Devil, would you like to explain that?"

"I don't care what they believe. In fact it has always been my preference that people believe nothing."

Laughter, applause, hoots and whistles.

"But you must be able to do all kinds of stuff, if you really *are* Satan. Give us a sign. Anything."

Tyler doesn't reply. He can't.

Got him! At last! Artorio sits back in his chair complacently, and nods to a floor-walker to get this one off and bring the next one on.

And that's when the incident happened. Perfectly on cue, as though an answer to "Give us a sign", a whole row of overhead studio lights blew, one after the other, like they did in "The Natural" when Robert Redford thwacked the baseball out of the stadium.

Which was enough for a significant proportion of the American People to believe, unhesitatingly, that Tyler was the Devil.

4

Hail Satan

In the natural world there is an overlap between day and night which has more to it than fading light being overtaken by deepening dark. It begins when the first of the daytime creatures make for their roosts and the first of the night-time creatures crawl from their caves, or from under rocks or from rotten holes in dying trees, places hidden from the sun and all that is wholesome, where they have half-slept the day away, waiting their turn to hunt, kill and feast.

So it is in the unnatural world. With Los Angeles' roads still busy, the shops not yet closed, and the cinemas and restaurants far from empty, at the 'overlap' there is a distinct sense of homeward-bound to be felt on every street corner, and a urgency of purpose—like that of so many birds flying through the dusk to a distant copse—as the day-people move quickly past the emerging night-people, glad to get to their cars and their gated communities, and yield the city to the night and all who inhabit it.

Didier, bored out of his mind, had slept on-and-off throughout the day (as much as cocaine allowed him to, and as fitfully as it insisted upon) to the inefficient lullaby of television. With darkness falling, he stretched his arms like a plump moth opening its wings, and showered and dressed with an indistinct memory filtering into his wakening brain that he had arranged to meet Tyler that very night, ideally sober, to discuss their 'big idea'.

It was a matter of controversy between them—and eventually the subject of an expensive lawsuit—which of them had the 'big idea' first, and who brought the other in on it. The truth of the matter, which the judge and jury never got to hear (they rarely do), is that the origin of 'the idea' was nothing other than a spontaneous and fantastic joke, bursting out more or less simultaneously from both of them, between guffaws of helpless laughter over cocktails at The Mondrian. In the days and nights following, when the joke had taken a serious turn, and they began to think 'maybe this could work', the contributions from each were as good as equal, and the legal system should never have been troubled with their squabble over the profits—and *would* never have been troubled, if the profits hadn't been enormous.

It all started when Tyler began to get fan mail from people across America who had been taken-in by his appearance as the Devil on 'The Artorio Collection'.

A corrupt employee at the TV station—possibly a vengeful Artorio himself—leaked or sold Tyler's address, and many a fervent believer wrote to him. Leaving to one side those correspondents who expressed an urgent desire to come over to Los Angeles and (mixing their mythology) shoot him with a silver bullet, or ram a wooden stake through his heart, there was an unhealthy number of fans—acolytes, even—whose letters began with the salutation "Hail Satan!"

The irony was that Tyler looked nothing like any depiction of Beelzebub anyone has ever committed to paper, canvas or celluloid. Rather short, pleasant looking, and with no sign of facial hair, he might have passed for one of Satan's little helpers, but not the fallen angel himself.

Tyler resisted the temptation to respond to his fan mail in character—temptation was, after all, his to trap others with—and he trashed all the hasty, albeit extremely funny, drafts he had composed in reply. It was only when Didier and he were off their faces in the Mondrian one night that the idea was conceived, and nearly aborted by laughter, of turning the preposterous belief that Tyler was the Devil into hard cash—by way of a mail-order anti-Christ religious sect, with Tyler's fans making the initial data-base of followers.

"You could pay thousands of dollars for market research like that," said Didier. In fact, for the database derived from all the mail Tyler ultimately received, they could have paid tens of thousands.

When Tyler and Didier heard their calling, the Internet was in its early days and there was only a modest handful of sites giving advice on how to finance and reap the rewards from 'spreading the word'—whatever word it was you chanced upon and looked like it could make a buck. But if today you were to 'Google' the phrase 'Setting up a New Religion', you would get no less than 240,000,000 'hits'. (Astonishingly, if you were to Google 'How to *Make Money* out of a New Religion' your screen would show more than *half a billion* hits. But on closer examination of the first few pages of the various sites, again and again 'making money' is the religion itself.)

"The key to it is pyramid selling," said Didier, deep in thoughts of printers, pamphlets and bank accounts, rather than cloven hooves, horns and a trident;

and they had parted on that first, momentous night, their narcotic-fuelled heads spinning with the absurdity of it all, and yet the possibilities of it all, and most importantly of it all, the money it might bring them.

For Didier's amusement, Tyler surrendered to a brief, blasphemous lapse into mock self-doubt, inspired by the passing desert trolley—

"*What does it profiterole if it gain the whole world . . . ?*"

"I shouldn't worry yourself about that, girlfriend," said Didier. "Your soul, if you ever had one, was lost a very long time ago."

* * *

The *locus* of their second meeting was again the Mondrian (which they affectionately called their 'boardroom'); and the refreshments they laid on for themselves, to sustain them through the rigours of it, were not materially different from those that had kept them alert through their first.

"You look like shit!" said the rested Didier to Tyler, who had only just driven back from the beach, and was dishevelled and sunburnt, and certainly tired; but to set the record straight, not otherwise faecal.

"I left something for you under the toilet-roll in the restroom. Go get it before anyone else does." Tyler went to do just that, returning suitably charged-up and sniffing; and with both of them at more or less the same place mentally, they began to pool the results of their investigations so far.

The founder of the most financially successful model was, of course, L. Ron Hubbard, and his followers seemed to Didier to fall into two broad types. There were those in the traditional, religious sense of the word, who followed his teachings. Then there were those of another kind altogether, who followed his extraordinarily successful formula for making money.

Didier gave a clear indication which of the two groups he should be counted amongst when he identified to Tyler the two cardinal principles underpinning their new religion; they being (1) that the profits should not be subject to tax, and (2) that the profits should go to the prophets.

In order to achieve the first, it was necessary to register the religion with the government, to do which required that they give it a name. 'Satanism' was not thought appropriate for their purposes, and was probably already registered with the IRS. They rapidly came to the conclusion that the name of their sect was far too important to be determined on a whim, and they put-off the decision (as in the coming months they were to put-off so much else) until they were more certain of their ground.

As for the second principle, Tyler told Didier that it was essential they both get ordained, legally, so they could call themselves 'ministers'—which allowed them to take a tax-free stipend. It wouldn't be far from the truth to say that this hurdle was the highest they had to jump, and the delay it occasioned was the longest they had to endure. To give an idea of the difficulties in their path, I will quote verbatim from the on-line 'Ordination Package' Tyler downloaded:

"GET ORDAINED ON LINE: no purchase is necessary in order to obtain the full legal benefits of being a minister. Just fill in the attached form. Our dedicated staff validates every application, and within 24 hours of your submission you will receive an email that confirms your ordination.

Please be sure to comply with the following instructions:

- **You must give your true legal name. Submitting your animal's name will invalidate your application.**

- **You must choose whether to be called a Minister or a Pastor. Be sure to check the appropriate box.**

- **Submission of an application in the name of a friend without his/her permission is a fraud, and in some States a criminal offence.**

Remember to create an account, which makes it easier to purchase inspirational products and church supplies with one click of the mouse. Substantial discounts are available only to ordained account holders. Look out for our special offers on holy grails (chalices), t-shirts, calendars, greeting cards and figurines printed or manufactured with the logo of your own design. We also offer a design service, details on request."

It should be mentioned that a Doctor of Divinity Certificate was listed under '**Best Sellers**'. It was too important an achievement merely to be given away.

Those vital matters being agreed upon, Didier raised two further issues, which he said they should try their best to settle before they next meet.

First there was the tricky question of who—other than themselves—would finance their enterprise. Even if he was loaded with spare cash Didier would have had someone else put up the risk-money; but the start-up would need to be found from a third party in any event, because neither he nor Tyler had a cent to his name, and each survived on the generosity of others and borrowed money that would never be returned. Tyler said he would give serious thought to approaching one of the 'Quakers', but he couldn't decide which. "Leave it with me" he said. And it was left with him.

Finally, if things kicked-off they would need premises. Didier said he had some thoughts about that, but wouldn't tell Tyler any more about them until he had made soundings of his own.

With those mysteries hanging in the air, they parted; resolving to get together again in two weeks, at the same place and time, and see what each other had achieved.

"We should be Doctors of Divinity by then," said Didier.

5

Rome

"I used to go drinking with Tyler at Yamashiro."

"It's a great place to go when you're high," said his godson. "The view downtown is awesome."

"I hope you are joking?" The old man was genuinely distressed. "Please tell me you don't take any drugs, and this is another of your bad jokes?"

"Everyone in LA does drugs. It's no big deal. Just a little weed, now and then."

"Oh Scott! Scott! The little boy I saw christened and confirmed!" (The old man's acting had not improved since he left a thankless Hollywood.) "Now he is a drug addict. Promise me you will get help?"

"I don't think that's a promise I can make," his godson said, with laboured insouciance. "And I'm not an addict. Don't worry about it. I'm no different than anyone else my age. Or a whole lot older, come to that. It's nothing. Really. I shouldn't have told you. *Forgive me, god-father, for I have sinned.*"

The master of the long sigh now gave a master-class demonstration.

"Alcohol is bad enough. Believe me." (Another sigh.) "So it becomes my turn to make a confession. I used to get a little drunk with Tyler, up there at Yamashiro, gazing down at the night-time view."

"Good boi!"

"And on one night especially, I became very drunk. Looking back at things, I am sorry to say I think it was Tyler who deliberately let me to get drunk. We had '*Mai Tais*' up there. And '*Zombies*'. We were young . . . "

"Who gets old in Los Angeles?"

"Where did you hear that?"

"How do I know?" said his godson. "Somewhere. Nowhere. I just said it, I guess."

His godfather eyed him suspiciously, then continued—

"And the view at night, as you like to say, was 'awesome'."

"You got that right." His godson grinned wider still. "Happy times!"

"At some point in the evening—I have no clear memory of exactly when it was—Tyler mentioned to me he was going into business with Didier. I was too drunk to understand why he was telling me this. A *Zombie* or *Mai Tai* later, or we may have gone back to beer by then, he asked me if I would like to invest in their business. He said that they needed some initial cash so they could get things going—you must have heard of such a thing?"

"Start-up."

"—and if I would like to invest they would pay me back within six months and I could have a ten per-cent share of the profits."

"How much did he want?"

"I did not fully understand what he was saying, I was too drunk, you see."

"How much?"

"And it seemed like a good investment, and I had only recently finished a film, so I had money in the bank."

"How much did he want?"

"Five thousand dollars."

"Which you did *not* give to him . . . I don't want to hear this . . . "

"The next day, I could not in fact *believe* I had agreed to give it to him—"

"To lend him. Please?"

"But I felt I had made a promise, so I—"

"Did you ever get it back?"

"The five thousand, yes. In bits. Most of it. Some of it. A hundred here, a hundred there. But not the ten per-cent."

"There was nothing in writing?"

"No." He gave a bitter little laugh—"And they are rich now, *si*?"

"You are sooooo dumb! You know that?"

"I am comforted by your compassion. *Grazie*. But when I heard more about the business I had invested in, maybe I am happier not having even one per-cent."

"Totally dumb."

6

Christ the Redeemer

Didier invited Tom to join him for dinner at a little Mexican restaurant in Laurel Canyon—'El Coyote'.

'El Coyote' was (and maybe still is) a quaint, hide-away place: not a tourist haunt; more like a cabin than a restaurant; single story, tucked away into the side of the hill, and surrounded by woodland. Two minutes from Sunset Boulevard, but to Tom it seemed like another country. It was no whim or accident that caused Didier to suggest 'El Coyote' as the venue for their little *tête à tête*.

Laurel Canyon winds up the Hills from Sunset Boulevard. It meets the western end of Hollywood Boulevard on its way, and further up it passes Mount Olympus on the right—with its classically named residential streets: Jupiter Drive, (Zeus Drive as well, to avoid discrimination), Venus Drive (but no Athena, oddly), Electra Drive, Achilles Drive, and the tucked-away Hermes Drive—which, perversely, the mail man sometimes skips. Over to the left, as you near the top of the hill, is "Wonderland Avenue Elementary School". Nothing to do with Michael Jackson (or Alice) but I would consider changing the name if I were the principal.

On their drive up the hill, Didier and Tom saw a large deer, with magnificent antlers, lying dead by the side of the road—hit by a truck, probably. Didier was concerned that the sight might turn Tom against an area he had intended him to fall in love with: but no—

"It's superb!" said Tom. "Don't think I'm not sorry for the animal. What a splendid beast he must have been! It's dreadful to see him lying there, dead. But it's superb as well, a sight like that. Here. Here of all places! Los Angeles. A man-made city in the middle of the desert, water piped from God knows where, and there's the Monarch of the Glen lying by the side of the road! I'm blown away."

Didier purred.

El Coyote did not exactly 'provide' parking for its customers. Parking existed, merely. On a dried-up quarter-acre of mud, or on rough weeds, or (which is where they settled) among withered leaves and pine-cones underneath the trees. As they strolled to the entrance, a real-live coyote appeared from nowhere, and just as quickly trotted away into the depths of the woods.

"Would you look at that!" said Tom. "I had no idea this place existed."

Didier purred again.

They were seated, at Didier's request, at a table far enough away from the other diners for them to have an intimate conversation without being overheard, but not so far from the entrance that Didier was denied the opportunity to nod or wave at anyone coming in who he knew, or wanted to know.

"They make the best Margaritas outside of Mexico," he said; ordering a pitcher without even asking Tom what he wanted. "You have to drive down to Tijuana to get anything even close—you ever been to Tijuana?" Tom said he hadn't. "We ought to go sometime. You can get anything you want there."

Tom had no idea what Didier was talking about, nor did he want anything in particular, but was happy to give his approval for a trip there sometime. He downed his first Margarita as though it was a beer.

"A couple of hours drive," continued Didier. "Max."

"How did you find this place?" asked Tom, sipping his second Margarita.

"We all use it. Because *they* don't." He meant anyone not in show-business. (Like which there is no other business.)

"I don't mean the restaurant, I mean the whole area."

"You like it?"

"I love it."

"You should move here," said Didier, pouring Tom his third Margarita

"I wish."

"The market's at an all-time low," said Didier. "After the earthquake. Prices fell along with the houses, if you know what I'm saying. You should think about it. You're too big for that B-list block in Larrabee."

"It's large enough for me . . . "

"Too big a star. You walked the Red Carpet dear," said Didier.

"I'm no star. Don't—"

"You're big in Hollywood. If you lose sight of that, it'll lose sight of you."

"Is it safe?" asked Tom.

"Safe? What do you mean?"

"Houses. After the earthquake. The houses. Strutrerly."

"Structurally? The ones up for sale are the ones still here, aren't they?" said Didier, helping Tom to his fourth Margarita.

"Safe as houses," thought Tom, and chuckled to himself.

When they had eaten, and Tom had drunk, and Didier had allowed Tom to pick up the tab, and they were heading home, Didier, instead of turning left down Laurel towards Sunset, turned right and motored up the hill towards Mulholland Drive.

"Where are we going?" asked Tom, happy to go anywhere Didier chose. Tijuana, even.

"I want to show you something."

Didier turned the car off Mulholland, onto a narrow trail that sent them down the other side of the hill—all the meandering way to Studio City if they had wanted to go that far. But after a hundred yards he took a sharp right onto a steep, stony path that seemed to lead nowhere, except into the pitch black of the night that had now fallen.

The track curved round to the left—and *suddenly*, immediately below them, *as though they had at that moment been switched on*, were all the million dazzling lights of the Valley.

"Fuuuuccckkkk . . . " breathed Tom.

Didier kept quiet, because the best was yet to come. He drove round a sweeping bend, and lying immediately in their path was the silhouette of a large house. Didier drove on, not slowing down, if anything accelerating, even though at any moment they would crash into the house—but they didn't: it struck out from the hillside on wooden stilts. Didier drove *under the house*, between the stilts holding it up, and parked the car with a little flourish of a skid.

"Fuuuuccckkkk . . . " breathed Tom again.

"It's for rent," said Didier. "Come."

He walked over to some wooden steps leading to the deck, and beckoned Tom to follow him up.

"Do you think it's OK?"

"Puleeeze. Don't be so English," said Didier and climbed onto the deck, with Tom not far behind.

"Take a look," said Didier, with all the pride of an owner—no, more than that: all the pride of a realtor.

The view was one of the most sensational in the city. The Glendale Mountains in the distance; the entire breadth of Ventura Boulevard and Studio City beneath them; Warner Studios and Disney to the Left, Universal almost straight ahead, the Hollywood Bowl and Downtown LA way over to the right.

And lying straight ahead of them was the famous Hollywood Sign itself: immediately opposite, the other side of the 101 Freeway, high up in Griffith Park, embracing the world of film like Christ The Redeemer over Rio.

"*He took him to a very high place, and showed him all the kingdoms of the world and their glory*," murmured Tom, incoherent and slurring his words.

"Sure," said Didier.

7
Monologue

"*When I was a kid I thought 'the benefit of hindsight' meant being able to see out the back of your head. That would be one great fucking thing to be able to do, wouldn't it? I wondered why the grown-ups kept saying about someone they didn't like who was right about something they were wrong about—'Ah, that's just with the benefit of hindsight.' OK, so the guy could see out the back of his head! What's so bad about that?*

"*I'll never get how no one saw what they were doing to Tom though. Out the front or the back. Or if they saw it, why they didn't do anything about it. Somebody should have stopped him. I mean . . . Why didn't they? None of our business? Was that it? That simple? The Quakers? So pleased with ourselves and our stupid name we didn't need to do anything? We were supposed to be friends, so why didn't anyone <u>do</u> anything?*

"*That's when it started. Damned if I don't think so, anyway. First off Tom goes up there. And soon we all drift away. I hated it. Like those plants the kids pick up, and blow the seeds off and make a wish and the seeds float away. Tom first, that's all it took. 'PUFF!' Then the rest of us. On the wind.*

"*Except Madison. She stayed. Madison was the best, you know that? Poor drunken Madison. Says something about us, huh? 'The Quakers'. I hated that stupid name.*

"*But why didn't <u>she</u> do anything about it? Do you think she was too proud? Same as Chloe? Letting bad things happen because you're too proud to stop them?*"

He turns from the bed, as though he can't bring himself to say it face to face—even to a still-as-death, expressionless, eyes-shut, comatose face.

"*Letting bad things happen because you're too proud to stop them. That's kinda funny. When you think about it. Oh boy! That is really funny.*"

Then he starts all over again, right from the beginning. Urgently. Almost manic -

"*January 1994 . . . The Northridge quake . . . Twenty or so killed outright . . . 'The seismic seven' . . . Can you hear me? . . . 'the Quakers' . . . Christ! I fucking hated that name.*"

His mind drifts towards things he hasn't yet spoken of; and he wonders if he has the courage to recall them, let alone talk about them.

"*Did you ever pick up that plant and blow the seeds off? And make a wish?*

   'I fell in love with James Tyrone and was so happy for a time.'

"*Remember?*"

8

Field-work

"It's a matter of timing," said Didier.

"Just get him drunk one night, and ask him," said Tyler. "Jesus! *I'll* do it!"

Didier suggested they should put in some field-work while they waited for exactly the right moment to push Tom into further recklessness. Tyler reluctantly agreed. They hit on the idea of attending a variety of 'crank-meetings', as they pleasantly called them, at which they could see for themselves, up close and personal, what the current trends were in the sale of spirituality.

Both had friends, or more accurately they knew people, who had taken up the fashionable pastime of 'chanting'; and Tyler had dated a girl who was intriguingly reticent when asked about the bi-weekly workshops she conducted at the Church of Cognitive Healing. After much discussion, and ultimately the toss of a coin, Didier was tasked with researching Buddhism, while Tyler took on the investigation of the Church.

It was the sheer tedium of his lot that caused Didier eventually to announce 'they just needed to get the flavour of the thing, and simply did *not* need to go into it in any depth'. He was, to be fair to him, unlucky in his initial selection of meetings to spy upon, because the first few of them were attended by genuinely devout followers of Nichiren, who asked for no money, made no money, and wanted no money, or anything else other than to assemble together and chant NAM-MYOHO-RENGE-KYO repeatedly ("endlessly" was the word Didier preferred) in order to obtain an inner peace and spiritual growth.

"The value of which is . . . ?" asked Didier of his mentor. The friend suggested that Didier leave.

At another meeting Didier held up his hand and inquired what NAM-MYOHO-RENGE-KYO meant. He was told "*I devote myself to the Lotus Sutra of the Wonderful Law.*" He replied "Uh-huh," and left without being asked.

After a half-dozen equally unhelpful assemblies, and when he was on the verge of giving up altogether, he at last struck a rich seam of inspiration. The session was conducted by a man and a woman to whom any casting director in the industry would unhesitatingly have given the roles of time-share sales-persons. It was from their lips that he heard the magic words: "*Before you chant, think of what you want, it can be anything you like . . . It doesn't have to be spiritual.*" Chanting for a specific material benefit was not something Didier had so far encountered in Buddhists, and his heart beat faster.

The evening began with timeshare-woman asking the neophytes (they were called 'our new friends') to stand and introduce themselves. Didier gave Tyler's name, as a precaution against any follow-up, and whispered to his host that he would explain later. There were twenty or so newcomers, and one after another they stood and said who they were. Each name was carefully written down by timeshare-man. Some embarked on additional details of their lives, and were listened to patiently, everything being written down.

After each person had said his piece, the timeshare team encouraged applause. Only when the introductions were over, and everyone seated, was the congregation asked to close its eyes and begin chanting.

"NAM-MYOHO-RENGE-KYO, NAM-MYOHO-RENGE-KYO, NAM-MYOHO-RENGE-KYO, NAM-MYOHO-RENGE-KYO, NAM-MYOHO-RENGE-KYO . . . "

Dider had no choice but to join in, because the timeshare team were watching:

"NAME-MY-RING-KEY-HOLE . . . "

The chanting lasted five minutes to the second, each one of which was a living hell to Didier, achieving an inner turbulence which was at bursting-point when a high-pitched jangling of Mongolian bells brought things to a halt. (Didier remarked to Tyler, later, how everyone was beaming and smiling and certainly *looked* happy. Tyler wondered if there were any difference between being happy and thinking you were happy—but Didier hadn't the faintest idea what he was talking about and that interesting speculation hit a brick wall.)

After the chanting, the sales-pitch began in earnest. One after another of the audience were called up on stage, from a list held by timeshare-woman, to tell the assembly how chanting had affected their lives. In short, how they had chanted *for* something, and got it. Whether or not they were 'plants' was a matter of hot debate between Tyler and Didier, provoked by the astonishing claims they made.

"*I started chanting for a girlfriend last month, and yesterday I got engaged!*"
Timeshare-woman clapped her hands and the audience followed suit.

"I've been chanting for a new job, and nothing much happened at first, but after a few weeks I got promotion."

Timeshare-man shook him by the hand. Didier had never seen a more moving display of feeling.

"Chanting has cured my insomnia."

That one Didier was prepared to believe.

A dozen or so similar endorsements of Buddhism were made by carefully selected audience members, so shining with enthusiasm they almost lit the hall. Every announcement was met with clapping, and even the occasional cheer. And Didier noticed that the claims ramped gently upwards, chanter by chanter, towards to the last and perhaps the most flagrant of them all -

"I started chanting for money only two weeks ago, and guess what? Three days later I won $163 on the lottery."

Upon which timeshare-woman turned to the audience and triumphantly proclaimed "You see? Chanting works!" Timeshare-man led the enthusiastic applause.

The last act in this little pantomime was, as in all good theatre it should be, what everything beforehand had been leading towards, inexorably. Two acolytes brought various articles from the wings and displayed them on stage. Some were indispensible to the practice of chanting, others were merely desirable—all were for sale. Introductory materials for the novices, including audio-tapes of NAM-MYOHO-RENGE-KYO. For the serious chanters, "The writings of Nirchiren Daishonin (abridged)"; and for the newcomers a book, "The Basics of Chanting", which it soon became apparent every guest that evening was expected to buy. There were prayer mats, even special chairs to chant from, bells and inappropriate incense sticks from Mexico, posters to mount on the wall of your dedicated chanting space, and tapes of Tibetan music. Numerous pamphlets and brochures caught Didier's special attention.

One by one, the names of the newcomers who had stood and introduced themselves, and now perhaps regretted it, were read out by timeshare-man, and each was made to stand again, and was asked if he/she wanted to buy "The Basics of Chanting." *It only cost a few dollars.* It may be that the first of the purchasers were indeed 'plants', to get the ball rolling: but it is certain that the first three bought the book and everyone thereafter was too embarrassed—standing up in the hall amongst so many seated, so many looking at them, so many waiting to hear their reply, waiting to applaud the initiation that was marked by the purchase of the book—everyone was too embarrassed to refuse to dip into his wallet for such a small sum. Everyone, that is, except

Didier. His only embarrassment was that he didn't answer to Tyler's name until nudged into a memory of his lie by his host. When asked if he wanted to buy "The Basics of Chanting" he said no, thank you, he did not. And the audience gasped.

"Why not?" asked timeshare-woman, visually radiant as ever, but with a new chill to her voice.

"Because I don't want to," replied Didier, bristling.

"You don't want to *today* friend, or *at all*?" said timeshare-man, slowly, with indisputable menace in his body-language. The entire audience stared at Didier, almost demanding from him the promise of a future purchase, at the next meeting perhaps, rather than an outright refusal. Those who had 'bought the damn book', and had not really wanted to, stared at him the hardest.

A weaker spirit might have caved-in for the sake of a few dollars. But Didier said -

"It doesn't do anything for me, chanting. It's not your problem." (With a smile that could freeze vodka.) "Have a nice night."

He stood up to leave—but they would not let him.

"It is customary for guests to make a donation. It doesn't have to be much. Whatever you can afford. I am sure you would like to say 'thank you' in *some* way to the organisers of this evening's meeting?"

Didier had to walk sideways past a whole row of seated knees, which appeared to have made up their minds not make his exit any easier. And when, *en route*, he gave a spiky "Thank you!" as his only response to that question from the stage, the knees seemed to get bigger, the legs longer, and there was less space for him to squeeze through the rows of seats blocking his way to the aisle.

As he was pushing past a particularly rigid pair of thighs, a woman two or three ahead of him began a quiet NAM-MYOHO-RENGE-KYO sequence, presumably for Didier's soul. Or maybe for him to go to Hell. Whichever it was, even Didier hadn't the gall to barge-by the chanter, who had her eyes closed and her feet stretched out in front of her.

"Excuse me."

"NAM-MYOHO-RENGE-KYO, NAM-MYOHO-RENGE-KYO . . . "

"Excuse me."

"NAM-MYOHO-RENGE-KYO, NAM-MYOHO-RENGE-KYO . . . "

"Oh for fuck's sake!"

Didier turned round (which was not made easy for him) and worked his way back along the row he had only just navigated, storming up the gangway to an illuminated 'Exit'—which to his fury was locked. He marched over to a 'Fire Exit' the other side of the auditorium, that even timeshare team dared not lock, and ignoring a sign that the doors were alarmed and should not be used except in an emergency, he flung them open, triggering a blaring claxon that sounded (so he ever after claimed) like someone yelling, rather than chanting, NAM-MYOHO-RENGE-KYO.

He left the hall with every eye darting hatred at him, and his host never spoke to him again.

But he had learned much, and imparted all to Tyler when they next met.

* * *

Tyler's account of his trip to the 'Celebrity Centre for Cognitive Healing' off Franklin Avenue, Hollywood, had traits analogous to Didier's experience with the time-team, but was rather more sinister. Of course he detected an *element* of timeshare sales in his conversations with the numerous church-wardens he was introduced to, but he thought their technique was more insidious. He was inclined to liken them to spiders—he told Didier he felt that he had entered a network of caves, with *Shelob* around every corner. But arachnids ultimately kill their prey, whereas the cognitive healers kept them alive—as long as there was money in their savings accounts. Tyler had seen a natural history documentary once, about a species of fungus that made zombies of the ants it invaded and then fed on their living flesh, and he tended to think there was little to choose between the fungi, the spiders, and the Cognitive Healers. Didier couldn't agree that the timeshare team were any better—but he was biased because of his traumatic experience, and Tyler's analysis is to be preferred.

His introductory session began with the screening of a short film, in a small theatre seating fifty or so which was almost filled to capacity with other initiates, eager to start healing. The brief title sequence was accompanied by a sound track that made subtle reference to the Church of Cognitive Healing's acronym—CCH—while reinforcing the Church's essential message of hope to all who wanted to turn their lives around—and wanted it so much they were ready to commit to a series of costly workshops, character assessments, self-help pamphlets, correspondence courses, and the ubiquitous audio-tapes.

The music and lyrics of David Bowie blasted out of the speakers -

"Changes..."

The music faced along with the name of the director (who had not, much to Tyler's surprise, insisted it be removed from the credits), and a little parable was performed for the edification of the audience:

A young married couple are seated on a park bench. They are in despair: he is out of work and she is pregnant. They can't pay their bills and don't know where to turn. An all-American, clean-cut, shiny-shoed, pressed-pants, white-shirted, blond-haired, Hitler-Youth type, comes up to them flashing his cognitive teeth and gives them a small CCH booklet. They read it (we aren't allowed to!) and all their problems seem to be solved. Exactly how this miracle is achieved is not explored by the film; but let no one be in any doubt, it has everything to do with the CCH booklet.

And that was that. Ten minutes, at most, of utter drivel.

The house-lights in the theatre came up, and the audience was organised into 'healing groups' of a half-dozen, seated around glass tables in small rooms, all of which inter-connected with other small rooms, each with a glass table, glass walls and a glass door. They had entered what were called "The Rooms of Enlightenment".

The pastor (always, always, always smiling) asked Tyler what he thought of the film. "Excellent," said Tyler, and a little alarm bell rang inside the pastor's head.

The group was handed two typed pages of a multiple-choice questionnaire. The questions were designed to tease out any self-doubt, parental or marital problems, likely sexual preference, hopes and dreams—and disposable income. The aspirants were asked to put their names in the spaces at the top, and to tick the boxes next to the questions that came closest to their *instinctive* answers. They were specifically instructed not to take time to think, but to go with the first response that came into their heads.

It would have been witty if Tyler had given Didier's name, not knowing Didier had given his; but because of the formality of his introduction to the Church, he was forced into truthfulness. Truthfulness as to his name only. As for his answers to the questionnaire, he understood what they were looking for and thought it amusing to give it them in generous helpings; so Truth made only a brief appearance on the papers he handed back to the pastor—on the first line: "Given Name . . . Last name . . . "—then it disappeared without a trace.

He hadn't got over the death of his mother. Had never had a relationship. Kept changing his job. Owned his house in LA, and a cabin in Aspen.

Travelled extensively. Didn't like to talk about his feelings. Usually placid, but when he did get angry it was sudden and could be violent. Feared rejection and disapproval. Preferred cats.

CCH gold dust!

When the pastor skim-read his group's answers (analysis would be overstating it) Tyler's inventions made that little alarm bell accelerate its tinkling into something a good deal more urgent. The pastor took the matter higher, and it was decided to remove Tyler from the group and interrogate him in a one-to-one session with a different and more experienced clergyman.

A common practice in situations like these was to leave the suspect waiting for up to half an hour, alone in a room *without* glass walls, or windows, hopefully to prey on his nerves and weaken his resistance to questioning. Regrettably, because attendance at the open-day was larger than expected, no rooms were instantly available, and Tyler had to be left alone in a waiting area to the side the main reception. It was there he observed a number of people coming and going, and (which galvanised him) making purchases over the counter. He shifted himself, seat-by-seat, closer to the action, in order to eavesdrop on what was being said.

The first thing to strike him was the breadth of the Church's congregation. There were the well-heeled and well-dressed; and there were the down-at-heel, badly dressed pound-shop people; and for every one of the rich, there were twenty of the poor. But whatever their position in the hierarchy of success, or the lower-archy of failure, most of them paid short visits and paid good money for something on display the other side of the counter. Cumulatively, they took away a huge variety of instruction booklets, self-help manuals, and graded educational treatises on cognitive healing; some modestly priced, some absurdly expensive for such a slim volume—one can only assume that the worth of the mysteries inside the covers was inestimable. The penitent manner in which followers of the Church came up to the counter to buy their useless pamphlets put Tyler in mind, and it was distasteful even to him that it did, of devout Christians approaching the altar to receive the Sacrament.

A recurring subject for discussion in most of the transactions Tyler could hear between priest and votary, vendor and purchaser, was the 'level' the money-spending disciple had reached, and how it disallowed him/her (but only temporarily) the prize of spending yet more of their money on *texts which were only available to those who had reached a higher level*. Again and again Tyler witnessed the minister offering the encouragement—"We're getting there, but there is still more work to do on your current level". Fortunately, there was always some piece of writing, for sale, that would be sure to assist the disappointed worshipper in attaining his goal. I should say his next goal—because whatever level anybody reached, there was always a higher one. Always. And there always would be. World without end.

Tyler likened one of the CCH salesmen to a sommelier in a fashionable restaurant, brow-beating a nouveau-riche diner into ordering an expensive wine he neither knew nor would appreciate. But the contracts of sale were not always as pleasant to watch as the mere parting of a fool and his money: other transactions saw the offering, in payment for the undrinkable house-wine, of the last few coins from the savings of the destitute, without a vestige of shame or hesitation in the servant of the Church whose hand accepted the quarters, dimes and cents making up the price.

Tyler was at last called away from this fascinating marketplace-cum-altar for his one-to-one session. It was destined to be short, for whilst the inquisitor kept a small number of brain-cells open to the possibility that Tyler might be genuine (because if he were the rewards would be plenty) the CCH had had its share of snoopers, investigative journalists and the like, and the inquisitor smelled trouble. He approached Tyler with caution.

"So," he said, looking over Tyler's questionnaire, on which someone had scrawled comments that Tyler could not read upside down. "You thought our film was excellent." He took a fountain pen from his jacket pocket, opened it, held it poised over the first sheet of the questionnaire, wrote nothing and looked Tyler straight in the eyes—"Why was that?"

Tyler hadn't expected a dart to be fired at him so soon. Now it was his turn to be cautious.

"I thought its message was clear, and uncluttered by irrelevant detail. Anyone would understand it."

"Are you in the business?" asked the inquisitor, eyes down now, and writing.

"Business?"

"The film business." (Still writing.)

"No. Didn't I put on the form I was unemployed?"

"Oh yes." His pen stops mid-word, and he looks up at Tyler. "But you haven't said anything about the jobs you keep changing. Between unemployments. What were they?"

"Anything to occupy me. Temporary jobs. This and that." Then Tyler threw him a bone—"I don't *have* to work, you see."

Nice try, but the inquisitor didn't bite. The open mind was closing fast, and the minority opposition brain-cells were crossing the floor to vote with the government. He returned to looking at the questionnaire, and deliberately wasted a few minutes re-reading material he had already digested, tapping the blunt end of his fountain pen on the desk-top, very slowly. When he had at last finished his charade-read he eyeballed Tyler again, and was pleased to detect signs of nervousness.

"We've identified some issues we could help you with," he said, pretty much going through the motions, but testing Tyler one last time, in case the opportunity really were there of fleecing him out of all he owned.

"Issues?" repeated Tyler.

"You have a mild Generalized Anxiety Disorder—not your fault—repressed emotions—very common." He was right about it being common: the CCH doctors found mild Generalized Anxiety Disorder in the vast majority, if not all, of those who turned to them for help. "Looking at some of your answers," continued the inquisitor, "it seems to me you don't have too high an opinion of yourself."

It is possibly the only miracle ever to occur within the walls of the Church of Cognitive Healing, that Tyler did not burst out laughing there and then. "Really?" was all he could say with a straight face.

"We could help you there. I think you would benefit from a course of Cognitive Therapy."

"Would that heal me?"

Tyler! Tyler! Have you become so complacent? That was too disingenuous by a mile, and your questioner isn't a fool!

The interrogator painstakingly screwed the top back onto his fountain pen. He had heard all he needed. To all intents and purposes the interview was over and the remaining volleys of dialogue were little more than damage-limitation on both sides of the table—the inquisitor trying not to give away anything that Tyler didn't know already, and Tyler trying to extricate himself from the web without making too big an enemy of the Church.

"I don't know about 'heal'," said the holy man, tightening the screw-top of his pen until it squeaked, and not saying another word until he had returned the pen to his jacket pocket. "We can't give any guarantees. But an intensive course would have aimed at identifying any issues much more accurately than this." He waved the two-page questionnaire in Tyler's face; closer, perhaps, and faster than he might have if irritation hadn't been building-up inside of him.

"*Would have?*" asked Tyler.

"I think so, don't you?" said the man, for that is what he had become: a mere man now, with an unpleasant forced smile. "And maybe would have rooted out whatever it is holding you back. Maybe. Who knows?" He almost sighed—an odd sigh, if that's what it was, with no inward breath before it—then stacked the questionnaire with some other loose papers, and rapped the sides of the bundle on the table to even the edges, and to signal 'the end', unequivocally.

"But that's what scares me," said Tyler, happy to be steered to his retreat. "Whatever I am—and sure, I accept it's far from perfect—I don't want to start changing any of it, in case I end up being someone I like even less." He gave an unconvincing laugh, and pushed his chair back.

"That is perfectly understandable," said the man, making no real effort to disguise what he thought the truth was. "Why did you come here?"

For the second time, Tyler was completely thrown by an abrupt left-field question, and every instinct screamed "beware!" at him.

"Listen. I think the work you do here is wonderful. I'm impressed." Tyler knew he was rumbled, but was not at all certain how much of a threat he might appear, or what kind of self-protection—or retaliation—these zealots were capable of; so he added, by way of a rather desperate insurance premium—"I have no doubt at all that you help a great many people. It's great work you do. But I don't think the Church is right for me." He shrugged his shoulders and slid his chair further back in preparation for imminent escape.

"No, I don't think so either."

They stood, shook hands, and what each didn't say out loud, the other understood perfectly.

When Tyler had left the building, his interrogator caused a number of inquiries to be made of him, as a result of which he learned for the first time about Tyler's appearance on 'The Artorio Collection'—and a great deal more. The girl who had introduced Tyler to the Church was threatened with the consequences of breaching the confidentiality clause in her contract of employment, and then she was fired.

Tyler heard from the girl herself, in tears, about her dismissal; but she clammed-up on telling him anything else, and after a while stopped taking his calls. He also got wind of the inquiries the Church was making about him, and in a drug-enhanced paranoia quit his Larrabee apartment, giving no forwarding address.

If he had known any more about the Church of Cognitive Healing, he would have done precisely the same, stone-cold sober.

9

A Gentleman's Word

Tom, being English, was by Californian standards an alcoholic. He had been known to have a beer with his lunch. And it was in recognition of that character flaw that Tyler found his passport to Tom's confidence. Tom and he became bar-buddies, meeting regularly for drinks at the wonderful Yamashiro restaurant with it's night-time view over LA, or at the Polo Lounge of the Beverly Hills Hotel, or at Trader Vic's in the Hilton, where they sometimes shared a whole cauldron of cocktail, each supping from a straw either side of the poison, embarrassingly like young lovers. Chasen's, with its horseshoe bar and self-important barman became a favourite playground for the two of them, and they placed bets as to how insolent they could goad the barman into being.

In the course of a few of weeks Tom and Tyler, Tyler and Tom, became inseparable. "Joined at the hip," said Chloe. And the sad truth was, that lurking alongside the guile and the manipulation, Tyler had a genuine liking for Tom.

Cocaine used to be passed around the polite society of Los Angeles like after-dinner mints. In less polite society Crystal Meth Amphetamine was making its debut; although it's rocket-rise to the drug of choice was yet to come.

It was no shock to Tom, therefore, when one night Tyler offered him a 'hit' of cocaine from a little silver spoon. Another night Tyler left Tom a line of coke in a rest-room cubicle in the Four Seasons—this became a pleasant little naughtiness they sometimes indulged in, because it added risk to the buzz.

It soon became a matter of routine that when they were out drinking together Tyler would give Tom a discreet 'bump' from a small glass phial he kept in his jeans pocket. The audacious public imbibing of narcotics quickly became a great favourite with them, in fierce competition with the line-under- the-toilet-roll.

They had a great many laughs on their boys' nights out, Tyler and Tom, Tom and Tyler; and they often remarked—not at all defensively—'What harm did it do them, going crazy once in a while?' In fact, it was actually good for them! You got that right! Clears away the cobwebs. Definitely! You know what? Coke made them feel *so* good, it should be perscribed! Deferetly!

"Wanna bump?"

"Cheers!"

"Here's one for Madison!"

"Here's two for Didier!"

Madison, ignorant of the truth, even encouraged Tom to set off with Tyler whenever a last-minute invitation came along: she thought it would loosen him up some. 'In a good way', as Scott might have said. She had her own girls' nights, after all, and they sure as hell loosened *her* up.

On one such jaunt, nicely relaxed, and stimulated not only by the substances coursing through their systems but also by the chance sighting of what looked like the handle of a whip sticking out of the leather bag of a high-class prostitute they 'clocked' sitting at the bar of the Peninsular Hotel, Tyler took Tom off to a 'Gentlemen's Club' on Highland Avenue for some illicit fun never to be told to Madison.

Los Angeles could boast a good few gentlemen's clubs in those days, as most great cities could—as they still can these days, I have no doubt. But whether it were Boodles or Whites in London, The Travellers in Paris, The Century Club in New York, or the Jonathan Club in LA, none of these grand old establishments had in common with the gentlemen's club in Highland Avenue the signage, which advertised 'Naked Girls', 'Live Nudes', and 'Private Lap Dances' in huge, bright neon lights, flashing all over the front and sides of the building.

The gentlemen inside were of all ages, but all were gentlemen. Young gentlemen, in groups that had assembled to bid farewell to one of their number as he deserted them for the joys of matrimony. Old gentlemen, who couldn't remember what the joys of matrimony were, and if their wives should ever discover where they had been that night would soon be experiencing the joys of alimony.

Tyler was the polar opposite of Didier when it came to parting with what little cash was in his wallet. Wherever they went, Tom had to fight with Tyler to pay his share. His admission to the gentlemen's club on Highland was settled without his having to find a cent—Tyler was a member, and Tom was his guest. Champagne, or something like it, was already on their table. (It was always on the tables the gentlemen were shown to.) Paid 'hostesses' were making a fuss of Tom, even before he had sat down. Lewd dances were being performed in front of his nose, literally, before Tyler could even place his little spoon of powder there.

Only now did Tom begin to pay for anything, by way of his brain-cells of course, but also dollar bills: fives, tens and even twenties, which he tucked into the little g-strings comprising the entire costume of whichever Salome was performing for him.

One hostess, sharing Tom's cozy chair, pressing close and filling his head with flattering nonsense, while she made sure he drank glass after glass of champagne, or sometimes beer from a bottle, or shots of Tequila, made the mistake of twirling the whisps of thinning hair on the top of Tom's head with her fingers, about which he was as sensitive any young man losing his hair, and many an older man too.

"Why are you making such a big deal with me?" he said. He's the good-looking guy," nodding towards Tyler.

"You're the one wearing a Rolex," she said, shamelessly.

A very lithe black girl (who was a student, working her way through business-school) had so clearly caught Tom's attention that Tyler took her to one side and arranged for her to give Tom a 'private dance' in a booth. (They cost extra, the private dances; and they are the heartbeat of any respectable gentlemen's club.) The student led our tipsy Tom by his neck-tie to a large roped-off pleasure-dome, calling him a 'naughty boy'.

The space inside was octagonal (though from the outside it looked like a circus-tent) with a low velvet bench running right round the perimeter, even along the inside of the door when the door was shut—which it always was but for the brief seconds when a new couple slipped in. Tom, having been offered a 'private dance', was disappointed that the booth to which he was taken was not in the least private; a half-dozen men were already there, young and old, each with his own hostess *in flagrante saltatio*, sinking lower and lower in his seat, ogling the naked body of the dancer straddling his legs and grinding her way down towards his crotch.

Some of the younger gentlemen took small spoons, like the one Tyler had, and from time to time sniffed a quick 'bump'. Tom was offered a 'hit' by a gentleman sitting (and sinking) immediately next to him, and took it. He determined that next time he would have a supply of his own—to take and to share. Even some of the girls took 'hits'—although the rules of that gentlemen's club strictly forbade it, as one might expect. The rules, indeed, strictly forbade practically everything that took place in that private booth; but just as most gentlemen's clubs have their ancient traditions, so did this, and the "*more in the breach*" tradition was closely adhered to.

Other couples arrived, and then more still, until the booth was heaving with men and women rubbing against each other, the air rancid with their sweat, the music drowned out by the groans and shouts of approaching orgasm.

Tom emerged looking, to Tyler's relief, delightfully unflustered, if a little *dishabille*. Whilst the experience was certainly not one he was going to enthuse about in a letter to his mother, Tom was not in the least ashamed of what had so obviously taken place during that dance—the dance that was ludicrously called 'private'.

"This place is *great!*" he said, far too loudly. (It is possible one of the 'hits' he had been given inside the room was MDMA.)

Tyler decided it was time to wind things down: indeed, it was well *past* time, if he were to bring the night to the successful conclusion he had planned all along.

"We need to get you home, old sport."

"Don't be so mean! One more dance."

"I don't think so," said Tyler.

"Is it past the little boy's bedtime?" asked an Oriental hostess, straightening Tom's neck tie, and pulling it tight up against his collar.

"Yes!" said Tyler, firmly.

There were sufficient fond farewells to satisfy a departing emigrant to Australia, and Tom said 'damn right!' he would see them all again soon, and took many a pecked kiss, and a few blown ones to make up the numbers.

In the blink of an eye (and there were many), Tyler was driving a blithely happy Tom up Outpost to the sanctuary of his new home. He helped him climb the steps to the front door, and having given him a pill he said would get him to sleep, and made him promise to take it, he casually dropped into the conversation—

"You know Tom, this place would be ideal for Didier and me to set up a temporary office. Do you think by any chance you could lend us some space? Just for a few weeks, until we get going. For our mail-order business? Like in the basement?"

"Sure!" said Tom. "When d'you want to move in?"

And it was done. As easy as that. The new religion had premises, even if it hadn't a creed.

Tyler returned to his car, extremely pleased with himself; and he set off for Larrabee very much looking forward to telling Didier exactly how he had softened-up Tom.

He was far up the hill, demanding more from his old Mustang than was fair to it, and therefore he never heard—he couldn't have, way up there, even if the Mustang hadn't been straining—he never heard Tom open the door to the workshop where he made his puppets—and he never heard Tom say to the lifeless forms inside:

"Wait 'til you hear what I have to tell you guys!"

10

Acts of the Apostles

Having taken so long to obtain a rash permission from Tom, they took no time at all to occupy the basement.

Tyler thought the Rubicon was crossed when they were given their own set of keys. Didier regarded the tipping point as their having a telephone installed—as an additional number on Tom's line: they would pay him whatever was owing each quarter. Of course they would.

They purchased a desk. Then a rug. Two office-chairs—high backs, for good posture. A desk-lamp. A portable filing system, with alphabetical dividers. A water-cooler, on a monthly contract. Biros and pencils—and a little pot to stand them in. Erasers. Pencil sharpeners. Paper clips. A hole-puncher. A staple-gun. Writing paper and envelopes. And pads of cheap paper, for jotting down ideas.

Then they ran out of ideas.

They held one meeting there, to take stock as it were, as soon as they had fully recovered from the exertions of setting-up shop.

"Right. So. Where do we go from here?"

"We take stock."

Stock was taken. Dider suggested -

"Why don't you bring all the fan mail you've been sent . . . "

"Our data-base!"

"Exactly. Our data-base. You need to file it alphabetically."

Good idea. In the pristine files, the dark green stacks of them, wrapped in cellophane and shouting efficiency at them from the unopened boxes on the floor.

"I'll go get the fan mail," said Tyler, and their meeting ended.

But Tyler didn't get round to accomplishing, or even embarking upon, his little filing task, not for a good few days; and when it was done (or soon after—maybe a week after—maybe a couple of weeks—it *might* have been a month) they met again.

"Right. So. Where do we go from here?"

Neither of them had anything fresh to bring to the table. After much soul-searching—an ambitious undertaking!—Tyler said :

"You know what?"

"What?"

"What we urgently need to do is to formulate, with much greater clarity dude, exactly what the Church's message is."

Didier agreed, but put it another way:

"You know what?"

"What?"

"The reason we're still struggling with a name for this fucking deal is that we have no fucking idea what we're trying to fucking sell."

Tyler agreed.

They then brought the second of the two meetings held in the crypt of their Church to an abrupt end; the notional minutes recording that they were to think hard about Didier's challenging analysis, and regroup only when they were absolutely clear in their minds about the nature of the product they were going to stack their shelves with.

They determined to meet soon. Really soon. They would *not* let this enterprise lose momentum.

They did not discuss the matter again for several weeks. When they bumped into each other socially, they tended to avoid the subject altogether, other than a non-committal "*I'm working on it*" or "*I think I might be onto something*" or "*We should get together*" and "*Let's do that.*"

And so their enterprise went into hibernation; and in dutiful observance of Nature's time-table it did not re-emerge until the following spring. But meanwhile Didier installed a sofa-bed in Tom's basement, and made occasional use of the Church's well-equipped vestry as somewhere to take tricks: it was a source of comfort to him that the tricks did not know his Larrabee address.

Four

1

No Cause or Just Impediment

Spring. And the whole of Los Angeles said he was getting married too young. The bride and the whole of Los Angeles fell out on account of this. The official version of LA's objections comprised a miscellany of the usually-given, frequently sound, and mostly ignored reasons why too-youthful a marriage can come to be regretted; but the simple truth is, deep down, that the girls didn't want Scott to marry anyone except themselves, and the boys didn't want him to marry at all. Los Angeles was somewhat put out, therefore, by his dogged pursuit of matrimony—and it found Valeria's happiness in her engagement a particular irritation.

The trap-door spider had pounced.

Many years ago, on one of her birthdays, the child-Valeria had been given a gas-filled balloon, which she prized above all her other presents. It was tied to her push-chair; but she bawled the deafening cries of demanding children the world over, until the string was wrapped around her hand and not around the push-chair: she didn't want people on the sidewalk just to see a balloon—she wanted them to see that it was *her* balloon. So it was with Scott, the most recent of her presents, negligently given her by Chloe. Mere engagement tied him to her pushchair, so to speak. She needed to clasp him in her hand; and she set about having a wedding ring placed upon it, just as the balloon-string had been wrapped around it, as soon as it could be made to happen.

She had been married before of course, and had married well. She had triumphed in her elaborate wedding-dress, with a train so long it had to be held up by two page-boys (in the silliest of clothes). She had revelled in the confidences of her maid of honour and her condescension towards the lesser bridesmaids. She had impressed the guests with a string quartet in the rose garden, and affected to have been wholly unaware of the dozens of young men in tuxedos admiring her, just as she was oblivious of the dozens of young women in Royal Ascot dresses envying her. She had suffered the embarrassment that her family did not move in the social circles in which the groom's family orbited so luminously, and that not one of her guests knew his guests. She had dominated the reception, dazzled at the dance and feigned a rapturous enjoyment of the disappointing honeymoon.

So when Scott proposed, and she accepted—almost immediately after he had said "*Will you*", and certainly before he had finished saying "*marry me*"—and when she sensed the censure of Los Angeles, and was haunted by the ghosts of past disapproval, she said to Scott—only a couple of weeks after he slid the engagement ring onto her finger—that she didn't want the fuss of a big wedding, and she suggested—

"Why don't we go to Vegas *now*, and get married right away?"

'Now?"

"Right now!"

It was the Easter weekend, and the University was on vacation. Scott smiled.

"You wanna be an Easter Bride?"

"Let's do it. Oh do let's! Just think, we'll come back husband and wife—no one will believe it!"

"Husband and wife!" He gave her a long kiss, and held her out in front of him, to get a good look at her—"Wife!"—then he wrapped his arms round her.

"Shall we?" she said, looking up from his embrace.

"Shall we?" he said, grinning the decision he had already made.

"Why not?" she replied, as though it had been his idea all along.

Valeria, as anyone who knows her from these pages will be aware, was not a fool; and she suspected that if her engagement to Scott was a long one, Chloe's engagement (if it were genuine) might turn out to be a short one. She wanted Scott signed, sealed and delivered, as soon she could bring it about.

The manager of the Larrabee apartment block agreed to look after Scott's dog while they were away; but to no one else, other than Billy, did they utter a word of their impromptu plan.

"Do you think it's quite right, Billy being there?"—said Valeria when they were alone, snuggling close to Scott and laying her head on his chest. "It doesn't *seem* right somehow," she added, playing with the hair around Scott's navel.

"I'd like him to be there," said Scott.

If anyone cares to fix the point in time, it was from that precise moment that the target of Valeria's jealousy began to turn from Chloe towards her own son.

"Then let's take him with us!" she said, in a burst of enthusiasm.

When Billy was told he was to have a dad sooner than he ever dreamed, he couldn't have been more excited or more happy. He was possibly the happiest of all of them.

The manager of the apartment block being a widow, three times, and recently divorced from her fourth, held a handkerchief to her eyes when they were departing, and—perhaps not realising the full significance of what she was saying—wished them all the luck she had had.

* * *

Easter is not recognised in Los Angeles as quite the same thing as it is elsewhere. The day of the crucifixion, for example, is scarcely acknowledged; but the Sunday following, on which one must presume the Disciples hunted for eggs in the Garden of Gethsemane, is observed religiously.

The weekend as a whole, however, has in common with Easter the world over that it is not a good time to travel; and it is an especially bad time to embark on a journey from the city of angels to the city of sin. A three to five hour trip can be multiplied to ten or even eleven hours' driving. The best time to go is on a Sunday afternoon, when you can glide over a traffic-free State border into Nevada, with the added enjoyment of seeing the long queues of cars in the opposite direction grinding their way slowly back to Barstow, and to LA, and to work on Monday morning.

Valeria, Scott and Billy set forth in the highest of spirits on Easter Saturday afternoon. They drove through the San Bernardino Mountains without any significant hold-ups, then hit the 15 Freeway across the Mojave Desert, stopping only for a steak at a dusty old roadhouse (with a pin-ball machine, and some cowboys playing it, delightfully evocative of the rape scene in the film "The Accused"). But the last forty miles—after they had passed Whiskey Pete's out-of-town casino in the improbably-named 'Primm', and pushed forward through the scorched landscape, with the hot sand making night's air shimmer even though the sun had long since set—the final furlong to the finishing post was slow going; and it was past eleven o'clock at night when they arrived in Vegas.

* * *

Scott had long been aware of a 'deal' offered by one of the old 50's casinos and advertised in every flyer that came stuffed inside the newspapers, and he had quickly made their wedding plans around it. He had telephoned ahead from LA, and booked them all into a large suite—with a Jacuzzi in every bedroom!—for a very modest sum: *the deal being that he had to play the tables in the Hotel casino for no less than eight hours*. If he fell short of that time, he would be charged the full the cost of the suite, which was astronomical.

"Sounds too good to be true," Valeria said. "Are you sure there isn't a catch?"

"Sure I'm sure," replied Scott. "The trick is not to try to *make* money. I can break-even easy, and then we get the room practically for free."

"No catch at all then," she said.

"Trust me."

She didn't, of course.

* * *

On arrival at the Casino Scott was given a card which the receptionist told him to hand to the croupiers at each table he played. The croupiers would sign for the times he spent at them. When he checked-out he would have to show a certified eight hours' play, or pay the inflated price for the suite.

They wove their way through the maze of slot machines between Reception and the elevator; and for a brief, accidental moment they found themselves, luggage and child and all, in the centre of the gaming-floor itself. What they saw was what anyone might have expected of a casino gaming-floor. Banks of eager faces packing the low-staking roulette tables. Solitary players wagering vast sums at the high staking black-jack tables, roped-off so they could lose in peace. A rowdy crowd geeing-on the couple shooting craps, with hoots and hollers at every throw of the dice. A typical casino gaming floor, you might say, like any other.

Except in *this* casino figures from history, ancient and modern, paraded around in full costume, like extras from a film set—or a number of different film sets, perhaps crossing paths in the commissary. They were a fascinating mix, please don't get me wrong, and I certainly wouldn't wish to be thought mean-spirited about the concept; but the casting of these actors was open to legitimate criticism, and the direction of them (assuming any to have been given) clearly lacked a sense of history. It must have been odd, for example, to see Helen of Troy leaning against the bar in conversation with Jimmy Durante. And whilst Age may not have been able to wither Cleopatra, one can't help but wish it had been able to persuade her not to chew gum.

The suite was as eclectic a mix of styles as was the mix of impersonated characters on the casino floor below. All was opulence; but the assertive shapes of Art Deco rubbed shoulders with a world-weary *fin de ciecle,* and neither was comfortable with the proximity of the other—although they were united in snubbing the brand new Louis Quinze chairs. Numerous reproductions of extravagantly framed paintings decorated the walls (where there wasn't a flat-screen TV, surround-sound speakers, or a coral-studded mirror). Occasionally there was an old master which wasn't a reproduction, but an ambitious copy—the best of which was a Venus who had an expression on her face that made her look less as though she were being blown shore-wards on a shell, and more as though she was stepping out of a stretch limo to the flash of paparazzi cameras.

There was, as promised, a Jacuzzi in each of the three bedrooms, with different-sized black candles on every ledge, and bottles of bath-gels, essences, trays of tiny soaps, and a remote control for the many TVs, at least one of which could be watched from any position in the Jacuzzi, provided one's head was above the water.

Even though it was coming close to midnight Scott said he needed to go down to the casino floor and put in a couple of hours or he would never be able to fit in the required time at the tables . . .

"And get married," Valeria reminded him.

. . . all on the same day.

How little Valeria knew Las Vegas! It would have been possible for her to be married whilst *playing* blackjack if she had wanted to.

Scott left Valeria to see Billy safely in bed, telling her he would be back in an hour to let her know how things were going.

"I'll heat up the Jacuzzi," she said.

"Half an hour."

But it was more like two. At one point he was $800 up, and couldn't leave on a winning streak; at another point he was $500 down, and couldn't leave before he had at least broken even. When he finally returned to their suite, carrying a bottle of champagne in an ice bucket, it was 2.45 a.m. And he was $200 down.

There was a note from Valeria -

"Your bride has gone to bed. Why don't you take the third bedroom? We can pretend you're marrying a virgin."

Scott put the champagne in the refrigerator and returned to the casino floor for another hours' payment for their accommodation. When he finally came back, after nearly two hours and very much in need of sleep, he had racked-up a grand total of five hours twenty minutes at the tables, and was a thousand dollars down.

* * *

The sound of a popping cork woke him up.

"Happy Wedding Day!" screamed Billy.

A huge breakfast was spread over a black marble table (with ugly cherubs for legs) that both reflected and amplified a vase of orchids in the centre of it. No expense had been spared. Valeria handed Scott a glass of champagne—

"The room is practically for free," she smiled. "You breaking even?"

"Yep," said Scott.

"How much longer to go?

"Couple of hours."

"I'm sure we can fit it in before our honeymoon," said Valeria, mixing Billy his very first Mimosa.

"Where are we going on our honeymoon?" yelled Billy.

* * *

Nevada marriage licences are all but given away—no waiting period, and no blood test—Las Vegas has smoothed out whatever residual difficulties, if that isn't too strong a word, are inherent in the State-wide regime: once you complete and submit a short form, together with photo id and $60 (cash), a marriage licence is yours for the taking, at any hour from 8.00 in the morning until midnight.

There is a snag, though. Having arranged the legal preliminaries with so little effort it is not at all easy to find a simple *wedding ceremony*: they are mostly 'themed'. You can be married by Elvis Presley. Or you can be married *as* Elvis Presley—both of you can. There are Pirate-Ship weddings (of course), and underwater weddings—after walking-the-plank to Mendelsohn? There are even drive-through weddings: it is pleasant to think of the happy couple driving straight onto the 95 Highway to Reno and an equally quick divorce.

Or you could be married at Denny's, where they advertise -

"Not only can you enjoy eggs and pancakes around the clock, but you can get hitched at the 64,000-square-foot-restauant."

It comes with a side order of bridesmaids. Over-easy, or sunny side up? Excellent choice!

Scott and Valeria eventually found a glamour-free registry office, and in as much time, and for less money (and with not much more ceremony) than it takes to pay a water-utility bill, they were married.

* * *

Two hours and forty minutes. Scott needed to put in another two hours and forty minutes, and not a second less, in order to avoid a room-charge he couldn't afford.

In search of a diversion from the enervating wait, Valeria took Billy to the free 'Buccaneer Bay' show outside the Treasure Island Casino; where, from the sidewalk, they watched a pirate ship sailing on a gigantic artificial lake, with a cast of stunt men who pillaged a mock-up Caribbean village, only to be engaged by a manned British Royal Navy sailing ship, 'the Britannia', with many a gas-fired 'powder magazine' explosion and sheets of flame, the spectacle ending with the sinking of the Brittania, her masts and all disappearing beneath the lake, along with her brave captain.

"Wow!" said Billy. And even Valeria was impressed. But she couldn't stop herself looking at her watch even while the Captain's bicorn was yet above the water: one hour and twenty-five minutes to go.

She took Billy for a skull-and-crossbones tankard of soda, and checked her watch no less than five times in the three minutes he took to drink it.

Strolling along 'the strip', with a loop of recorded advertisements yelling at them from loudspeakers hidden in the bushes, they reached the 'Circus Circus' casino, went inside and saw a high-wire act performing right above the gaming tables.

One hour. Just one more hour. How was Scott doing? It was possible, of course, that he was winning. Possible. Unlikely though. But why unlikely?

Valeria's mental state was a mix of growing resentment that ***this*** was how she was forced to spend her (second) wedding day, and a genuine apprehension on behalf of Scott—or rather, on behalf of his 'worldly goods', with all of which he had, that very morning, her endowed. After a brief glance at the trapeze act she took a protesting Billy, who had been hoping for tigers, back to their hotel, and she began to pack their cases. And re-pack them. And re-pack them again.

Half an hour.

She made Billy 'go wash his face', while she 'changed into something else'.

"Go on. Go wash your face."

A quarter of an hour.

"I've *scrubbed* my face."

With only a few minutes to go, there was a knock on the door. Valeria called to '*come in*'. No-one did. Another knock on the door. Valeria asked Billy to '*go see who it was*' and continued packing.

"It's Dad!"

Scott, and two men supporting him, staggered into the room. He had collapsed at a low-stake roulette table.

"Scott! What's wrong?"

"Nothing."

> He had wanted to continue playing the tables 'for just ten minutes more', but they wouldn't let him.
> They said 'he was drunk'.
> He said 'it was only lack of sleep'.
> They said 'sure it was, and hadn't he better go to his room and get some?'
> He said 'he couldn't afford to stay another night in the suite'.
> They said 'there were cheaper rooms available.'

The two men sat Scott down in a chair by the black marble table. Even the cherub-legs seemed disapproving of him. The men asked Valeria if she would like a doctor sent up to the room. Scott shouted 'No!' and the men left, telling him to '*take it easy*'.

"When's check-out?" he asked.

"Half an hour," said Valeria. "Have you been drinking?"

"Can I get a coffee?"

In Vegas they give free liquor to anyone playing the tables.

* * *

They wove their way from the elevator back through the banks of machines towards Reception. Things were pretty much the same as they had been when they arrived: except Marc Antony had grown at least six inches from the night before, his tattoos were gone, and he had something going with Marilyn Monroe. Jimmy Durante was dressed up as George Washington, but had made no change to his prosthetic nose, and the founding father's dignity was not enhanced by a suspicion that at any minute he might break into "*Inka Dinka Do*". Helen of Troy was for some reason accompanied by seven dwarves.

Scott told Valeria and Billy to '*go wait for him at his truck*'. He only needed another ten minutes.

Close on half an hour later Scott arrived and gave Valeria the keys, saying he didn't feel well, and would she do the driving.

"How much did you lose?" she asked.

"D'you mind if we don't talk about it?"

* * *

When they quit the parking lot Valeira made a right into the busy traffic of the 'strip' and missed the turning onto Highway 15, setting off in completely the wrong direction. Scott was too distracted to pay attention and the mistake wasn't rectified until they had driven a few miles through town. They passed 'Vegas Vic' on East Freemont Street, the giant neon sign of a cowboy, grinning inanely and seeming to wave "*Hi! Nice to see you!*" or "*Goodbye! Come back soon!*"—depending on whether you were entering or leaving Vegas. And on the bleak northern outskirts, where there were no bright lights or street shows, no hotels or casinos, but a straggle of cheap food outlets and 'dollar shops', and a signpost to the Valley of Fire State Park, Valeria realised they were on the wrong road and wheeled the truck around in an illegal U-turn. A weather-battered bill-board outside one of the pawn shops proclaimed—in fading colours, but without any shame—"*We can turn your wage-packet into chips*".

They needed to stop on East Freemont Street so that Scott could throw-up in the gutter. A couple of passers-by 'tut-tutted', but Vegas Vic couldn't have cared less -

"*HI! Nice to see you!*"

2

Rome

"The manager of the apartments told me Scott and Valeria had gone to Las Vegas to be married. Married! She was supposed to keep it a secret until they returned, but she said she couldn't—it was such happy news! Can you believe that? '*Such happy news*'! And we all assumed Scott only became engaged in retaliation to Chloe, eh? Not a single one of us thought that a wedding—a wedding between Scott and Valeria!—No one thought it would really happen.

"I ran upstairs and told Madison; Madison telephoned Tyler; and Tyler told Didier before any of us thought of stopping him—to prevent Didier from being the one who told your mother, you can well understand why. But he did tell her, of course, *subito*, and with a little suggestion of '*you brought this on yourself . . .* ' in his voice, perhaps?

"Chloe '*disappeared off the Radar*', as you like to say, almost immediately. She never picked up on the phone, and her answer-service was cancelled. Your poor mother. The best thing, so we decided, was to leave her alone for a day or so. To get all the crying done, *sì*?

"Madison was the obvious choice for the first face-to-face and heart-to-heart. She sent Chloe a note—which we all had written, of course, but it was sent as though it was only from Madison—saying she would call round the next morning, and she was going to bring some coffee and doughnuts, like they used to. It was Madison's turn, the note said.

"The next day, mid-morning, Madison tapped at the apartment door (and I was hiding down the corridor, listening)—and she tapped so very, very softly, as though if she was any more loud she might wake up the whole block—she tapped at the door at eleven o'clock precisely.

'*Chloe, it's me*,' she whispered.

"But there was no reply. She made another go at it, with a slightly raised voice. But Chloe didn't answer. Madison came back to where I was listening, and we decided to give it just one more day. So we took the coffee and doughnuts to my apartment, to think what was the best thing to do. We didn't eat them.

"The next morning—

'Chloe. Are you awake? It's Madison. Come to the door honey, and we'll both have a good old cry.'

"But again, no reply.

"Images of an empty bottle of sleeping pills, and your mother lying on her bed in the most final of sleeps flashed into my head, but were just as quickly dismissed. That wasn't her way. Not if I knew your mother. Eh?

'CHLOE! CHLOE! ARE YOU THERE?'

"I shouted, and Madison shouted, both of us together shouted, and it was most certainly enough to wake up the whole block!

"We went down to the manager's office and I asked, as carelessly as my present state of mind would allow, if she had seen Chloe because we needed to speak to her about this or that.

'She's gone home. Didn't she tell any of you guys?'

"Madison rushed in with—

'She mentioned something about it. I didn't know she meant so soon."

"Why Madison thought she needed to lie is as much a mystery to me, sitting here now, as it was to me then. But she lied just the same. I asked -

'How long did she say she would be away?'

'You mean she didn't tell you?'

'She only said—'

'She's quit. Gone home. The apartment's up for rent.'

'I'll call her at home then', I said, trying to look nonchalant.

'You do that,' said the manager.

"It was much, much later that we discovered where your mother had gone, and what she did there.

"One thing is for sure, she didn't go home."

Five

1

The Evangelists

Like many a project before it, Tyler's and Didier's had stalled because of indolence. They could hardly blame its inertia on a lack of funds: even though little was left of the Dutch guy's start-up money, they didn't have anything to spend it on—anything, that is, for which it was lent to them.

They had not met since Christmas, and when they *had* met neither had a sensible word to offer as to the furtherance of their great enterprise. The office in Tom's basement became Didier's habitual overnight accommodation, and he quit Larrabee altogether when he could no longer afford the rent there.

It was in late March, in the same spring that saw Scott take the plunge into matrimonial bliss, that their new religion, cursed by procrastination but blessed with an unshakable belief in itself, and sustained by the certainty of resurrection, decided it needed to get out of bed one morning and give itself a jump-start, or it would atrophy into nothing.

Tyler had slept well and awoke with renewed energy (possibly because he was neither drunk nor stoned the previous night) and with a determination to undertake, *that very day*, the in-depth, serious theological study that he and Didier had been putting-off for so long. '*It had to be done, and today he would do it!*'

He called Didier and told him he was going to the public library –

"*My dear. Are you crazy?*"

– and he set off, light of heart, with a spring in his step and a burning zeal to understand the scriptures of those who had gone before, on whose sacred writings they would lay down the foundations, the very cornerstones, of their new *credo*.

Or as Didier put it, they would answer the question—"What are we trying to sell?"

Tyler's research could be described as a day-trip to Theosophy, stopping off for a quick lunch with Epicurius. The two most important revelations, his twin Epiphanies, were that 'Lucifer' actually means 'the bringer of light', and that 'pleasure' is to be equated with 'good'.

On those two rocks did he build his Church.

As the day wore on he became ever more galvanised by what he read, turning pages faster and faster, his table piled with vast ecclesiastical tomes. After a few frenzied hours' reading, and without any warning, there came to him a blinding moment of revelation, when the utter simplicity of their message was revealed as though by divine inspiration. He closed all his books and replaced them one by one on their dusty shelves, wondering why it had him taken so long to see *the truth*.

* * *

"We need to project an image of Satan, and Satanism, that is the antithesis of Christianity, but at the same time isn't *malign*."

Tyler and Didier were back at the Mondrian: they couldn't be bothered driving all the way up to Tom's canyon house, and it was the matter of a five-second discussion that decided them to blow the last of the Dutch guy's money in style.

To summarise Tyler's research, in the tone in which he relayed it to Didier: -

Christians (and their spoil-sport predecessors) had thrown every hurdle they could lay their hands on between man and pleasure, even persuading him that most of the things he enjoyed were wicked—for no reason that could survive scrutiny; and when Lucifer tried to shed some light on their nonsense he was demonised by them, literally, as the embodiment of evil. The Christians had had better PR: but the tide was turning, and Mankind was demonstrably better off as a result.

"You know what I'm saying?" said Tyler.

Didier said to Tyler that he *didn't* know what he was saying, not quite.

"It is so important," enthused Tyler. "I can't tell you. I know I'm right: I got a gut feeling. The devil thing, and all the Hail Satan shit, it's not going to make us a dime. We want to sell something that makes out *Christianity* is the bad guy, get it? How it has mind-fucked people all this time, and stunted their potential, deliberately, ruthlessly, for its own goddam purposes. For its own goddam *enrichment*."

"Disgraceful," said Didier, helping himself to another quail's egg from a little cut-glass bowl half-filled with crushed ice.

"How come the Vatican is loaded? Hey? And the overwhelming majority of the Church's followers poor? Ever thought about that? "*Sacrifice yourself for the benefit of others*"—that's more or less how it goes, isn't it? The Crucifixion, for Christ's sake. What was that all about? We want to make our followers unashamed of putting themselves first. Jesus! That ought to be easy enough."

Didier raised an eyebrow and nodded mute assent, dipping the last of the shared order of quails' eggs into the celery salt, even while he was licking his lips from the second-to-last. He was becoming interested.

"The more I think about it," continued Tyler, on an apostatic roll, "the more I can't understand how the '*love thy neighbour as thyself*' deal ever got off the ground. You *gotta* love yourself more than the next guy, right? Duh! It's kinda obvious."

"As the horns on your head," said Didier.

"I'm serious, man. We need to show them how to rebuild themselves, free from all the self-sacrificing crap the last two thousand years have filled their heads with. And held them back them with. Turned them into slaves. Really. I mean it. Fucking slaves."

Didier clicked his fingers for another round of Manhattans. Tyler's fire had reignited his religious fervour.

"Before they rebuild themselves, dear," he said, "don't forget it's we who demolish them. We have to empty their heads of the *existing* crap before we fill their heads with *our* crap. It's called a 'cognitive review'—but we may have to invent another title, for legal reasons. They're very litigious, your new friends. But whatever label we give it, it's got to cost them. That's the beginning and end, the alpha and omega, the . . . "

"I got the point."

" . . . the entire business model. And it costs. That's all that matters. It costs. A *donation*! Maybe we should call it a donation?"

Tyler scribbled away on his notepad, furiously transcribing every word, a Joseph Smith to the angelic Didier.

"We have to get them to see how the people who make it big," said Didier, with increasing passion, "the ones who have everything, the large houses, the fancy cars, the promotion, whatever, *always* put themselves first."

"Every time," agreed Tyler. "*Help yourself, before you help anyone else.* If we can get them to see that, then they'll see the light, huh?"

"If we shine it directly into their eyes," said Didier.

"The Church of Self Help," said Tyler. "Hey! *We got ourselves a name*!"

"The Church of Self Help," repeated Didier, slowly and with reverence.

"We need to make them see that they *can*—and *will*, if they follow . . . help me out here," said Tyler. "If they follow . . . "

"The word."

"The WORD . . . " repeated Tyler, and wrote it down. (And the word was good.)

"Faithfully."

"Of course," said Tyler, earnest and upright and everything that is virtuous. "To the letter. Only then will they will reap the rewards from the new person we turn them into—or better still the person we *help them to make of themselves*—or even betterer still (fuckin' Hell, this is so good!) the real person inside of them that has been *held back* by the biggest load of crap ever dumped on mankind –"

He paused, smiled at Didier . . . and then in unison they said **"The Ten Commandments!"**—and laughed out loud, delighted they were singing from the same hymn-sheet. But Tyler attempted a 'High Five', while Didier went for the linking of their little fingers, so their hands mangled together rather painfully, and a good deal less triumphantly than had been their aim.

"We have to get them to *trust* us that *we*—"

"And *only* we," put in Didier.

"Sure," Tyler grinned. "*We* have the tools to release them—and quickly too—from all the brainwashing. Show them how to discover their *true potential*. Hang on, I gotta get some of this on paper."

Tyler frantically scrawled on his pad, while Didier corrected him with –

"*Over time*. Screw 'quickly'. He will reap the rewards of what we tell him *over time*. Over a long, long time." Didier savoured the thought, and murmured, almost overcome by the beauty of it, "While we drip-feed him the secrets of self-help."

"I said to hang on," moaned Tyler. "'The *secrets of self-help*.' OK, I got that. That's really good." (And they saw that it was good.)

"Don't forget 'drip-feed'," said Didier, snapping out of his reverie. "Whatever he buys, there always has to be something left on the shelves. Something he wants. Something he *needs*, to get to the next level of . . . whatever the fuck it is we dream up. It's like I always said, it's about pamphlets. *We* make money out of telling *him* what's holding him back from making money for himself. It's a winner. Always has been. *Plus ça change*."

"Yeah, yeah. But not just money," said Tyler. "Health and happiness. They fly off the shelves! Did you know Hubbard claimed to cure arthritis? And leukaemia? And people *believed* him?"

"Why shouldn't they?" Didier drifted back into his dream world. "*Blessed are the sick*."

"What about relationships?—Sex? Can you give me a single reason in Hell why I shouldn't lust after my neighbour's wife?"

"Or his boyfriend," suggested Didier.

"Gimme a break, I'm brainstorming here."

"There's a lot of competition," warned Didier. "We're not exactly at the head of the gold-rush."

"There's always competition. Whatever you do, there's competition, right? If you get stuck on that, dude, you may as well not try anything."

"Have you been reading one of your own pamphlets?" asked Didier.

How they laughed.

2
Luke

When it came to the crunch, neither Didier nor Tyler could face the prospect of writing the all-important tracts. Didier ducked out of it completely, on the implausible basis that English was not his first language. Tyler spent the better part of April trying to come up with the goods, but gave up altogether after one night in which he squandered a couple of hours sitting sideways in front of his computer, drinking beers and writing desultory sentences during the ad-breaks in back-to-back episodes of 'Jeopardy' on TV; and when he found he had not progressed any further than typing "*What is Jesus?*" there was no escaping the awful reality that they needed to bring someone else in on their scam.

Once again, the project stalled.

And then (as irony would have it, on Independence Day) a possible candidate stepped into the frame, on whom they came to be wholly reliant.

Luke was a student of creative writing who waited tables at night, and who Didier had unsuccessfully tried to pick up on a number of occasions. The boy was straight but flirted shamelessly nonetheless, with his eyes (if Didier had only opened his) on the tip rather than on Didier.

He had a quiet insolence about him, which made him many an enemy and many an admirer too. Nothing he said or did was untouched by it. Didier recognised it, disliked it, but was drawn to it. Tyler adored it.

Luke's final-year project, a full-length screenplay, was an insulting parody of "*Lord of the Rings*", unashamedly derivative of "*Bill and Ted's Excellent Adventure*", with a nod to "*Stanley and Livingston.*" The story revolved around a couple of surfers from Topanga Canyon, who had travelled many miles North and South along the Pacific Coast Highway to catch waves, but had never in their lives ventured further east than Brentwood. Then one day they set off on an epic journey—to trace the source of Sunset Boulevard. (Between which and the Ocean there are things much more frightening than Orcs and Nazguls.) The script would never be filmed, as Luke knew even while he wrote it. He deliberately made it ten pages longer than the statutory 120, as a personal gesture of contempt for the industry, not caring that it had little chance of being recognised as anything other than an amateur's mistake. The line "Dorothy Chandler, I presume?" did, however, raise a smile.

His creative writing also found expression in the on-line dating sites that were starting up around then—there are millions of them now. His postings said –

'Looking for dirty girl for a one-night stand of shallow, meaningless sex.

Or less, with the right person.'

He never received an answer; and the invigilators removed his ad within a few days because of complaints. But whenever Luke bothered to look, if he found it wasn't there, he immediately re-posted it.

Someone as indigent as he, and educated, was exactly what the founders of The Church of Self Help needed, because as yet there had been no collections from their congregation—there *was* no congregation—and the start-up cash they had borrowed from the Dutch guy had trickled through their fingers, and down their throats, and up their noses, to the extent that it had become necessary to invest their own money. A sacrifice too great to make, even for the glory of their Church and the fat-cat life ever after.

An unlooked-for blessing, which no one could have anticipated, was that Luke was completely amoral. He already supplemented his income as a waiter by attending AA meetings as a dealer—there, herded together in one room, was a ready-made customer base, standing up and announcing to the world they were addicted to crystal meth. He didn't, of course, stand up in his turn and say *'My name is Luke and I am a dealer.'* He proclaimed a non-existent addiction and 'hey presto!' the bond with his customers-to-be was made.

Whether or not to increase his earnings by penning the seductive gibberish Didier and Tyler wanted from him was a no-brainer so far as he was concerned. He understood perfectly what was required and he had no qualms in producing it. He was naturally creative, articulate and prolific, and he fostered no illusions that he would be paid anything more than a pittance for writing the texts; which did not trouble him in the least, since he had no intention of spending more than a few minutes on each and claiming he had spent hours. His first-draft uncorrected test-pamphlet secured him the position. Indeed, the first two sentences gave it to him.

"Have you ever thought why the Bible tells you how hard it is for a rich man to enter the Kingdom of Heaven? Someone wants you to be poor, my friend."

The entire document was only a few pages long and told the reader nothing, while hinting at the promise of everything. Can't get a job? Can't get promotion? Can't pay your rent? Can't pay your taxes? *Can't get laid?* It was all down to the people who said YOU wouldn't be allowed into heaven unless you were poor. The Church of Self Help offered an alternative view, without specifying precisely what that view was. But it was definitely a better alternative.

The journey of Self Help was an easy one. The path was *not* stony, like they'd been led to believe. The Church was there to guide its congregation through the maze that rich people, governments, corporations, their spiritual leaders, their schools and colleges, their doctors, *anyone* in a position of authority or trust, had carefully constructed in order to confuse them and keep them from everything good that life has to offer. Each of us has it in us to succeed, we just need to cast-off the old belief that we are here on earth to look after someone else, and start looking after ourselves.

As Tyler said—"He's got a point."

3
As Ye Sow

In the fall of 1998, at the Department of Microbiology at the University of Chicago, a post-graduate research student looked at bacteria in a Petri Dish through an electron microscope. So powerful was the microscope, the student was able to single-out just one bacterium and watch it sub-divide into two, and then into four, and then into eight—until in no time at all there were so many squirming around in the dish it was impossible to count them. It only takes 20 such sub-divisions for two bacteria to multiply into a million.

On the same day, at around the same time, not too far away, Deondra Singleton of Altgeld Gardens, Riverdale, stepped out into the miasma that is the morning air of South Chicago and walked the short distance from her low-rise housing development, along the bank of one of the many toxic rivers in Riverdale, towards a trailer—the home of her only two friends in the neighbourhood. She clutched The Church of Self Help pamphlet in both her hands, tight, as though she might at any moment be mugged and its precious content lost to the thief. It had been sent in a letter addressed to her deceased husband and opened in the unlikely off-chance it might contain a benefits cheque. When she read the contents, and again a second time, she recovered from her initial disappointment as the false hope took its hold that her life might at last be turning around. By the time she left her apartment with her news, she was so excited that her angina kicked-in and she had to make frequent stops along the riverbank to catch her breath.

The two friends had little difficulty in identifying themselves (as well as Deondra, and a host of others) as amongst those who *"someone wanted to be poor"*; and they were happy to fill-in their particulars on the slips of paper Deondra had brought with her, and to mail them to the address in California.

"There might be somethin' in it, and there might not, but there aint nothin' to lose but two dollars and the cost of a stamp."

In less than a week the two friends had received their own Church of Self Help starter packs, and their own little slips of paper with which to proselytise others—who were not difficult to find amongst the humble folk living around the manufacturing plants, former steel mills and waste dumps of Altgeld Gardens.

And so, a little more slowly than the bacteria but just as steadily, the followers of the Church of Self Help began to multiply. In Illinois and Texas, Florida and California, and any other of the fifty States that can boast healthy numbers of the deprived and ignorant amongst their populations, who have all but given up hope in their penniless, hungry lives. You have to understand that at that time the lawmakers in America were preoccupied with a civil trial, manufactured for the purposes of cornering their President into defending himself with a lie about a minor sexual indiscretion, in order that the second term of his presidency should be futile and nothing useful done in it. During those heady constitutional times the plight of Deondra Singleton and the few like her (anything between thousands and millions—no-one had counted) were way down the lists of political priorities; and it is to be doubted if they have made their way up the lists since.

4

So Shall Ye Reap

There had never been any letter like it delivered to Tom's canyon house, so when Luke collected the envelope from the mailbox he at once realised this was no ordinary morning.

He scanned through Tom's mail to check if there were any similar to it, and being satisfied there were not, and also that none of Tom's other letters was worth his steaming open, he called Didier. There was no answer: there never was with Didier, which is why Luke perversely called him and not Tyler: Didier was permanently on the run from his creditors, and always call-screened. The answer-machine kicked in, and Luke left this tantalising message –

"I am holding a letter addressed to The Church of Self Help."

Didier and Tyler arrived within twenty minutes.

They found the letter, unopened, propped-up in the centre of the desk in their office, with a lit votive-candle either side of it. What promise Luke made when he lit them, and to whom, are questions best left unanswered...

The three men stared at the letter, almost afraid of it, as though it might do something of its own accord. No one stepped closer than a few feet. There was a hesitation to open it—yet the certainty that it *would* be opened—something of the kind I imagine lingers with archaeologists who find an ancient, sealed sarcophagus.

Tyler at last took the initiative and tentatively, respectfully, reached for it. Luke handed him a small kitchen-knife (it was all he could improvise on short notice). With the two others crowding in on him, Luke biting his bottom lip, Didier almost salivating, Tyler slit the envelope, painstakingly, and with exaggerated ceremony.

He looked at each of the others in turn, slowly and deliberately building the tension to the point where if he didn't reveal the contents, Luke might have slugged him. Then he ripped the envelope apart, so suddenly and so savagely that Didier jumped backwards. A two-dollar bill floated to the floor.

"We said to send no cash!" Didier barked, discomforted by the shock Tyler had given him.

"Shall I return it?" asked Luke sweetly.

"It might have been stolen!" said Didier. Indeed it might, thought Luke. But it was too small a theft to be of the least attraction to him.

Tyler scanned the scrap of lined paper in which the bill had been sandwiched, and on which there was untidy writing. Then he re-folded it, with meticulous care, and looked up at Didier—I can only describe him as leering.

"What? *What*?" shouted Didier.

Tyler took his time, before saying –

"She wants the introductory booklet."

"Then I suppose I'd better go write an introductory booklet," said Luke.

A moment's pause—then the three men linked their arms and '*whooped*' for joy.

"This calls for a celebration."

"I have just the thing," said Luke.

Once again, the dispenser proved himself indispensible.

* * *

Luke completed the manuscript over the weekend. The most economical print-run they could find necessitated a minimum order of two hundred and fifty copies. They pooled every last cent they had, borrowed what they could from the few remaining banks crazy enough to yield cash at an ATM, pawned their watches, pawned Tom's watch (which they took from him when he was asleep), and instructed the printers.

Money orders and two-dollar bills soon trickled in at an ever-increasing rate of flow. Didier and Tyler began to use their offices, daily, for the first time since taking possession of them; addressing, stamping and posting Luke's introductory booklet, '*The Church of Self Help: First Steps*', all over America.

Within two months they had sold every copy, and had enough cash to order a run of a thousand more (and to redeem Tom's watch: but they put that particular task on hold: he hadn't said anything about it being missing).

Within another month it was necessary for Luke to pen 'Self Help: The Manual'. The manual, it hardly needs mentioning, was a big word for a little pamphlet; but it cost more nonetheless: five dollars.

Within six months they had recruited a second writer, who together with Luke created a pyramid of paper that led the Church's eager followers, at greater and greater cost, towards (but never reaching) the celestial '*Seventh Level of Self Help*'. The print-runs were in the thousands.

"Alleluia," said Didier.

"Amen," said Tyler.

"Want a little something to celebrate?" asked Luke.

Six

1

Domestic Bliss

Valeria found the prettiest little house you can imagine, in Abbot Kinney: a short walk from Venice Beach. It had a kumquat bush in the front, and a grapefruit tree which was picture-postcard, sprinkled with white blossom that smelled beautiful—even though the fruit tasted vile. The entire back-yard was overhung with a huge Avocado Pear tree which, in season, rained pears down like an eleventh Egyptian plague.

Sure, the location was not too convenient for Scott's teaching job at the new UCLA extension; but it has to have been *the* most *spectacular* drive to work—"*up the Pacific Coast Highway and along Topanga Canyon, then straight onto the 405*"—she said.

Scott spent increasingly more time with his family, and less with his friends, until such encounters as he had with the old Larrabee set tended to become a little strained—with not much remaining by way of shared experiences between them, and diminishingly little in common to talk about. At their worst, conversations dried up altogether: no one knew what to say: their socialising became less frequent, and shorter. Sometimes it was as though Scott had never really known them.

These things happen, and it was inevitable that the Quakers would lose Scott when he married. They perfectly understood, sad though it made them, that a newly-wed man's duties, as well as his desires, would always take precedence over his bachelor friendships, and they gradually let him slip out of their lives.

Being a step-father to Billy was a particularly strong pull away from them. But I don't want to exaggerate that side of things: Scott should not be thought to have loved Billy any more than the most loving dad in creation ever loved his most perfect, adorable son.

* * *

A new baby. A girl. Scott would have showed her off to the whole world—but Valeria, as we have seen, had fallen out with the world. In addition she was, in a curious way, again jealous of her own child, and how she took centre-stage in their little family road-show.

She strongly disagreed with the world that the girl had her father's eyes.

"Anyhow", she said, "everyone knows the eyes totally change in the first year."

Naturally, the world got to see the baby girl just as soon as she had completed the nine-month journey from '*the tedious shores of Lethe*'; but the world was not allowed to pick her up (not even the girl-world), or do anything else that might frighten her, bruise her, or infect her with the latest fashion in germs, or play with her arms and legs or her little wandering, wondering fingers—or enjoy anything at all of the innocent delight new-born babies return to fondling adults.

Scott and Valeria didn't exactly fight over what to call her, but they disagreed. Valeria had her way. It was to be *Isabel*. She chose it not because it was a pretty name, but because she had already planned a wholly fictitious family-shortening of it to '*Bella*'—she had even invented a history along the lines that Billy had said '*Bella*' first of all, not being able to cope with three syllables; and it was for no other reason than to impose her little conceit on the world that she determined to have the baby Christened '*Isabel*'. You may easily imagine, therefore, that Valeria was not at all pleased when Scott lifted his daughter above his head, waved her in the air as though she were flying, and called her '*Tinkerbell*'. Ever after, Billy called her '*Tinkerbell*'. All Scott's friends called her '*Tinkerbell*'. The whole hateful world called her '*Tinkerbell*'—except Valeria, who stuck to 'Bella'.

After all, it was a family name. Billy had called it her first. '*Billy*' and '*Bella*': wasn't that cute?

If Billy was thrilled to have a dad, he was bursting with pride to have a sister. He was more solicitous of his helpless little sibling than any parent is of their first-born child. He hushed Scott and Valeria if he thought their chatter might wake her. He even made them creep around the house. He watched over her milk when they were warming it. He played with her, dangled her toys in front of her, and often just gazed at her. Never once—I am sure that is right: never once—did any accident of his making cause her to cry.

She gazed back at him too, and always smiled when he peered over the side of her cot.

2

Domestic Fury

It was an implied term of their marriage, and a fundamental one, on which Valeria's undying love for Scott was dependent, that he maintained good health; so she was unsympathetic towards Scott's thoughtless decline into illness, when it was clear to her he was in breach of contract.

It began with headaches; which, as Valeria pointed out, everyone had, she more than most, and she let it be known that she thought he was making rather a fuss. The occasional dragging of his right leg required more thorough investigation, however, because it was difficult for Valeria to sustain the argument 'everyone had that'.

The investigation was fortunately inexpensive because of Scott's health insurance, but unfortunately inadequate because of the low level of premiums. He was given a course of neuromuscular therapy, at the end of which no honest observer could report any improvement, but the therapist was very positive.

The insurance premiums were raised.

* * *

The tempest began in earnest in August when Scott fell over while taking a class at UCLA. It wasn't that he fainted—it was something different, a sudden loss of balance—'*for no apparent reason*'. He picked himself up and continued with the class, his normal self again, in less than a couple of minutes; but word got around, and a close colleague persuaded Scott to see someone at the medical school; which led to tests, which led to more tests, which in the course of several weeks led to the thunderbolt of diagnosis.

One morning, having been asked to see the guys at the medical school (yet again), and been greeted so pleasantly, so attentively; and having been asked to sit down, and the door being closed gently behind him, and after an introductory few words of how very sorry they were, he was told he had one of the many variants of multiple sclerosis, and needed to seek specialist help.

Valeria's fantasy ideal of marriage, gleaned from magazines and the girl-friends who read them, imploded when she realised what Scott's illness meant for *her*; and the nightmare that replaced her shattered dreams dominated her every waking moment as well as her sleep, until it had lured her beyond reach of the remotest chance of being able to come to terms with the complications real life throws at us.

At first she was supportive, undeniably, with only comfort-breaks for impatience. But support lasted no more than a few weeks, and was soon overtaken by complaint. Complaints behind his back, initially—need it be said? Sighs and scathing remarks to her circle of girl-friends about the inconveniences she had to suffer—they could not *imagine* how Scott's growing infirmity affected her!—and all received with the '*poor Valeria*' sympathy she was angling for; no thought being given, by Valeria or her girl-friends, to the tragedy endured by 'poor Scott' himself.

She *knew* he should have had a blood-test before they were married. Why did she listen to him? What a foolish idea it was to get married in Las Vegas! With no blood test! Utterly foolish! Unforgivably foolish!

The slow regression of his disease showed no mercy. From time to time dragging his foot and clutching the back of a chair to steady himself, Scott might knock something over, a spoon might fall from the edge of a table, or a *glass* might fall—which was intolerable! And how annoying it was, as his speech deteriorated, for her to have to ask him, with increasing frequency, to repeat what he had just said. Even if she understood him on the second pass, she sometimes feigned incomprehension and made him write it down, to emphasise how impossible he was making things for her. Once he was incapable of holding a pen steady enough to write and she walked out of the house, making no further attempt to understand what he was trying to say.

Her exasperation escalated into major rows between them. At first these occurred only when they were alone. Then it became a matter of indifference to her whether Billy were there or not, or if Bedlam should break out because her shouted duet with Scott had a screaming *baby-obligato* to accompany it.

After putting-up with things for some six or seven months (if you are content to characterise her irritation, temper, cruel remarks, and occasional storming out of the house, as 'putting-up with things') Valeria decided that Scott's shaking limbs necessitated separated sleeping arrangements; and it even became her habit to go to what she called 'her' bedroom to watch television in the evenings. She would not be seen again until morning. Billy had sometimes made Scott breakfast by the time she appeared. She ate hers in silence.

Whether she fully knew it or not, she was subtly encouraged by her girl-friends (and it was not much later that she had secretly determined so for herself) to start all over again, *before it was too late*, with a new and as yet unmet man—like the ones she saw every day, healthy and handsome, on every sidewalk she walked, and every magazine she read.

She was particularly fortified by a little booklet one of her circle showed her, published by 'The Church of Self Help'. It made total sense. It was as though the Church knew her personally, and understood the heavy burdens she had to bear. She had spent her life so far in abject slavery to others: to no less than the husbands of two failed marriages, and no less than the two children born of them. How right the Church was! The world is divided into two broad types: those who look after others, and those who look after themselves. Valeria knew in which group she had so far wasted her life, and to which group she *should* belong! And she dreamed replacement dreams of a new life with her new Adam, life as it was always supposed to be, and *should have been already*, if life was only fair. But it wasn't fair, '*and she wasn't going to sit there and lie down under it*'—which, conceptually, had to be right. She would put these last few years entirely behind her, and with any luck forget they had ever been.

Quite how little Billy fitted into her plans, less still baby *Bella*, she and her confidants hadn't thought-through, and never did.

* * *

There was a different philosophy at UCLA, where Scott continued to give classes on the history of art. Everything was done to make things easier for him. They changed his room to the ground floor. They gave him smaller, more intimate classes, so that his growing difficulty in speaking was minimised. There was concern—with good cause—about his driving, so a colleague who lived a couple of miles south of Venice chauffeured him to and from work every day.

Eventually, though—mainly because of his failing speech, about which student complaints (not unkind, justified) were ever-more frequent—it became indefensible for him to keep his job, and towards the end of the summer vacation Scott was told they were 'letting him go', with the greatest of reluctance, and the smallest of pensions.

* * *

The sudden plunge in their disposable income forced Valeria into a part-time clerical job with a law firm. Scott, alone in the house on Valeria's working days (in the first few months she took her new-born baby with her), and frequently alone on her non-working days, tried to pass his time painting.

What a valiant challenge to the diminishing control he had over his limbs! And what a mess Valeria had to clear up! It was beyond endurance! Was she making herself clear? Beyond endurance! And it had to stop!

On the infrequent occasions Scott couldn't manoeuvre himself into his truck and get to the corner store, feeding himself was a problem—but that only troubled *Scott*. There were no visible signs of concern on Valeria's part when she returned home and found he had not eaten all day. During his periods of remission, when he could manage to get around and to drive, the complaint was that he might have been less selfish and shopped for the household while he was out shopping for himself.

Surprisingly, what stung Valeria more painfully than anything else was the growing fondness between Scott and Billy. Valeria never rose to it or in any way dealt with it head-on, but she resented every last detail of it nonetheless, and resented Scott all the more for being the cause of it. When school ended, and Billy was home before Valeria, and had run an errand to get Scott some food, and she returned to find the two of them sitting on the same sofa—watching the TV, eating a TV meal, with Scott's dog asleep at their feet—she was driven to distraction. Must she carry the whole household? Weren't there chores for Billy to do? Something has to be done about that animal: it smells, and it's shedding hairs all over the kitchen!

Billy became a constant companion to Scott. He sat and talked to him, fetched him food and drink, read bits out of the newspapers to him when his eyes failed, walked the dog three or four times a day, and was in every way remarkable for a boy scarcely nine years old. Loved by the man and his dog, and loving them both in return. But instead of softening Valeria's heart, it heaped coals of fire upon it and added fresh causes of jealousy to the many other burdens she had to bear. Slowly, there grew something like revulsion towards the three of them; towards Scott, towards his dog, and even towards her own son; a hatred of everything they shared, and everything she felt herself excluded from—although she could easily have been a part of any of it, any time she chose.

* * *

Valeria returned home from work one late afternoon and found Billy and Scott sitting together watching 'The Flintstones'. The dog was with them, asleep at Scott's feet, as he usually was. He opened one eye for Valeria's entrance, then closed it.

"Have you tidied your den like I told you?"

"Yes mom," said Billy.

"Hmmm," she murmured, clattering about the room adjusting things.

The dialogue in 'The Flintstones' isn't Neil Simon, but the cartoon is believed to be funnier if you hear the words. So Valeria continued her cross-examination.

"Have you fed Bella?"

"Sure," said Scott.

"Did she need changing?"

"Ugh," said Billy.

Scott cut him off with—"No, she was fine."

"When did you last look?"

"Twenty minutes ago. Half an hour. She's fine. She's sleeping like an angel."

"Did you get everything on the list?"

"Yes," they said in unison.

Undefeated, Valeria marched between the sofa and the television, blocking their view while she checked the sideboard where the shopping list lay under a few dollar-bills and a pile of change. She scoured the till-receipt.

"They charge whatever they like because they know you can't be bothered to go all the way to Jon's," she said. "They certainly got the two of you worked out."

Neither replied and she went upstairs.

"*Yabba Dabba Doo!*" said Fred Flintstone.

Then they heard Valeria's scream.

* * *

Sudden Infant Death Syndrome - or SIDS (since everything must have an acronym, so we needn't trouble ourselves with what it means)—is given not as the cause of death, but as the verdict when no cause can be found.

Poor Isabel! I am allowing her such a brief life, and have consigned her role in this little drama to a bit-player, a catalyst, whose function is only to be born and to die. What she experienced in her few months' visit, what thoughts she may have had, what sounds she heard and stored, what sights, must be invented by someone with the effrontery to pretend a knowledge of such things. That Isabel did see, think, hear, and in her new-born brain begin to make shapes out of chaos, is indisputable—but we must let 'Ghost Trail' invent a story for her, which Courtney can relay to us as soon as she decides it is expedient to have a fit.

The parental torment inflicted by authority in cases of Sudden Infant Death Syndrome is unforgivable. The investigation, the unspoken suggestions of fault, the autopsy, the inquest—the review of clinical history...

"No. We were married in Las Vegas. There were no blood tests."

The doctors assured Scott that his medical condition was irrelevant, a red-herring, and he must not allow himself to think for one moment that it had anything to do with Isabel's unexplained death—but Valeria insinuated otherwise. Scott's multiple sclerosis was the key to the whole tragic business. Sure it was! Isn't it obvious?

The experts said Scott had done everything he should have, text-book perfect: he had lain Isabel on her back, on a firm mattress, with no pillows, quilts, comforters or stuffed toys—but Valeria said the room was *too warm*. She lied (and soon after, believed the lie) that she had thought so the moment she entered the nursery.

Not for the world would I suggest otherwise than that Valeria suffered the unimaginable agonies of any mother who has lost her new-born child: without artifice or agenda: a deep, genuine grief that scarred her heart for all time. I cannot take that from her—would that I were able to!—and we must feel for her, acutely. But her chosen escape-route, and it was not many days before she found it, ran along a path paved with Scott's fault, and all the sign-posts on that route pointed to the divorce courts.

At the very moment divorce crystalised in her mind as the solution to her problems, her marriage to Scott was effectively over.

* * *

The most terrible thing of all was that Scott, as he deteriorated, was less and less able to cope with Valeria's days of sullen silence, or put up any defence against her weeks of ranting. He even became afraid of her.

What a euphemism 'irretrievably broken down' is for a marital wreck such as theirs!

One gusty morning some two or three weeks after the funeral, with a Santa Ana wind blowing the leaves off the only deciduous tree in Abbot Kinney, the weather was brewing up a storm inside the matrimonial home. While Billy was at school Valeria orchestrated a stand-up row with the ailing Scott, alone and defenceless against her; a row which had been long in the planning and went as well as could be hoped in the execution.

She had waited for a spillage, or a broken vase or glass; and when Scott eventually, inevitably, *splendidly* obliged her, she tore into him. How much longer could she be expected to take all this? How much? How much? When he mumbled a confused, incomprehensible reply, she pulled at her hair, like a melodramatic heroine in Dickens, and threw a kitchen pot-scrubber at him, yelling—'She was going mad'. He was driving her mad. Did he hear her? MAD!

"Say something sensible for Christ sake," she yelled at his mumbled response.

At the height of her rage, words and objects flying at him, the words hitting harder than the objects, Scott shaking head to foot and crouching in the corner of the kitchen, she screamed at him to leave the house. NOW. Before she killed herself—or both of them! And he obeyed. Whatever it was he said—almost simpering—(Scott, simpering!)—she *made sure* she couldn't understand.

So wrecked that he could only manage to pack a few, inadequate overnight things, and his eyes so swollen he surely couldn't see well enough to drive, he left the pretty house in Abbot Kinney like a turned-away beggar; and it is truly astonishing that the self-martyred Valeria could find not one ounce of pity for him. But she couldn't—she wouldn't—and slammed the door behind him, hard, so she didn't have to watch his failed attempts to start his truck—she certainly wasn't going to let him have *that* as an excuse for staying!

But he did manage to get the truck started, eventually; and to drive—slowly, quickly, slowly again—sometimes veering off-road altogether and hitting trash cans—miraculously not catching the eye of a passing patrol car or motorcycle cop—all the way up to Larrabee, and to the door of Chloe's old apartment.

The new occupants had no idea who Chloe was, or where she had gone.

* * *

It was August 17 1998. President Clinton had that day become the first sitting President to testify in front of a Grand Jury investigating his conduct, and had broadcast to the nation that he had had an "inappropriate relationship" with Monica Lewinsky. Madison, the last of the Quakers still to live in Larrabee, saw the headline on a window-display television in the Beverley Centre and rushed home to catch-up with and try to make sense of the news that had stunned America and much of the world besides.

Scott had been in the elevator for some while when she returned, having in his confusion and through blurred vision pressed the button for the underground car-park, then pressed the button for the mezzanine where the gym was, then in anger wildly stabbed at all the buttons, and was taken up to the penthouse, where the doors wouldn't open—because you need a key for the penthouse—and there he had given up altogether.

Madison found Scott sitting on the floor, his head in his hands—where he might have been carried up and down all day if she hadn't rescued him. She took him back to her apartment, sat him down in her kitchen, and gave him a whisky and water.

President Clinton, the House of Representatives, The Senate, and Chief Justice Rehnquist himself, took a back seat while Madison listened to quite another, albeit just as depressing, version of the events of the last couple of years; and when Scott had run out of words—any words: his speech had become utterly incomprehensible even to kind ears—she put him onto a bed in the spare-room.

As soon as she was sure he was asleep she made a number of telephone calls.

And one by one they returned to the place where all of them had first met.

> *'Met properly'.*
> *'The night of the Northridge quake.'*
> *'Greater than the sum of the parts, and all that crap.'*

Seven

1

Rome

"It was late in the afternoon when I arrived to Madison's apartment. You realise I had not been there for—well, it was since many months. It felt strange, let me tell you, pressing a bell on the wall to be allowed in—to be allowed in to Larrabee! Think of it! Where I used to pass through—without asking permission!—with my own key to my own apartment. When all of us used to live there... and we were such friends, you see . . . and everything was perfect. Or maybe I pretended it was perfect. Maybe I turned away from the imperfections, eh? Such a depression fell on me, *Scottino*."

The muted sound of midnight chimed on church towers near and far.

"*Francesca da Rimini*," said his godson.

"Now you are going to quote Dante at me? To make me feel better?"

"I only know it from a DVD cover." (He tended to belittle his privileged education.) '*There is no greater sorrow than to remember happy times . . . in bad times*', or something like that."

"In grief . . . *Nella miseria*."

There was a long silence. Each of them, perhaps, remembering happier times.

"I took the elevator up to the third . . . the third…the third what? The word!" (A flash of anger—an escape from the grief.) "What is the word? *Il piano?*"

"To the third floor."

"And I used to live there! God help me! Tyler had already arrived. And Tom was sitting at the table—looking very grey and thin, I thought. Didier was not answering his pager. Did he ever answer his pager? We sat around in Madison's kitchen, speaking *sotto voce*—Scott was asleep in the next room—and all of us in shock—we hadn't seen Scott for so long. We had no idea.

"Time passes too fast, *Scottino*. Pay attention to every moment. Listen to me. Soon there will be no moments left, or very few. But how can you possibly understand?"

There was no performance, no acting, in the deep breath and the sigh that followed.

"No one even knew he was ill. No one had any idea . . . – ill! God in heaven!"

"What about my mother?"

"Your mother?"

"Didn't she come?" he asked, almost pitifully. He seemed to have had all the joy knocked out of him. All his youthful high spirits, in one long day.

"How could we tell where to find her? She could have been anywhere. We had seen *Scott* more recently than we had seen your mother! Is it possible? Wasted…wasted! Madison called Chloe's parents—but the difference in clocks, eh? East and West. She left a message on their answer service—but Madison did not say what had happened. *Dio mio*! She said only that Chloe needed to call her back.

"I could not promise you, now, how long we were there that night. Slowly drinking through the bottles of wine Madison brought to the table. From the wine-rack screwed to the wall. Remember the wine-rack? We had no thought for the wine's quality—or even its colour! It might have been vinegar . . . White vinegar. Red vinegar. It didn't matter. Madison made little attempts at the preparation (or the heating if I am truthful to you) of pieces from her refrigerator. But we didn't eat.

"There was so much change in Scott! I cannot bring myself to look back on it. He was very handsome, you know."

"I know."

"Then came the strange moment again. Don't think me an old man with a feeble brain, because I am only one of those things. I am saying that the moment, it was odd, that is all. *Strano*. You understand? It happened just as I told you before, at the time Madison emptied the bottle of red wine into her glass and stood to take another from that same wooden wine-rack screwed into her kitchen wall. It was, exactly as I have told you, when we sat around the same table, after your mother left the message she was engaged. I can't find the words for it. It was so . . . But it was more . . . *There was almost a shudder*, do you know what I am trying to describe to you? As though time himself suffered his little earthquake. I am not making sense. But the moment, the moment itself, it again said to me: '*Remember!*'—That is for sure.

"I broke out of my dream when the intercom buzzed. We thought it must be Didier. Tyler answered it –

'*That you Didier?*'

"There was no reply. The intercom buzzed again. Tyler said -

'*I'll go let him in.*'

"When he came back, he wasn't with Didier: he was leading a dog; or I should prefer to say the dog was leading him, pulling at his leash to get to the door of the spare bedroom. You are there ahead of me, eh?"

"She threw the dog out, too?"

"*Essatamente.*"

2

Monologue

He sits up suddenly. He doesn't know how long he has been asleep, or *if* he has been asleep. Or if he is asleep still, and all this is a dream.

He continues as though he had never stopped speaking…

"Squid! The dog's name was Squid! But you knew that. Weird name for a dog. But great, huh? I loved that name.

"I was with Scott when he went 'to get himself a dawg'—that's what he said: 'I'm gonna get myself a dawg"—after his first one got hit by a car. (Scott was awful cut up about that. Tell you the truth, I didn't like it too much myself.) Tom came along, because he hung out with Scott back then. Tom wasn't too much of a dog-guy. But he hung out with Scott. Back then, anyway. Before he hung out with Tyler.

"Scott got him from the rescue center run by a woman who played the double-bass in the orchestras that played all the movie music. Tom kept calling her double-bass a 'bull fiddle' like Jack Lemon did in 'Some Like it Hot', but she never got the joke. Maybe she thought the joke was on her. I hope not. She was a nice lady.

"She had a place in the Valley, jam-packed with mutts she'd rescued from the street. We nearly turned up on her doorstep after the quake—remember?—to ask her to take us in too; but then we thought better of it. There was quite a few people on the LA streets in those days, needed rescuing; and like you said, it was obvious she only rescued dogs.

"Well, we was sat down and shown a few mutts, and they seemed OK to me. But Scott said they was nothing special, so the woman who played the bull fiddle brought out some more. No go. One after another—nothing doing. Then this dog was brought out and let off the leash. He was just a medium-sized weird mix of a pooch, with a cute face and two enormous black eyes, like a panda. Tom said he looked like a cuttlefish he'd seen swimming around the water-bungalows some- where in the Gulf—or maybe it was Hawaii, it doesn't really matter—with its big eyes out the water, all lost and lonely. I thought the damn dog looked more like

a Panda. But Scott called him 'Squid' because of what Tom said, and because they hung out together. It's a great name though, isn't it?

"At first Squid took no notice at all of Scott. Couldn't be less interested. Once he was off the leash he ran three or four times round the yard like a 'wild thang', and the nearest he got to paying Scott any attention was to take an extra long whizz against the wheels of his truck. It was me he went to, which really bugged Scott, big time. Or he pretended it did. Tom laughed like he was fit to bust. The damn dog leaped up onto my knees and licked my face with one big slurp, leaped off again and shot behind the Hibiscus bushes for a quiet few moments of his own. When he eventually decides to re-appear he trots back, mighty pleased with himself, and this time stands right next to Scott, looking up at him with his tongue hanging out, panting and grinning—I swear to God, he was grinning—like all the time he'd been playing a joke on him.

"Then for no reason he shoots up like a vertical take-off airplane—Squid never jumped, believe me, he never jumped: it was vertical take-off, every time: I seen it for myself: vertical take-off: straight into the air—and he lands 'plop' in Scott's lap, snuggles down with his head on his front paws, closes his eyes and falls asleep. I swear to God! He falls asleep.

"'That's my dawg' says Scott."

* * *

"One day, that awful sad time when Scott was real ill, and Tom went kinda crazy—you know, that shouldn't have happened—how could we not see what was going on? Beats me. Every time I think about it.

"Anyhow, one day around that god-awful miserable time, I was walking Squid—we used to take turns, then, looking after him, remember?—and I was walking him and his big panda eyes down the jogging track in Runyon Canyon, when these two men—probably in their mid-eighties, or older, wearing torn cut-off faded jeans that must have measured no more than four inches down from the waist-belt to the frayed ends, hiking boots, and t-shirts a couple sizes too small—these two gay guys came striding towards us. Right as they were passing, and without breaking step or looking at me, one of them said "Your dog's wearing too much eye-shadow", and they disappeared off into the Park . . . into the 'never to be seen again' . . . like . . . I don't know. But I never saw them again.

"I wish I could have met those guys. I should have stopped and talked, or something. I would have, if there wasn't that god-awful unhappiness dragging us all down. They were funny. I wonder who they were, what they did. But you know

what? The sadness disappeared along with the gay guys. For a while, anyway. For a time.

For a time…

> *'I fell in love with James Tyrone, and was so happy for a time.'*

"It was your favourite line in all the plays and all the movies you'd ever seen. It made you cry.

"Jesus Christ! I don't know what I'm trying to say. Why don't you just wake up and tell me what I'm trying to say?"

3

Someone Special

Chloe was a long while in returning the call. Madison had given a sufficiently truthful version of events to ensure Chloe would come over; but she held back on the detail. The idea was they would break it to Chloe face-to-face: but Chloe's fear of what lay behind Madison's Delphic words was every bit as bad as the reality, if not worse; and she was sick with worry by the time her plane touched down at LAX.

She had not been out East, as they had thought, but had been living and working in Seattle. The working part was waiting tables between poorly paid stints as production assistant on a couple of local TV children's specials: the living part we don't want to look at too closely. She arrived at the airport in the morning. Tyler met her in his beat-up old Mustang convertible; and they drove to Madison's in the LA sunshine, with the roof down and the wind blowing in their faces.

"So where the hell did you go?"

"Back to Canada. Where we were filming," she said. "Where's Scott staying?"

"With Madison, until an apartment comes free."

"He's not going home?"

"His dad died in the summer. Doesn't even remember his Mom. Why Canada? To be with your fiancé?"

—That was cruel of Tyler.

"I wanted to go back to where I made it all happen."

"Explanation?"

"Where I took that stupid job, and went on that stupid skiing holiday, and sent all those stupid postcards."

"It's the stupidest place you could have gone," he said.

"Not if I wanted to make things as bad as they could possibly be."

"Oh, Chloe." There was real compassion in Tyler's voice, which would have surprised those who only knew the surface of him.

"When's there going to be a vacancy?" she asked.

"There's a couple moving-out in a few days. The manager's holding the apartment."

"Just one?"

"Only one I know of," said Tyler.

"Can I stay with you while I wait?"

"I quit Larrabee," he said; and it was clear to Chloe he was not going to say why.

"Didier?"

"Left ages ago. Can't afford the rent. He's more or less living in Tom's basement."

"Alone?"

"What d'you do in Canada? Quebec, right?"

"I went to the jeweller's –I'd paid a week's earnings for that stupid ring, and I wanted to return it where it came from. Like the Ring in that stupid movie."

"You get your money back?"

"I didn't *want* my money back. I gave it to him."

"Jeez!"

"Can I sleep at your place for a night or two?" she asked.

"It's a dump."

Then he added, as if of no consequence, "Why not with Scott? I know Madison wouldn't mind—until he gets his own place. Her apartment's big enough."

Chloe made no reply.

"You can bunk up with me if you *like…*" said Tyler.

"We'll work something out."

They drove in silence for a while.

"The ring stunt must have taken all of five minutes. What did you do for the rest of the year?"

"You don't want to know."

"Sure I do."

"You won't want me sleeping-over when you hear. You'll be disgusted."

Chloe's little laugh was mirthless.

"Disgusted? Gimme a break!" said Tyler.

"It's worse than anything you can imagine."

"Then I definitely want to know."

"Brace yourself," said Chloe.

"If its been done, I done it."

"I don't think so, Tyler."

"Truth is," said Tyler, with a sly smile, "you *want* to tell me, don't you?"

"Damn right I do," said Chloe. "Not just you. I want to tell the whole world. Pass it on to as many people as you can. I'd like to be pointed at, as the girl who..."

"So why don't you just take a deep breath and tell *me*."

"I found the cheapest motel in town that smelt of . . . it smelt, right? And it had bugs—I saw them. The bathroom was vile."

"Why there for Christ sake?" asked Tyler.

Chloe's reply was slow and deliberate. As though she was living through the decision all over again, and approving it thoroughly.

"I needed it to be devoid of any comfort or consolation—or anything, no matter how small, that could give me any relief, any refuge, or peace or . . . whatever. Anything good. Anything that allowed me to forget. Anything that had the slightest chance of letting me escape thinking about what I had done. What I'd lost. The . . . enormity of what I'd lost. What I'd thrown away."

She turned and faced Tyler.

"I went *looking* for a cheap, smelly, bug infested motel."

"Oh Chloe!" he said, for the second time, and with even greater feeling. "How long were you there? What did you do?"

"Well here's where it gets a little . . . I'm not proud of myself, Tyler; and you're going to wish you never heard it."

"Sure."

Chloe gave another humourless laugh.

"I bought a local paper and looked up the classifieds . . . you ready? . . . to find an escort agency. Does that shock you?"

"Listen, I *been* an escort."

"Really? I should have stayed in LA."

"I'd have given you a great price."

"Another lost opportunity."

Where Tyler's interjections were meant to lighten things up, Chloe's replies came from the depths.

"I don't understand," said Tyler "Why a hustler? I thought you were avoiding everything nice."

"For me, Tyler, it was not nice. Not at all nice. The idea was, it sounds crazy I know, but the idea was . . . I suppose . . . I suppose it was to degrade myself. Amateur psycho-analysis. Don't you love it? To punish myself. I wanted to sink into the gutter—and I did. For sure. I did exactly that. Into the gutter. And there was this side to it too, if I'm honest . . . I hate myself for it . . . for the weakness . . . Fuck! Fuck! Fuck! Fuck!—But . . . I couldn't bear to be alone. How feeble is that? I hired a male whore so I wouldn't be alone. Laughable. Pathetic. God! But thankfully that little self-indulgence didn't last very long!"

"What happened?"

"I found this ad in the papers, and called up the number. The ad said an escort agency: so I asked for an escort."

"Makes sense."

"To escort me. Sounds so proper, doesn't it? Old fashioned almost. 'To escort me.' Like out of Jane Austin. Except I wanted a dinner-date first, and to be made a fuss of in public, everyone looking at me being taken out by this stud, then afterwards...I wanted . . . you know..."

"I know," said Tyler. "Out of Jackie Collins. You don't need to beat yourself up about *that*."

"The guy at the other end of the phone was totally matter of fact. I could have been ordering a pizza. He said I had called at *just* the right time, and they had *exactly* what I was looking for. An *exceptionally* good-looking young man, he said. *Real* considerate, *impeccable* manners, and they could guarantee me an *excellent* evening. He was very much in demand, apparently."

"Impeccable manners? I didn't do that one."

"Oh he did. Big time. And as good-looking as the man said. He drove a nice car, and picked me up, and opened the door for me and everything, yada yada. I'd booked him for the whole evening, dinner at a smart restaurant first, as though it was a real date. Someone sitting at the table with me, like I was his girl, or just . . . Oh God! I don't believe I..."

She stopped for a while. Tyler waited.

"Anyway, he made them put us in a cosy little banquette, so we were sitting next to each other, not on opposite sides, right up close, like we were a couple. Except it must have looked like he was having a meal with his mother."

"Yeah Yeah."

They drove on in silence. Chloe with her head turned sharp right, pretending to look out of the window. Until Tyler said –

"So you finish dinner."

"But there was *much* more to it. It was perfect. He ordered the wine, tasted it—like he really knew if it was good or bad. Asked for one bottle to be chilled, and the other to be decanted. When the girl comes round selling roses, he bought one for me, and pinned it to my little jacket. I never had so much attention in my life. Not even with..."

She didn't choke. Her lips didn't tremble. She didn't say 'excuse me' and put her sleeve to her eyes. She just couldn't speak his name.

Tyler came in quickly—"You went to your bug-infested place, or did he have his own base-camp?"

"My place."

"And?"

"That's when I realised why he wouldn't stop talking all evening. He didn't want us to get round to discussing Act Two."

"Excuse me? He's an escort. Act Two goes with the territory."

"Not that night it didn't. He'd spent the whole meal avoiding any hint of it. He pulled up outside the Motel, and nothing could be clearer than he wanted me out of the car fast as possible."

"He took one look at your sleazy Motel, that's what happened," said Tyler.

"No. It was a one-act show. I brought up the subject as delicately as I could, but he always managed to skirt round it. When I fast-forwarded through the delicacy and brought it up in plain English, he said he was sorry, *it was embarrassing for him*, so he said, but all I had booked was a companion for the evening. That was all. He was lying, of course. I sure as hell hadn't booked 'just a companion'. I kept calm though, and didn't make a fuss. But nothing could be more certain: this escort, this handsome young man with impeccable manners and the gift of conversation, who was paid to have sex with anyone they sent him to, just couldn't bring himself to have sex with *me*."

"You got that wrong," said Tyler. "I been there. It doesn't work like that. There was some kind of misunderstanding when you spoke to the guy at the agency."

"There was no misunderstanding, Tyler. I told them exactly what I was looking for, and they said they had just the thing. I'm not going to kid myself there was any *misunderstanding*. That's way too easy. It's a lie. Fact is, I was so repulsive to him he couldn't bring himself to do it. Not that night. Not even for money . . . Not with me, anyway."

"Don't do this, Chloe. I'm telling you, that isn't how it works. There'd been a mistake. Trust me . . . It just doesn't work like that."

"It's exactly how it worked. The relief on his face when I got out the car. He even forgot to open the door for me. His tyres squealed when he drove off."

"Did you ask for a refund? Or did they offer you an exchange?"

"I made no complaint at all."

"You gave it to them, like the ring? You a *professional* victim, or what?"

"If that's what you want to call it. But we haven't reached the climax."

"You already said that."

"Hilarious. The next day I telephoned the agency again, and made another booking."

"Go girl!"

"This time I spelled it out so clearly, it couldn't have been more graphic if I sent them a drawing. I even got them to repeat what I had asked for, word for every disgusting word. The guy, who had obviously had the low-down from the escort, tried to put me off by saying that because last night had been a dinner companion, this would be much more expensive. I repeated I didn't want a dinner companion, so there could be no mistake, and I'd pay whatever the price was. He gave up and we made the deal."

"At your place?"

"Oh yes. I wanted it to be special."

"Did it work out?"

"Hold your horses. I haven't told you the best bit."

"Which is?"

"I asked for the same escort."

"What?"

"The same escort. The talker. They tried offering me someone else, in fact they became quite insistent, but I said it was him or nothing."

"In the name of . . . Why?"

"I knew he would loathe having to screw me."

"Chloe!"

"Even while he was doing it, I wanted to appreciate—no, to enjoy—the fact that he must be hating every minute. And boy, did it take him a long time."

She broke the long silence, while Tyler was trying to get his head round what he had just heard –

"Disgusted yet?"

Tyler said 'of course not' with as little conviction as ever a man has spoken.

"Disgusting," said Chloe. "It's a great word, don't you think? Dripping from the sewer. Every syllable. *Dis-gus-ting*. I am disgusting. *Chloe is disgusting*. I want everyone to know. *Chloe is disgusting*."

"Stop."

"*Dis-gus-ting*."

"Stop it!"

"It's quite something, let me tell you, to see that staring back at you from the mirror."

With an ill judged, ill-timed, and high-risk attempt at humour, Tyler said -

"I don't know how you can bring yourself to shave."

At last he thought he saw something that could be mistaken for a smile on Chloe's face—which, in fact, was wracked with pain.

They had reached Larrabee.

4

The Gardening Angel

Tyler took Chloe up to Madison's apartment, where Scott was staying until he and all of them had worked out what he was going to do and where he was going to do it. He was asleep in the spare room when Chloe tip-toed in and took a peep at him, opening and closing the door as you would on a sleeping baby. She turned to Tyler -

"I wasn't expecting …"

But she didn't finish—as though she needed to! Her handsome Scott was thin, haggard, with sunken cheeks, sores on the arm that dangled over the bedside, and breathing with great difficulty—possibly having a nightmare, the way he let out little yelps like dreaming dogs do.

"I know," said Tyler.

Chloe covered her face with her hands –

"God! What a mess I made of it. What a mess. What a terrible mess."

Tyler pulled her to him, as he had been aching to all afternoon, and kissed the top of her head.

"It's not your fault."

He led her to the kitchen and shut the door. They spoke in near-whispers.

"Drink?"

Chloe nodded, and Tyler went about the preparations while he teased-out the rest of her story.

"How did you end up in Seattle?"

"Another film job. TV. Didn't last long, but I had nowhere else to go, so I stayed."

"Doing?"

She never got to answer.

"Hi Chloe."

They hadn't heard him, nor seen him open the door—but there he was, supporting himself on its frame. Chloe ran to him, clung to him, and wept profusely against his chest.

* * *

He took her back to the lovers' car-park off the service road behind the Hamburger joint North of Holloway, where they used to sit on the wooden bench and plan their futures, to tell her what he had decided to do now their futures had not turned out like they were supposed to.

Scott was walking very slowly these days, with the help of a stick. Kerbsides were a major problem, because he couldn't look down without losing his balance. Chloe assisted him as best she could, trying to ignore the drivers who blasted their horns at him because of the time he was taking to cross the road.

He couldn't tilt his head *up* either, for the same reason; but there was nothing much to see if he had—no star or planet, not even the moon, had come out into the pitch black sky to look down at their misery.

The LA smog meant you couldn't watch the aeroplanes coming in to land over the ocean, or rising into the night on take-off: it even smothered the pretty street-lights, so you couldn't see them three blocks away, let alone stretching all those miles to the airport. There were no cars parked in the dirt-yard either, with their steamed-up windows and creaking springs. Scott and Chloe stood by the edge of the precipice completely alone—in a place where they had come to be alone, yet felt abandoned.

"I'm dying, Chloe."

It was an age before she could find something to say.

At last she turned to him, and even though she realised the banality of it as the words fell from her mouth, she said "We're all dying"—as if that were any consolation, or ever could be—and she instantly regretted speaking. But Scott looked fondly back at poor Chloe as though her tired cliché was the greatest possible comfort anyone could have given him.

No one but he knew, then, that his double-vision had become so bad that he found it next to impossible to make the two images of whatever he saw slide into a single picture. The only way he could drive his truck was to keep one eye shut. He didn't tell them, because he was afraid (and with good reason) they would take away his licence. And it was a strain to look at *anything* for any length of time, because the images drifted further and further apart. So he looked away from the two Chloes and let his eyes find rest in the indistinct smog, which was the same whether doubled-up or in focus.

She broke the long silence with -

"When I was a girl—I mean a really little girl—it's the first memory I have of anything—I thought I had a guardian angel." She stared at the ground while she made her awkward confession. "My mom told me."

'And when you go to sleep Chloe, with your eyes tight shut, your guardian angel will watch over you, and protect you, all night long.'
'My Garden Angel?'
'Your Guardian Angel.'
'My Gardening Angel?'
'Yes my darling…your Gardening Angel.'

"And I believed her. Isn't that silly? Every night I thought of him. He never had a face, or any shape. He was just . . . there. Mine. My own angel. Even when I started to grow up, I always fell asleep thinking of him—watching over me—protecting me. Sometimes I used to let myself imagine the comforter was his wing stretched across me." She glanced at Scott and mistook his squinting for something very different, so she looked down again quickly. "And then, when I met you Scott, after I met you up there on the roof, all of a sudden . . . my guardian angel had a face."

Scott clenched his jaw, staring—or seeming to stare—straight ahead of him. Now, maybe, it wasn't just a squint she saw in his eyes.

"And even after all our fights; after we split, and I went away, and you got married; every night, ever since we met, my guardian angel has had the same face."

"You know we can't get back together," said Scott, still staring straight ahead of him.

"I love you Scott, that's all that matters," she continued, as though he hadn't uttered a word. "I used to think it was the hardest thing to say—but it's the easiest. I love you. I always have."

He turned towards her, and with all the strength remaining in his weak eyes he forced the two Chloes to become one, saying –

"And I've always loved you, Chloe. 'Course I have. Christ! What did you think? Maybe not as much as I should. Not as much as I do now. But I screwed up, didn't I?" He stared into the smog again. "And now's too late."

Although she knew it was coming, she couldn't face it when it came. She gripped hold of his arms, in denial as to the hopelessness of her pleading -

"Please let me stay with you."

"I'm dying, Chloe. And every faculty I have is dying ahead of me."

"I can look after you. Please Scott."

"Dear, darling Chloe. You got to see—I could never do that to you."

"It isn't fair," she sobbed.

"It's how things are, how the cards have fallen."

"Fallen for *us*. Together."

"No, for me. For me . . . For me . . . Dear God! I'm not going to let it be the way they fall for you."

"There is no God."

"Don't say that . . . Guardian angels, and no God?"

"I hate you." She clutched herself even tighter against the man she hated.

"I know." He lifted up her head and mopped her cheeks with kisses.

"You remember me telling you once, right here where we are, on this very spot, that I was one of 'the lucky people'?" She nodded and blinked her huge dark eyes at him. "I still am," he said, and let go his stick and steadied himself against his luck.

She laid her head on his chest and he rocked her quietly back and forth, deep into the night, heaven knows for how long until she began to fall asleep, and they made their slow way home as the first light of day looked like it might be showing in the East.

* * *

"*Sadly, sadly the sun rose…*"

And it has risen on many thousands of mornings since. But on that grey dawn it rose on no sadder sight than Chloe and Scott locked in each other's arms, sharing a bed for the last time; the pillow, on which both their heads lay close, damp with the secret tears of her gardening angel.

5
Disabled Friendly

It was Tyler who arranged the lease for Scott's small studio apartment in Larrabee.

It was Tyler who arranged for the sale of Scott's truck when he could no longer climb into it—and he got a good price, too.

But it was the Dutch guy who researched the best disabled-friendly replacement vehicle, with features for access and driving that Scott didn't need right away, all of them built-in for when the time came that he couldn't drive without them; and with space for carrying a wheelchair-bound passenger, for when he couldn't drive at all.

Everyone had been shocked, in the first days of his return to Larrabee, to see how badly Scott sometimes dragged his right foot. It was intermittent—it came and it went; but when it did come it seemed to stay for longer and longer before taking its leave; until, like many an unwelcome visitor, there was no getting rid of it. And everyone saw the implications for Scott's driving, except Scott himself—especially for his driving that heavy truck: the truck that was as instantly associated with Scott as mirrored Ray Bans are with Californian motorcycle cops: the four-by-four that never needed to be shifted into four-wheel drive, not even to get up Coldwater Canyon in the rain: the pick-up truck with a load capacity of half a ton, that had rarely picked up anything more than a pizza. Jet black, with all coloured signage sand-blasted from it; extra-wide wheels that lifted the cabin a metre and a half off the ground; and extra-large 'kick-ass' bumpers that said '*don't fuck with me*'. A must-have LA vehicle as iconic as Madison's Hummer. When two LA trucks drew up alongside at traffic signals, they growled at each other like pack-dogs.

Many a distraught conversation they had, the Quakers absent Scott, on the broad subject of 'what could they do?' about the truck.

"One of these days," said Tyler, "he's going to kill himself in that damn truck."

Chloe rushed from the room.

When Scott clipped the wing-mirrors of a parked car—which he did more often than he admitted even to himself—he never told any of them. And when his right foot stuck on the accelerator, and he couldn't brake and sailed through a red stop sign, luckily suffering no worse than a chorus of car-horns, he pulled up by the sidewalk as soon as he had the use of his foot again, shaking, soaking in sweat; and he had to wait a full half-hour before he regained sufficient composure to risk setting off. But not one word of the incident did he let slip to any of them.

Scott was all-too aware that there was behind-his-back concern about his driving, and he became crafty as a result; which was not like him, and for that reason alone it was upsetting to those who noticed it. He took elaborate pains not to be seen driving—making no end of excuses for not giving any of them a ride, or going on a trip with them, or arriving in their sight.

One day in the Larrabee parking lot he was struggling (and failing) to haul himself into the truck's impossibly high driver's seat, when he heard a familiar voice:

"Need a hand, buddy?"

Tyler came striding over from his old Mustang.

"You keeping tabs on me, or what?" said Scott, sourly. A good question nonetheless, because that is exactly what Tyler had been doing.

"Lighten up! I'm visiting with Chloe," said Tyler.

"I'm doing fine. Thanks."

"OK" said Tyler, making no attempt to appear convinced.

Scott ignored him and tried yet again to lift himself into the driver's seat.

"You sure?' said Tyler.

"I said I'm fine," snapped Scott. He stood by the open door, making no further assault on the out-of-reach cabin.

"Are you going to stand there and watch?" he said, without looking at Tyler.

For all his good intentions, Tyler was rattled. He turned his back on Scott, tossing a provocative 'Have a nice day' over his shoulder as he sauntered towards the exit.

After a third failed attempt, while the exit door was still swinging behind Tyler, and a fourth not long after, Scott swallowed his pride, steeled himself and called out -

"Tyler! I'm sorry."

Too late. Tyler was out of earshot. With no hope of any reply—with no hope of anything—Scott yelled:

"I do need help!"

* * *

He knew he couldn't follow Tyler to Chloe's apartment—that is, he couldn't bring himself to do so, and have to explain what Tyler had just seen, and have to submit to all the supplementary interrogation, and have to lie. Anyway, he couldn't think of any lies just then. Neither could he get into his truck and escape them—*his friends*, who wanted nothing but his well-being. He leaned against the vehicle for a few empty minutes. Then he sat on the oil-stained floor, defeated, little more alive than Nimrod when the power is off.

He was forced to pull himself to his feet when a young family came chattering towards the car next to his truck. He couldn't deal with any 'are you alright?' questions, and he stood as quickly as he could manage, shut the truck door, locked it, and limped away with a nod to the parents and a short shared smile with the children.

Where next? He hobbled his painful way to his old haunt, "*The Santa Lucia*", the idea being to while-away enough time there as was consistent with his having driven on an errand, accomplishing it, and returning.

"Just a cappuccino," he said to the waiter—the same who had given Chloe and him the unwanted *Limoncello*, but did not recognise Scott as the young lover of such ancient history. The waiter removed the menu with that feigned surprise they put on when they want you to know they think you probably can't afford the food. The cappuccino was eventually brought to the table, it having been pointedly delayed in the making, lest Scott should suppose that by not ordering food he was saving time. Scott reached for it, but 'intention tremor' set in and he immediately gave up trying.

Intention tremor is common in multiple sclerosis. It occurs when the muscles the brain is asking to do something take too long in sending feedback to the brain that the task has been accomplished, or is under way. The brain thinks it has to send the instruction a second time, which *en route* passes the delayed 'mission accomplished' message, which is at last on its way to the brain from the muscles. So the brain panics and quickly sends out an 'abort mission' message to compensate for the redundant, duplicated, 'do it' command. The cycle is repeated, mercilessly. It throws the muscles into spasm and they vacillate, sometimes wildly, between obeying the repeat 'do it' messages and the contradictory 'abort' messages, as if telling the brain '*for Christ's sake, make up your mind!*' If Scott had tried to take a hold of the coffee cup, his intention tremor would probably have flung the contents across the table.

After many minutes had passed, with Scott staring out of the window and not touching his drink, the waiter came fussing over and said he was sorry, but if Scott was not going to eat, he would have to ask him to drink his coffee and leave. They did not accept drinks-only orders between twelve and two, he said. '*He was so sorry. If they didn't get quite so busy at lunchtimes, he could stay there as long as he wanted. But they would need the table.*' Scott asked if they served Lasagne, without taking the proffered menu. (The intention tremor would have made that difficult.) '*Yes, they served lasagne.*' It would have pleased the waiter if they didn't, and he could have brought this strange interaction to an end—but, alas, of course they did at the 'Santa Lucia' café/bar, and Scott ordered it.

Unaware of the torment he was inflicting on Scott, who only wanted to be left alone to think, the waiter fired-off the few remaining rounds of ammunition in his gunbelt.

"Would that be with fries?"—"Could I interest you in a side salad?"—"Some bread and olives, perhaps"

Scott answered 'yes' to every suggested extra the waiter piled on his notional plate.

And still there were decisions to torture him with:

"What dressing on the salad? Thousand Island? French? Ranch? Blue Cheese…"

"*The first one.*"
"*Was that the Thousand Island?*"
"*Sure.*"
"*Or was it the French?*"
"*It doesn't matter.*"
"*But you must choose.*"
"*The French.*"
"*Not the Thousand Island?*"
"*Both. Bring both.*"

With doubt entering his mind whether all this food would be paid for, and in a escalating state of suspicion that it wouldn't, the waiter asked Scott if he would like to keep a tab behind the bar.

"A tab?"

It meant Scott had to hand over his charge-card in advance of anything being prepared for him.

When the card was safely swiped, and the food brought to the table, it was simply a question of experience and timing how long the waiter should leave things before asking Scott if 'everything was to his satisfaction'. The timing was made slightly more delicate than usual, however, because Scott left all the food on his plate as untouched as the cold coffee sitting beside it. He had made a stab at picking up a fork, but quickly gave up when his waving arm, like the arm of an out of control puppet, tipped over a glass of water, which the waiter mopped up with the maximum fuss, protesting it was no trouble at all, and bringing another very full glass despite everything Scott could do to persuade him he didn't want it.

Scott made no further attempt to eat or drink, and might have been a dummy in a shop window, staring blankly into the street outside—and through, rather than at, the passing traffic and the people scurrying by, who never once tempted his eyes to follow them.

'*Everything was excellent. Thank you.*' (A surreal conversation at best; but can you imagine how much more so if Scott had *complained*, nothing having been tasted?)

When sufficient time had passed for an errand credibly to have been run, Scott signed for the meal and retrieved his charge-card. He unwittingly threw down dollar bills amounting to a forty per-cent tip, upon seeing which the waiter succumbed to the worst in himself and gave not the slightest tell-tale sign. Scott left the café/bar having both triumphed and been vanquished in a conflict he was scarcely aware had taken place.

He limped his way back to Larrabee, up the steep hill, and into the apartment block, dreading the likelihood of having to meet any of those whose only interest was helping him.

6

Rome

"Scott would have seen it as an informal gathering of friends, but we had planned it in advance.

"I think it had been a specially bad day for him. At the table he didn't eat or drink—and he refused all help in doing either, as was typical of him.

"The others asked me to raise the subject—because I was the oldest they said. I suppose I still am the oldest, eh? The oldest of us who are still alive. Someone said in a film that dying is the oldest anyone can get—so perhaps the young ones are older than me now, *si*?"

"Catch 22."

"Is that so? Catch 22. *Va bene* . . . So. I took up my task and I delicately mentioned to Scott the difficulties he sometimes seemed to have with his truck, and if there was anything I could do to help him. To my surprise he did not explode, like I feared he would."

> *'Sure, what did you have in mind?'*

"I offered to take him to a dealer in Glendale who specialised in made-to-measure disabled-friendly cars—if he wanted to go, I said quickly—just to have a look."

> *'Do they do conversions?'*

"Tyler told him converting the truck was probably out of the question. We waited for Scott's reaction. But Chloe rushed in and said it would be far too *espensive* anyway, which was not helpful because it diverted Scott from the little journey I was taking him on."

> *'How much is expensive?'*

"Tyler said it wasn't a question of money."

'*They only do cars. It isn't an option. I'm sorry buddy.*'

'*I can ask.*'

'*Sure.*'

"Everyone agreed, immediately, and with great enthusiasm, piling in, one on top of ourselves—"

'*Of course, you have to ask.*'

"The answer came as soon as we arrived at Glendale. The dealer told Scott that he must understand conversion involves 'major surgery'—does that make sense?"

"You bet it does," said his godson. "You have to cut the whole chassis out and totally reconstruct it, even heavy-duty parts like brake lines and the fuel tank need to be shifted. Major, major surgery. A guy at McGill had his Chevvy done after he snapped his spine in a skiing accident. He told me all about it. Then the car has to be specially approved by the DMV—which adds up to mega bucks. That's why they convert a whole load in bulk. Saves on cost. What was his truck?"

"I have no idea."

'*A Dodge Dakota,*' said Scott to the dealer.

'*You got to be kidding. No-one will undertake the bespoke conversion of a Dodge Dakota. I'm sorry.*'

"The salesman said he could show Scott some of the more popular wheelchair-friendly cars on the market. Wheelchair! Without a word of warning, Scott turned away and dragged his right foot out of the showroom. He stood the other side of the plate-glass with his back to us, hands in his pockets, looking up at the Glendale Mountains. I tried to apologise for him. The salesman said it was usual and I must be patient."

'*It's tough, I know, but I find it's better in the long run not to wrap it up. He's coming back.*'

'*So. How do I get a friendly wheelchair into one of these then?*' said Scott.

"The man took Scott through all the recent advances they had made in technology. He showed him foot controls that could be made hand controls, and hand controls that could be made knee controls, or elbow controls, *é cosi, é cosi*. I didn't know they had such things! To reduce the effort, steering can be done with something he called—and I shall never forget—a '*steering wheel spinner knob*'."

"A 'Brodie Knob'," said his godson. "They call it the 'suicide knob'."

"So much he did not tell us," said the old man. "But he demonstrated how getting in and out can be obtained by ramps and pulleys and fulcrums and only God knows what else—it is quite astonishing—all motorised as necessary. A *permanently* wheelchair-bound driver, the salesman told Scott, without mercy emphasising the word *permanently*, can be lifted, chair and all, into the driver's position, without any additional assistance. *Miraculoso!* The chair is secured at the pressing of a button, *et voila!* The disabled driver is able to take full control of the car.

'*Cool,*' *said Scott. 'Except I'll have to learn to drive all over again.*'

"That was no problem, said the salesman; there were specialist driving lessons—which he could arrange—in vehicles fitted out so the instructor can seize control instantly from the passenger seat, if it so happened that he needed to, eh? The salesman showed us just such a car in the parking lot, and he let Scott try it for himself—with the instructor next to him having to take over within seconds, you can imagine! It was a disaster!"

'*You see?*' said the dealer, almost by way of a boast.

"He was sure Scott would pick up the new controls in a very few lessons. He asked if Scott had informed the DMV? If he hadn't, he should do so without delay.

'*Obviously, you will have to re-take your driving test and obtain a new drivers' licence. It would probably be a restricted licence, but it will enable you to get around. You'd better get used to not driving on the Freeways. But that should be no problem. There are compensating advantages, you know. Such as Handicap Parking Permits.*'

"Scott recoiled as though he had been slapped in the face by the Invisible Man.

"After we were shown a number of choices, with Scott less and less interested in any of them, we found what I thought was the perfect car. But Scott was not happy. He wanted time to think about it, and the salesman said he understood. He gave Scott his card, and I think he would not have made a bet on seeing him again. I drove us back to Larrabee."

'I'm not taking any test,' said Scott.

'I don't think you have a choice, my friend.'

'And there's no way I can have special lessons.'

'What are you saying to me? It is perfect.'

"Scott replied in a flat monotone, with no emotion, a recital of the dull facts."

'What I'm saying to you is that I have to close one eye when I drive, and the other one's blurred. I won't <u>pass</u> any test, it's a joke to even think about taking a test, and the instructor would report me to the DMV before I even started the car. I'm talking about losing my licence.'

"I pulled-up by the sidewalk."

'Are you telling me you have been driving your truck around Los Angeles, looking out of one blurred eye?'

'That's what I'm telling you.'

'Serio?'

'Yep.'

"I think I exploded. I told him he must stop driving, altogether."

'Not until I have to.'

"You can imagine, I told him in the strongest language that he most certainly <u>did</u> have to, now."

"Are you going to report me? I'd totally understand. In fact, I think maybe you'd better report me."

"I said of course I was not going to report him: but it was imperative for him to stop driving. It was not fair, not so much for him, I said, but to anyone he might cause an accident to."

'Been managing so far, haven't I? It's not that blurred.'

"I was in despair!"

'And I recon I've got a few months before it gets any worse. Safe months. Maybe a year. A year could be long time—for me. It might be all there is.'

"I banged both my hands on the steering wheel."

'Listen to me' said Scott. *There's some driving in me yet. I know there is. Can't say how long, but there's some driving left in me. You have no idea how careful I am.'*

"I think I swore at him, holding the wheel tight in both my fists."

'When the day comes, and you tell me for real I have to stop, I'll stop. I'll give you the keys, for Christ's sake, the moment you tell me. I swear to God. You have my word.'

"I banged both my hands on the steering wheel again."

'I <u>am</u> telling you for real! You have to stop driving!"

'The day I give up driving, it's all over for me. You gotta know that as well as I do.'

"I started to say something . . . I can't remember . . . It doesn't matter. He interrupted, angrily…"

'Don't? Don't what? Don't bullshit each other? You figure it out. I'll be waiting for the end. Am I wrong? There'll be nothing else to do, 'cept wait.'

"I said to stop talking like a madman. He had a duty. We both had a duty. Something like that…"

'Yeah, yeah, yeah. I'll be sitting and waiting. We both know it's true.'

"Then his anger went—suddenly—and it was unbearable, *Scottino*."

'Please. Please don't take me off the road while I have life in me. Not while I have life.'

"I pulled my hands through my hair—don't be funny now. Not now."

'I'll be so careful. You'll see. I've been careful up to today, haven't I? You didn't know, until I told you. Huh? You didn't know, right?'

"I looked at Scott, but I made no reply to him. He was not being fair to me. It was impossible to know what to do."

'I'd go down on my knees, but you'd have to help me up.'

"Scott smiled at his own weak little joke, and I was the one who became onion-eyed. Is that an expression here?"

'What do you want me to do?

'You could teach me in one of those damn cars the instructors use.'

'They weren't for sale.'

'They make 'em. Someone's gotta sell 'em.'

'And suppose it doesn't work?'

'It will. I promise you.'

'And you'll stop driving, the moment I say?'

'I swear to God.'

'No arguments?'

'No arguments.'

'My decision?'

'Your call.'

"I pulled my car out into Brand Avenue –

'I need my head examined.'

"Scott reached behind his seat, I think it was so I would not see his trembling hand. But I did see it."

'Yeah. That you do,' he said.

7

Monologue

"Guess what it is next week? Halloween. Comes round every year.

"I used to love Halloween. We all did, 'cept some of us pretended we didn't. Like it was childish an' all. But they still got dressed up, didn't they? You did. Don't say you didn't. I got the pictures.

"Tom said it was his favorite out of all the seasons in the year, because it was the longest. Tom was real pissy about Halloween. He said it lasted from the end of September through to Thanksgiving. Ha frigging Ha. I recon it never lasted much more than a month. Depending how it fell, maybe another weekend. You got to sympathise though. After you've taken all that trouble with the costume an' stuff, and you only get to wear it a few times beforehand, maybe one or two nights mid-week, Halloween itself obviously, the weekend after for sure, and if there's a party maybe even once more. If you're lucky. I totally get it that no one wants to pack it up in a trunk for a year.

"Some people keep their Christmas lights up until Valentines. I like that.

"It was great the way everyone dressed up for Halloween. Adults acting like kids. Maybe some of them never got to be kids? But I didn't think the bank clerks should put on face-paint. It didn't seem right. Not the bank clerks.

"You remember that waiter, dressed up as Dracula, who didn't get it when Tom wanted to know if he recommended the Borscht? And when he asked Tom if they had Halloween in England, Tom said no, he believed it was a Cherokee word.

"I didn't like the way Tom got all smart-ass 'bout the way we said it though. Like the English way was right, and the American way had to be wrong. The English can be real pricks, can't they? 'Halloween.' Like in 'Ha Ha'. That's the way we say it, so Tom can just stick his way. What do the English know? It's a Cherokee word.

"Madison said the October special they did was real funny, because the guys behind the cameras, all in their Halloween gear, were way more frightening than anything they could dream up for the audience. The tough guy, Bradley, gave an excuse, which I though was real lame, that the spirits were busy that night, it being Halloween an' all. Wasn't that pathetic?

"*The best times was when we were all down in West Hollywood, watching the parade—which I always thought was pretty damn scary, that parade they do, what with some of the stuff they put on the floats. I don't think kids should be allowed to see that kind of stuff—and what the hell has it got to do with Halloween?*"

"*But there's that one time you gotta remember, when we were all down at a sidewalk cafe on Melrose, or maybe it was Third, and we'd seen the parade go by, in all these scary costumes, people with axes through their heads and stuff, which was great. How do they do those? Remember how it was so frigging obvious the cops had been told to be gay-friendly, because there'd been some bad publicity the year before in West Hollywood, and there'd been a new Mayor or something? And the cops were putting a brave face on it, pretending to be in the spirit of it, and smiling at the cameras like they'd been told to, but it was obvious as shit they didn't like it. Not one little bit.*

"*Then these two huge guys dressed as women cops came along, they must have been seven feet tall—why is it so many transvestites are seven feet tall? You ever noticed that? Or are they cross-dressers? Do you know the difference? Damned if I do. Got nothing against them, but I don't know the difference and it pisses me off.*

"*Anyway these two cops were sitting on the front of their patrol car, uncomfortable as shit, and the transvestite cops were chucking them under the chin and flirting with them, which the real cops definitely did not like. But the crowd loved it, so the real cops kept their cool. And the gay cops went on and on making jokes about what the 'serve' bit of 'protect and serve' meant. And when they handcuffed the real cops to each other, it got a bit ugly, and the real cops said it wasn't funny. But the gay cops wouldn't take the cuffs off the real cops, and everyone was laughing 'cept the real cops.*

"*Now that was what I call a really good Halloween.*

"*I could do without some of the stuff on the floats, though. I got to be honest with you.*

"*Then there was that night Scott was in his wheelchair, which was more or less all the time those days, and people thought it was a Halloween thing, because there was a fair number of 'Baby Janes' wheeling Joan Crawford around, and it was really sad some of the people on the sidewalk thought Scott was in costume, 'cos he was in a wheelchair an' all.*

"*Worse than sad. Truth is, I couldn't bear it, if you want to know.*

"*He didn't seem to mind though, and started making out he was a Zombie, which was actually genuinely scary, but we all laughed, just like the passers-by laughed, and Madison was laughing but told him to 'stop it' cause it wasn't nice. Then it turned out he wasn't acting, and Tyler had to take him to A&E. Remember?*

"It has to be the worst Halloween ever. I never much liked Halloween after that.

"Anyhow, it's next week.

"Weird, huh?"

* * *

"A thing that really bugs me 'bout Scott is he always left it one step too late.

"'Course I was sorry for him—Sorry for him? Christ! There isn't a word gets close. He said once, when I was sitting with him on Santa Monica pier watching the dolphins, he said imagine what it'd be like if you was a dolphin, and couldn't swim.

"But if he'd just accepted that's how it was, and—here's an example—if he wore his first pair of glasses when he should've, instead of putting up that fight, there's no end of stuff he could have done. He stopped going to the movies—did you know that? Because he couldn't make out the picture; and by the time he caved-in and finally got himself some glasses, he couldn't walk—not far, anyway—not without a frame; and then he wouldn't go to the movies because he needed to take a piss every five minutes.

"Boy was he angry if ever someone even hinted he should try a wheelchair.

'Maybe you should.'—'Perhaps.'—'You ever tried one?'

"Didn't matter how they led up to it, did he get ansty!

"Never got himself a hearing-aid either, not before his hand shook so much he couldn't work the TV remote or tape-deck. And he never asked anyone to put on any music for him. And Scott loved his music. Remember? But oh no! He'd not ask! Not Scott!

"I wonder what kind of world he ended up living in? Not hearing too good. Not seeing much that wasn't doubled up, or blurred. Towards the end, not even being able to speak. Not so you'd understand. Least, not so I could understand. Most of the time, anyway.

What kind of a world d'you think that was?"

Not for a moment does he pause to consider that he's talking to another human being deprived of all faculties, who is trespassing on such life as is within reach in total reliance on doctors and nurses and the miracles of modern medicine. Unable to see, or speak—perhaps unable to hear. *'Sometimes they can'*, the nurse had said.

"Even after he was persuaded to buy a top-of-the-range motorised wheelchair, it was days before he used it. And by the time he gave up the fight, he couldn't hardly

work it. It was stupid. I really liked Scott, but it was plain stupid, the way he made things worse for himself.

"I hated seeing him struggling in and out of that car. When the wheelchair arrived he almost stopped driving. Would you believe that? Gave up altogether for a while, until he came to terms with the chair. Scott! Giving up driving! Needed someone else to take him around. Totally dependent. Couldn't get anywhere otherwise. But he never asked, did he? The other guy always had to make the move. I get mad when I start thinking 'bout that. What he missed out on. 'Cause he was so fucking stubborn.

"So when he finally caved-in and got himself a wheelchair, it was way too late to be much use. Always a step too late. Always fucking always. And wouldn't it have been so easy if he'd taken that step when he should've? He could've done all kinds of stuff he never got round to, because he never took any of those steps when he should: never: not a one of them: because he wouldn't ask anyone to help him, because . . . I don't know. I don't understand it.

"There's things I wish I'd done with Scott. Places I wish we'd gone, all kinds of stuff; when he could do them easy, when he could go there and no problem, when we could have gone together, all of us, or just him and me. I liked that, when it was just him and me. But he had to make it hard for himself, didn't he?

"That's what bugged me about Scott.

"You know what bugs me more than anything else? After all that fuss, I think he only used the motorised goddam chair a half-dozen times. Maybe a couple times more.

"A half-dozen times . . . Beats everything, doesn't it?"

8

The Dolphins

It would be wrong to say that as he deteriorated physically, Scott also deteriorated mentally. One of the many curses of multiple sclerosis is that the inability to control limbs, the shaking—and especially the slurred speech, the wild intonation, suddenly loud then inaudibly soft—are too readily assumed by the inexperienced and ignorant, no matter how well-meaning they are, to be signs of mental infirmity.

It hurt Chloe more, perhaps, than it did Scott himself, when a waiter taking an order talked-down to him, kindness itself, but speaking so slowly, and choosing such simple words and basic syntax—as though Scott were retarded. Too often a waiter would ask "what does he want?" and Chloe would bristle and say "ASK him!"—with an unsaid "for fuck's sake!"

All that being so, if not a deterioration there was a strange emotional progression running alongside Scott's inexorable physical debility. An ever-more-exposed rawness. A tendency to cry, at the oddest things. Whether it was something he found funny, or sad, or beautiful, his emotional response was increasingly extreme, and more often than not it ended in tears. Tears of laughter, tears of sadness, or tears because the thing—whatever it was—was to him so beautiful, so wonderful, he shook his head first of all, in awe of it, and then he cried—but happily: that's the important thing: whatever it was, it filled him with so much happiness, his tears burst out from him.

It could be something as mundane as a joke in an episode of 'Friends'—Scott would laugh himself into tears. Or the sight of a child in the sand-pit helping his father build a castle—Scott would smile himself into tears.

When they went down to Venice Beach, he liked to be taken onto Santa Monica Pier and to be left in his wheelchair to watch the pelicans diving for fish, and to look out for dolphins, while the rest of the Quakers rollerbladed on the cycle track. You might say it was insensitive of them to underline his incapacity by doing what he hadn't been able to do for so very long: but Scott was alive to all of that, and impervious to it, and it was usually he who came up with the suggestion that they all go down to Venice and enjoy themselves on the track while he looked for dolphins.

They often talked about it, how much he loved to see those dolphins swim by. The strange way he came to stare at them when they made an appearance (which wasn't by any means on every trip), with such veneration in his eyes, as though he were looking at creatures from mythology or from heaven itself; and how his tears started to flow when they 'showed their backs above the water'.

"*Look at them. They're incredible*," he used to say, his face contorted with delight, and sometimes amazement—as though he'd never seen them before. "*They're beautiful.*"

It was not at all easy for any of the Quakers who was with Scott at such a time—smiling and agreeing the dolphins were indeed beautiful, or the joke on 'Friends' was indeed funny; but falling far below the emotional benchmark Scott had set, however hard they tried to match him, and feeling they were disappointing him by their more measured response.

The time came when Scott couldn't say anything at all when he saw a pod leap through the waves. He pointed at them and made a peculiar noise, as though he were in pain . . . "*Ah . . . ah . . . ah...*" and he burst into unashamed tears and laughter, turning round to make sure they had seen them, and that they fully appreciated the miracle swimming by, leaping though the air, as much as he appreciated it himself.

The truth is, it was acutely embarrassing for them and they didn't know where to look or what to say, and they came to wish that the Pacific had been devoid of all dolphin life.

"*Ah . . . ah . . . ah...*"

9

A Little Accident

As head-on collisions go, the accident was not a serious one; and no-one was badly injured. The cars took the brunt of it—and horrific as the broken fenders and the dented and seared bodywork might have looked, neither vehicle came even close to being written-off; and when the time came to clear the road of them each could have been driven to its own garage, easily and safely, instead of being hauled onto the tow-away trucks they used to deliver them back home.

The other driver didn't get as far as insisting that the traffic cops were involved—even though he was bursting to, being for the first time in his driving life the wronged party in a traffic accident—because a CHP officer was passing and had dismounted from his Kawasaki before the driver had unstrapped his seat belt.

They exchanged insurance details, names and addresses, in the usual way. The officer took brief statements from each driver and from passers-by, and the majority voice was that Scott had approached the junction with half of his car on the wrong side of the road.

The officer at first mistook Scott's speech defects for drunkenness, and arrested him. Then the involuntary shaking of his head, his fluttering eyes, and his inability to stand, were diagnosed as signs of concussion—maybe much worse—and the officer radioed for an ambulance. All Scott had suffered was a graze to his head: the rest of the 'symptoms' were everyday Scott.

The game was up, and he knew it. The wheelchair and the specially adapted car should have been a give-away before he even opened his mouth. He put up no resistance to the ambulance, submitted to the medical examination, answered the unending questions, and was unsurprised at the disbelief his answers generated. So much was inevitable: but it was the *kindness*, oddly, the *kindness* that he hadn't expected, and which pained him the most.

He gave Chloe's details as the person to contact. When he was asked who was his next of kin he said he didn't know—and on saying so, said it again, and nearly broke down at the realisation of it. They told him not to worry and that they were sure his friend would know, speaking to him as though he were mentally impaired.

10

Rome

"You wouldn't exactly call it a party, *Scottino*, but it was a celebration of sorts. And Scott was determined to have it, that you can be sure.

"I picked him up from the hospital, and we drove back to Larrabee without mentioning the unmentionable subject. I had not even tried to work out in my head the best way to approach it. But one thing I was certain, and had made up my mind: Scott must now keep the promise he had given to me—and so earnestly, *si*? In exactly the same car, sitting in the same seat—not too far from the same road, if I am right—all those weeks ago."

> *'No arguments?'*
>
> *'No arguments.'*
>
> *'My decision?'*
>
> *'Your call.'*

"I am sure of it that Scott perfectly understood it was inevitable, what lay ahead. There was something about his manner—I don't know, I can't 'put my finger on it', as you like to say—he had no 'ifs', or 'buts', or other excuses, or any more of his emotional blackmail: remember that nonsense? Nothing left in his little store of word-weapons to keep away what neither of us had the courage, or inclination if I am honest with you, to mention in our conversation.

"So if there were more silences on that drive home, than talking, you will appreciate why.

"But every silence had the 'unmentionable' hammering at its doors; and each of us spoke as soon as we could think of something to say, at the speed of machine-guns, to drown-out the terrible noise of that silence.

"The advertisements by the road—what do you call them?"

"Billboards."

"The Bill Boards were determined to remind us –

'*Come to the Florida* **KEYS**!'

"The word leapt out at us, the way cartoon eyes do when they are astonished.

"A West Hollywood 'Lock and **KEY**' *soirée* shouted at us from the side of a passing bus.

"Every other shop was a 24 Hour shoe-repair that cut **KEYS**—'*at any time of the day or night*'

"Even when we approached Larrabee, where I thought we might be safe on the Strip, there were flying-posters all along the way, advertising a concert by '*A Perfect Circle*', at Gazzari's old **KEY** Club on Sunset.

"A perfect circle," said his godson. "What about that, huh?"

* * *

"My car, of course, was not 'wheelchair friendly' like the cars the dealer had shown us in Glendale. It was a sports coupé."

"I just can't see you in a sports coupé!" said the young man.

"What is so funny?"

"I just can't see you . . . getting in and out…"

"Well try to imagine what a tortured business we had of it, positioning Scott into the front passenger seat, even with the lid open –"

"Roof."

"Securing the wheelchair into the little back seats of my car, my sports coupé that is so funny it makes you laugh, it was a nightmare task, let me tell you. And the whole business of it had to be repeated, *in ordine inverso*, when we parked at Larrabee.

"The moment I was in dread was approaching fast. We took the elevator without speaking, except as to little politeness such as '*come on up*' from Scott, and '*let me do that*' when Scott couldn't press the right button.

"Once inside Scott's studio apartment, I closed the door, making something of a statement out of it, eh?

'*I guess it's time then*,' Scott said.

"I nodded back to my friend. His speech was very slurred, but I got the meaning of it.

'*Do me this one favour.*'

'*You said 'no argument'.*'

'*No. Listen. You got me wrong. 'Course I'll give 'em to you, like I said I would. But I don't want to just hand them over. Now. Not like this. Like I'm beaten. I want to . . . kind of make a big thing of it . . .*'

"I agreed, of course, to 'let him make a big thing of it'. How could I not agree?

"It became, perhaps, the worst night of my life."

11

A Good Thing, Not a Bad Thing

"The Ceremony of the Keys!" proclaimed Tom.

The cork was popped. The sparkling wine overflowed. The Dutch guy played his part and knelt in front of Scott's chair, presenting him with a velvet cushion for the keys—and everyone cheered.

"This is getting ridiculous," muttered Didier.

Scott could not have been more delighted with the charade. He dropped both sets of car-keys into the cushion, and Chloe ceremoniously cut the cake.

They clapped, and hurrah'd, and laughed, and hugged Scott, and hugged each other, and took flash-photos, and cheered again, and were about as depressed and miserable as they had ever been. When it came to a point where Scott was enjoying it so much he might just laugh himself into embarrassing everyone, Tyler collared Billy and asked –

"How old are you now?"

"Ten Sir."

"A boy of ten doesn't have to call me Sir," said Tyler.

"I like it," said Madison.

"It's cute," said Chloe.

"It's how he's been brought up," said Scott.

Then Billy added—"It's a good thing, not a bad thing," and everyone laughed and clapped all over again, though Billy didn't quite see why. Scott was so proud of him he pulled Billy into a hug, and cried over his shoulder.

Billy thought the 'hug-deal' went on far too long, and far too tight, and he couldn't wait to wriggle himself free from it.

* * *

It is hardly surprising that Scott's speech deteriorated after all that had happened that day, worse and worse throughout the night, to the point where it was difficult, even for those who recognised the patterns of it, to understand a word he was saying.

The party dwindled until nightfall, and it was only Chloe who remained. When Scott asked her to come out for a 'walk', she correctly interpreted the '*alk*' sound and they left the apartment, alone together like in the old days, and headed down Larrabee towards Sunset and the majestic jacaranda trees now in their full blue mist of bloom in the streets below.

She had long ceased to be sad at his calling these little excursions 'walks'—Scott driving his motorised wheelchair at a snail's pace through the neighbourhood, in the patient company of whomever would accompany him. He loved them so much, she would have called them anything he wanted.

It used to be, when he could still walk, that *she* dictated these journeys, having the final say of the helper as to what streets she took him across, and how far she was willing to go before she turned him back. But the imprisonment of his wheelchair had paradoxically given Scott a new independence; and that night *he* did the steering of Chloe, much against her inner wishes, towards their old haunt behind the little strip of shops with the laundry and Jerry Seinfeld's photograph in the window, where once they had dreamed—and had since awoken.

Everything conceivable was different from how it was when they last visited the lonely, lovely, sad old place. The dirt-yard was tarmacked over and was used as the official parking-lot for the restaurant, with marked-out bays. Their wooden bench was gone. There was no view across the long miles to the airport, and a high brick wall protecting cars from the precipice was as far as anyone could see, unless they stood on tip-toe and looked over it. The quiet of lovers' trysts was replaced by the to-and-fro of valet parking, and they were asked to leave almost as soon as they had arrived, by a valet who needed the space so he could park, of all vehicles—a black truck.

Neither cared, but each was disappointed for the other. Scott shrugged a resigned shrug at Chloe, and they left. As they trundled up the steep slope of Larrabee Street, Scott said something to her—though she understood not a word. It would be heartless, shameful, and I wouldn't do it under any compulsion, to set down on paper a phonetic reproduction of the wild sounds he made; and you, the reader, shall see what Scott thought Chloe could hear -

"It keeps changing, and it's never what you expect, but it's not bad, is it?"

She hadn't a clue what he had said, and gave him a quizzical look which he interpreted as "What isn't? What isn't bad?"

"Life," he said.

She couldn't have begun to guess what he was trying to tell her: but the tune of it, the rough melody of his incomprehensible mumbling, all vowel sounds, suggested that an appropriate response might be 'No', and that's what she hesitatingly replied: "No."

"No. It's not that bad," he said.

They returned to the apartment block in silence, '*said their goodnights, their good lucks and felt their different ways into the dark of their different rooms, and the comfort of their different beds.*'

And they never spoke again.

* * *

Just before dawn the following morning, Scott dressed, fed Squid, took a third set of car keys which had been secretly cut, and just as secretly hidden, and drove his damaged, disabled-friendly car to Santa Monica. He parked as close to the pier as he could, lowered himself in his motorized chair down the motorized platform onto the sidewalk, and drove up the ramp onto the deserted pier, across to where a gap in the railings was ribboned-off around some incompleted repair.

Looking straight ahead of him, with no expression either of resolve or despair—or anything at all—Scott aimed the slow-moving, monotonously whining, electric-powered chair through the ribbon, through the gap in the railings, up to the edge and over the side of the pier into the swirling Ocean.

It is unforgivably sentimental even to allow it in a fleeting moment of weakness, but wouldn't it be wonderful, and fuel an absurd and irrational hope of things better than we dare dream of, if it was out of pity that the sharks and sea scavengers left Scott's body untouched? He was washed up on Huntington Beach a couple of days later, unscathed, at peace, and strangely beautiful as he lay dead in the sand.

Immediately before he was discovered by an early-morning jogger, a pod of dolphins swam by, very close inshore.

Eight

1

Nella Miseria

Scott was not known to have been in recent contact with any of his immediate family, and when the Dutch guy went about the task of trying to find relatives to inform of Scott's death it began to look as though there *was* no immediate family. He found a distant cousin who in turn offered to coordinate the promulgation of the news to all other known relations, whether immediate or not, whom decency and formality required telling. The day after they first spoke, the distant cousin telephoned to ask if a cremation could be arranged in California, adding *'whatever expense was involved would of course be met'*.

No kin of Scott's felt they were close enough or knew their drowned cousin well enough for their presence at the service to be necessary, or anything other than mildly hypocritical. So it came to pass that the last remains of Scott were turned to ashes with only Chloe, the Dutch guy, Tyler, Madison, Didier and Tom to bear witness.

. . . And Squid. Tom had Squid in the back of his car, staring at the crematorium through the rear window.

Valeria did not attend, nor did she tell Billy that the funeral was taking place. When she casually slipped it into conversation the next day, Billy burst into tears and locked himself in his room and stayed there two whole nights. He only came out after a desperate Valeria had called Tyler to drive down to Abbot Kinney and coax him out with some food and a soda. Billy opened the door slowly, backed away from any kind of physical contact—from either of them—looked hard at his mother and said:

"I ain't never gonna let you see me cry again. Ever."

Valeria said:

"'I'm not. I'm not going to'. Not 'I ain't never'."

Then she had her own emotional moment, of a kind, and walked away from her son with a handkerchief at her nose.

After the awful service, and the piped organ music, and the coffin disappearing like luggage at the airport, or a magician's trick, and the mauve smoke (that only Squid saw billowing from the chimney), they made their way back to Larrabee: Madison driving Chloe, and the men following, each in his own car. For the remainder of the day and deep into the night they sat around Madison's kitchen table, once again working their way through the miscellany of bottles she kept in the little wooden rack screwed to the wall.

When Madison emptied a bottle of red wine into her glass and stood to take another from the wine-rack, the Dutch guy jumped to his feet and snatched the bottle from her hand. No one understood why.

"Don't. Please. Ti prego. Let me."

He pulled the cork, put the opened bottle on the table, and left the room. He returned a couple of minutes later, red-eyed. But they were all red-eyed that night.

It is commonplace at times like these for the qualities of the deceased to be slightly exaggerated, and it is poignant, not foolish, that it is so: it should be so. But when the surviving Quakers shared their remembered praises of Scott it was difficult for them to say anything that didn't seem to sell him short. Many a choked sentiment ended with a tearful Chloe finding solace in Tyler's arms, or a tearful Tom in Madison's.

Squid lay in his re-housed basket, his head on folded paws, looking at one of them, then another, aware that things were terrible, and needing repeated assurance that he had done nothing wrong. He picked-up on the fact that he was the theme of many a worried conversation, and that distressed him even more—with good reason: Valeria was adamant that 'no way' would she take Squid back:

'What part of 'no way' do you not understand?'

—as though she had thought of that silly little put-down herself.

As they all knew, and she knew they all knew, her house was perfectly large enough, and the yard more than ample—Squid had lived there before!—and Billy was desperate for her to say 'yes'. Many a smaller house in that street had a larger family and a bigger dog; which might, by anyone other than Valeria, have had to be excused-away with some weak lie. But the hardness of truth gave Valeria an even harder pleasure—certainly no embarrassment—because it spelled it out in plain English, to the adults as well as to the child, that she simply didn't *want* the animal and all its associations back in her house. She rather wished she lived on a ranch, so her point could be less ambiguous.

Valeria never came out of these hurtful gestures with any identifiable harm to herself: her suffering was more subtle, to be found in the overarching damage done her every day in the dreadful world she had created for herself. But she was adept at cutting off someone else's nose to spite yet another person's face. She knew her rejection of Squid would disappoint Billy deeply—bitterly, uncomprehendingly—and she didn't care. It was important to her, and she had a perverse comfort in it, that Billy saw how much she hated Scott for becoming ill and ruining her life; how much she regretted ever allowing him back *into* her life; and she was determined Billy should not be able to salvage even a dog out of it, when she had lost everything. She never thought it a possibility that the loss of his surrogate father might have devastated Billy as much (if not far more) than the loss of her actual husband had devastated her. A great many times did she have to say—and when she didn't have to, she brought the subject up so that she might—that her final answer was 'NO!' And she revelled in her ever-repeated question, predicated on the absurd proposition that there was a part of 'no' they might not understand.

So as the remaining Quakers—without Valeria—sat in Madison's kitchen, slowly drinking more than they should, eating less than they needed, talking away the interminable hours before they could leave and go to their beds (Chloe sedated and sleeping—and Tyler at last being able, alone in his room, to let go his self-restraint in a way he thought impermissible in company). And with one or another of them going to the forlorn dog to pet him, and tell him *'it was alright'*, the talk reverted again and again to *'what were they going to do about Squid'*. And again and again no one could think of an answer. Before parting they decided on the temporary expedient of lodging Squid up in Tom's place in the Hills while they wracked their brains for a permanent solution.

When she heard of this, Valeria was somewhat vexed: she would have preferred, indeed she had assumed it would be so, that Squid be forced to return to the rescue centre (as though he had broken the terms of his parole)—which, unless another rescue were forthcoming, was but a staging-post to the pound and a lethal injection.

Irrespective of Valeria's elegant solution, however, up to the Hollywood Hills went Squid. His dog-bed was put in the hallway, where Nimrod sat in his chair guarding the house and now had canine support. Squid, alone in his basket at night, stared at Nimrod often and long, never quite 'making him out': but Nimrod never paid any attention to Squid—so far as I am aware.

In the short-term it worked out pretty well. Up on that large deck with its panoramic view of Studio City, and the amazing quiet of night—yet only five minutes from Sunset Boulevard—and stars in the sky above as well in the houses down below, Squid had found a more splendid accommodation than many a human manages for himself, let alone for his dog. With a large kennel for shade, and plenty of gophers and squirrels to chase-off, the occasional skunk, and the comings and goings of devoted men of the Church, he had a good time of it boarding in the Hollywood Hills with Tom, who over-fed him in about the same ratio as he under-fed himself.

They took turns walking him—in Runyon Canyon, not far from Tom, or in the Laurel Canyon dog park further along Mulholland—just as they had when Squid lived with the ailing Scott; and Squid himself seemed wildly enthusiastic with the arrangement, scraping Tom's front door with his paws when they arrived back home.

But even Tom, as obliging a man as you could wish to find, made it clear that the solution was temporary, and they would have to work out something more permanent, whatever that might be.

"Nimrod might get jealous," he said feebly. "So we'd better sort it out soon."

They didn't have to: events overtook the need.

2

Rome

"It may be I am the only one who thinks so—which is not likely—but if the trip was meant to lift our spirits, it was a failure. A disaster. '*You get the picture*', as you like to say?"

"I don't think I have *ever* said—"

"It was Didier's idea. To go down to Tijuana. '*We needed to do something to cheer ourselves up*', so he claimed. Hah! To use your favourite expression—'*yeah, right!*'"

"Why do you keep—"

"I am certain he only wanted a free car-journey. Tijuana was, as you would say,—"

"*I* would say…?"

"—it was his 'one-stop-shopping destination' for the uppers and the downers. You understand? You know Tijuana?"

"So I am allowed to speak?" said his godson. "Sure I know Tijuana."

"I was simply asking," said the old man.

"Everyone in LA goes there for steroids and sleeping pills and valium and shit. I mean everyone—*You get the picture?*"

"I am not impressed, *Scottino*. I hope you do not buy the sleeping pills and the steroids and the shit? Or perhaps it is worse, maybe?"

"Most revered godfather . . . back off! Please? I'm cool. I'm good."

"I hope so."

"But your loving godson has to laugh (if he is permitted) at the way I can just go to a doctor in Tijuana and he'll write me a prescription . . . for anything. In Tijuana, twenty dollars and it's yours."

"It's disgraceful."

"It's awesome. You see a doc in LA, and he says '*so what seems to be the problem?*' In Tijuana the doc says '*so what do you want?*' Now that's what I call healthcare."

His godfather clucked disapproval, and continued—

"The insignificance of the border-crossing amazed me. The divide between one of the great civilisations in history, and the USA, was *unmanned*. How do you call it? Swinging metal bars, eight feet or so in height, like the gates at a Zoo, with horizontal iron teeth that move in one direction only, so you can enter—but not exit. How do you call it?"

"A turnstile."

"They made a fuss of it, Didier and Tom. I think they were drunk, or high. They were like a Laurel and Hardy film, the way they pushed and pulled at the bars, and got stuck, and fell through the other side.

'*Welcome to Mehico!*' said Didier, in a ridiculous Austro-Latino accent.

'*Is this it?*' said Tom.

"Tom could be forgiven for asking, in my view, because there was nothing to see but wasteland, crudely fenced off, and a little pathway leading to nowhere.

'*Sure,*' said Didier. '*This is it. Follow me. Mehico is beeg country, señor. Eez beeg!*'

"We took the path for fifty or so metres until it opened onto a small *piazza*, which had a peculiarity about it, to my mind, perhaps unique amongst the *piazze* of the world, in that every other shop was *una farmacia*, with a green cross hanging over the sidewalk, you know the one I mean? Of course you know: you purchase your steroids and sleeping pills and shit there—"

"You got that right."

"And next to every *farmacia*, it will be very familiar to you, there is a doctor's surgery.

"That's where you can get anything you want," said his godson.

'*Where can I get something to drink?*' asked Tom.

'The sombreros and the Mariachi bands are the other end of a cab ride,' said Didier. *'This is the medical quarter. They cater for a different kind of tourist.'*

"You will appreciate how much I was reassured when Didier explained to me that these descendants of Hippocrates would not prescribe drugs for pleasure . . . *ricreativo...*

"You have to go into the main square for those," said his godson.

"Didier told Tom he should limit his request at the doctor's surgery to the more acceptable shopping-list of sleeping pills, Valium, Xanax, steroids, horse-tranquilizers, phials of stem-cells for the intra-venous injection, and anti-ageing products made from aborted foetuses."

"Wow!" said the young man. "I missed out. I only ever got myself steroids—"

"And *'sleeping pills and shit'*. You are not at all funny."

His godson seemed to think otherwise. The old man shook his head and continued -

"We agreed to part and meet again at a *ristorante* in the main square in a half-hour: Tom was no more than twenty minutes. When Didier found us (late, of course) at a pavement table I saw that his sports bag was stuffed—I must presume with sports gear. *'Yeah right'*, eh? He was very edgy, even more than he had been on the drive down, and he wanted to set-off immediately. He told Tom to ask for the remainder of his *tortilla* 'to go', because we needed to beat the afternoon rush back to the USA. At least, that is the reason he gave.

"If the journey into Mexico was down a little pathway in the desert, the journey back into America was an epic battle in a jungle of glass and steel, against an army of *poliziotti* who had pre-decided to stop *anyone* crossing the border. We entered a huge fortress of a building, the largest Immigration Hall you have seen anywhere in the world, divided into lines of first-time entrants, as well as *supplicanti* for re-admission like ourselves. The lines were separated from each other by ropes—with no easy identification of which lane to join, and numerous shouted orders from angry uniformed *poliziotti*—whichever lane we joined, it was the wrong one!

"Tom was immediately spotted as someone attempting to take *food* into America! How could he dare to do such a thing? Eh? Not making any sense to me as English, and defying analysis in any language I think, the crude, barked-out orders Tom received from a uniformed woman—who, I should mention, was squeezed into tight-fitting striped pants, and when she walked . . . what is it that ducks do?"

"Ducks?"

"What is the word for what they do? When they walk."

"Waddle."

"*Perfetto*. She 'waddled' over to Tom and shouted something at him which I guessed to be a command that under NO circumstances was he to take his half-eaten tortilla across the border. This Harpy, this over-weight Gorgon—"

"This duck."

"She was not at all pleased that Tom's solution to the problem she had made for him was to eat his tortilla; which he did right in front of her eyes; not intending defiance, I am sure—but looking like it, I am equally sure. Tom was dragged out of the line for more detailed investigation, and so were we all, because we were with him. It was terrible. We emptied our pockets and I was strip-searched."

"You weren't!"

"I almost was. Nothing was found, of course, not even on Tom, and we were allowed to re-join the line—all the way back at the end of it, naturally.

"But Didier . . . *mio Dio*! He was required to unzip his sports bag—and out there spilled, as from *una cornucopia*, a cascade of forbidden narcotics."

"Fantastic! Was he arrested?" asked his godson.

"The importance of the written prescription now became clear to me: Didier waived pieces of paper that accounted for every single drug. He said (and I think it was truthful) they were all prescribed by a qualified doctor: he claimed (he was lying of course) that as a US citizen he believed he was entitled to bring back any medicines a doctor had prescribed for him. He was taken away for further questioning by a tough-looking man who I heard say:

> *'This is not my first time at the rodeo.'*

"All we could do, after we had had our documentation checked and double-checked, and mysterious entries were made onto a computer screen, and after we were fingerprinted, photographed, asked why we had been to Mexico ('I'd never been there before' was regarded as *'smart-ass'*: that was what they said: and Tom's documentation was checked again)—all we could do when we had survived the terrible ordeal, was to wait on the American side of the border and hope everything would work itself out for Didier—who, you will understand, must have been through this process a hundred times and must *'know the ropes'*? Eh? But I was concerned for him."

"Who had the keys to his car?"

"So we did not wait for him out of loyalty or friendship. You have made your point. Eventually, after it seemed to me more than an hour, Didier walked through the gates, one in a crowd of twenty or so, shaken, and a little dazed—remember how they came out of the spacecraft at the end of 'Close Encounter of a third Kind'?

"Close Encounters—"

"And this is how he greeted Tom:

> *"What the fuck did you think you were doing? You nearly got me fucking arrested, you fuck!"*

"Which is not polite, eh? Even in America?

"Tom said nothing; and even though I could not help notice that Didier no longer carried his sports bag, or anything else, I kept my curiosity to myself. We walked to the parking lot in silence—*un silenzio totale*—and we drove for some minutes without speaking. It wasn't until we were approaching the road to Laguna, and the car stopped in a jam of traffic, that the silence finally broke.

> *'So how come you were so fucking clean?'* asked Didier.

> *'I ditched my stuff before we went into immigration.'*

> *'You WHAT?'*

'*I didn't like the look of all those uniforms.*'

"It seemed to me Didier spent the next minutes in despair, or disbelief certainly, which he demonstrated by noises through the nose. Finally he said:

'*So you just dumped everything?*'

'*Like I told you.*'

'*In front of everyone?*'

'*No. Discreetly. In a trash can. I may be a 'fuck', but I'm not a stupid fuck.*'

'*You know what you ARE? You're crazy. Totally FUCKING crazy.*'

"A few minutes more, again in silence. Then Tom tried to make it better:

'*I didn't have that much stuff.*'

'*Jesus!*' Didier shook his head.

"If only Tom had stopped there, I think it might have gone away. But, Tom being Tom, he had to say—

'*And discretion is the better part of Valium.*'

"I think at that moment Didier hated Tom, *visceralmente*, perhaps more than he had ever hated any other human being. It could be—I have often thought it might be so—it could be that Didier decided then to make his *vendetta* on Tom."

3

Laguna

As the traffic slowed, once again to a complete halt, Didier's edginess increased. And when the parallel lines of cars at last began to creep forward, without any warning Didier snaked his Landrover across two lanes of stop-start vehicles, and with the gridlocked drivers blaring their horns at him, he headed along the hard-shoulder for the next available exit, which was signposted to Laguna Miguel. "*Bette Davis said it's the only place she was ever happy,*" was the only explanation he gave.

If that was true, it was not difficult for them to see why, as soon as they reached the Ocean. Fresh and salty, healthy, sunny Laguna by the sea. Young men playing volleyball on the beach, vying for the attentions of the groups of young girls watching them—who were evaluating them and chatting not-too-discreetly about who was the 'hottest'. Well-behaved children, every one of whom seemed to be holding a parent with one hand and an ice-cream cone with the other. The great Pacific crashing down on the sand, bringing in the surfers on its back. A strut of land jutting into the waves, with a house built on top of it and blow-hole through the middle of it, where adults and children alike ran the gauntlet at low tide and dashed through, *always* getting soaked, *always* laughing.

And in the centre of Laguna, at the very heart of the freshness, the whole-someness, the perfect families with perfect children, the sun, the beach-sports and the laughter, Didier found a seedy sea-front hotel with an even seedier bar beneath it.

"*What do you say we crash and set off early tomorrow? I can't take this traffic.*"

But the Dutch guy said he needed to get back to LA. They dropped him off where he could pick up a bus.

* * *

Didier put up some resistance, but didn't press the point, and he and Tom took separate rooms. They agreed to meet 'in five', and go shopping for over-night necessities.

It was a hot afternoon, and it had been an enervating drive, so when on their return from the quaint little mall where they made their purchases Didier suggested a beer in the bar beneath the hotel, Tom took him up on it—and, being Tom, he was the one to ask '*what would you like?*' even as they were walking through the entrance—from the brilliant sun into the dark.

The saloon was almost empty—only a handful of men sitting on barstools, each of whom looked over at Tom and Didier with the mild contempt regulars often have, and make sure it is known they have, for strangers. The lighting was low, the sawdust floors dirty, the heavy wooden tables and chairs scattered along the walls uninviting and unoccupied.

Didier sloped off—he said to the rest-room—while Tom bought the beers. But when Tom carried two ice-cold bottles (no glasses were offered) over to the corner where Didier was now sitting, he found him neatly adjusting four lines of white powder on the table-top, so they were approximately the same fatness and length.

"Are you crazy?" whispered Tom, looking round at the men at the bar.

"Don't be so fucking English," said Didier. "It's kewl."

Indeed it was. As a kewcumber. The bartender caught Tom's eye and gave a knowing nod. One of the men on stools turned round to see what was going on, turned back, and downed his shot-glass in one. The strangers, it would seem, were becoming acceptable to the regulars.

Didier thrust a rolled-up twenty-dollar bill into Tom's hand, and Tom dutifully took one line in each nostril.

"Congratulations," said Didier. "You've just taken your first hit of crystal meth."

"What's it do?" grinned Tom.

* * *

It would be tedious to map their progress that night—as tedious as it is for any sober person to arrive late in the company of drunks. Suffice it that Didier—having got Tom 'off his face'—further off than he had ever been in his life—on a drug he had never previously taken, and to a point where he was in some need of chaperoning—Didier deserted him entirely to chat-up a young man who was leaning against the bar, looking every inch the hustler he was. After not too long in negotiations, Didier left the building with the young man—never once looking back at Tom, who sat in his chair as though glued to it, confused and dismayed at the departure of his mentor, his tempter, his corrupter.

How long he sat there, wondering when Didier would return, or *if* he would return, Tom could never afterwards work out. What is certain is that by 2.00 a.m. or so, when the bars were closing, and the town quietening, Tom could be seen wandering along the beach where the sand met the water, clueless as to how to find his way back to the hotel.

The sluggish sea looked to him as thick as tar; and on occasion Tom thought he could see a whale leaping out of the waves and slapping back into them with a gigantic, slow-motion, viscous splash. He stared at the blackness for minutes at a time, waiting for another whale—which would never come: there were no whales: only the surf.

Tiny orange-red lights, wandering a few feet above the sand, pulsing brighter for just a second or two, then dimmer again, fascinated Tom and drew his dilated eyes away from the ocean. He pondered them for an age, wondering if they might be scaled-down alien spacecraft: why, he reasoned, should aliens be the same size as humans? Sometimes a light would move horizontally towards another light. Sometimes the lights would disappear altogether. Then one of the lights floated slowly towards him.

"Are you OK bud?" asked a guy with a cigarette.

"I'm looking for Didier," replied Tom.

In a sane world that insane reply would have had no hope of being of any assistance at all to the stranger: but in that quarter of Laguna, on that stretch of beach, it met with—

"Didier? Are you staying at the hotel?" (There was no question in the man's mind as to which hotel that might be.)

"Yes," said Tom. "I can't find it." He stumbled in an oncoming wave, and stepped further out to sea.

"Here. Get out the water and I'll show you the way."

How easily Tom might have been set upon, beaten, robbed, or even drowned! How little Didier thought of, or cared about, any such possibility! Although in justice to him, he would certainly have cared if even one of those things had actually happened. We mustn't think of him as devoid of decency

But fate had put Tom in the path of a truly Good Samaritan. He led the bewildered, abandoned ingénue to his Hotel, which was only yards away, woke the night porter, located Tom's room, and left Tom lying on his bed, having taken off his wet shoes and socks.

"He's with Didier," he said to the night porter as they closed the door on Tom: which seemed to explain everything.

* * *

"You smell like cat-piss," was Didier's encouragement to Tom to get off his bed and take a shower.

That Didier could manage to be up and ready to go so early in the morning, when he had imbibed, ingested, and even injected, more narcotics in one night than Tom had had in his life, was in large part due to his never having been to bed.

One of the many positive sides of Didier's character was his ability to organise others into doing things for him. A Mexican bus-boy (odd name for someone in their fifties) from a nearby diner arrived at Tom's room with orange juice, doughnuts and hot coffee—the hotel had no facilities for eating, notwithstanding it had facilities for just about everything else. The Mexican set the tray down and waited for payment. There was a little hiatus of embarrassment before Tom nodded towards his wallet, from which Didier took the required sum, rounding it up to the nearest twenty so as not to have to do any maths, and to tip the bus-boy generously. For which the ancient boy thanked Didier profusely in Spanish. When he realised his Spanish was not understood, he told Didier his friend smelt like cat-piss.

Showered and re-hydrated, jump-started by the sugary doughnuts, and smelling more human, Tom settled their account with the hotel and joined Didier at his car.

"I'll drive," said Didier, in a tone that implied it was to be his only contribution to the day, and an excessive one at that.

* * *

Didier dropped Tom off at his hillside home, and gave him a small quarter-bag of white powder.

"It'll help you come down," he said.

4

A Broken-Hearted Heart

Kate Morgan was a woman who is said to have committed suicide at the Hotel Del Coronado, San Diego. She was found on the steps leading to the beach one November morning in 1892, with a gunshot wound to her head, assumed to have been self-inflicted. In spite of evidence being given at her inquest that the bullet could not have come from her own hand-gun, a verdict of suicide was recorded.

Her spirit walks the Hotel, and many claim to have seen her. It is widely believed that she will continue to haunt the seaside steps until the mysterious circumstances of her death are finally resolved.

She is the focus of great pity, and an ever-increasing concern, amongst a host of other spirits, who, like she, are condemned to an interminable delay in their journey between this life and the next. Her anguish is painful to them. Her torment unbearable. Nothing they can say or do seems to bring any comfort to her, and her fellow spirits have held many a long meeting to discuss how best to ameliorate her suffering.

At one such spectral gathering in the mid-1990's, a young-blood with fresh ideas, newly arrived from a car-crash on the 10 Freeway, made a radical proposal which, after hot debate, was adopted by large majority as the course of action most likely to offer a complete solution. Kate Morgan was to go to the Hotel, on a night when 'Ghost Trail' were making a program about her, and knock over a chair in a different room.

Contrary to all expectations, the action failed to give any relief to poor Kate, and she haunts the Hotel del Coronado to this day, as certainly as she ever did.

* * *

The episode was dull. It is difficult to blame it on the total absence of any sign of any spirit making any effort to communicate with any of them—because in all conscience there was little difference between it and the most enthralling episodes of 'Ghost Trail' ever broadcast, if that were the benchmark. Nor was the episode lacking in shrieks (at nothing), off-stage bangs (for no reason), green light from night-vision cameras (for no discernable purpose), or fascinating pseudo-scientific explanations for the various things that had not, if you paid attention, happened at all (surreal is too tame a word)—which were the staple diet for the fans of 'Ghost Trail'.

No. The problem was Madison. She was distant, abstracted—sometimes as though she really were in a trance. But not in an entertaining way (as people in trances or having fits so often are). The spark had gone out of her. Or as her agent, Wendle Stein would have put it—'the heat'. Her mind was somewhere else, and it wasn't anywhere that made good television. Her lacklustre performance was dragging the show down to the very depths of the shallow little pond in which 'Ghost Trail' and a handful of like programs competed with each other. It is just as well that her dead twin sister, Alice, had never existed and was therefore unlikely to be *goin' a hauntin'*, because Alice would have been very worried about Madison. Very worried indeed.

When the recording was over, Courtney asked her new friend for a drink at a local Western-themed bar, and Madison accepted readily—even more readily, you must understand, than she would at any other time when offered a drink.

"There's something wrong, honey, and you just let it all spill out," said Courtney, settling them both down in a snug corner as far away as possible from the line-dancing starting up the other side of the premises. "What can I get you?"

"Anything," said Madison.

"Boy, there sure IS something wrong," said Courtney. "What'll it be?"

"Just a soda," said Madison.

"I think you'd better …"

"Long Island Iced Tea, easy on the cola."

A few minutes later, with her own drink hardly touched, Courtney made the pointed observation—"That's a long iced tea to slip down so fast!" And Madison, apologising for her empty glass, meant to reply that she really should have had a soda first to quench her thirst, but she said—

"I should have had a soda thirst, to quench my first."

"I think you need another, hon. Don't move, I'll get them." Courtney, downed her own liquor in one gulp—an *homage*, maybe, to the line of cowboy-hatted men stamping their boots the other side of the saloon and singing along to a recording of the country and western song "*I can't feel my heart*."

"It's like a soda…" Madison's voice trailed off as Courtney went to the bar. When she returned, she found Madison sobbing.

"*My broken-hearted heart…*" sang the Cowboys.

Courtney let Madison be for a moment, carefully placed the drinks on the table, sat opposite her, and with a sisterly intimacy asked—"Now what's this all about?"

Madison looked up, and one might have thought from the delicacy of her doing it that before replying she took just a modest sip of her drink—but the level of booze descended to about half-way down the glass (and half of what remained was ice) in one unbroken slurp. She leaned forward, as though she was about to speak—but said nothing.

Even the huge stuffed buffalo-head above the table seemed to stretch down towards the pair of women and try to listen-in, it's saucer-eyes goggling at them; and the antlers hanging on the opposite wall might just as well have had ears either side, flicking forwards as they did on the shot moose that used to own them, in order not to miss a word of the impending revelation.

The Cowboys filled in with -

"*And if you find my heart
My broken-hearted heart…*"

But still nothing from Madison. And somehow her glass was now empty, except for a puddle of melting ice.

"*Then tell my eyes they needn't cry no more.*"

It became increasingly likely that Courtney and Madison had stumbled into a *gay* Western Bar. No women were dancing with the men; but the greater giveaway was perhaps the manner in which the Cowboys sang the next line of the lyric—

"*Oooo*"

Madison stared at the dregs in her glass, swilling them around and smiling tipsily at them, as though they had a bitter symbolism only she understood. Once she uttered a scarcely-audible "Oh yes!", laughed quietly, closed her eyes and sank into silence again.

At the words "*You stole my heart and walked right out the door,*" the stamping of cowboy boots was so loud that even from the other side of the saloon it woke Madison from her stupor, and at last she began to tell Courtney her woes.

"It's Tom," she said.

"What about him?" asked Courtney.

"He isn't the same."

"As what?"

"As Tom."

"Now just slow down, honey, and tell me what you're trying to say."

"He's changed."

"How has he changed?"

"I don't think he likes me any more."

"Don't be a silly," said Courtney. "I've seen the two of you together. He's crazy about you."

"I was wondering . . . you know . . . about maybe having some work done..."

"If that's what I think it means, NO."

"Just my nose?"

"NO."

Madison did not press the argument any further; nor did she, internally, strike out the possibility that surgery might be the solution to her perceived unattractiveness. It would be unfair to call good-natured, kind-hearted, generous Madison peevish at *any* time, but she tip-toed towards pouting when she continued -

"He doesn't talk to me."

"He ignores you?"

"No. But he just kind of sinks into his own world and I can't get through to him. I think he may be seeing someone else."

"When did you last have sex?"

Madison blushed.

"Come one honey, I'm a grown up."

"A couple of weeks."

"When did you last get together—I mean see each other, face to face?"

"A couple of days."

"When did you last talk? On the phone?"

"A couple of hours."

"Hon, I don't think you have too much of a problem."

"But it's the *way* he talks. Sometimes he doesn't make sense at all. Sometimes he takes an age to answer. Sometimes he forgets what I've been saying to him. I think he may have forgotten I'm even there."

"I get the picture." Courtney pursed her lips and swilled her drink around, making up her mind how to put—what she *did* put, in these words:

"OK. Now don't take this wrong, but I seen this kind of thing before. Is he on anything?"

"*On anything?*"

"Oh give me a break! Is he on anything or not?"

"No . . . NO! That's not like Tom. That's not like Tom at all. What would he be on?"

"Maybe you better ask him."

"He'd be mad at me. Anyway, he isn't."

"That ain't how it sounds to me. Sounds to me like he may have a little problem. He wouldn't be the first. Who's he hang out with?"

"Didier and Tyler, mostly, when I'm recording."

"Didier? And you think he's clean? Are you kidding me?"

"It's not *that*. I know it's not. But I was wondering . . . if it was something else. What with Didier and all. "

"What else? Spit it out."

"Do you think . . . do you think Tom might be gay?"

"Honey, if he's gay, I'm straight."

It may be my imagination, but I think at that point the Buffallo and the Moose shrank back and minded their own business.

"You mean you didn't know?" said Courtney.

"No . . . I never . . . " faltered Madison.

"C'mon! Everyone knows! Take that scared look right off—I'm not going to eat you. I'm happily married with a beautiful daughter who has two moms. Now. You go and speak direct to Tom and find out what in heck's going on. You go do it. Understand?"

"I guess so."

"Definitely so."

"You really think that's it?" said Madison, slipping back into doubt.

"We'll soon know, won't we?"

"I guess so."

"Would you stop saying that? It's annoying the tits off me. Finish your drink and join me and the boys for a dance."

(Madison's drink had been finished some fifteen minutes.)

"It'll do you good," said Courtney, knocking back her third slug of Southern Comfort and dragging Madison to her feet.

"I don't think..."

"You'll feel a whole lot better. Come on girl. Do what the boss says."

Courtney led Madison over to the line of cowboys, and alongside them they stamped their feet in perfect synchronisation, like a *corps de ballet* at a truck stop. The song continued, relentlessly -

> "*And if I lose my heart, my broken-hearted heart,*
> *I might just lose my mind for evermore.*"

After which, and the cowboys' careless loss of their hearing, their sight, and a miscellany of vital organs for good measure, Madison did indeed feel a whole lot better, and resolved to bring up the difficult subject with Tom, as delicately as she could, at the earliest opportunity.

5

Bad Stuff

"Who's there?"

A voice came from the other side of the door, but it was muffled by the steel plates Tom had recently installed against burglars.

"Who is it?" shouted Tom. "Stand directly in front."

A ghostly image appeared on the CCTV monitor: it was Luke. Tom un-slid the miscellany of bolts and mortice locks that kept the front door secure against an army of imaginary intruders. Then he eased the door open a crack.

"Mornin'," said Luke, unfazed on the other side. "I left my keys back at the apartment. You OK?"

Tom opened the door fully. His haggard face, bloodshot eyes, grinding teeth, the sweat-soaked t-shirt—did Luke need to see any more?

"What time is it?" said Tom, looking over Luke's shoulder—at nothing, that had not moved in the bushes and had made no sound while doing do.

"Just gone eleven. You alone?"

Was he alone? Tom had been unable to answer that question all night long!

"Yeah. Why?" said Tom, still searching the middle distance for an explanation for the movement he had not seen, and the sounds he had not heard.

"I think maybe you need somethin' to eat," said Luke, walking right into the hallway and peering round to see if there were signs of anyone but Tom.

"I'm not hungry," said Tom.

"I'll make you some eggs, while you take a shower maybe?" said Luke. "Have you slept?"

"A little," said Tom, putting up no resistance to Luke's quiet assumption of control—but lying nonetheless.

"This is what we'll do. You clean up and have somethin' to eat. Just as much as you can manage. Don't worry 'bout what you can't. But you got to eat somethin', trust me. You'll feel a different man and it'll help you sleep. And we'll get some liquid inside of you. You got juice, water in the fridge?"

"I think so."

"OK so why don't you go rehydrate while I rustle up the eggs? Then we'll get you to bed."

With one last look into the bushes, Tom closed the front door.

"There's no-one there, Tom. And no-one's goin' to arrive I don't know about."

* * *

Tom gave up the effort of eating after only a couple of mouthfuls of scrambled eggs, and part of a half-slice of buttered toast.

"Good man," said Luke. "When you wake up you'll be wantin' to eat some more, then we'll get you to bed again. You're goin' to be fine. Take one of these, and you'll sleep like a baby. An' I won't leave, so don't you worry."

He handed Tom a small blue pill.

"Thanks," said Tom.

"*De nada*," said Luke.

"I mean it," said Tom.

"I know where you're at, pal, an' I'm here to help."

"I feel…"

"Hey. I don't wanna hear it. You got that? There's nothin' to be ashamed of. Half of LA is on meth." Luke's smile was not in the least patronising. It was almost approving.

"Poor baby Tom. Everythin'll be fine after you get some sleep."

Tom popped the pill, swilled it back with some juice, and went down the stairs to his bedroom.

"An' listen," his ministering angel called after him. "I think you've taken some bad stuff. Next time you better come to me first. D'you hear?"

* * *

He woke up in the dark. Lying on his bed, dripping in sweat. His eyes twitched rapidly. A quiet buzzing pulsed inside his head; like a hornet trapped at a window, but with the rhythmic precision of a metronome.

A black shadow crept up the side of his bed and over his body.

He watched in mute terror as the shadow crawled across the pillow. He slid away from it, quiet as he could, out of the bed and onto the floor, into the corner of the room. He breathed short shallow breaths, so as not to make a sound. His eyes were fixed on the window.

Impenetrable blackness. But something was definitely outside. From the dark emerged an indistinct form. It hovered at the window then moved away.

Tom suffocated a shout. He covered his eyes with both hands. Through the night noises, barely audible, like distant sounds carried on the wind—whispered voices.

'He's on the floor. On the floor. There he is. On the floor.'

'We've found him. He's on the floor.'

'We've found him.'

'Found him. There he is.'

'On the floor.'

Tom curled into a ball, like a hedgehog.

Shadows flitted across the ceiling. A petrified Tom peeped at them from behind his fingers. Standing at the window was the silhouette of a man. It stepped forward just one pace, and stopped. Tom shrank back, hyperventilating. The buzzing in his head crescendo'd to full volume, then died away, slowly, as the dark of the night was pierced by daylight, and he drifted once more into a fitful sleep.

Bright sunshine. Normality.

The figure of the man is only a tree, swaying in the wind. The voices are only the sounds of an air-conditioning unit, with repeated machine noises in the same pitch and the same rhythm of '*We found him*' and '*On the floor: On the floor.*'

6

Bereft

When a dog loses its owner, and after a period of what can only be described as mourning—somehow the dog knows his master isn't away on just another holiday—the dog eventually pulls itself together and gets on with its life, without (we presume) other dogs counselling it to do so. A great many of us humans, however, need extra help and support before we can pull *our* lives together after the death of a loved one. Heaven only knows where we might sink without it.

Valieria was very different from most dogs, and from many a human too, and had been wise enough to have 'got on with her life' some months before Scott died; indeed, she had begun to 'get on with her life' soon after Scott became ill; with the happy consequence that when the inevitable day dawned, albeit before God had intended it, and she became a widow, her prescient action did not merely cushion the awful blow—it meant there was no blow to cushion. In fact, throughout the short time of bereavement (I can find no suitable alternative), although she had sufficient sense of decorum not to go out every night in her party dresses, she could be described as surrounding herself with a luxury of cushions dedicated solely to her pleasure rather than to any 'blow softening'.

She lost no time in spreading news of her loss, and *availability*, amongst the stable of hopefuls she used to take out for regular exercise. But when she was corralling them in her lasso got caught on an unexpected rock.

If she was nothing else, Valeria was industrious. The hours she put in to attract the attentions of unattached men, and—while he lived—to keep the unattached men away from Scott, and from each other, would have been rejected as implausible by a honey-bee. But Valeria's efforts were, as so often hard work is, misdirected, and as a result futile.

When Scott died the reality came bursting rudely into her life that, putting it bluntly, one of her chief attractions to all those unattached men had been that she was attached. And when she gave them the good news (each of them in order of preference, the richest first over a candle-lit dinner, down to the poorest at Hamburger Hamlet) that she was recently widowed, the lukewarm responses of '*I'm so sorry*', '*Isn't that rather sudden?*' and '*What can I say?*'—with no other words to fill the dreadful silence—needed all the blow-softening cushions she could find.

Their faces were ashen. A comforting hand was sometimes placed on hers: either the palm was sweaty, or simply cold. It wasn't unknown for the other hand, at the same time, to empty a full glass of wine in one gulp. It was only a matter of days before her no-longer-clandestine telephone calls to these unattached men were cut short because '*This isn't a good time. I'll call you back.*' Which, with increasing frequency, they didn't.

She finally worked out that the reason they might be meeting less often, or not at all, at the usual bars, was because her men had stopped *using* the usual bars. One of them was so terrified of Valeria's predatory powers, he accepted a job-offer the other side of America and left California without telling her.

Whether it is natural or unnatural, and however much it is to be deplored, it is what happened, and so I shall set it down: Valeria dealt with her bitter disappointments and frustrations by making life as miserable for Billy as it was for herself. The first and the most obvious punishment inflicted on him for having been loved by Scott, and for having loved him in return, was to put a stop to Billy's taking Squid for a walk.

Of course she hadn't the time to drive Billy all the way up to Tom's house just to see a wretched animal that wasn't even his! It was really quite ridiculous. Beyond ridiculous. What was she supposed to do while he walked it? Sit in the car? All that way, just for that? *Did they have any idea how far away she lived?* No one remarked that the journey-time would be about half that which she had forced Scott to travel in order to get to work, every day while his health lasted, as well as many of the days while his health deteriorated.

"He needs to grow up," she told a disbelieving Tyler when he telephoned her to ask what the hell was going on. "Pandering to him every time he throws a sulk isn't going to help."

Tyler said *he* would come and drive Billy up there next Saturday.

"He has chores to do. I can't run this house by myself." Then, waspishly, "I don't have a maid, Tyler." Then, as unpleasantly as possible, "Female or male." Tyler slammed the phone down on her and arrived early the next Saturday morning, unannounced, to collect Billy. Surprisingly Valeria put up no resistance, though her face was thunder. Billy was returned before lunch.

They came to an arrangement by which one or other of the Quakers would take Billy over to Mulholland every other Saturday; the manufactured 'chores' which for some reason could not be undertaken on any other day of the week were done on the Saturdays in between. When the fortnightly pattern of Saturday morning collections was well established, Tyler telephoned late one Friday to say Luke would be picking Billy up the next day instead of him.

"I'm sending my maid", he said.

The truth, not told to Valeria, was that Chloe was waiting in her car with Squid (once her natural enemy, and now her 'darling dog'), around the corner and unseen by Valeria, for Billy to be transferred to them.

It was not long before Luke was turning up at Abbot Kinney on a Saturday morning on a regular basis—more often by far than anyone else.

7

Hector's

"You look GREAT!"

She looked awful.

Hector's was the 'breakfast-meeting' place of choice. With so much to do in the working day, Hollywood gathered there at dawn, and did those things which were less important.

It was somewhere for agents to pretend to their middling-clients that they were active on their behalf; and many a breakfast heard of an actor's name being put forward for this film or that film (and breakfast saw the actor believing it), or of a script enthusiastically received by a studio (upon which it was promptly shown the back door—but the writer wasn't told—not yet—not at Hector's.)

Hector's was also somewhere to have a Bloody Mary at 7.00 am, and Madison sat sipping hers, waiting for Tom to join her for a 'quick bite' before she set off to record the next thrilling episode of 'Ghost Trail'.

She had noticed—she couldn't help but do so—a woman sitting on her own at an adjacent table, who looked as though she might have been in a car accident, or suffered third degree burns in a fire. She thought: "How courageous, to step into the public eye and brave all the staring and the whispered comments!"

But Hector's clientele paid no attention at all to the disfigured woman; nor were there any whispered asides—none that Madison could hear; and she felt guilty for taking frequent peeps at the warped mask which was once a face. But she was drawn to it, time and again, and couldn't keep her eyes from it. Until she heard:

"You look GREAT!"

A creature of similarly mutilated features joined the poor woman at the table. And still no one but Madison stared at them.

Because I don't know their names, I shall call them Accident 1 and Accident 2.

"When did he take the bandages off?" asked Accident 2, her lips achieving a kiss notwithstanding the rest of her head was never closer than six inches.

"About a month ago," said Accident 1. "I been keeping inside…"

"Well, you *got* to! said Accident 2 emphatically.

"Sitting by the pool, you know."

"In the shade I hope!"—this woman was the 'alpha accident'.

She scanned her friend's face, and neck, and behind the ears:

"I told you he was good."

"He said we'd do the nose in stages. D'you think maybe it could still *shave-down* some?" asked Accident 1.

This might have been thought a cruel question, since Accident 2 had no nose at all. The area of her face customarily assigned to the nose was, if anything, concave.

"Give it a couple of months. I waited six before getting my cheeks lifted."

"And they look GREAT!" said Accident 1.

Cosmetic surgery survives in Los Angeles because its victims indulge in a communal lie—namely, that each other looks 'GREAT'. If the truth were told, the whole edifice of plastic surgery (like its reconstructed features) would collapse. If only Los Angeleans were bold enough to say -

"Dear God! You look hideous!"

"So do you!"

—Then the surgeons might have to return to medicine, and making sick people well.

The phenomenon—a determined refusal to admit the truth, sustained by the mutual support of like-minded liars—is not peculiar to the re-adjustment of faces: many interior designers, film makers, *avant-garde* composers, even some modern democracies, are wholly dependent on it; and without it we would not have *"Downton Abbey"*.

Madison's eavesdropping was timely, and her secret toying with the idea of *'having some work done'* ended abruptly, never to recur. Tom joined her at the very moment she resigned herself to her God-given looks.

Tom thoroughly enjoyed breakfast at Hector's. When he went there for the first time and was served a huge, steaming plate of 'Pasta Mama', with thick linguini and soft-cooked eggs, rivers of melted cheese and tangled strands of spinach—at 7.30 in the morning—he knew he had found his perfect restaurant. So when, that morning, he ordered 'just a black coffee', Madison thought it might present exactly the kind of opening she needed—

"Just a coffee?"

"That's what I said."

They sat in silence until the coffee was brought to the table.

"Tom, I've been meaning to ask . . . is there anything wrong?"

"Wrong?"

"With work, up there in the Hills, I don't know . . . with you? Is everything OK?"

"Everything's fine." (A rather flat laugh.)

Again, they sat in silence, Madison taking small bites of her almond croissant and even smaller sips of her Bloody Mary, and Tom doing nothing except stir his coffee.

"Why do you ask?" he said suddenly.

She waited a long time to answer, nearly saying something then sinking back into thoughtful silence a half-dozen times.

"Christ! It's an easy enough question!"

"Tom . . . Don't be angry with me or anything, OK?"

"What about?" said Tom, putting his coffee spoon back in the saucer, then lifting it out and stirring his coffee again.

"I've been worried, that's all. About *you*."

"About me?"

"Are you . . . " she hesitated.

"Am I *what*?"

She still couldn't find the way to put it...

"For crying out loud!" he fairly shouted at her. "What? What? What?"

She *withered* in front of his eyes—it's the best I can do to describe her reaction to his cruel words, and his even more cruel tone of voice. She shrank from him, and withered. Then she leaned towards him, confidentially, and just a little pathetically, and very quietly—

"Doing stuff. You know."

"Ahhhh! I see. That's what this is all about! No Madison. No. I'm not 'doing stuff.'"

He stirred his coffee again, faster. Then he downed the entire cupful in one action.

"I have to go," he said, getting to his feet. He paused at the table, red in the face, and added—

"It does occur to me, though..."

He made a pointed nod towards Madison's Bloody Mary. And if living in America had dulled the edge of his Englishness, his accent, his autocratic manner, then the last few minutes had honed all three again, razor sharp—

"Do you really think you are in the strongest position to be making accusations of that kind?"

With which he left Hector's, letting the door slam behind him.

It was perhaps from that moment that the lines time had traced on Madison's lived-in face sank deeper, and the little channels alcohol had etched on her cheeks became chasms, as though her head were made of plaster-of-Paris and had cracked while it set. And no lotions or mud-baths, not even her dreamed-of surgery, would ever smooth her skin again.

8

More Bad Stuff

On the occasions Didier's discrete 'by appointment' dealer failed to answer his calls, it was likely he was indulging in his own product and would not be available for a day or two; and Didier was forced, if he couldn't wait a day or two, to turn instead to the less than discrete suppliers who regularly set up shop in one or other of the bars along that strip of Santa Monica Boulevard between La Brea and Fairfax where the male prostitutes used to solicit for customers. Maybe they still do. It was known affectionately as '*The Boulevard of Broken Boys*', and the bars which served it did not fail in their duty to be appropriately sleazy.

On such a night—that is, Didier having run out of product and his discrete dealer not answering—he and Tyler cruised eastwards down Santa Monica in search of a 'bump'. Although the car was Didier's, and he was by far the more *au fait* with the locality and all it had to offer, Tyler was driving, because (a) he had to keep his eyes on the road while Didier kept his eyes on the sidewalk, looking for a familiar face, and (b) Didier had already ingested more than enough narcotics to incapacitate him from performing any function traditionally associated with getting a motor vehicle from one place to another.

Rather than park in an area where there was no guarantee the car would still be there when they returned, Didier suggested that Tyler pull up alongside the most likely bar, wait in the drivers' seat, engine running, while he went inside, hopefully to do some quick business. (He had been told, on a failed mission elsewhere, that '*this one was a sure thing*').

He wasn't two seconds gone before one of the hustlers who had been leaning against the wall the opposite side of the road recognised Didier's Range Rover and jay-walked through the traffic purposefully towards it. At the same time, a police patrol car taxied slowly, but intimidatingly—like a manta ray into a bait-ball—westward down the Boulevard. Tyler yanked the gear-box into first and drove-off (as did a number of other vehicles) just as the patrol car twirled its blue lights and let out that odd baby's hiccup of a siren the LA police use to call attention to themselves; and all the hustlers on foot scuttled away as well, *fast*, down side streets and into the shadows of service roads, like seaside crabs into holes in the sand.

Tyler drove round the block, passing the bar twice; but the police were parked opposite and he daren't risk a third circuit. He found Didier, furious and paranoid, some distance along Santa Monica looking for him.

"Where the fuck have you been?"

"There was a cop car."

"You could've got me arrested."

"You could've got *me* arrested!" retaliated Tyler. "You scored?"

"Crap." Didier held up a quarter-bag of white-ish powder.

"You're sure?"

Didier sniffed the top of the bag.

"Crap."

They drove on in silence for a few minutes, each angry with the other, aimlessly eastwards along Santa Monica, until Tyler said—

"I got an idea."

—and made a sudden left up Vine Street.

* * *

It was 2.30 in the morning when they free-wheeled down the steep track off Mulholland; headlights off, engine off, and only the crunch of tyres against stones to give them away—should Tom be awake and listening at that hour. A feint red glow from the ever-booted computers in his workshop spilt out onto the undergrowth that lay below and beyond the deck. Otherwise there was complete dark. No moon. No stars.

They pulled-up fifty or so yards from the house and crept, silent as mice, towards the basement entrance. A sudden scratching and snuffling sound close by, the animal completely hidden in the murk, made them start—and stop.

"Skunk?"

"Deer," said Tyler. "I read in the paper a jogger got himself killed by one recently. Antlers went right through his chest. You shouldn't go out jogging in the dark. Not in the Hills."

Tyler enjoyed panicking Didier when he was high.

A shadow slid across the track. "And there's mountain lions too," said Tyler.

* * *

"He's asleep. I can see him."

Tyler lowered himself noiselessly down onto the mud outside Tom's bed-room window. Didier slid his key into the lock and turned the tumblers with all the delicacy of a life-long safe-breaker. The door inched open. Emboldened by the sound of heavy snoring, they tiptoed into the dark of the basement.

"Luke told me he keeps it in his workshop," whispered Didier.

Tom always locked his workshop. His approach to high-security, however, and he was by no means alone in taking this precaution, was to hang all his keys on a hook in an unlocked cupboard in the hall. The cupboard in the hall was but a short flight of stairs leading up from the basement. And there was no impediment between basement, stairs, and the cupboard in the hall.

* * *

When, after a few failed experiments, they found the correct key and crept into the workshop, motion-activated lights 'popped' on, bulb by bulb, as though the room itself were blinking open its eyes and staring at them. More disconcerting still to the amphetamine-charged minds of the intruders was that Nimrod was sitting on a bench directly facing the door as they entered; and if anybody (or anything) was looking at them—he was.

Every box, jar, caddy, canister, drawer, cabinet, bench, ledge, shelf—every last container was searched, and every surface was swept—but they did not find what they had come for. Even the movie-posters hanging on the walls were eased-out from their hooks to see if anything fell from behind them.

They eyes of a puppet don't, as the eyes of a painting are said to, 'follow you around the room'; but neither Didier nor Tyler, high as kites, could escape the uneasy sensation that Nimrod was watching them, and they were increasingly unnerved by it.

"Sorry dude," said Tyler. "I can't stand this." He took hold of Nimrod and sat him facing the wall.

"Shit!" he said suddenly, and far too loudly, but with a glint in his eye and a premature hint of triumph in his voice.

"*Guess where we haven't looked?*"

He lifted Nimrod off the bench, stood him upright on the floor, and went through each and every one of his pockets—as though Nimrod had failed a preliminary frisking at airport security. Then he held him upside down by his feet, and shook him…

The quarter-bag was filled to about a gram with white crystals of varying size. Tyler waved it in front of his nose, nodding his approval to Didier.

"And such a sweet looking boy!" he said.

Didier took the bag and smelled it too, passing it by his nostrils like a sommelier. Then he opened it, and dabbed the inside with his spit-wet thumb and tasted the dust.

"This is quality. It is *very, very* good!"

Exultant in their success, they tidied the little disturbances they had made, closed every drawer, returned every box and jar to its original position, and were about to replace Nimrod on the bench where they found him when Didier had a brainwave—

"Shall we leave him like that?" he grinned at Tyler. The 'that' being Nimrod standing upright on the floor, facing the door, his head leaning back against the wall, his eyes staring at the ceiling, his jacket undone and his arms outstretched. "It'll freak the shit out of him."

They thought that was an extremely amusing and worthwhile goal, and left Nimrod where he was, their only regret being that they would not be around to see the shit freaked out of Tom as Didier had confidently predicted it would be.

Not at all displeased with themselves, they returned the keys to the upstairs cupboard, sneaked out of the house like the burglars they were, walked back to the car as though on hot coals, and drove their contented way towards the two day's oblivion which Tom's 'quality' quarter-bag promised them.

The mood broke without warning. (Didier had the distressing habit of going from sublime joy to abject misery in a space of time shorter than any science has yet been able to measure.)

"We shouldn't have left him like that," he said in a panic—perversely paranoid in the safety of Tyler's car and a mile from Tom's house, when he had been utterly reckless in the workshop and a hair's breadth from discovery.

"He's going to put two and two together when he can't find his stuff."

"No he's not," said Tyler. "I exchanged it with *our* stuff. Nifty, huh?"

"But it's crap!"

"Do you think Tom's going to know the difference?"

* * *

Although it is hardly worthy of comment that Didier had been unobservant, it has to be said that it was uncharacteristic of Tyler not to have noticed. Maybe it was because he was pre-occupied with his substitution of the street-narcotics (God knows what chemical it was he left for Tom); but if he had for one moment paused to ask himself why Nimrod was down in the workshop and not in his customary seat in the hallway, and if he had looked at all closely at his face while searched his pockets, he would have seen that Nimrod had a .22 calibre bullet hole in his left temple, just behind the ear.

9
Lost

It wasn't as though no one had seen Tom getting more and more weird over the last few months; or that they hadn't talked about it, and often; but no-one fully realised just how much of a mess his head was in. And because no one saw any—or enough—of this (except Luke, who was the principal cause of it; and perhaps Didier, who was indifferent; and Tyler, who of all of them should have done something about it), it never occurred to the remaining Quakers that it might not be such a good idea for Tom to dog-sit Squid while they looked for a permanent home for him.

When Madison arrived one afternoon to pick up Tom and take Squid for a walk in Runyon Canyon, she was shocked—and scared—to find Tom as she'd never seen him before—unshaved, unwashed, eyes like saucers—wandering aimlessly amongst the wild goat-grass below his house, shouting:

"Squid! Squid!"

Tom had been out all night, and had left Squid on the deck with just a bowl of water and some dried food; and when he came back in the early morning, Squid wasn't there. He'd searched the Hills all day, and couldn't find him.

"Squid! Squid!"

Madison, eventually and with great difficulty, took a shivering Tom back inside; his face bright red, as though he had rubella; his scared eyes darting around looking for something, nothing—it didn't really matter what, because it wasn't there. He kept telling Madison to 'hush' because he could hear something outside the window—but of course she couldn't hear anything, for the same-old reason that there was nothing to be heard, except the leaves rustling and the air-conditioning rattling.

Try her best, Madison couldn't get any sense out of Tom, who rambled on and on about people being outside, *if only she would be quiet and listen*. When Tom went out onto the deck, for the twentieth time, to look for these people, sometimes peering through binoculars, Madison called Tyler in a panic—who didn't pick up: he wasn't in a much better state than Tom.

It was an hour of hell for Madison, before Luke arrived in Tyler's car.

He asked Madison to heat some soup, and they *made* Tom drink it—or half of it. Luke gave Tom a little blue pill (Xanex) as an *aperitif*, and a couple of sleeping pills (temazepan) after the soup as a *digestif*. Madison asked if that was OK, and shouldn't they get a doctor, but Luke said he knew what he was doing. Which he did. He'd done it for Tyler a half-hour earlier.

They finally got Tom onto his bed, and went upstairs to discuss what to do next.

"One of us has to stay and look after him," so it seemed obvious to Madison. But Luke said there was nothing more they could do, and his usual unnerving calm escalated to something that lingered on the borders of *a reaction* when Madison disagreed with him. Eventually, they settled it that Luke would stay with Tom while Madison drove around to see if she could find Squid, and make inquiries at neighbouring properties—and the pound if it came to that. Madison set off as agreed.

As soon as her car had disappeared up the track, Luke locked up, left the house, slid into Tyler's car and drove back to his own apartment in the Valley, where an important customer was expecting to pick up a delivery.

10

Dog-Napped

Back then in Los Angeles, and maybe nowadays too, if your dog went missing for any length of time, it could just as easily be it had escaped from the yard and been run over by a car, as it could that it had been eaten by coyotes. Or it may have been kidnapped—'dognapped' they used to call it. Dog-owners would come out of supermarkets to the place in the shade where they had tied their faithful pal to the railings, and find he was not there. They'd shout his name, absurdly, for a half hour or so, then give up and go home. The next day they'd put up notices round trees and lamp-posts, with a bad photograph of the dog, possibly his name, a telephone number, and the offer of a reward. A day or so later they would get a call from someone saying they'd found the dog, and arrangements were made for the 'drop'. There was a tacit understanding that the finder/caller had abducted the animal in the first place, but the pantomime was acted out with no mention of the reality, and grateful thanks were given to the criminal, along with the reward money.

A fraternity who were truly offended to be classed with the dog-nappers were the 'opportunists'. They never *took* a dog, they wouldn't dream of doing such a thing, but if they found one they kept it until the offer of a reward was put about, and then called the owners, as though they had only that moment found the animal; and they claimed the reward accordingly. The 'latter-day opportunists' went a step further and waited a few days until the owners were, hopefully, desperate, and then they telephoned to negotiate a higher sum of money than the advertised reward. For some reason the dog-nappers rarely stooped that low, and tended to ask only for the reward as stated on the 'missing' posters. Maybe they thought dog-napping was as far as they could decently go.

The lowest life in this field of human endeavour were 'the scavengers'—a group who had evolved over time, Darwin–style, from the latter-day opportunists. They found a dog roaming the streets, waited for the 'missing' posters to be put up, and focussed only on the posters offering *no reward at all* and were, for that reason, of *no interest at all* to the opportunists. The scavengers took the initiative in the matter by telephoning and, not to put too fine a point on it, telling the owners that if they didn't pay so many dollars ransom money, the owners would never see their best friend again. More often than not they drew a blank—the reason no money was offered was that there was no money to offer. But every now and then they struck lucky and squeezed a small sum from an impecunious owner.

As it is with their distant and more respectable cousins, the kidnappers of humans, payment of the ransom was a delicate business—satchels left on park benches, etc.—and it didn't always result in the return of the dog. The scavengers were regarded as scum, and the dog-nappers would challenge you to 'settle it outside' if you dared to suggest their simple, honest trade could sink to a *modus operandi* so vile.

When Squid jumped over the rail fencing-off the deck from the Yukka bushes, the goat-grass, the brome and starthistle, and all the creatures that snuck around them at night, he did so not because (as they liked to think) he was looking for Scott, but because Tom was now behaving so strangely he spooked even a dog, and Squid was scared of him.

Squid ran off into the gardens the other side of Mulholland, and soon found himself in the familiar territory of Runyon Canyon, Billy's favoured walking-choice. Nosing around on his own, and exploring places hidden from the well-worn paths, he soon fell into the company of a small pack of coyotes, and he had a whale of a time chasing squirrels with them. Coyotes are cunning animals, bigger than foxes but smaller than wolves, and like to befriend domestic dogs and gain their trust by playing with them—tearing their throats out and eating them only when they become hungry. It keeps the meat fresh, as good as if it were refrigerated, to make sure it stays alive until needed. (I am sure there is human activity of an analogous kind, but I can't quite put my finger on it.)

There was a film crew in Runyon Canyon that day. When Squid and the Coyotes ran by them in the late afternoon the crew weren't shooting anything, just setting up for a night scene. Jeeps and trucks bounced up and down the track from Franklin Avenue, sending clouds of dust and stones into the air behind them. A large lorry with a load of scaffolding, straining up the hill with a groaning engine, and headlights full-on in the dusk, sent the coyotes running to one side of the track and Squid to the other—which saved Squid from the coyote stock-pot he had been earmarked for later that night, but drove him into the hands of a sinister looking vagrant who had walked up into the canyon to see if he could beg or steal some food from the film-crew, and was happily diverted to the possibility of barbequed dog instead. The vagrant took the string tied around his pants and made one end into a small noose. Squid was too friendly to resist a 'here boy!' but too quick for the drunken man when he tried to lasso him, and he slipped easily out of reach with that sideways skid dogs are so adept at.

He trotted back towards the film set, and was made a good old fuss of by some of the crew, until he snatched a sausage-roll from an unguarded table-spread, quickly followed by a slice of pizza (with anchovies and extra cheese). He was contemplating desert when he was chased away by the best boy—(only the best for Squid)—and he scampered off, tolerably well fed, out of the Canyon and into La Cuesta Drive, looking for water to quench the salty aftertaste of the anchovies.

Many a fine film-star's house in the Hollywood Hills has many a fine swimming pool, and Squid was too thirsty to be over-particular about a chlorinated beverage as a complement to his pizza. He was in mid-slurp when a particularly ugly, un-stereotypical pool-boy jabbed at him with the handle end of his long pool-net, and Squid went scurrying away, eastwards and upwards through the grounds of the big houses, taking the odd chlorine-refreshment as he went, sometimes lucky enough to drink from one of those sunken sinks of tap water for rinsing the dirt off feet before swimming. Speculation as to what film-star's foot-dirt he might be privileged to have sent to his stomach entirely eluded him.

He soon found himself back on the broad sweep of Mulholland, which he followed until he came to the Hollywood Bowl Overlook. There he picked up a scent that instantly turned him into a very strange, rather wild creature, wholly unlike the Squid we know: not so much savage but odd, undomesticated, suddenly under the influence of ancient, inherited instinct, quietly following the scent and loping through the Hills—as though he were auditioning for a walk-on part in 'Call of the Wild', but not truly authentic with his loping and unlikely to be cast.

We will jump-cut to the cause of the scent. It was heralded to the brave Hollywood Bowl audience that was gathering for an evening of popular classics and film-scores (without even the promise of fireworks, with which the Hollywood Bowl often rewarded its patrons for staying until the end), by an announcement over the loud speakers:

"Ladies and gentlemen, there is a skunk making its way from the ticket-office to the car park." (Some wit, too near the microphone, remarked that the skunk had obviously purchased a ticket for a better night.)

And sure enough, there was the handsome little animal, for whom the large crowd parted like the red sea, strutting along with his head held high, apparently indifferent to the attention—and respect—he was receiving, except for the *slightest* hint of self-consciousness at the occasional bursts of applause, which he controlled with remarkable aplomb, all things considered.

If only Squid had not, a few minutes earlier, picked up its scent! The skunk would have disappeared into the car park and the bushes beyond it, and the audience would have filed into their uncomfortable seats, envied each-others' picnics, and fidgeted through *Eine kleine Nachtmusik* being played by an 80-piece orchestra. But Squid came charging down the avenue created by the parting crowd, heading straight for the plucky little skunk, making a low gurgling growl that had a primeval menace in it that no-one had ever heard from Squid. (No-one had seen him chase a skunk.)

On sensing the approaching enemy, the skunk lost all sense of decorum, stopped in his tracks, turned and squirted his foul-smelling urine—presumably at Squid, but achieving the kind of widespread spray we associate with a loose length of hosepipe flaying around the flower-beds when the sprinkler has blown off it.

The crowd went wild. There might have been a mass-murderer with an assault weapon firing at random amongst them, and the chaos could not have been greater. A couple of minutes of glorious panic, a lot of shouting, more screaming and running—then the all-too-short entertainment was over.

No-one saw the skunk again, nor Squid—they disappeared as quickly as they had arrived. And no-one was actually splashed with the skunk's urine, either. But a number of music-lovers feigned the necessity of returning home and spreading tomato ketchup over themselves according to the old remedy, rather than endure the concert.

Squid didn't catch the skunk, and continued nose to the ground, following the skunk's and others' scents, until he found himself a mile or so to the West, at the lower edge of the Laurel Canyon dog park, which was closed for the night. But the gate was swinging loose.

There was a notice at the entrance warning dog-owners about sightings of mountain lions. Squid paused in front of it, almost as though he could read it.; and while he was to all insane appearances preoccupied with it, a sack was thrown over his head and he was seized—not by a 'dog-napper' (of whom the park knew plenty) but by a 'scavenger' who had driven by the park on his way home, like a fisherman heading for port who keeps a line trailing behind the boat on the off-chance.

Barking, snarling, yelping, kicking-out with all four of his legs, Squid was manhandled into the back of a van and driven away with a couple of other unfortunate bagged-up mutts to keep him company, to some hide-out we shall never be taken to—although we shall hear a good deal more about Squid, in due course.

11

Rome

"We put posters on all the lampposts, and in all the shop-windows in the area—then on the lampposts and shop windows further away—then (so it seemed to me) we pasted them over the whole of Los Angeles.

"Madison paid for an advertisement, full page, in all the local newspapers, but with no result. I told the papers to run it for a second week . . . *ma non ho fatto niente.*

"We toured the area in our cars, day after day, sometimes with Billy, sometimes without him, sometimes in pairs, sometimes on our own: but there was never any sign of Squid.

"In my eyes, it seemed that Chloe, for no good reason, had a deep-down guilt that she was the cause of everything that had gone wrong. And Tyler thought *he* was to blame (with better reason, eh?). Even Madison felt guilty, or responsible for Tom it may be—she told me she was sure she could have stopped it '*if only she had done something sooner*'. She kept saying it. "*If only I had done something sooner!*" Again and again. *Come sempre.* But it 'hit a raw nerve', as you like to say, with me also. I had seen things with my own eyes . . . and I did nothing. Nothing, *Scottino*—Nothing.

"And although we were so sorry for young Billy, and felt for him so badly—*mio Dio!* Is there language for it?—and we would do anything we could to help him . . . our endless search for Squid—relentless, it was: *ossessivo*—it was not about our guilt, or about Billy. Now I look back on it I can see it was about something very different. There was an unborn thought in our minds that somehow, in some strange way . . . what is it, when you can never manage to touch the idea, to work out what it means? It is always near you, but you can't hold it?

"Elusive?"

"*Sfuggente*. I had this strange, 'elusive', half-born thought, that we weren't doing all the things we did, night and day, for the sake of Squid, or Billy, or even in memory of Scott—we were doing it *for ourselves*. We could not permit it—do you see?—we could not bear it—to let Scott die twice."

12
An Acrylic

Billy looked at the address on the business card and made sure he had enough change for the two busses he would need to take him to the junction of Sunset and Eastern Avenue, and then back again. He'd tried telephoning the number a couple of times, when his mother was out, but he never got an answer.

He was told by the charming Motel receptionist to 'scram before she called the cops', but he gave the card to her, and like Madison before him but with even less grace, he was shown into the great man's offices.

"Of course I remember you my dear boy!" Wendle was telling the truth, strange though it was for him to find himself doing so.

"Does your mother know? Of course she does! Or you wouldn't be here, would you?"

"I…"

"I'll tell you what, Johnny, don't say anything more about your mother, OK?" So far, Billy had not mentioned her.

"It's enough she's given her permission, and I don't need to hear any—what more is there to hear? Nothing I can think of. Can you?"

"Nothing, Sir."

"Good boy. So you'd like to be on WEB NBC? And why shouldn't you? Is your dog signed up with anyone?"

"I don't think so. No Sir."

"Well we'll need to get you both an audition. But I'm sure that'll just be a formality. I can't tell you how pleased…You are *exactly* what the show . . . I don't know what it is, but you are it. No doubt about that. You are *it*, dear boy. Where is your lovely dog? You say he's not represented?"

When at last he was allowed to speak, Billy told Wendle a very different tale from anything he had imagined he was going to hear. As he might have said—how could he have predicted it? You tell me.

"Oh. I see. I see. That is . . . well, it's some story. I wasn't expecting . . . not quite…why should I?"

He thought, long and hard—for a couple of seconds.

"But it's *splendid!* I mean it's terrible, of course. But that is definitely some story! It's got *legs* dear boy. If ever anything had legs, it's got legs."

"It's a dog."

"You mistake me my dear. The story. It's got . . . what's the word? But it's got it. Heart. That's the word. Heat. Splendid! I mean it. Terrible! You're going to be famous, my dear."

"I just want my dog back."

"Of course you do. And that's what I want too. My dear boy! *Everybody* wants your dog back. What else would anybody want? You tell.... This is splendid! And terrible. Awful. Couldn't be worse."

Wendle was getting over-excited.

"Now. What's your number? Is it OK to call you at home?"

"Not really, Sir."

"Of course it isn't. Why should it be? I understand. Can you call *me*, then, at twelve o'clock exactly, tomorrow morning? Do you think you can do that?"

"No problem Sir."

"Good boy! You really are a remarkable young man!"

Billy blushed and looked at his sneakers.

"Well then. Off you go. Leave everything to me. Tomorrow it is. Of course it is. I can't think what *else* it is. Can you?"

"No Sir," said Billy, having as little idea what Wendle meant as Wendle did himself.

"Goodbye," said Wendle, shooing Billy out, desperate to be rid of him and to set up an audition and get this splendid story, with such legs, on the move.

"Goodbye Sir," said Billy.

Although Billy was waiting on Sunset for a bus home in little more than a minute from the time he turned his back on the offices of Sunset Creative Arts, Wendle had already dangled his tempting tit-bit of a story (inasmuch as one can do such a thing over the telephone) in the face of a *very* interested researcher at NBC; and Billy was booked into a recording session, with no need for any audition, before the bus had even arrived.

"If anything's got legs," said Wendle to himself, abandoning his usual metaphorical reliance on temperature, "it's gotta be this. It's got legs coming out of its butt."

* * *

After the recording, they thought the piece was too good to take its place in the queue, and they squeezed it into the very next broadcast later the same week, removing a touching segment about every boy needing an iPlayer, and rescheduling it until nearer the Holidays.

Billy's moment of fame went along these lines—

Sue, the young female anchor-woman had presented a clip of a boy who (if you asked me, what he really needed, more than anything else, was a sound thrashing and to be grounded for a month) had been complaining why he needed the newest games' console; and in demonstrating it for the cameras he had crashed a cyber-airplane into an unidentified Middle-Eastern village, killing not only the enemy (civilians to a man, woman and child) but the All-American hero of the game, as well his entire crew.

"Oops!" said Sue. "That's wasn't supposed to happen!"

"It sure wasn't," said a laughing Matt, the young male presenter. In a nano-second he changed his broad smile and his deep laughter into an even deeper sincerity.

"And now a heartrending story you may find it difficult to believe."

"That's right, Matt," said Sue, nodding at him with a face as compassionate as any ever seen on television.

"The saying is that what every boy needs is a dog," said Matt.

"And we have a young man with us this afternoon who *had* a dog," said Sue. The camera cut to a close-up photo of Squid.

"That's right," said Matt. "Some of our younger viewers may find this story upsetting, and parental guidance is advised," he added, disconcertingly quickly. But you don't get more sincere than Matt. He's probably the nicest man on television.

"That's right," said Sue, looking at the camera and nodding, with a grim turn to her mouth—out-sincering Matt as good as she could give. She's probably the nicest woman who ever existed.

"Why don't you tell us what happened Billy?"

To see the broadcast programme you might have thought Billy was with them, maybe on a sofa next to them. In fact, what he said had been pre-recorded, and heavily edited. I don't think he ever saw Matt and Sue. They didn't like children, and met as few of them as they could without being in breach of contract.

Billy said—

"Well, I have this dog, he's called Squid."

What he had actually said was "Well I have this dog . . . he's not mine . . . he belongs to a friend of mine . . . but I walk him . . . and it's like he's my dog.

He's called Squid." They edited out the detail because it muddled the story line.

"*One day he got lost.*"

"That's awful," said Sue. And they cleverly spliced it in as though she had said it to Billy's face.

"*We thought he'd run away, but it looks like he was stolen.*"

"Stolen? Why do you think that, Billy?" intercut Matt.

"*A guy called-up the number on his collar, but it's an old number, and we didn't know about it for a while. It's a long story…*" (You can imagine, they edited out most of the long story.) "*Anyway, they wanted a hundred dollars, or I wouldn't see my dog back. That's what he said.*"

Matt interjected, sternly to the camera: "I want to make it clear this is *not* a request for donations. The LAPD have said under no circumstances should anyone make any payment to these kind of people."

The LAPD had said no such thing. When Billy had gone to the station, they said they were sorry but 'they didn't do lost dogs. Had he tried the pound?' They weren't interested in the ransom demand, and made no suggestion either to pay it or not to pay it, other than the desk sergeant asking "Have you *got* a hundred dollars?"

"Go on Billy," said Sue. And the TV recording cut back to Billy:

"*My mom says it's too late now, and anyway we can't afford a hundred dollars. So I hope if anyone sees him…*" (Cut back to photo.) "*He's called Squid. If anyone sees him wandering around, all lost, call out 'Here Squid!' and he'll come over. He's real friendly, he don't bite or nothing. And if you see someone with him call 911. You can get me on this number. Not the number on his collar. Ok? My name's Billy.*"

The Abbot Kinney telephone number went up on screen, superimposed over the photo of Squid.

"Well that beats everything doesn't it?" said Matt.

"I don't know how some people can live with themselves," said Sue.

"We wish you all the best, Billy. What a brave young man!"

"How could they do a thing like that?" said Sue.

"Beats me. But someone out there must have seen him," said Matt.

"So please, please, please call this number, if you have seen Squid," said Sue, on the brink of a tear. The picture of Squid went back on screen, with Billy's telephone number superimposed again. "Hasn't he got the cutest face though?"

"He sure has," said Matt. Then added—"You mean the dog?"

(Studio laughter in the background.)

"And here's something every boy is going to need this Fall…" said a smiling Sue, with a flick of her long hair.

* * *

It didn't have as many legs as Wendle thought. A couple of local papers picked it up; it provoked some gossip in the shops and streets and on the busses, about how shocking it was for anyone to do such a thing—and that was that.

Or nearly that.

The scavenger who had taken Squid, and had him tethered in his back yard, heard a couple of women talking about the TV show in a local convenience store. He became nervous. He would never have admitted it, and it was somewhat out of character considering the many other things he had done in his life, but he felt bad about himself when he saw Billy's sad face in the torn-out scrap of newspaper his accomplice showed him, and when he read the story underneath it.

Perhaps most important of all, he realised there was never going to be a hundred dollars coming his way. In the dead of night he seized Squid and took him back to where he had 'napped him', tied him to the railings, went to a public call-box, dialled the number on Squid's collar (the accomplice had failed to tear out Billy's number from the paper), and left a message 'where they could find their damned dog, and they were lucky he hadn't slit its throat.'

13

A False Lead

Tyler was not comfortable listening to Madison's concerns about Tom (although he played less of a part in things than he thought: Luke and Didier had made most of the running), and he shifted in his chair when she told him Courtney thought the problem was substance abuse.

They were in Madison's kitchen, again sitting at the table Tyler now associated only with bad news. A number of empty beer bottles and vodka-miniatures lay spread in front of them. Tyler had steered Madison away from red wine because of the Dutch guy's irrational superstition about the wine rack—which he had begun to share. He took a Budweiser from the 'fridge, flipped the top, and drank from the bottle. His cool performance was never going to get him an Oscar, but it was good enough for a nomination, and Madison was taken in.

"Drugs?" he said. "Is that what she thinks? First I heard of that."

"She's sure of it. She's seen it before. I guess there's not much Courtney hasn't seen before. Where would Tom be getting drugs?"

"Damned if I know," said Tyler, managing not to choke on his beer.

"I'm so naïve, Tyler. I wish I knew more of the world," she sighed.

"You seem to know a heck of a lot about the next one!"

She managed a faint smile back at him—exactly as Tyler had meant her to, hoping to shift the conversation away from narcotics.

"Have you ever taken drugs?" she asked him.

It was only a slight retch, because Tyler's swig of beer was at that moment safely passed his oesophagus.

"I smoked grass at school. All the kids did. Didn't you?"

"Grass?"

"Grass. Weed."

"Oh. Cannabis. No. That was mostly the boys. Very few of us girls did anything like that. Unless... I couldn't have been the *only* one who didn't? Could I?"

"Maybe. What school were you at?"

"A convent."

"Boys?"

"Maintenance. Gardeners. The gardeners' kids. The cook's kids. My oh my! Did I have a crush on the janitor's boy!"

"Did you... You know . . . Do it?" A wide-eyed Tyler nodded his head enthusiastically, and a little ridiculously, rather than complete his prurient question verbally.

"Of course not. He broke my heart, like all boys did: but from a distance. Don't think I spoke to him, not once in all that time. Isn't that sad? I wonder if he noticed me. We called them 'oods' - objects of desire. They were boys of steel, like superman, but made of unobtainium. That's what we used to say."

She slipped into the strange *Blanche Dubois* voice she used on TV sometimes—

"Un-ob-*tai*-nium. Objects of *dee-zire*."

—then she let out a tipsy giggle and took a swig of neat vodka.

Madison saw something through the blurred glass of her hip flask, that few would associate with Tyler: a cloud passed over his face and for a moment he looked almost vulnerable. It lasted for a split-second, and then it was gone, and Tyler became Tyler again.

"It's not cannabis," she said in her normal accent. "I've seen that. It's something else."

"What does Courtney think?" asked Tyler, desperate to take the focus away from himself.

"What do *you* think?" said Madison. "And where's he getting it from?"

All Tyler could do was shrug, behind the shelter of another gulp of beer.

"Do you like that Luke?" asked Madison, out of the blue. "Where did you find him? What's he do up there? I don't get him. He kinda scares me."

Before Tyler could stammer out any diversionary answer there was a knock at the door.

Madison went to investigate and a woman's voice said '*I won't come in*' as she strode into the kitchen in front of Madison.

"We had another call," she said, with a nod to Tyler, and a nod back. "It must have been a couple of days ago. I'm sorry, but we try to spend as much time as we can in the desert, what with the weather and the Impeachment."

"How...?"

Tyler was fascinated to know, but never got to ask, how Palm Springs, even with its mists of water, and cubic miles of outside air-conditioning, managed to distract this strange woman in the matter of President Clinton's Impeachment.

"Becky took over Scott's apartment..." began Madison.

"And his telephone number," added Becky. "It was the same voice as before. He said they'd left the dog tied to the railings."

Tyler leaped to his feet. "Where?"

* * *

It was some hours before he returned from the dog-park. Empty handed.

"I looked everywhere," he said. "Top to bottom. I called and called for him. Not a sign."

"Poor Squid" said Madison. "It's been two whole days! Why did she have to be in Palm Springs?"

They decided not to tell Billy. What was the point in raising his hopes, only to dash them? Tyler had found the remains of string tied to the railings, under the sign warning about mountain lions.

"Gnawed through," said Tyler. "It looked fresh."

"No blood though?" asked Madison. Tyler had said so a dozen times, but he said it again.

"No. No blood."

"We'd better tell Tom to keep a look out," said Madison, ploughing on through the fatuousness of it as though the reality had not been so very clearly signalled. Of course the absence of blood militated against the mountain lion theory; but it had been raining hard, night and day in the forty-eight hours since the message was left on her neighbour's answerphone.

"I'll let him know," said Tyler.

"Tell him there was no blood," she urged, trying to recruit him to her optimism.

"Two whole days," he said, looking at the rain beating against her windows.

14

The Secret of the House Next Door

If it is harsh to comment that 'Ghost Trail' had not distinguished itself in terms of good taste in the choice of some of its investigations, it is only fair to counter-balance the criticism with an observation that the program sank no lower in the estimation of right-thinking people when it embarked on a series of broadcasts to mark the thirtieth anniversary of the 'Manson Murders'.

Any haunting of the very spot where Sharon Tate and four others had been slaughtered was a delicate subject to document, even for the hardened sensibilities of the 'Ghost Trail' team; made no easier by the fact that the Cielo Drive house in which the murders took place had been demolished five years earlier. An impediment, it should be pointed out, that had not stopped a rival program investigating Sharon Tate's alleged haunting of *the house next door*.

The Marx Brothers would have approved -

"Go to the house next door."

"Suppose there isn't any house next door?

"Well, then of course, we gotta build one."

For the purposes of their 'Manson murders' anniversary series, 'Ghost Trail' could be thought of as having built houses-next-door all along Mulholland Drive.

Abigail Folger and her boyfriend Wojciech Frykowski had rented a property in a quaint backwater called Woodstock Road, and they had even dined, along with the other Manson victims, at El Coyote in Laurel Canyon, on the night before their dawn murders. Ghost Triail's very own Bradley said he would stake his reputation—yes! his reputation!—on there being, technically, 'a shit-load of energy in that house in Woodstock Road'.

Unused energy, no doubt.

Nobody could legitimately complain that the plan was anything worse than obscenely distasteful, but its path was littered with difficulties and failure nonetheless. The idea was to film an episode in the Abigail Folger house itself. Madison's dead twin, Alice, was to hint at certain shocking revelations about Sharon Tate, most of which had already been published in the National Inquirer; but that was not thought to matter too much, the assumption being Ghost Trail's core audience didn't take a newspaper.

The first problem was the house. It was never likely they could get permission to film there, and they didn't. So the location scouts found a property near enough to lay claim to a Manson Murders connection (a house next door to the house next door). Their initial visit found the place adequate, if not perfect: they had been told 'derelict', and found only a house that had been vacant a few weeks, and was shuttered-up. But it was huge, and of a somewhat Gothic interior design; and the smothering of the whole building with tarpaulin while it was being treated for termites was an unexpected bonus, giving the place a distinctly sinister look, and going a long way to make up for their initial disappointment at losing the Folger dwelling itself.

There was uncertainty, it has to be said, as to whether it was yet safe to enter the house after its chemical treatment. The warning signs were still in place, and despite several calls to the owners, and to the termite-treatment company, a definitive answer was never obtained. Undaunted by the toxic dangers, and with no Alice to warn them "Don't go in there!", and driven by desperation to come up with *any* plausible location, the scouts recommended the spot, lied about its safety, and a crew began to set things up accordingly.

The next problem was the format of the show. The initial idea had looked good on paper, but their comedy instincts were drawn to the absurdity of what was required of them, and every script the writers worked on (scheduling the impromptu down to the last detail) came out as though Alice and Sharon each thought the other was rather fun and were having a girlish laugh at the expense of the other spirits.

The writers settled on leaving more than was usually the case to the improvisation talents of the cast. A foolhardy experiment, you may think, and destined for failure.

* * *

It had been raining heavily for almost two weeks, and they could not put-off the filming of the Manson Murder special for another day if they were to meet the scheduled broadcast.

The rain hit the ground like bullets. The kind of downpour that has some people say '*the heavens have opened*', as though there is a celestial reservoir up there and the angels have raised the sluice gates. Rain so heavy and cold it kept the newspapers away from the shoot, despite an intriguing press-release which in dry weather might have tempted a good few from their desks—but every one of the local hacks sheltered in front of their typewriters, except for a single cub reporter and his unimpressive camera, which did not look at all likely to give them the colour-splash on the front page of the gutter tabloids they had been hoping for, any more than did the boy look capable of writing the short, sensational headlines they needed to boost their TV ratings. Disappointed by the absence of the professionals, they (particularly Bradley) were rather too dismissive of the cub-reporter; and as things turned out they might have wished they had been a little less condescending and made a friend of him.

The constant hammering of the storm was so loud it became necessary for the 'Ghost Trail' team to go deeper into the bowels of the rambling house than they had ever intended, in order to get a recordable sound level. Much deeper. Then deeper still. And what awaited them there, wholly unscripted, was to frighten them far more than they had ever frightened their audience.

The yellow fumes that had eradicated the last mortal struggles of termite-life had also poisoned every other living thing in the building—and because of the recklessness of the location-scouts might well be poised to poison the entire production team as well. The floor was littered with dead vermin and the crisp remains of flying insects twenty times the size of any termite. Corpses of spiders—some of them quite large—dangled down on the strong-as-steel strands of web dragged from their dying abdomens as they dropped from their secret places in the ceilings—the house could have had been decorated for Halloween, and by a very macabre mind.

The darkness inside, when they went deep, was darker than any dark they had known. The tarpaulin was stretched over the entire house; and Madison, perhaps remembering a scene from '*Fantasia*', said that it was as though a bat the size of a mountain had folded its wings over it. Vince added '*and was not going to let any of them out again*'.

The brass rings, with rope pulled through, which anyone could see from the outside held the tarpaulin sheets together, looked, in the blackest of blackness inside, like eyes—terrible eyes, because when a gust pulled the ringlets across a beam or window-frame, the light was blocked and the wandering eyes blinked shut - and open - and shut again. Then open again.

Worst of all was the wind. Not howling like a ham King Lear, nor whistling, nor even moaning as the Brontës might have had it. It was the sigh of remembered pain, given a voice that wandered from room to room yet seemed to come from nowhere. Nowhere on earth, that is.

"This house is evil," said Courtney, when they had descended almost to the lowest level of the cellars, where there was no longer flooring, but dry mud and grit. Perhaps buried coffins. Perhaps unburied coffins.

And each of them shared the same thought, though no one articulated it: that it would be better not to ask any spirit to show itself in the shuttered-up, tarpaulin-covered, spider-cemetery of a house on Woodstock Road, because for the first time in the history of 'Ghost Trail' a spirit might actually comply with the request.

Even Bradley was cowed, and used ordinary words and made sentences, like a sane adult.

"Let's just set up, do what we have to, and get out of here," he said calmly; and they went about doing just that, in total silence.

Total Silence.

Then what was that sound?

They were all in the same room (if 'room' is the right word for a hollowed-out cavern to side of the dirt-floor). Cast and crew. All together. In the same room.

Then what *was* that sound?

"I can hear footsteps!" said Courtney, not quite believing her hackneyed announcement was genuine.

"So can I!" said Madison.

But neither of them screamed '*Oh my God*!'. The footsteps were very soft, but real. They hushed each other and stood listening. Every person went deathly quiet, keeping perfectly still, not breathing, trying not to make the slightest noise.

"Who's there?" said Vince into the dark of a passageway that sloped deeper-still into the underground mysteries of the old house.

The footsteps stopped. Or had they ever been? Had they? If anyone entertained any doubt, it was quickly resolved by the unmistakable sound of breathing, coming from the same place.

"Who's there?" repeated Vince, the bravest of them all, inching towards the sound.

Now the breathing stopped—but everyone had heard it.

"Ok. We all leave. Slowly. Now," said Bradley.

"Who's there, Dammit?" said Vince, and threw a shard of brick into the blackness.

An unearthly howl, followed by rapid footsteps rushing at them from the abyss.

Now they screamed. Even Bradley. Especially Bradley. The lighting man dropped his kit and ran for his life. None of them was carrying a torch, and none of them could lay a hand on one in the dark.

Vince threw a lens-hood into the void and it hit Courtney, who screamed and ran off in the wrong direction, towards the thing—whatever it was.

Another howl from the depths, while they bumped into each other trying to feel their way to the exit. Madison fell onto the floor and Bradley tripped over her. While they dithered and clambered, and went this way then the next, the awful breathing came closer, and their panic turned to mayhem. The footsteps were almost upon them when they stumbled through a door into a corridor semi-lit by a pair of those ringlet-eyes, which on the way in had unnerved them but were their blessed saviour on the way out.

They rushed up a short stairway towards the light of an open door, with the rapid footsteps gaining on them fast and the hideous breathing louder and closer. Madison sobbed pathetically, while the rest shouted or screamed various permutations of "Jesus", "Fuck", "It's right behind me", "Run", "Christ", "Faster", "It's here", "Get out of my way!", "Help!", "It's got me!", and a long "Noooooo!"—sprinkled (perhaps out of loyalty to their calling) with liberal proclamations of "*Oh My God!*"

The belittled cub-reporter, despite the inadequacies of his camera, took a great many photographs as the terrified team ran from the building; and his copy proved punchier than any of them had given him credit for having the wit to compose. In fact it kick-started a successful career.

Two of his pictures were syndicated. One was of Bradley, scared out of his wits, pushing Courtney down into the mud as he careered from the house, with little Squid running up behind him. The caption read—

"*Spooked by a Pooch.*"

The other photo was a close-up of Squid, taken through Vince's open legs, gaining on him; with the black rings around what they used to call his 'panda eyes' prominent on his cute 'too much mascara' face. Beneath the picture, in a camp font that dripped red like horror-film blood, was written—

'*The Clown of the Baskervilles.*'

Squid, scared and hungry, living rough since his release by the scavengers, suddenly woken from a deep dog-sleep in his lonely hiding place, and by an army of unfamiliar sights and sounds enough to frighten a wolf, had single-handedly chased the Ghost-Hunters to the end of their trail.

15
Closing In

Madison put up a short pursuit, shouting for Squid to 'come here boy!' Vince joined her, we must hope without vengeance as his motive. The terrain was impenetrable, with gardens and shrubberies and pools and locked gates and barbed fences and a thousand other things between them and Squid that a dog can leap over, but they had to climb over, or take a detour round, or even wade through. It didn't much matter, though: the driving rain was unforgiving and would have slowed their progress on a flat race-track.

Squid was too scared, from the moment of his capture to the hounding of him from his lair by the film crew—and he didn't know Madison well enough to have confidence in her—and he only knew Vince as someone who threw missiles at him—he was too scared to come running up to them wagging his tail, like the 'good boy' they were so desperately trying to persuade him he was. He turned round though, and suddenly too—maybe recognising Madison's voice; and from only about fifty yards away he stopped and stared curiously at them, as though he might after all be tempted to trust them.

They crept closer—coaxing him with a soft 'Here Squid!' and a friendly 'That's a good boy!' No shouting. No running.

Squid stood his ground. They crept closer.

"*Hey! Squid!*"

They almost whispered the words. His ears pricked up and forward.

"*That's my boy!*"

They advanced another few feet—but got no further than a pace or two before Squid bared his teeth and snarled at them. They stopped in their tracks.

"*Good boy!*" urged Madison, somewhat hopelessly.

Squid barked a couple of times, but stood stock-still. Then he barked again—as though he might have been expecting a barked reply from them!—adding a particularly savage snarl that seemed aimed specifically at Vince; who, when he inched another half-step forwards, with the quietest 'Good boy!' of all, sent Squid running off into the bushes, tail down and fast, deep into the Hollywood Hills, out of sight and beyond rescue.

* * *

Madison drove over to Tom's house, the other side of the hill from where she had been filming: but there was no reply from her hammering on the front door. She checked the basement: Luke was not around either. None of the Church's workers had ventured out into the storm: their teaching of self-help had been put on hold while they practised what they preached. Madison took her cell phone and called every number she knew, including Tom's, before the battery failed.

No one was at home or at work and all she achieved was to leave half a dozen messages on half a dozen answer-machines. Close to despair, she drove up and down the streets leading off Mulholland, on the slim chance she might find Squid before he found another hide-away.

* * *

Billy returned from school late, but his mother was out. She usually was these days. He saw the red light flashing on the handset, punched the pin number and heard Madison's recorded voice -

> *"Valeria. Billy. I've just seen Squid up near Outpost. He's alive and looks well..."* (It was probably best to lie.) *"...but he's a bit scared. He ran away from me—I don't think he recognizes me—that's so sad!—he's somewhere here. D'you think you could bring Billy? Would you mind? The weather's hell, but what can I say? I'm sure he'll come to Billy. Isn't it great news though? I'll keep looking and let you know. God bless."*

Billy grabbed all the loose change he could find in his and his mother's pockets, striking lucky with a five-dollar bill in one of hers; and with scant protection from the incessant rain, he left the house. He ran back immediately, dashed up stairs and took a scoop of dog-treats he kept in a tin box, and shoved them in his jeans' pocket.

Valeria was about to put her key in the door when he opened it to run out.

> *"And where do you think you're going?"* she said.

He brushed passed her without replying.

"Billy! Come back here!"

He ignored her and ran down the path where the grapefruit tree dropped its vile fruit, and out onto Abbot Kinney.

"Billy! What's happened?" (Now she was anxious.) *"What's happened? Answer me!"*

He turned and shouted at her

"This is your fault!"

He tore down the street until her screams of 'Come back!' became indistinguishable from the storm closing in on him from every direction.

A pedant might say, with some justification, that *'This is your fault!'* was not an answer to Valeria's question—*'What's happened?'*

But she was never to hear a better answer—or any other answer—from Billy's lips.

16
El Niño

They blamed it on El Niño. A naughty little boy, who legend has it flies over the Pacific and, for want of anything more amusing to do, puffs the sea onto Mexico and Southern California. His appalling upbringing is all too obvious, but the regrettable lack of any or any sufficient parental control came to a head in 1998/99, when his most unruly behaviour to date seemed to have made him determined to blow the entire Ocean onto the Western Seaboard of the Americas, not for one moment sparing Los Angeles from the deluge—in spite of all the good deeds that might otherwise have mitigated his punishment of the City of Angels.

The storm drains at the Sunset end of Larrabee blew geysers as high as 'Old Faithful', and the tracks that ran under Tom's house, down towards the Valley, and under all the other stilted houses on the Hills, became so like mountain streams that it would not have been surprising to see trout and salmon leaping their way through the spray up towards Mulholland Drive.

It was through the unrelenting rain and against the torrents gushing down the hillside that Billy scrambled, wildly, searching for Squid—running sideways along the slanting ground, frequently slipping in the mud and tumbling through the chest-high thistles, picking himself up and clambering through the scrub again, cut and bruised, t-shirt torn, grabbing bracken and thorns to pull himself over the steepest slopes.

He screamed Squid's name so loudly they could hear him inside the houses he ran passed—and sometimes ran under—despite the thunderous battering El Niño was giving their windows and decks. Prudent householders, protecting themselves against the unusual without caring to find out what it was, drew their blinds and locked their doors against it, giving no thought to whether or how they could help a frantic child, so clearly in need of help.

* * *

Tom lies awake his bed, huddled under the comforter. His eyes are shut tight. The phone rings and the message service kicks in.

"The subscriber you are calling is pretending to be asleep at this time. Please call back later."

(According to Tom.)

A whispered voice comes from outside the window -

"He's pretending to be asleep. He's only pretending. He's pretending. He's pretending to be asleep."

Tom opens his eyes but only looks at the window via its reflection in a mirror. He doesn't dare look straight at it.

"He's looking at us. He's looking at us in the mirror. He's looking right at us."

Tom jumps out of bed, slams shut the window blinds, and jumps back. He pulls the comforter over his head.

The phone rings incessantly.

* * *

If you imagine a ball of tangled string, sliced through the middle with a sharp blade and allowed to spread out wide on a table; or if you think instead of a mess of spaghetti spilled on the floor, lying no more than one strand thick; you might have some idea of the equally tangled, equally messy, network of roads leading up from Ventura Boulevard to the ridge of the Hollywood Hills.

There are a few routes that wind all the way from bottom to top, and from top to bottom—although when you are half way up you begin to lose your nerve and doubt if you are not going back downhill again. As well as the through-routes, there is a multitude of other streets, avenues and trails, some long, some short, each leading to its own unexpected dead end: the maze at Hampton Court, or the Labyrinth at Knossos, might have been modelled on an ancient map of them.

* * *

Someone has broken into his house while he was asleep. They've done it before—it is impossible to ignore the evidence. He would be <u>mad</u> to ignore the evidence.

The light in the kitchen—who has switched it on? And why have they gone into the kitchen? To get a knife? Are they going to kill him?

*"**Are you going to kill me**?" he defies the emptiness.*

The door to the bathroom - open! Open! What do they want in the bathroom? Are they in there?

—"Lock the door!"

Or are they in the kitchen?

—"Lock the door!"

* * *

They divided up the territory so that they didn't duplicate each others' searches, but they sometimes crossed paths, one or other of them having inadvertently gone off-route.

Even Didier was patrolling in his Landrover; but there was little risk of crossing paths with Didier because he stuck to the safety of Mulholland Drive and drove back and forth along the same short stretch between Runyon Canyon and the track leading down to Tom's house—about a dozen times, without seeing Tyler, Madison, Chloe or any other person or animal doing battle with *El Niño*.

* * *

Every door in Tom's house is fitted with a mortice lock. Each door has its own key—for security reasons. Important, security reasons. The dangers if each door could be unlocked by a single key are too obvious, and at the same time too complex, to be rehearsed here: it is enough that Tom understands them, perfectly.

* * *

Now the rain was beating down on the roofs in stair-rods. It cascaded over the gutters and onto the waterlogged mud, overflowing the blocked drains, racing down the hillside, the little rivulets getting wider and faster as they joined forces, until a malevolent army of swollen rivers roared towards Studio City, in search of somewhere to flood or an overhang to collapse or maybe someone to wash off-balance and drown.

* * *

Seven keys on seven key-rings, hanging out of sight in a broom cupboard in the hall.

Tom runs upstairs to get them—but what if the broom-cupboard in the hall is the very place they are hiding?

* * *

Madison's 'stars and stripes' Hummer was unmistakable even in the dense rain and fog, and Tyler flashed his headlights wildly as they careered towards each other. They stopped alongside, blocking the entire width of the road—no one else would be crazy enough to be out!—and continued the search together in his Mustang. Madison looking, Tyler driving.

The worn windshield wipers were turned-on 'fast', and they belted from side to side as hectic as everyone and everything else, scratching and squeaking on the glass with a "*There he is. There he is. There he is,*" until Madison could bear the noise no longer and begged Tyler to slow them down, even though the windshield became opaque with rain.

But the wipers still said "*I can seeeeeee him. I can seeeeeee him.*"

* *

"Back back back back." The rain pelts against the windows as though a battalion of El Niños were firing stones at them.

Tom flies downstairs.

The air-conditioning screams at him—"Lock the door! Lock the door!"

Tom flies upstairs.

* *

They almost collided head-on with Chloe. She yelled at them through their half-opened windows—

"Billy heard Madison's message and set off on his own. No one knows where is he is. Valeria's somewhere up here, off her head with worry. She bust up crying when she thanked me for helping. Imagine! Valeria!"

* *

He grabs every key he can. Five. There should be seven. They've taken two of them. But which two?

Two of the keys are in the doors. The doors for which they were made, Tom.—Can't you see them?

He searches on his hands and knees. From the depths of the cupboard, barely audible, whispered voices -

— *"Can't you see?"*

— *"He can't see!"*

— *"He's on the floor!"*

* *

Valeria saw a flash of a something or someone running through the mist about a hundred yards ahead of her. She raced forward at breakneck speed—but the trail came to an abrupt end and she leapt from the car and gave chase on foot.

"Billy?—Billy!"

*

The bathroom door! One of the missing keys! They've taken the key to the bathroom door!

The key is already in the door, Tom. Why can't you see that? Look!

He drags a chest of drawers from his bedroom and pushes it hard against the bathroom door.

"Now try!" he shouts at the people who aren't in the bathroom—and aren't in his house, and aren't outside, or upstairs or downstairs or anywhere else except in his chem-crazed head.

*

"Over there!" shouted the Dutch guy to Madison.

"Can you see him?"

"He's over there!"

"SQUID!"

*

Tom keeps his gun in a drawer by the bed. Locked. It's always locked. So why does the drawer pull open without a key? Were they trying to get his gun as well?

They <u>are</u> going to kill him!

Who, Tom? Who's going to kill you?

*

"I can see him!" shouted Madison.

Tyler braked to a halt and skidded a good ten feet down the track.

"Billy! We're over here!"

*

The sliding doors to the deck. They weren't like that. Why aren't they secured?

They've gone outside!

He can see them. In the rain. Shadows hiding in the thick rain.

*

Squid stopped running at the sound of his name; and from the landslides below Tom's house, all familiarity swept away by the tumbling mud, he stared up at the car, hungry, frightened, confused.

"He's seen us," yelled Madison. "Squid!" she screamed again. But he came no closer.

"Billy, we've found him. Billy! BILLY!"

*

Tom slides the glass door open and the tempest bursts inside the house, drenching him in an instant, flooding his eyes and his mouth and his ears as though he is walking into a waterfall.

—*"He's over there!"*

—*"I can see him!"*

It's Billy, Tom. Don't you recognise the voice of a child?

Tom shouts, roars, into the blinding rain—"WHAT ARE YOU WAITING FOR?"

The shadows close in on him, and he empties his gun in an arc of bullets, sweeping the entire breadth of his deck from Universal Studios to Downtown LA.

Nine

1

Departures

A helicopter-ambulance touched down on the clearing next to Tom's house, its mini-hurricane blowing over the trashcans, spilling bagged-up kitchen waste, empty quarter-bags and used hypodermics into the ponds and rills the rain-storm had made in the muddy ground. Seconds later, a police patrol-car raced down the track, siren blaring, blue lights flashing.

Only one bullet had engaged. It entered through Squid's shoulder and lodged in his heart, killing him instantly. Billy, carrying the limp corpse in his arms, the dog's blood all over his T-shirt and jeans, stumbling up through the Yukka bushes to the house, sobbing, wailing, *howling* an anguish unbearable even to write about—and pray God none of us should come close to knowing it—Billy trod on a drowning rattlesnake and was bitten on the ankle.

The paramedics tornaqueed the leg and pumped serum into Billy's arm just as soon as they could leap out of the still-landing air-ambulance. They strapped him into a stretcher, wrenched him up inside, rose skywards, and vanished into the night.

* * *

Tom was arrested at gun-point—a necessary precaution: he was huddled in a corner, unarmed, and crying like a baby in its pram. They manhandled him, handcuffed, into the back seat of the patrol car, and raced up the cascading waterfall that used to be the track to Mulholland—all sirens again, and flashing blue lights—heaven alone knows why.

Tom never returned to his canyon home, or saw his creations 'the Nurslings', not even Nimrod, ever again. A week or two later, in the middle of a hot night in the hospital wing of the prison, awaiting pre-trial psychiatric assessment, he fell victim to his last seizure, a bad one, and no-one came to him—just another screaming lunatic in his cell—and he died, although he could easily have been saved, alone and frightened.

A cynic might say that those in whose care he was placed were in dereliction of duty: but that is wrong. The date of Tom's death explains it all—February

9, 1999. On that day the staff in the hospital wing could be forgiven for sitting in front of the TV in thrall to the final stages of the Impeachment of President Clinton. The climax, around which advertising revenues were their highest, came when Chief Justice Rehnquist declared:

"Senators, how say you? Is the respondent, William Jefferson Clinton, guilty or not guilty?"

Clinton was acquitted, of course. Only the Republicans voted 'guilty'.

As a finale to the proceedings, which were broadcast across the world, Senators of all political persuasions united, laughing and joking with each other in the most amiable way; and they presented the Chief Justice with a Golden Gavel, as though it were his consolation prize at the end of a game-show. The judge's acceptance of it was as pleasant as could be, and everything was in accordance with the majesty and dignity of the Highest Court in the free world.

At such an historic moment, the staff in the hospital wing of the prison in which Tom was held could hardly have been expected to abandon the TV simply to answer the desperate calls of a dying man.

* * *

Madison had arranged for Tom's legal representation, and she visited him as often as she had been allowed to—if he was sufficiently in his right mind to receive a visitor and know who it was. She was given the news they were axing 'Ghost Trail' the same day she was told that Tom had died.

When members of Tom's family came over from England they took immediate possession of his house and cut Madison and all Tom's 'Quaker' friends out of everything that followed. They didn't answer a single enquiry. No one knew when or where Tom was buried, cremated, or if he was left to medical science to save on funeral expenses.

Madison wasn't the brightest, but she wasn't stupid either. She saw that LA had nothing left to offer her; and to her credit she saw that she had never had much of any value to offer LA. She had come to hate the Hummer, and didn't even bother to sell it. She abandoned it in the parking lot, key in the ignition, for anyone to steal and maybe have their own fifteen minutes; and she didn't look back at it once, briskly stepping out to her waiting taxi, carrying fewer bags than she arrived with, bound for the relative sanity of Wisconsin.

Back home she discovered was a minor celebrity, and had the sense not to let her distaste for the reality of things stand in the way of an enjoyment of that, for as long as it might last. She didn't flaunt her small-pond importance, not for the world would she have done so—her intention had been to kick the last spec of Los Angeles dust from her heels as she boarded the aeroplane home. But she found an innocent pleasure in the occasional recognition of her, and the slight sense (it was never to be improved on) that she *was* somebody. And for my part I would not deny her a single second of it.

A week after she set foot in her parents' suburban home, and had slept in her old bedroom for the first time in a pocket-lifetime, in a bed she had forgotten how small, two letters from LA arrived in the same mail: two postal aftershocks, as it were, from the turbulence she had left behind her.

One letter was scented, and we can guess from whom it came. The other was in handwriting she didn't recognise. Driven by her instinct for suspense, she opened Wendle Stein's letter first and kept the mystery of the other alive for a little longer.

Wendle's letter was obviously dictated by him, probably into a machine; then, almost certainly, transcribed word for word by somebody who was either stupid or malicious—maybe his 'secretary' (stupid *and* malicious); and it was sent to the post without any critical revision. With illuminating consequences. But at least it was correctly addressed, and for the first time in all that time as her agent, Wendle Stein's salutation properly identified her as -

"*Madison my dear,*

I've been trying to find you everywhere. They told me you had taken off home for a short break with your family, and who can blame you? But don't rush off like that without letting me know, sweetheart. Sure it was disappointing for all of us that 'The Ghost Train' came to such a sudden stop, but these things don't last forever, and everyone agrees it wouldn't have run as long as it did without your—what can I call it? The energy had gone out of it Madeline, and as Brandon said, no energy means the spirits have gone somewhere else. Or words to that effect. To another Network if they got any sense. Christ! The fuckin' spirits 'll be wanting a percentage next! Don't put any of that in.

I've managed to get you a spot on a 'Ghost Hunter' celebrity special for 'The Artorio Collection'. There isn't much money in it my dear, but it will keep the flame burning until—you tell me! The sky's the limit! We record the show a week Thursday. NBC, Studio City. 10.00 am.

With every fond wish, etc.

That's not right. I don't like 'fond', but I want it to sound affectionate. Think of some other word. Fifty per-cent of not much is better than—you know what I'm saying?

Wendle.

ps. I have held back your final cheque in lieu of the cancelation fees for the billboard campaign, which I am sure you'll agree has no heat left in it.
  WS"

His name was typed, as were his post-script initials. Let us assume in his favour he never read the letter before the malicious slut at the front desk put it in an envelope and posted it.

Madison was too polite, and too kind-hearted to ignore Wendle altogether, even though she perfectly understood the insult inherent in the sentences not meant for her eyes; and, in spite of everything, she had genuine affection for him, and gratitude, even, for his sleight-of-hand manoeuvrings on her behalf in tinsel-town. But once she had written a few lines in reply, in which she declined his kind offer of another chance to prostitute herself, she discarded the scented paper and its scented envelope without a second thought—and she never heard from Wendle again, not even to give her the remainder of the money she was owed.

The second letter was quite another matter. She turned it over, felt the thin contents, and looked at it quizzically for a moment or two before opening it—to get the fullest enjoyment of its mystery. Even when she had slit the envelope with a knife, and pulled out the few sheets it contained, she peered inside to see if there were any other preliminary business to delay the reading of it. But there wasn't, so she laid each page flat in front of her, pressed away the creases, wiped clean her reading glasses (again), and at last succumbed to the inevitability of learning who the writer was, and what he had to say. And in stark distinction from her treatment of Wendle's letter, once she had finished this one she read it a second time, and a third; and ever afterwards she kept it safe amongst her private things, took it out and re-read it now and then, and will probably keep it, and read it, again and again, 'til the day comes that she needs someone else to read it for her—but by then she'll know it by heart, and will mouth the words along with the reader.

It was written in untidy manuscript, with no corrections, and this what it said:

"I couldn't come and say goodbye. I hate goodbyes. I can't shake off a fear they might be the last.

  "The reason I'm writing is some suits from England have been asking around for your forwarding address, and you can expect to hear from them real soon. I think they already got it but I gave it them anyway. I hope that's OK. It's not a bad thing—remember how Scott used to say that? I miss Scott.

"The bottom line is, I know what it's about. I read the Will when I was up at the house looking for this and that. I shouldn't have, but I came across it, and read it. I wish I was a better person Madison.

"It says 'To my Darling', which is a pretty nice start, isn't it? Don't cry. If I was going to write a will, which I won't, ever, I can't think of better words to begin it with. He left you everything. I mean everything. The house, the puppets, the patents—and what's laying there in the bank is a tidy enough sum, you better believe it. But I want to prepare you, and you mustn't let it upset you. The English are going to fight it, because they say he wasn't in his right mind. Sorry. I can't think of other words. But don't worry about it. A lawyer at the gym told me they haven't a hope in Hell. Tom wrote it way before all of that, and we can prove it easy. It's dated a week or so after you met him in the Larrabee parking lot, first time since the awards, all those years back.

That's <u>way</u> back. Do you remember that time? You used to talk about it enough Madison!"

Did she remember? It was on that same evening Tom showed her his studio in West Hollywood; and she woke up by his side the next morning, and a couple of times in the night too, as happy as she had ever been. Now, sitting in Wisconsin in the most merciless of winters, she truly thought she could smell orange blossom.

"Take my advice (from bitter experience) and settle. They'll let you have half, trust me. If you offer half they'll be back to England in a New York minute.

"I'm so happy for you Madison. I hope we meet again. You were a star in ways Hollywood doesn't understand, and never will. You were the best of us. Please don't think too bad of me.

"God bless you."

And it was signed by—of all the people to invoke the name of God!—Tyler.

Madison didn't settle for half. She accepted an offer of a third, and it was more than she ever needed.

* * *

Billy lived. But being so young, and so slight, he was a long time recovering. And when at last he opened his eyes again on the strange world of Los Angeles, he was unable to speak. That is, he wouldn't speak. No coaxing could draw him out of his self-imposed dumbness. Perhaps 'numbness' is the better word.

After months at a special school, and session after session of therapy, one spring morning he opened his mouth, without warning, and turned to the therapist -

"*It isn't like the movies, is it. Where you shout at me, I cry, you give me a hug, and everything's better.*"

From that day on he spoke: to anyone who spoke to him first. Except to his mother. He refused point-blank, no matter what the situation, to speak to her; whom he unfairly blamed—no one else—for the deaths of Scott and of Squid. He didn't ignore her: he looked her in the eye when spoken to, but never answered. And when she had finished speaking, whether it were to help him, to reprimand him, plead with him or merely to question him, he turned and walked away.

They thought it would pass in a few days or so: but it didn't. They said it had to pass in a week or so: but it didn't. Not in a month or so, or a year or so, or at all before he left home as soon as he was old enough and California State Law permitted him.

For those half-dozen years the atmosphere in the pretty house in Abbot Kinney was unendurable, and it damaged both of them irreparably. Valeria was driven to a depth of despair not even she deserved; sometimes tearful, sometimes hysterical, sometimes kneeling at his feet, weeping, begging him to speak to her. And Billy, growing through his teenage years into a young man, just stared back at her, unmoved, unmovable. Numb.

Valeria aged prematurely, and rapidly—little wonder, living a daily life of mute condemnation from her only surviving child; and when he'd gone, living a life of mute condemnation from herself—and she never remarried, not any of the handsome men she saw on the sidewalks and dreamed of a fresh life with, nor anyone else. She kept the house on Abbot Kinney and lived there alone, with few friends and little contact with the outside world.

* * *

Chloe married her Canadian after all. He existed, but she was never engaged to him—not back when she left the fateful message that she had 'wonderful news'. He came to LA expressly to find her, almost a year to the day after Scott died. At the end of the winter she followed him to a lakeside fishing hotel he owned and managed up in the Algonquin Mountains, and began a life as far removed from the LA smog, and all that lies within it, as could possibly be imagined.

All the remaining Larrabee set were invited to the wedding, but only Madison and the Dutch guy came. As a wedding-present Tyler sent a water-colour which was very like (but even better) one which in another life she had admired in the window of a fashionable Melrose art dealer, and had said "*who can afford to have a painting like that on their wall?*" Tyler's gift-card read: "*I can. Which means you can. All my love.*" But Chloe didn't remember the Melrose incident, and never understood what Tyler meant.

Chloe asked the Dutch guy and Madison to be godparents to her first-born child, a boy, and they saw him christened 'Scott' with stoic faces that betrayed nothing of the name's forbidden back-story. Chloe's husband didn't fully know why she was so insistent on calling their boy Scott, although he had an inkling: but he didn't need to know the whole story, didn't want to, and it is best he never did. Anyway, he liked the name Scott: it was a good Canadian name for a healthy boy, running around in the great outdoors with his dog—who they called . . . do I need to spell out the oddball name she persuaded them to give him?

* * *

Luke lost his job as writer-in-chief of the continually evolving tracts and booklets sent out in the name of 'The Church of Self-Help'. To be frank, even he, the writer of its Genesis, was not quite up to the challenge of its Revelations—the aliens-from-outer-space explanation for mankind, which was the turn of non-events their invented religion had taken. But there were two more compelling reasons for his dismissal.

Firstly, the team of writers now employed by the Church was more than capable of churning out the stock-in-trade tracts and pamphlets without Luke's input, for less money cumulatively than Luke had recently demanded for himself alone, and they could be relied on to do so until the Day of Judgment (when Heaven help them all).

Secondly, and it was thought decisive, Luke had begun to find inspiration for his creative writing in the company cheque-book and accounts. When caught, he was summarily excommunicated from the Church and all its good works—although after a few months in the wilderness he was allowed limited access back into the fold (because his Austrian employer, a Doctor of Divinity, was a forgiving man), but only for the purposes of supplying drugs and procuring boys for Didier, and with no responsibility for anything else, fiscal or pascal.

* * *

Didier and Tyler settled their lawsuit, and bit the bullet on the legal fees they had wasted: but they never forgave each other, indeed they came to hate each other; and they resigned themselves, commendably in the circumstances, to a half share each of the massive profits that continued to roll in, and probably do to this very day, from the sad, stupid, profligate followers of their sham religion.

2

Monologue

"It would be kinda funny, wouldn't it, if they were right and we were wrong? If all that shit Tom got hooked on opened some door we don't understand—not yet, anyway—that let Tom look inside, along with the other crazy crack-heads, and see and hear things we can't. Not imaginary things. Real things. Things that are actually there, invisible to you and me. Whole worlds of things.

"What if Madison really did have a dead twin, who stayed alongside of her, always?"

He looks at the pale face on the pillow, and the gentle rise and fall of the bed-sheet, and wonders if maybe there is such a place; where words like his, spoken to sleeping ears and minds, can be heard—by the dead as well as the dying—and whether unearthly replies, spoken in silence, could be heard by the likes of Tom and Madison.

Twenty seven years old, and handsome as his father, all the nurses in love with him, Billy speaks to his dying mother just as he has spoken to her throughout the night, such a long night, for the first time since he made up his child's mind never to speak to her again, all those long years ago.

"So that's it, I guess. Our story. You and me. You and me! That's kinda funny too . . . The Quakers. Weird, huh? The Seismic Seven? Squid? Do you remember? Any of it? Scott?—Scott, mom! Can you even hear me?"

There's not the remotest sign that she can. Nothing. No change in the slow rhythm of the bed-sheet, or in the height or the pace of the thin green traces her pulse leaves on the screen beside her.

"The thing is, I sometimes wondered . . . "

A nurse opens the door, peers in, and quickly backs out, as hushed as hushed can be.

"It's about Scott, mom. I often wondered, you know, how close you were . . . you and Scott . . . at USC, I mean . . . before. You know? First time round.

'I fell in love with James Tyrone and was so happy for a time.'

"Remember how you used to say that? Was that Scott, mom? . . . First time?"

Now the rise and fall of the bed sheet begins to slow down . . .

"It's just . . . they say I'm getting to look awful like him."

. . . and the on-screen pulses sink towards a horizontal green line . . .

"Am I?"

. . . and the rhythmic 'bleep' flattens, pulse by pulse . . .

"Was he?"

. . . to a long, dull monotone. There is no possibility, now, of her ever answering him.

"Mom?"

Billy leans forward and places his hand on her cold, limp arm. Then he breaks.

"Oh Mom! . . . I'm so sorry!"

He takes hold of her stiffening fingers, like a child again clinging to his mother's skirts.

"I'm so sorry what I did!"

It is several minutes before he moves. He stands, leans over her and kisses each of the eyelids that had never opened for him all night. After another long pause, he kisses her forehead.

"I hope . . . "

He looks at the careworn face until it melts out of focus. He turns away, and his moist eyes rest on the blurring image of the window. So softly -

"I hope . . . "

The first feint signs of morning glow behind the venetian blind, and a pale ray of sun makes bands of light and shadow dance on the wall.

3

Rome

The taxi sounded its horn again, and for much longer. A torrent of abuse flew through the open window of an apartment the other side of the street.

"Ma la vuoi smettere con questo cazzo di clacson!!"

The driver shouted back at the window:

"CHE CAZZO VUOI?"

—then he called up to the old man:

"Sbrigati!! Che io sto lavorando. E non ho tempo da pedere!"

It was early morning, and the Dutch guy's tales of Los Angeles, so far as he knew them, and with very little invented or held back, were at last told.

"You look disappointed."

"Not at all," said his godson. "*No. Not at all.* It's just that I thought . . . "

"Because your mother called you Scott?"

"Of course . . . of course that . . . and the fact that no one would *talk* about him. About *them*. It got to me, I guess. More than just my name. More than anything. It was taboo . . . off limits . . . and I wondered. That's all. I knew there was something. I needed to know what."

"Now you do. You are half Canadian. Your mother loved your father; and he loved her; and they both loved you. Very much."

His godson smiled at him, a sad smile, and said nothing.

"You must not worry that she loved someone else before. It troubles you? I am right, *si*? Don't let it, *Scottino*. It is natural. It's good. You will come to love many women, many people I hope, in your lifetime—and more than '*just a glance*'."

"Sure."

"But you are not thinking to yourself, secretly, it has been a waste of time? Eh? Coming all this way? Sitting up all night, and this is all you learn? I have told you everything I know, but perhaps it is not what you thought you would hear?"

"C'mon! It wasn't a waste of time . . . 'Course it wasn't. What are you saying? And I wanted to see you."

"As you keep telling me."

The taxi blasted its horn in repeated short bursts. Now, two or three windows were thrown open –

"Ma si può sapere che cazzo hai da suonare cosi!!"

"When you return to Los Angeles you must try to find Billy," said the old man, opening the door from his apartment.

'If you say so," replied his godson. "Why?"

"You need to ask? *Non ci credo!* Don't you . . . 'get it'—as you like to say? He is the son of Scott! You are the son of Chloe! Together, you are the children they never had! Don't you find that . . . interesting, at the least?

"He's gotta be ten years older than me."

"Does that make any difference? *Scottino! Scottino!* In my eyes, and maybe in the eyes of—who knows if they can see?—*you are like brothers.*"

"Brothers? My most . . . wonderful, sentimental godfather! No way! And suppose I *found* my make-believe brother? We've never met. Does he even know I exist? It will be kind of odd, don't you think? For both of us? A little embarrassing? And then what?"

"Tell him. Tell him who you are, and who he is—and rescue him."

"What's that supposed to mean?"

"You don't know?"

Billy said there were quite a few people in LA needed rescuing.

"Suppose he tells me to get lost?"

The old man seized hold of his godson's hands –

"Suppose he doesn't?"

In a momentary reversal of their roles he calmed his godfather's quavering fingers; and in a voice one might use to comfort an anxious child, he said –

"I'll look out for him, sure."

"Will you?"

"Of course."

"But do you want to?"

"Why wouldn't I?"

"But *do* you?"

What a night, a single night, to ask him to grow older by so many years!

"*Con tutto il mio cuore*," he replied

"With all your heart?" said his godfather. "Now it is you '*going all Italian on me*'."

"As I like to say."

"As you like to say."

The taxi-driver yelled up at them from the foot of the stairs –

"*Deficiente arrivo!*"

"Go, Go, Go," he said, pushing his godson through the door.

"Next year then . . . And thank you." He kissed him on both cheeks.

"*Certo*," said the old man. A moment's hesitation, then—"Next year."

He watched him run down the stairs until, at the mezzanine, he turned and called—

"You never said who."

"I told you everything."

"No you didn't. Who was it you fell in love with?"

"*Non ti capisco.*" (Which was often his refuge from the truth.)

"The reason you stayed out there so long. The love-hate thing. Who was it?"

"*Imbecille.* Isn't it obvious?"

"Not to me—."

The taxi driver slammed the heel of his hand on the car-horn, and left it there.

"—I won't go until you tell me!"

"You have all the pieces: put them together," he shouted back at him.

"I can't. Who was it?"

"Are you completely without a brain?"

"Yes. Tell me! Who with?"

A long sigh. Eyes raised to heaven. Hands thrown up in exasperation. The old actor was notorious for milking his curtain-line.

"*Ridicolo giovane!*—With Los Angeles, of course."

His godson laughed out loud, shook his head, and ran from the building into a cacophony of shouted profanities and the constant blast of a taxi-horn.

The End

About the Author

Jed Hamilton was born in New York City in 1963 to a Scottish mother and Canadian father; the family immigrated to the UK in 1970.

Hamilton qualified as a lawyer in 1988 and was employed as in-house counsel for an American production company. In 1991, he moved to Los Angeles and worked as a composer in the film industry. After eleven years, he returned to England in 2003.

Aside from his debut novel, Hamilton has also written three screenplays.

www.ingramcontent.com/pod-product-compliance
Lightning Source LLC
Chambersburg PA
CBHW031254170626
46807CB00001B/147